THE ATLAS PARADOX

TOR BOOKS BY OLIVIE BLAKE

The Atlas Six
Alone with You in the Ether

OLIVIE BLAKE

THE
ATLAS
PARADOX

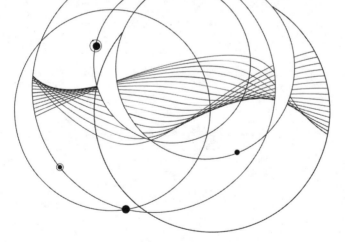

TOR

A TOM DOHERTY ASSOCIATES BOOK
NEW YORK

THE ATLAS PARADOX

Copyright © 2022 by Alexene Farol Follmuth

Interior illustrations and endpaper art by Little Chmura

A Tor Book
Published by Tom Doherty Associates
120 Broadway
New York, NY 10271

www.tor-forge.com

Tor® is a registered trademark of Macmillan Publishing Group, LLC.

The Library of Congress Cataloging-in-Publication Data is available upon request.

ISBN 978-1-250-85509-1 (hardcover)
ISBN 978-1-250-88223-3 (signed)
ISBN 978-1-250-85512-1 (ebook)

Our books may be purchased in bulk for promotional, educational,
or business use. Please contact your local bookseller or the Macmillan Corporate
and Premium Sales Department at 1-800-221-7945, extension 5442,
or by email at MacmillanSpecialMarkets@macmillan.com.

First Edition: 2022

Printed in the United States of America

0 9 8 7 6 5 4 3 2 1

For my talisman,
Henry Atlas

THE ATLAS PARADOX

PERSONS OF INTEREST

CAINE, TRISTAN

Tristan Caine is the son of Adrian Caine, head of a magical crime syndicate. Tristan would resent having his father as a point of introduction, but there is little Tristan does not resent. Born in London and educated at the London School of Magic, Tristan is a former venture capitalist for the Wessex Corporation as well as the estranged former fiancé of Eden Wessex. Trained in the school of illusion, Tristan's true specialty is unknown, though his talents include seeing through illusions (See also: *quantum theory; time; illusions— seeing through illusions; components—magical components*). Per the Alexandrian Society elimination terms, Tristan was tasked with killing Callum Nova. For reasons ostensibly related to his conscience, Tristan did not succeed.

FERRER DE VARONA, NICOLÁS (may refer to DE VARONA, NICOLÁS or DE VARONA, NICO)

Nicolás Ferrer de Varona, commonly called Nico, was born in Havana, Cuba, and sent to the United States at an early age, where he would later graduate from the prestigious New York University for Magical Arts. Nico is uncommonly gifted as a physicist and possesses several capabilities outside his specialty (See also: *lithospheric proclivities; seismology—tectonics; shifting—human to animal; alchemy; draughts—alchemical*). Nico has a close friendship with fellow NYUMA graduates Gideon Drake and Maximilian Wolfe, and despite a long-standing antagonism, an alliance with Elizabeth "Libby" Rhodes. While Nico is extremely skilled in hand-to-hand combat, this did not prevent him from losing his ally in the end.

KAMALI, PARISA

Little about the details of Parisa Kamali's early life or true identity is known beyond speculation (See also: *beauty, curse of—Callum Nova*). Parisa was born in Tehran, Iran, and attended École Magique de Paris. She is a telepath of great proficiency with a variety of known associations (*Tristan Caine; Libby Rhodes*) and experiments (*time—mental chronometry; subconscious—dreams; Dalton Ellery*). It would be inadvisable to trust her. Undoubtedly, though, you will.

MORI, REINA

If little is known about Parisa Kamali, even less is known about Reina Mori. Not that it's a competition, but if it were, Reina would win. Born in Tokyo, Japan, with astounding naturalism capabilities, Reina instead attended the Osaka Institute of Magic and studied classics with a focus on mythology. For Reina alone the earth personally offers fruit, and to Reina alone nature speaks. It is worth noting, though, that in Reina's opinion, she has other talents (See also: *amplification—energy; combat experience—Nico de Varona*).

NOVA, CALLUM

Callum Nova, of the South Africa–based Nova media conglomerate, is a manipulist whose powers extend to the metaphysical—that is, in layman's terms, an empath. Born in Cape Town, South Africa, Callum studied very comfortably at the Hellenistic University of Magical Arts before joining the family business in the profitable sale of medeian beauty products and illusions. Only one person on earth knows for sure what Callum actually looks like. Unfortunately for Callum, that person wanted him dead. Unfortunately for Tristan, he did not want it badly enough (See also: *betrayal, no fate so final as*).

RHODES, ELIZABETH (may refer to RHODES, LIBBY)

Elizabeth "Libby" Rhodes is a gifted physicist. Born in Pittsburgh, Pennsylvania, USA, Libby's early life was marked by the loss of her older sister, Katherine. Libby attended the New York University of Magical Arts, where she met her rival-turned-ally Nicolás "Nico" de Varona and her erstwhile boyfriend, Ezra Fowler. As a Society recruit, Libby conducted several notable experiments (See also: *time—fourth dimension; quantum theory—time; Tristan Caine*) and moral quandaries (*Parisa Kamali; Tristan Caine*) before disappearing, initially presumed by the remainder of her cohort to be deceased. Libby's current location is unknown (See also: *Ezra Fowler*).

FOR FURTHER READING

ALEXANDRIAN SOCIETY, THE
    Archives—lost knowledge
    Library (See also: *Alexandria; Babylon; Carthage; ancient libraries— Islamic; ancient libraries—Asian*)
    Rituals—initiation (See also: *magic—sacrifice; magic—death*)

BLAKELY, ATLAS
    Alexandrian Society, the (See also: *Alexandrian Society—initiates; Alexandrian Society—Caretakers*)

Early life—London, England
Telepathy

DRAKE, GIDEON
    Abilities—unknown (See also: *human mind—subconscious*)
    Creature—subspecies (See also: *taxonomy—creature; species—unknown*)
    Criminal affiliations (See also: *Eilif*)
    Early life—Cape Breton, Nova Scotia, Canada
    Education—New York University of Magical Arts
    Specialty—Traveler (See also: *dream realms—navigation*)

EILIF
    Alliances—unknown
    Children (See also: *Gideon Drake*)
    Creature—finfolk (See also: *taxonomy—creature; finfolk—mermaid*)

ELLERY, DALTON
    Alexandrian Society, the (See also: *Alexandrian Society—initiates;*
        Alexandrian Society—researchers)
    Animation
    Known affiliations (See also: *Parisa Kamali*)

FOWLER, EZRA
    Abilities (See also: *traveling—fourth dimension; physicist—quantum*)
    Alexandrian Society, the (See also: *Alexandrian Society—uninitiated;*
        Alexandrian Society—elimination)
    Early life—Los Angeles, CA
    Education—New York University for Magical Arts
    Known alliances (See also: *Atlas Blakely*)
    Previous employment (See also: *NYUMA—resident advisors*)
    Personal relationships (See also: *Libby Rhodes*)
    Specialty—Traveler (See also: *time*)

PRINCE, THE
    Animation—general
    Identity (See also: *identity—unknown*)
    Known affiliations (See also: *Ezra Fowler, Eilif*)

THE ALEXANDRIAN SOCIETY
FELLOWSHIP COURSE OF STUDY

YEAR ONE

Directives:

Candidates for initiation to the Alexandrian Society will rigorously contribute new and innovative research to the archives of knowledge herein. They will also protect and care for the archives throughout the duration of their residency, pending satisfactory completion of initiation terms.

Core Curriculum:

Space

Time

Thought

Intent

Further details of study to follow, pending terms of initiation.

Modules for first year study and completion of initiation requirements to conclude by 1 June.

Initiates will each contribute a treatise of significance to the archives, the topic of which is open to their choosing.

Independent Study Proposal:
Minimum requirements denoted with *

    Research topic title*:_____

    Aims:_____

    Methodology (list any relevant texts):_____

    _____

    _____

Timetable:
    Completion of Proposal: Indicate timeframe for any intended data collection, review, and/or analysis. To be delivered no later than 1 June.

Initiate signature:

Approved by:

Atlas Blakely

· BEGINNING ·

Gideon Drake shaded his eyes from the red-burning sun and swept a glance across the scorched and blackened hills. Heat rippled in the air between particulate clouds of ash. Little moth wings of debris floated delicately across his limited vision. The smoke was thick, chalky enough to stick in his throat, and if any of it was real it would constitute a medical emergency on the spot.

But it wasn't, so it didn't.

Gideon glanced down at the black Lab beside him, frowning at him in contemplation, and then turned back to the unfamiliar scene, pulling his shirt above his mouth to manifest a thin veil of semi-breathable air.

"That's very interesting," Gideon murmured to himself.

In the dream realms these burnings happened from time to time. Gideon called them "erosions," though if he ever met another of his kind, he wouldn't be surprised to learn there was already a proper name. It was common enough, though almost never this . . . flammable.

If Gideon had a philosophy, it was this: No sense despairing.

There was no telling what was real and what was not for Gideon Drake. His perception of dreamt wasteland might be a completely different scene to the dreamer. The burnings were a fine reminder of something Gideon had learned long ago: there is doom to be found everywhere if doom is what you seek.

"Well, come on then, Max," Gideon said to the dog, who was coincidentally also his roommate. Max sniffed the air and whined in opposition as they headed west, but they both understood that dreams were Gideon's domain, and therefore their path was ultimately Gideon's decision.

Magically speaking, the dream realms were part of a collective subconscious. While every human had access to a corner of the realms, very few were able to traverse the realms of dreams as Gideon was.

To see where a person's own consciousness ended and others' began required a particular set of skills, and Gideon—who knew the shifting patterns of the realms the same way sailors know the tides—had even keener senses now that he rarely left their midst.

To the outside world, Gideon presented as a fairly normal person with narcolepsy. Understanding his magic, though, was not straightforward at all. As far as Gideon could gather, the line between conscious and subconscious was very thin for him. He could identify time and location within the dream realms, but his ability to walk through dreams occasionally prevented him from making it all the way through breakfast upright. Sometimes it seemed he belonged more to the realm of dreams than to the world of the living. Still, Gideon's apparent somnambular flaw meant that he could make use of the limits others faced. A normal person could fly in a dream, for example, but they would know they were dreaming, and therefore be aware that they couldn't actually fly in real life. Gideon Drake, on the other hand, could fly, period. Whether he happened to be awake or dreaming was the part he couldn't always figure out.

Gideon wasn't technically any more powerful than anyone else would be inside of a dream. His corporeal limitations were similar to those of telepathy—no magic performed in the dream realms could possibly harm him permanently, unless his physical form suffered something like a stroke or seizure. Gideon felt pain the same way another person might feel it in a dream—imagined, and then gone when they woke up. Unless he was under unusual amounts of stress that could then cause one of the above bodily reactions, that is . . . but that he never worried over. Only Nico worried about that sort of thing.

At the thought of Nico, Gideon suffered the usual twinge of something exposed, like having misplaced one shoe and carried on trudging without it. For the last year, he had trained himself (with varying degrees of success, depending on the day) to stop cataloguing the absence of his and Max's usual companion. It had been difficult at first; the thought of Nico usually came back to him reflexively, like muscle memory, without preemption or forethought, and therefore with the unforeseen consequence of disrupting his intended route. Sometimes, when Gideon's thoughts went to Nico, so did Gideon himself.

In the end, the pitfall and the providence of knowing Nico de Varona was that he could not be readily forgotten, nor easily parted from. Missing him was like missing a severed limb. Never quite complete and never whole, though on occasion the vestigial aches proved helpfully informative.

Gideon allowed himself to feel the things he tried (under other circumstances) not to, and like a sigh of relief, he felt the realms shift courteously beneath his feet. The nightmare gradually subsided, giving way to the atmosphere of Gideon's own dreams, and so Gideon followed the path that came to him most easily: his own.

The smoke from the dream faded as Gideon's mind wandered, and as such he and Max found themselves moving through conscious perception of time and space. In place of scorched earth, there was now the faint suggestion of microwavable popcorn and industrial-strength laundry detergent—unmistakable top notes of the NYUMA dorms.

And with it, the familiar face of a teenager Gideon once knew.

"I'm Nico," said the wild-eyed, messy-haired boy whose T-shirt was inadvertently folded up on one side from the presence of his duffel bag. "You're Gideon? You look exhausted," he decided as an afterthought, tossing the bag below the second bed and glancing around the room, adding, "You know, we'd have a lot more room if we bunked these."

Was this a memory, or a dream? It was hard for Gideon Drake to tell.

It was difficult to explain what exactly Nico had done to the air in the room, which Nico himself didn't appear to have noticed. With mild claustrophobia, Gideon managed, "I'm not sure we're allowed to move the furniture. I guess we could ask?"

"We could, but asking so diminishes our chances at a favorable outcome." Nico paused, glancing at him. "What is that accent, by the way? French?"

"Sort of. Acadian."

"Quebecois?"

"Close enough."

Nico's grin broadened. "Well, excellent," he said. "I've been wanting to expand linguistically. I think too much in English now, I need something else. Never trust a dichotomy, I always say. Though on a relevant note, do you want top or bottom?" he asked, and Gideon blinked.

"You choose," he managed, and Nico waved a hand, rearranging furniture so effortlessly that in the span of a breath, Gideon had already forgotten what the room looked like to begin with.

In real life, Gideon had learned very quickly that if there wasn't space, Nico made some. If things sat still for too long, then Nico would inevitably disrupt them. The school administrators at NYUMA had felt the only necessary accommodation for Gideon's presence was to label him "in need of disability services" and leave it at that, but given everything Gideon had observed about his new roommate within moments of meeting him, he was uneasily certain that it was only a matter of time before Nico found out the truth of him.

"Where do you go?" Nico had asked, proving Gideon right. "When you sleep, I mean."

It was two weeks into the school year and Nico had climbed down from the top bunk, manifesting at Gideon's side and startling him awake. Gideon hadn't even known he was sleeping.

"I have narcolepsy," he managed to say.

"Bullshit," Nico replied.

Gideon had stared at him and thought, I can't tell you. Not that he thought Nico was going to turn out to be some sort of creature hunter or someone planted in his room by his mother (although both were a distinct possibility), but there was always a moment when people started to look at him differently. Gideon hated that moment. The moment when others started to find something—many somethings—to reinforce their suspicions that Gideon was repulsive in some way. Instinctual knowledge; prey responding to a threat. Fight or flight.

I can't tell anyone, Gideon had thought, but especially not you.

"There's something weird about you," Nico continued matter-of-factly. "Not bad-weird, just weird." He folded his arms over his chest, considering it. "What's your story?"

"I told you. Narcolepsy."

Nico rolled his eyes. *"Menteur."*

Liar. So he really was planning to learn French, then.

"What's 'shut up' in Spanish?" a former version of Gideon had asked in real life, and Nico had given him a smile that Gideon would later learn was exceptionally dangerous.

"Get out of bed, Sandman," Nico had said, tossing aside the covers. "We're going out."

Back in the present, Max nudged Gideon's knee with his nose, just hard enough that Gideon had to stumble for balance. "Thanks," he said, shaking himself free of the memory. The dorm room faded back into the erosion's distantly blazing hillside as Max supplied him with an unblinking look of expectation.

"Nico's this way," Gideon said, pointing through the thick brush of smoldering evergreens.

Max gave him a doubtful look.

Gideon sighed. "Fine," he said, and conjured a ball, tossing it into the woods. "Fetch."

The ball illuminated as it picked up speed, dousing the forest in a low, reassuring glow. Max gave Gideon another look of annoyance but darted ahead, following the path that Gideon's magic had created.

Everyone had magic in dreams. The limitations were not the laws of physics, but rather the control of the dreamer. Gideon, a creature who constantly wavered between consciousness and unconsciousness, lacked muscle memory when it came to the limitations of reality. (If you do not know precisely where impossibility begins and ends, then of course it cannot constrain you.)

Whether Gideon simply *had* magic or was *himself* magic was perpetually a subject up for debate. Nico was adamant about the former, Gideon himself not so sure. He could scarcely perform even mediocre witchery when called upon in class, which was why he had stuck primarily to theoretical studies of how and why magic existed. Because Nico was a physicist, he saw the world in terms of pseudo-anatomical construction, but Gideon liked to think of the world as something of a data cloud. That was all the dream realms were, in the end. Shared space for humanity's experience.

The real Nico was closer now, and the edge of the burning forest quickly dwindled to a thin stretch of vacant beach. Gideon bent down to brush his fingers over the sand, then plunged an arm through it, testing. Things were not burning here, but his arm did disappear instantly, swallowed up to the cuff of his shoulder. Max gave a low, cautioning growl.

Gideon retracted his hand, reaching over to give Max a little chin scratch of reassurance.

"Why don't you stay here," Gideon suggested. "I'll come get you in an hour or so."

Max whined softly.

"Yeah, yeah, I'll be careful. You're really starting to sound like Nico, you know."

Max barked.

"All right, fine, I take it back."

Gideon knelt on the beach with a roll of his eyes and submerged his hand again, this time leaning into the sand until it overtook his body and he slid fully into the other side. Instantly there was a shift in pressure, high to low, and Gideon found himself tumbling headlong into more sand, dropping from the sky onto the rolling hills of an arid desert.

He hit the sand face-first and spat a bit out of the side of his mouth. Gideon was not what one might call a lover of nature, having been exposed to a few too many of its less pleasant gifts. Were there worse things than sand? Yes, definitely, but still. Gideon didn't think it was entirely out of line to find its effects offensive. He could feel it everywhere already, in the lining of his ears and in his teeth, taking residence in the rivulets of his scalp. Not ideal—but, as ever, no point despairing.

Gideon dragged himself upright, struggling to maintain his balance in the endless ribbon of sand that rose to the top of his calves. He peered around at the dunes, bracing for something. What it would be, he had no idea. It was different every time.

A buzz in his right ear had him pivoting sharply (or trying to) with a yelp, swatting blindly at the air. Anything but mosquitoes—Gideon did not care for bugs. Another buzz and he flicked it away, this time suffering a needle prick to his forearm. A welt had already started to show, a plump tear of blood pearling up from the puncture. Gideon brought his arm up to inspect the wound more closely, brushing away an exoskeleton of metal, the minute trace of gunpowder.

So. Not bugs, then.

Knowing what type of obstacle came next was usually a mixed relief, because it meant that Gideon now had both the ability and the necessity to plan his defense. Sometimes entering this particular subconscious was a tactical matter. Sometimes there was combat, sometimes there were labyrinths. Occasionally escape rooms and chases and fights—those were preferable, owing to Gideon's general proficiency (up to this point) at eluding death and all its horsemen. Other times it was merely about the sweat of it, the strain, which was a matter of simple but terrible endurance. Gideon couldn't die in dreams—no one could—but he could suffer. He could feel fear, or pain. Sometimes the test was just about clenching your jaw and outlasting.

This dream, unfortunately, was going to be one of those.

Whatever tiny weapons were being fired at Gideon now were too small to dodge and too quick to fight—probably nothing that could exist on Earth or be operated by humans. Gideon took the blows like the unavoidable bites that they were and dove into the whip of the wind, closing his eyes to guard against the sting of sand. It mixed with his open wounds, blood streaking across his arms. He could see the blurs of red between slitted eyes, bright and relatively benign but still ugly. Like tear tracks on the statues of martyrs and saints.

Whichever telepath had set up these wards was without question a sadist of the highest, most troubling order.

Something pierced Gideon's neck, embedding in his throat, and Gideon's airway was instantly compromised. Choking, he rushed to apply pressure to the wound, willing himself to regenerate faster. Dreams were not real, the damage was not real—the only thing real was the struggle, and that much he would give without question. That much he would always give, always, because in the deepest caverns of his heart, he knew it was justified. That it was not only righteous, but owed.

The winds picked up, sand crusting his eyes and lips and adhering to the sweat in the folds of his neck, and Gideon, summoning the volumes of his pain, let out a scream—the primal kind. The kind that meant the screamer was giving in, letting go. He screamed and screamed and tried from somewhere inside his agony to offer the proper capitulation, the secret password of sorts. The right message. Something like *I will die before I give up, but everything inside your wards is safe from me.*

I am just a man in pain. I am just a mortal with a message.

It must have worked, because the moment Gideon's lungs emptied, blistering with pleading and strain, the ground gave way beneath him. He fell with a slurping sound of suction before being delivered, mercifully, to the sudden vacancy of an empty room.

"Oh good, you're here," said Nico with palpable relief, rising to his feet and approaching the bars of the telepathic wards that separated them. "I think I was having a dream about the beach or something."

Gideon instinctively glanced at his arms for evidence of blood or sand, indulging a testing inhale to check his lungs. Everything appeared to be in order, which meant that he had made it inside the Alexandrian Society's wards for the hundred and eighteenth time.

Each time was a little more nightmarish than the last. Each time, though, it was worth it.

Nico smiled as he leaned against the bars with his usual smuggery. "You look well," he remarked in playful approval. "Very rested, as always."

Gideon rolled his eyes.

"I'm here," he confirmed, and then, because it was what Gideon had come to say, he added, "And I think I might be close to finding Libby."

THE PARADOX:

If power is a thing to be had, it must be capable of possession. But power is not any discrete size or weight. Power is continuous. Power is parabolic. Say you are given some power, which then increases your capacity to accumulate more power. Your capacity for power increases exponentially in relation to the actual power you have gained. Thus, to gain power is to be increasingly power-less.

If the more power one has, the less one has, then is it the thing or are you?

I

DAZE

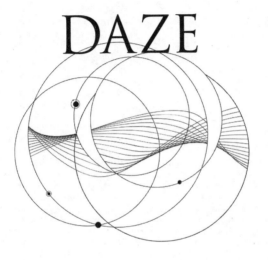

· LIBBY ·

The moment Ezra Fowler left her behind, two things became clear. The first was that the room—with its sparsely made bed and neatly folded clothing and orderly collection of prepackaged food—was meant for someone to live in for months, perhaps years.

The second was that Libby Rhodes herself was the room's intended occupant.

· EZRA ·

She would forgive him, Ezra thought.

And even if she did not, the alternative was still the end of the world at Atlas Blakely's hands.

So perhaps forgiveness was better not asked.

II

INITIATES

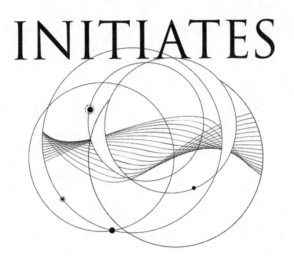

I t was nearly a year to the day since the six of them had set foot in the
Alexandrian Society's manor house and been promised, elusively, power.
All the world's knowledge under one roof. A lifetime of prestige, to crown
the privilege of having access to the universe's greatest secrets.

And all they had to do was survive a single year until the date of their
initiation.

There was unity in that—as there had been over the course of the year in
which they'd been modified and mutated and changed—and so where there
had once been six was now, irreversibly, one.

Or something.

Reina cast a glance around the room and wondered exactly how long their
unity would last. Presumably less than an hour. Already the energy in the
room had begun to shift as Atlas Blakely, their so-called Caretaker, stepped
quietly through the painted room's door, observing them in silence.

Beside Reina, Nico de Varona was fidgety as usual, glancing at Atlas and
then away. Tristan Caine was brooding silently behind them. From Reina's
periphery, she could see Parisa Kamali's features remain placidly unchanged
upon sight of the Caretaker, while Callum Nova, behind Parisa, did not even
acknowledge Atlas's entry. Callum stood at a distance from the others, chin
angled slightly outward, as if to signal that his mind was on other things.

"Try to think of everything that follows as a game," suggested Dalton
Ellery, the bespectacled researcher who was presently filling the role of initiation concierge. He nodded in Atlas's direction, then continued addressing
the other five. They stood against a bookcase, waiting, as Dalton directed
their attention to the center of the room.

The painted room had been cleared of its furniture, aside from a series of
ordinary dining chairs. The five chairs, placed several feet apart, all faced
inward and addressed a circle of empty space.

The loss of their sixth member was, by then, no longer fresh. It was, however, still noticeable. Like an old war wound that pained them only when it
rained, the missing hum of Libby Rhodes and her anxiety seemed to haunt
the standing space between the five initiates, unspoken—existing only in

the promises they had made to one another. From somewhere beneath the floorboards, her absence pulsed.

"You've come this far," Dalton continued, stepping into the center of the empty circle, "and you are no longer being tested. There is no passing or failing. However, we do feel an ethical obligation to warn you that while you are safe from bodily harm, that does not guarantee your comfort during this ceremony. You will not die," he concluded. "But, all other outcomes are plausible."

Beside Reina, Nico apprehensively shifted against the shelves. Tristan folded his arms more tightly across his chest, and Parisa slid a glance to Atlas, who hovered near the door. His expression had not changed.

Or perhaps it had. It was possible Reina was imagining it, but the Caretaker's customary look of bland attentiveness seemed a touch more marble than usual. Fixed, in a way that suggested curation.

"*All* other outcomes are plausible?" Callum asked, voicing the room's collective doubt into the empty space. "As in, we won't die, but we could conceivably wake up a giant cockroach?" ("Beetle," murmured Reina, which Callum ignored.)

"It's not a known outcome," Dalton said, "but neither is it technically impossible."

There was another intangible shift among the soon-to-be-initiated. Nico, sensing the potential for discord, glanced at Reina before saying, "Initiation means more access, doesn't it? And we've clearly all made choices to get here." Nico carefully directed his comments to the room at large rather than any specific candidate, though he lingered a moment on Atlas before turning to Dalton. "Seems like the intimidation factor isn't really necessary at this point, right?"

"It's really more of a disclaimer," Dalton said. "Any other questions?"

Several, obviously—but Dalton wasn't known for being forthcoming. Reina snuck a glance at Parisa, who was the only person who would know if there was anything to be suspicious about. She didn't look concerned. Not that Reina made a habit of being nervous, but she certainly wasn't going to waste her time on fear if Parisa wasn't worried first.

"The initiation ceremony requires you to leave this plane," continued Dalton. "The constraints of your transition will be defined for you."

"This will all be in our heads?" asked Tristan gruffly.

A tick of distress manifested on Nico's brow; ever since they'd witnessed Parisa's death at Callum's hands, they had all—but Parisa, ironically—been rendered skittish by the prospect of telepathic counterfeits.

Dalton paused. "No," he said, "but also yes, definitely."

"Oh, good," Nico exhaled in an undertone to Reina. "And I was so worried he might be unhelpful."

Before Reina could respond, Parisa said warily, "What exactly are we doing on the Society's astral plane? And no, that does not give me an advantage," she added, cutting off any further questions with an impatient sweep of the room. "If there are constraints, then I am also constrained," she said conclusively to Reina, who surely wasn't the only one thinking it. "Just because it's within the realm of my specialty doesn't mean I have any significant advantage."

Reina slid her glance away. *Touchy,* she thought in Parisa's direction.

She felt Parisa's posture shift stiffly in reply. *I don't appreciate the accusation. And suddenly you care what I think?*

Parisa didn't respond. From the far corner of the room, the potted fig unhelpfully cackled.

Dalton cleared his throat. "The construct of your initiation is not a secret—"

"How charming," muttered Tristan. "Something new and different."

"—it is simply a simulation," Dalton finished. "Within the simulation, you'll be faced with a projection of someone else in your initiate class. Not as they are, but as you perceive them."

He paused to observe the expressions of the others, which varied from marked indifference (Callum) to resigned ambivalence (Nico). If anyone felt a hint of distress, none who remained were willing to show it. Atlas, for his part, merely raised a hand to his chin, scratching an itch. It seemed an odd thing to notice, but Reina felt sure his suit looked more glaringly pristine than it did usually. Pressed within an inch of its life, like he'd known someone would be looking. Or perhaps it was just a trick of the light.

"This is not a test of what you've learned," Dalton added. "It is not a test at all—merely a formality. For the last year you have studied what we asked of you. Soon you will have the right to ask of the archives yourselves, wherever your paths of study take you." There was a brief shiver up Reina's spine, propitious and fateful. "As initiated members of the Society, the contents of the library will be yours to use, and to contribute to, as you wish, until your obligations to the archives are fulfilled and your tenure is at an end. You have earned your place here, but every bridge has two sides. Cross it."

He withdrew a file from nothing, catching it as if it had been tossed aloft.

"We'll start from youngest to oldest, which means Mr. de Varona will go first." Dalton glanced up at Nico, who nodded. It would always be Nico's preference to go first. He was built that way, always rushing into things. Without Libby for a counterweight, there was nothing to temper his recklessness. Nothing to anchor him at all.

Nico wasn't the only one left unbalanced. They were all slightly different without Libby Rhodes. Without them realizing it, she had established herself as the "but" in their collective conscience, their measure of morality. *But what if this happens, but what if something goes wrong, but what if someone is hurt.* The effects of her displacement from their anatomy as a group seemed imperceptibly compounding, like an infection that went undiagnosed. They could go on without her, of course, but the loss would surely prove significant given enough time. Slow internal bleeding, the toxification of a kidney. A tiny puncture somewhere in the constitution of an otherwise healthy lung.

A beleaguered fern sighed out *doomdoomdoom,* commentary that only Reina could hear and frankly did not appreciate.

"All right." Nico took a step toward Dalton. "Where am I going?"

"Nowhere. Sit." Dalton gestured to the five chairs, leading Nico to the one at approximately twelve o'clock. "All of you," Dalton clarified, "in order."

They each sat. To Reina's right was Tristan, to Tristan's right Callum, to Callum's right Parisa. Nico closed the circle on Reina's left.

There was a brief moment after they took their seats when they all collectively braced for something—something to fall from the ceiling or rise from the ground. There was nothing of the sort. The plants in the room bristled and yawned, Atlas took a seat among the anterior bookshelves, outside of Reina's view, and Dalton took his place behind Nico's chair, clipboard in hand.

Nico, fidgeting, glanced first at Reina and then swiftly over his shoulder. "What exactly am I supposed to d—"

"Begin," said Dalton.

Nico's head snapped forward—struck like a match, a corporeal off switch—while his consciousness slid out from beneath him. The air of the room crackled momentarily with static—with magic or life or some intangible wave of Nico himself. The uncanny energy pebbled their skin, lifting the hairs from their arms, the backs of their necks.

Within seconds, the sensation of unbridled electricity had resolved itself, becoming palpable condensation—a fine mist, at first, and then a cloud—and then, like the crack of a whip, a spectral image of Nico rose up from the center of the circle. His conception of the painted room blanketed the initiates as he stood within a projection of the furniture's usual arrangement: the table beside the bookcase, the sofa across from the hearth. He seemed incapable of seeing his four peers and two initiators as they sat in a circle around the room. In the projection, it was high noon, the heat of the sun emanating from the windows. The drapes were thrown open, the weather outside a clear, bright contrast to the wet summer gloom of their physical reality.

From the corner of Reina's eye, Tristan leaned forward, bracing his forearms on his knees with apprehension that read like disgust. "We're going to be able to watch each other's initiation rituals?"

"Yes," said Dalton, and just as he spoke, a spectral version of Reina materialized across from the projection of Nico, who grinned.

"Excellent," Nico said, clearing the projected room of its furniture with a wave of his hand. Like all of Nico's magic, it was difficult to see in proper sequence. There was simply a blink, and then all the furniture lined the room's perimeter. As if that were the layout as it had always been.

Nico put forth a hand to be shaken, offering it to his projection of Reina. It was the beginning of any standard sparring match. Even now, after a year of recreational combat, they still commenced every match that way.

From across the translucency of the projection, Reina caught Parisa rolling her eyes.

What? Reina demanded.

Parisa's dark gaze met hers. *If I wanted to spend my time watching the two of you behave like children, I'd have done so by now.*

But even before Parisa had completed her thought, the projection-Reina had already lunged. Nico's head narrowly slipped to the side as he pivoted out and threw a straight punch, testing his range. The real Reina would have known to expect that (and likely done the same herself), but the projection of her slipped the punch as if it had been thrown at full strength. Her hand fell low enough for Nico to give her cheek a light tap in warning; a reminder to stay light on her feet.

Projection-Reina threw out a series of single jabs; one, two, then a third, then a fourth, which Nico parried with his right hand, catching her forearm. The motion rocked projection-Reina forward, setting her off-balance, and Nico took advantage of the drop in levels to aim a hook at the side of her head, which she rushed to block with her forearm rather than roll beneath—a poor choice, Reina thought with a grimace. Her projected self succeeded in preventing the majority of impact, but she still took at least half the punch's intended force, if not more.

Nico and projection-Reina circled each other, each testing the other's footing. Nico worked his way to the inside of her wingspan, then swung easily to the outside of Reina's close hook when her projection took the bait. Nico's knuckles tapped her kidney as he slid deftly out of range. She responded with a blind swing for his head, catching the tip of his ear. He laughed. Her projection didn't.

Parisa suddenly sat up straighter, a thought creasing her brow.

Now you're suddenly interested in combat strategies? Reina scoffed in her direction. Reina couldn't see Atlas from where she was sitting—he was obscured by one of the room's many bookshelves—but she had a feeling he had taken notice, too.

Parisa shot her an irritated glance. *Please. This isn't combat. As usual, you're missing the point.*

What point? This was all so obviously pointless. Reina could witness this exact scenario in real life at any time—though she wouldn't, if given the choice. It was uncomfortable to watch herself fight, if only for the awkwardness of being forced to observe her usual shortcomings. Like this, in the audience, her failures seemed more exaggerated than usual. Movement came fluidly, naturally, to Nico. His rhythm—his orbit of the space—was always light and never stiff. He was never in the same place twice. Reina, by contrast, seemed stocky and immobile, a cliffside being steadily chipped away by Nico's tide. Reina found herself repeatedly looking away from the ritual's projection—though, in doing so, she noticed Parisa's attention still intently on her projected counterpart.

What exactly is so interesting to you about this? Reina asked grumpily, and Parisa stared at her from across the simulated combat, apparently no less annoyed by having to answer.

Don't you get it? This is a projection of what he thinks of you, Parisa said in Reina's head.

Reina thought she saw Parisa glance in Atlas's direction. If she did, though, it was brief and uncommunicative. Parisa's primary concern was the projection of Reina, not Atlas—which was, if anything, the most disconcerting thing currently taking place in the painted room. Being the object of Parisa's concentration couldn't be a good thing. (The potted fig agreed.)

So? thought Reina.

So, first of all, nobody said we couldn't use magic, but Nico isn't—and neither is his version of you. A flicker of a smile crossed Parisa's lips. *And I don't know if you've noticed, but he doesn't seem to find you dangerous at all, does he?*

Again: *So?*

For a year, we were all tasked with killing someone. We only recently learned who that might be. Parisa gestured with a glance to Nico's dancing form. *Does this seem like someone concerned with your threat to his life?*

Projection-Reina staggered, caught in one of Nico's usual traps: a jab that distracted her, causing her to miss Nico's hook from the edge of her periphery. He'd thrown a hard right cross and then an uppercut, the latter of which she'd been unable to block. These were all errors, but specifically they were *Reina's* errors. They were mistakes she'd made before.

Ah, you see it now, Parisa observed with a keen, disturbing satisfaction, and though Reina made every effort to clear any outside commentary from her mind, Parisa came through like white noise, radio static.

He thinks you're vulnerable.

And then, more derisively—

He thinks you're weak.

Reina bristled and forcefully thought of nothing, queuing up the usual punitive earworm of an old toothpaste ad from her youth. Parisa's smile turned tightly to a grimace of *touché, asshole* and then her attention drifted away, no doubt to some other game of amateur psychoanalysis. Projection-Reina slipped a right cross from Nico and dealt him a reasonable double jab in return, though he countered with a combination of punches she wasn't quite fast enough to fully block. Reina—the *real* Reina, who was growing increasingly annoyed—kept her expression still, realizing that Parisa wasn't the only one watching for her reaction. From the other side of Nico, Callum's gaze had slid surreptitiously to hers, observing her for a long, discerning moment before glancing away.

She wondered what her feelings were doing at that particular moment. Typically she did not concern herself with these things, believing herself to be a person of no great feeling. (Annoyance, irritation, impatience did not count. They were the mosquito bites on the emotional Richter scale.) Still, she could feel in some unpracticed, prickling way that she was wrestling with something. Not anguish, not fear . . . and certainly not betrayal, because despite Parisa's tacit claim to comprehend every nuance of all humanity, she was definitely wrong about that.

Though, in typical Parisa fashion, she wasn't quite wrong *enough*. Reina, who unlike certain people (Libby) was not completely subject to every whim of her own insecurity, knew that Nico didn't actually consider her weak. In Nico's mind, which Reina already understood to be a lawless and cluttered place, she knew that he did not consider *anyone* enough of an enemy to actively try to destroy them. That was both the charm and the rub of him: confidence that was also arrogance. To hold that against him would be to fundamentally misunderstand who he was. To care about his arrogance would only be an exercise in emotional fragility, and thus a waste of both their time.

Still, seeing herself through his eyes, it did seem that Nico considered Reina . . . predictable. Slightly inferior. Good, but not quite good enough. An impression that, to be fair, was accurate in certain areas, combat and physical magic included. Reina had never pretended it wasn't. Her concern with regard to the Society had always been access, not clout.

Had she considered that her obvious ambivalence to her own abilities might have struck the others as a reflection on her lack of skills? Yes. But if it were Tristan, or Callum, or Parisa who saw her this way, it might not have mattered. Reina had successfully revealed nothing of herself to them. Not to Nico either—not really—but he had spent far more time with her than any of the others. Hadn't he been paying attention?

Reina's mind served her an unwelcome flashback then. Tea with her grandmother, which had taken place after an especially fruitless dinner with her mother. *Someday they will see,* Baba had said with her gentle softness that had easily given way to forgetfulness, and then to mindless fluff that was sometimes connected to reality and sometimes not. *Someday they will look at you and see everything I see.*

MotherMother? the corner fern asked doubtfully.

Reina, despite herself, agreed.

Reina's mother, whom Reina generally did not think of and whom she most certainly did not speak of, had been the middle of three daughters and two sons. (A troublemaker in her youth, Reina's grandmother had always said fondly, as if she had watched an entertaining but unrealistic drama instead of her daughter's unfolding life.) Baba, an eccentric woman already with her odd penchant for kindness, had not wanted her daughter's whole life destroyed by one little indiscretion, so she had taken Reina in as an act of apparent generosity. Within one or two years, Reina's mother was successfully married to a mortal businessman, someone whose family had profited from the electronics boom that gave way to the medeian technomancy age. Reina always thought of him in the formal sense—the Businessman, who had no true name or meaning outside of his profession. He was not her father, merely the man who had married her mother after Reina was born. He knew that Reina lived in his mother-in-law's house only because he asked a lot of questions about her. At first he had thought she was a child of one of the staff, perhaps the housekeeper, and therefore someone he could ultimately control. Reina often wondered about the conversation her mother must have had as a result of this ironic turn of events. (Perhaps nothing had been said. Reina's mother did not talk much. She had the air of someone who had seen a lot and decided to simply close her eyes and stop looking.)

The point was the Businessman must not have been informed about Reina's true identity, because he was the one who began the habit of summoning her for monthly dinners. By that point there were other children—who were actually the Businessman's—although they, like their father, were mortal and not as powerful as Reina. He wasn't unkind. He took his business calls at the table but he didn't shout. He was just very, very transparent. During these dinners, when he would praise Reina's elegant kanji or her dutiful performance in school before transitioning to the subject of naturalism, Reina's mother would push food around her plate and practice her usual custom of saying nothing at all.

In any case, Reina's mother died two years before Reina's grandmother, when Reina was fourteen. At her funeral service, Reina's mother was described as a dutiful wife and mother. (Not as *Reina's* mother, of course. Reina sat in the back row, unobtrusively, and if there was any question of who she belonged to, no one asked.) Reina hadn't known her mother very well, but she was pretty sure that this speech was a very sad way for her story to end—that all that could be said of her unremarkable life was that she was proficient at two of her jobs. Nothing about whether she sang off-key in the shower or was fearful of garden snakes, or anything to give her any real shape at all.

Shortly after, the Businessman remarried. Life, as it usually did, went on.

Remembering was like quicksand, deeper and deeper with no escape. Reina was struck with another unpleasant recollection, a shudder of repulsion from the void of her subconscious.

Not long before the visit from Atlas, the Businessman had come to Reina's café by chance. He was angry about something, busy on his phone. So busy that despite many years of regular entreaties to meet, he had failed to recognize Reina at all. Granted, it had been over a decade since they had seen each other, but the irony was not lost on her. Once a month for many years he had sat across from her at her mother's table and pretended to find her interesting; just some weeks before, he had managed to find Reina's former roommate and ask for Reina's phone number, which, as of one hour and a new phone purchase later, the roommate no longer had. But that day, the Businessman had been busy cursing someone, a foreigner. The name sounded cumbersome on his tongue. "He did it before, he can do it again!" shouted the Businessman, who had looked through Reina when she handed him his coffee. She was, in that moment, better than invisible, which was a particularly bitter dose of triumph. Some validation for the worst part of herself. Her tangible transparency was proof that things were just as she'd always thought.

Reina had always known there was an ulterior reason the Businessman was so interested in her. He certainly did not want to meet because he missed her personality or her handwriting. It was also the reason that Reina's mother's lilies seemed to recoil from him while he ate. Reina had assumed as a child that plants' aversion to him was a symptom of her dislike, but there was something specific about him that day in the café that made her rethink her childhood assumptions.

No, not about him. *On* him.

Destruction. It was clear now in her memories, like a thin film through which to alter her lens, to view her childhood experience over again. It was obvious and unavoidable in the sepia tones of retrospect, a faint dusting along his shoulders, like dandruff or lint. She knew his business was more insidious than the agricultural benefits people typically wanted her for. But then, so was anything that yielded that much wealth. The destructive nature of his business lingered upon him like a particularly hazardous cologne.

She shook herself, casting off the lingering effects of the usual shame spiral that came with remembering anything about her past. The point was that Reina's grandmother had always said that someone would someday see her, and it was true, or mostly true, though not in the way she had meant. People did look, eventually. The Businessman was merely the first. In a sinister way the attention was inevitable, because by a certain point in her adolescence, what Reina was—what she could *do*—could not possibly be ignored, whether someone chose to look closely at her or not. But by then, Reina no longer wanted to be perceived at all.

The power she had was not simply profound for a naturalist—she was naturalism itself. That alone should have made her valuable, or at least useful. But why should she have ever had to prove her usefulness to anyone? She had not asked for the circumstances of her birth. She had not asked for her powers, either. If her so-called family could not offer her the dignity of acceptance, much less love, then they did not deserve the fruits of her worth. This, at least, was what she had told herself as she sat across from the Businessman during their monthly dinners.

It became easier over time to deny others the right to know her, to look too long at her. She developed a talent for isolation. She did not need to perform her own abilities or prove her own worth. Without fail, she knew it would happen just as her grandmother had said: They would see. They would see, specifically, power. Opportunity. Naturalism unconstrained, magic of an unprecedented magnitude. When Reina recognized herself as an object—a tool for others to use whenever they had the opportunity to profit—she took great care to isolate herself, to hide, to keep herself preserved. She never spent too long being herself where anyone could see, because it always resulted in her objectification at the behest of another's greed.

Except for Nico. Nico, whom Reina had chosen to spend time with as openly as she had ever spent time with *anyone,* and who she believed had wanted nothing from her. How rare! What a *blessing.* Except now, while watching him fight her rather weak-willed projection, his arrogance did deny one of Reina's fundamental self-held truths: that there was something about her to merit being seen.

She was built on a foundation of avoidance for the sake of self-preservation, but intentionally or not, she had opened a window for him.

He had seen her weaknesses, her inflexibilities, her defenses and mistakes. He had noted and remembered them. He had made use of them, those things about her that no one else had ever been given the privilege to get close to, and he had not done so in any great way. His perception of her was remarkably mediocre. He had no ambition to make use of her for any reason. His only application of what he had learned of her selfhood was being used to preserve his own ego, to service his own strengths.

Reina shifted in her chair.

Ah. So this feeling was disappointment, then.

In Nico's simulation, they had expanded their martial arts repertoire by then. They progressed from blocks and punches to kicks and holds as projection-Reina elevated the stakes of combat, perhaps choosing more challenging maneuvers out of some sense of inadequacy that Nico attributed to her. (Ah, but wasn't she just projecting now? Reina looked briefly at Parisa for confirmation and then turned quickly away, furious with herself.) Nico went for a grab, faking a knee to projection-Reina's face, and as she reeled out of reach, he knocked her off-balance, landing a hard kick to the weak spot in her thigh. In short: projection-Reina had fallen for another of Nico's usual traps, and the real Reina, who sat simmering in place, felt a little brush of resentment. Something gently insistent, like a tendril or a vine.

(How, exactly, was Reina any different to Nico from his friend, the dreamer? How had Nico failed to see that Reina, like the person he'd come here desperate to protect, was yet another tool that the wrong hands desired to use? Not that it mattered, of course. Not that she needed him, or anyone, to find her valuable. Not that she was upset.)

As far as Reina could tell, this initiation ritual was designed to punish the person being projected, not the one doing the projecting. Dalton had said it: there were no constraints. Which meant that Reina could have shown up in a vehicle and kidnapped Nico. She could have fought him with magic; could have pierced him with a lightning bolt through the center of his chest. She could have strangled him with a plant, and that was just within the realm of reality. What might she have done *outside* of it, in a magical projection inside a magic library, where reality as they had known it did not exist?

But Nico had not considered that. The possibility that she might beat him or surprise him had clearly never occurred to him. And so it was Reina who suffered, not him.

She tightened a fist, and the fern in the corner unfurled with the sound of a cracking whip, the branches propelling out like tentacles. There was something growing in her now, festering. Something softer than betrayal, but only in a rotting way, like a translucent peach fuzz of mold. Maybe she was annoyed with him. A spidery bite of something pestering, like the insistence of an itchy tag or whining insect hovering just out of sight. Maybe she was irritated by the discovery that apparently Nico de Varona saw nothing of consequence in her at all.

From the simulation, Nico again worked his way into close range, tangling up with Reina's projection. They grappled briefly before projection-Reina threw him off, and then Nico, as usual, danced away from her with a buoyant series of backsteps, eyes twinkling with mischief as he went.

For what it was worth, Reina did not need Nico to see her in any particular way. They were friends—or perhaps colleagues, nothing more. She had never thought of him romantically and certainly not sexually. She never thought of anyone sexually. That she possessed any sexual organs at all was of as little interest to her as it would have been to any other nongerminating plant. And of course there would be no reason for Nico to imagine her that way, aside from the fact that they had spent nearly all their time together and apparently—*apparently*—the only thing he'd learned about her was how likely she was to get caught by the exact same punch.

Well. Reina grimaced, folding her arms over her chest. Surely Parisa had put that thought there, somehow. It wasn't a thought Reina would have on her own. She cared absolutely nothing for what other people thought of her, and in any case, she especially did not need Nico's interest or approval. Yes she had trusted him more than anyone else in the house and yes she had never questioned whether she could rely on him. He had told her first, hadn't he, about the qualifications for initiation? The little murder game that had been left to the very fine print? And she had known he wouldn't kill her, and he hadn't asked her if she had ever considered killing him, but—

Nico dealt projection-Reina a hard blow that left her stumbling, bleary-eyed.

He hadn't asked her, Reina realized. Of course he hadn't. Because he had already known she wouldn't.

Because maybe he didn't think she was weak, but like everyone in Nico de Varona's life, he knew he had her loyalty.

(He knew he had hers, but did Reina really have his?)

She shifted in her seat again, unsettled and instantly suspicious of her own suspicion as the simulation went on. What *was* the point of this particular ritual? Dalton had said it wasn't a test, so what was its purpose? Was this supposed to be a revelation—some meaningful slice of perspective into what each of them really was—or was it somehow a trap?

And if it was, was Reina the one being caught, or was Nico?

Projection-Reina reeled back, visibly winded, and Nico immediately stopped. "Are you okay?" he asked her. Forgotten was the lesson her projection had taught him earlier—that she wouldn't wait to be told when to start, wouldn't hesitate to escalate the stakes. Nico promptly abandoned any fear of her retaliation, showing nothing but concern for her as if she'd never posed any threat to him at all. "Reina, are you okay?"

Projection-Reina didn't hit back. She straightened and met his eye.

"I'm fine," she said flatly. Toneless. Mechanical.

(Was that how she sounded to him?)

"We don't have to keep going," Nico assured her, practically puppy-eyed with compassion. "I don't really know what the hell we're doing here to begin with, but I don't want to hurt you."

Hurt her? As if she didn't know what she was doing? As if they had not been doing this exact thing for *nearly a year*? Their very first interaction had been in combat—had he been so concerned with her then? Did he think she would simply roll over and *die* if not for his merciful instruction?

Not that she was angry, of course.

Across the circle, Parisa smiled at Reina with positively gruesome implication.

"You can't hurt me," said projection-Reina. So at least there was that. (Though, wasn't there something odd about "you *can't* hurt me," which was false and somewhat delusional and by the sounds of it something to be discussed with a clinical professional, and "you *won't* hurt me," which at least implied some degree of skill at preventing said hurt?)

(By this point, Parisa was laughing into her palm.)

"I know," insisted Nico. "But still, I won't."

The image of them warped, dissolving. Nico woke again in his body with a choking gasp, the effect of renewed consciousness poured into him like water in his lungs.

For the first time, Atlas spoke.

"Sixty seconds and then we'll move on to Miss Mori," he said.

Dalton nodded, glancing at his watch.

Reina, meanwhile, turned to Nico, whispering as low as she could over the sound of him dragging in breaths. (Evidently the physical strain of the simulation transferred to his physical state, so at least in thoroughly humiliating her he'd managed to break a sweat.)

"Did you know it was going to be me?" she asked him. "Like, did you think of me in advance, or . . . ?"

"You could see the whole thing?" asked Nico, bemused but not guilty. So he felt no shame, then. No surprise there—Reina knew what he was—but once again, the reminder was starting to rankle. "No, I wasn't thinking specifically about you. Actually, I was thinking about—"

But Reina wouldn't get to hear what Nico was thinking about. Dalton had shifted behind her chair, and in a sensation less tactile than falling asleep, Reina felt a piece of herself come loose. One moment she'd been looking at Nico, who was still panting and midsentence, and the next she saw only the opening of an endless abyss, which became—after another moment of adjustment—the painted room.

Her ritual was taking place at night, the drapes of the painted room securely shut, the fire blazing from the hearth. The air was almost soggy with heat. Slick with it.

After another moment, a bright white robe stepped out from a cavernous dark.

"Hello, Reina," came Parisa's low murmur.

Fuck, Reina said in her mind, and projection-Parisa thinly smiled, letting the white robe fall.

· TRISTAN ·

Interesting," Callum remarked blandly, observing the specter of Parisa from his vantage point between her chair and Tristan's. The projection of Parisa that Reina had conjured was completely naked, having discarded the robe. She was fully exposed, which apparently was one of the "well, you won't *die*" initiation possibilities with which Dalton—and, by extension, Atlas, who looked as unapologetically smarmy as ever—did not feel the need to interfere.

Tristan, refusing to comment, shifted away from Callum, which only directed him unintentionally to Nico. Nico's expression seemed tense for a moment with conflict—something hesitant on the tip of his tongue—before Tristan dismissively looked away. Whatever it was Nico wanted, it was pointless and could wait.

The real Parisa observed herself from Reina's simulation, then shrugged.

"She's got my tits wrong," she said.

"True," Callum agreed. "And if I'm not mistaken, that's not the only inaccurate detail." He glanced sideways at her. "Don't you have a scar at the top of your thigh?"

Yes, thought Tristan. In the puckered shape of a sunburst. Unwillingly, he remembered running his fingers over it, feathering the edges lightly with his thumb.

"It's a burn. And you're disgusting," Parisa offered to Callum without any particular feeling.

Callum slid lower in his chair, smirking. "Am I supposed to limit my powers of observation? You don't bother hiding it."

The projection of Parisa advanced toward Reina, who stepped back. "Unlike you," Reina said to her version of Parisa, "I don't need to sexualize myself just to feel something."

"True," said projection-Parisa. "You need a lot more than that to feel anything."

"Zing," murmured Callum.

"Shut up," said the real Parisa, though again, there was something vacant in her tone. Unconfrontational. Tristan pondered the possibility of pondering it, then immediately threw it out. Whatever he thought about, Parisa would surely hear it.

She slid him a glance.

Indulge me anyway, she commented in his head.

He looked at where she sat with her eyes on Reina, arms folded. The trace of amusement in her tone had been reserved for his thoughts.

"Seems a bit low-stakes, doesn't it?" was what Parisa commented aloud.

"Why," drawled Callum, "because everyone else in the house has witnessed this before?"

"No," she said dismissively. "Because Reina's going to stop it before it goes any further."

"True," Callum agreed. "But then why—?"

"Well, that's the question, isn't it?" Parisa cut in.

"Ah," said Callum, nodding.

They'd been doing that lately. Nodding. Chatting. *Agreeing.* It set Tristan's teeth on edge. He had never paused to consider what it might be like if Callum and Parisa ever decided to make use of their complementary abilities, and it turned out that what it was like was annoying. No, distressing. Also, he was pretty sure Atlas was watching him. Probably waiting to see what Tristan might do in his own projection. Whatever it was that Tristan was supposed to already be able to do but obviously wasn't capable of, much to his frustration.

Tristan shifted, crossing left leg over right.

No. Bad.

He uncrossed his legs, switching. Right over left. No. Worse. He planted both feet on the ground before becoming aware of a loose thread near his sleeve. Then an itchy tag. Also, there was a twinge in his neck. He lifted his right hand to his mouth and chewed on the dry edge of a cuticle.

Beside him, Callum's mouth quirked.

"Interesting," Callum said again.

It was unclear at first whether Callum meant that Tristan's fidgeting was interesting, that Parisa was interesting, or that Reina's projection of Parisa was interesting or if he meant the opposite and was immensely bored with all of it—though the possibility remained that actually, Callum *did* find this very interesting, because it seemed the type of game that he enjoyed playing. A little psychological warfare, as a treat. Tristan shifted again, then realized Callum was still looking at him.

"What?" Tristan muttered.

Callum's smile shot up at the corners like the flick of a lighter.

"I could fix that for you," he said.

Yes, Tristan thought, he could definitely feel Atlas watching.

The shorthand between Callum and Tristan had been long enough established that Tristan did not require clarification. Callum meant that he could cure the fidgeting. The anxiety. He'd only said it to be fucking annoying, of course, because in the absence of Libby Rhodes, Tristan had obviously filled the role of person most likely to spontaneously combust. Maybe he'd known it all along, really, that the person most like Libby was not her counterpart in Nico, but the sliver of perpetual inadequacy she had in common with Tristan. At the thought of it, the itch of his collar worsened.

He curled a fist. Released it.

"Thought you were punishing me," he remarked to Callum, who shrugged. "Now you want to help?"

"Of course I'm not punishing you," said Callum smoothly. "Though, if I were, I imagine this would work quite well."

Lately Tristan, the resident failed murderer of the house, had been having daydreams. More like fantasies, really. Where he didn't hesitate. Where he simply killed Callum with the knife in the dining room for the good of the group, as he had been so auspiciously assigned. One month had passed since that night, the same night Libby Rhodes had disappeared—coincidence? cosmically speaking, Tristan doubted it very much—and still Tristan imagined things. Instances where even if his worst friend and closest enemy did not *die,* then at least *something* unpleasant befell him. As a form of quasi-meditation, Tristan entertained little reveries where he rose to his feet and socked Callum brutally in the jaw.

Every time, though, he imagined Callum laughing, or turning his head and spitting blood onto the floor, saying something like "So he has a spine after all," at which point Tristan would think okay, give me the knife, let's try this again, but then he remembered that no, he could still feel the shape of the handle in his palm. For the rest of his life he would remember the smoothness under his thumb, the exact frequency of his own doubt.

From afar, Tristan thought he saw Atlas shift in his chair.

"Leave Tristan alone," said Parisa to Callum. "He's melting."

"I'm aware," said Callum.

"Very helpful, Parisa, thank you," muttered Tristan.

"Of course," she replied, her gaze still fixed on the projection of herself.

Across Reina's unconscious—well, *half*-conscious—form, Nico looked up and caught Tristan's eye with a questioning glance. Something akin to *you good, mate?* Only they weren't mates and in fact Nico had not been very helpful at all in the aftermath of Libby's disappearance. Because apparently, suggesting they all bind together as a team to avenge her implied that Tristan was meant to have done more, or emoted more convincingly, or simply given up on life to take on the nightly ritual of howling at the moon in devastation at her absence. Or that was how Nico's gaze seemed to Tristan, anyway. Of course there was always the possibility that Nico was being sympathetic because Tristan seemed like he needed sympathy. Tristan decided he could probably stand to sock Nico in the jaw, too.

So. Things were going well, then.

Helpfully, things were not much better in Reina's projection of herself. Unlike Nico's initiation ritual, Reina's had scarcely any motion. No open threats, no violence. Probably for that reason it was unbearably worse. Tristan just had to sit there and *watch.*

"Tell the truth," said projection-Parisa. "You want to know why I take no interest in you."

"No," said Reina, which even Tristan could see was a lie.

"You do interest me," projection-Parisa told her. "You think I can't see that you're powerful?"

"I don't need you to tell me what I am," Reina replied.

"Actually, you do." Projection-Parisa stalked around Reina in a slow circle, prowling like a jungle cat. "You're desperate to know. And terrified to find out."

"Sounds like you," Callum commented to the real Parisa beside him.

Parisa said nothing. Tristan could see the evidence of calculation on her face, the gears turning. Not for the first time, he wondered what it would be like to read *her* mind.

Tristan jiggled his knee in place. Picked at the cuticle again. Caught Nico's questioning glance and decided that was the most annoying thing currently happening to him. Difficult to decide, really, what with all the things to be annoyed with. Callum maybe still trying to kill him. Parisa accusing him daily of having an acute existential crisis. Reina, who apparently had no trouble saying no to Parisa, making her possibly the most powerful person in the room.

There was also himself. Tristan, as ever, topped his own list of things to be annoyed with. Part of him felt that in some ledger of the universe, Libby's disappearance was his fault. If he'd just killed Callum, would they be in this position? He had liked it better over the last month, when Nico was holding Libby's disappearance against him wordlessly. Implying with his face and his tone and his eyebrows that Tristan had *failed.* This new change in opinion—the sense that Tristan was owed some sympathy—was either unbearable or infuriating. Yes, that's what it was, infuriating. Angering. That was a familiar feeling for Tristan. Comforting, almost. He was practically soothed by the taste of it. Fuck Nico. Fuck Callum. Fuck Parisa, too. Fuck Reina because why not? Sincerely, what was he still doing here? They'd almost gotten him to kill someone and then look, here he was, nearly the victim instead. That's what Callum had called him: a victim.

Would you be quiet? said Parisa. *I'm trying to pay attention.*

"Fuck off," said Tristan aloud, rising to his feet. Nico's eyes followed him. Callum's did not. Dalton, who was seated in the corner observing things, opened his mouth, and Tristan said, "Fuck off, Dalton, I know," and then Dalton said nothing. That Atlas was in the room had not escaped Tristan's notice, but for general purposes of righteousness, he was bent on behaving like it had.

Tristan paced around the outside of the circle of chairs, watching Reina's initiation hologram. The projection of Parisa was standing perilously close to Reina. Close enough that if Reina looked down, she would see the pebbled gooseflesh on Parisa's bare torso, too.

"Tell the truth," whispered projection-Parisa. "Are you afraid?"

"Of what?" said Reina scornfully. "You?"

"You could disappear," projection-Parisa murmured. "Do you realize that? Nothing you do will ever make an impact. At best you'll make somebody a lot of money. More likely you'll make a nice, decorative pet. You're not afraid of me, Reina, you're afraid of *becoming* me," she said, brushing Reina's cheek with a little laugh. In the projection, Parisa and Reina were the same height. In real life, Parisa was substantially smaller.

"You think what you're doing is rebelling," projection-Parisa said. "But you're not. You're just *not mattering.*"

"What does this have to do with sex?" Reina muttered, gaze fixed straight ahead.

"It's not about sex," said projection-Parisa. "You know that. It's never about sex."

"Then what's it about?"

Projection-Parisa's lips twisted upward. "Power."

Tristan glanced at the real Parisa, who looked newly troubled.

"In that case," said Reina. She glanced down through her lashes, taking in the presence of Parisa's projection inch by inch. Cataloguing the landscape of her, first with her eyes, then with the slightest motion of her hand. She reached out slowly, eyes falling on the curve of Parisa's neck. There was a heavy silence as the projection of Parisa inhaled sharply.

Then there was a glint of silver from between Reina's fingers. A thin blade, barely longer than Reina's palm, kissed the edge of Parisa's hip.

A knife.

(A swollen, elongated pulse from the clock on the mantel.)

From a distance of days and weeks and hazy recurring nightmares, Tristan blinked away a similar glint and forced down an all too accessible pain.

"There are other kinds of power," Reina cautioned softly. She pressed the blade slowly into Parisa's skin.

Parisa smirked, leaning forward to touch her lips to Reina's throat, and with a quick upward jab, Reina took the knife and—

Tristan turned away, sickened by the unmistakable sound of blade meeting flesh.

(There it was again—the flash of cold steel. The taste of wine and anguish. The right moment looming, then faltering. The thud of his heart. The clock on the mantel.)

Then the simulation went dark, blinking out.

"Sit, Mr. Caine," said Dalton.

Tristan, who had forgotten he was standing, glanced at the real Parisa as Reina's body seemed to come out of its trance, air refilling her lungs so abruptly she choked on it. She raised a hand—empty, no knife in sight—to her jaw, closing her fingers lightly around the curve of her neck as if to check that it was real.

(The flash of his blade. The thud of his heart.)

(Tick.)

(Tick.)

(Tick.)

"What the fuck was that?" demanded Tristan as the others turned to look at him. For once, Parisa did not look as if she'd known it was coming. Probably because Tristan had not known it was coming, either.

Reina's brow furrowed. "What?"

"Mr. Caine," warned Dalton. "Sit down."

"The knife," snapped Tristan, ignoring the flicker of something that crossed Atlas's brow. "Is that supposed to be some kind of joke?"

"Tristan," Callum murmured. Another infuriating cautioning tone.

Reina folded her arms over her chest. "If it's a joke, what's the punch line? This isn't like what happened with the two of them," Reina added, gesturing stubbornly with her chin to where Callum and Parisa sat beside each other. "It wasn't real. And in the ceremony I did warn her."

"Mr. Caine," said Dalton. "I really must advise you to take a seat."

"No, it's not—You know what? No," said Tristan, his agitation rising. (Tick.) "Are you trying to prove something to me? That I'm weak?" (Tick.) "Is that what this is?" Was this what they thought? That he was a coward? That if he had not done what he had done—if he had not failed as he had failed—then maybe the night, the year, their very *lives* might have turned out differently?

(Tick. Tick. Tick.)

"You're the one who made it about power, aren't you?" Tristan demanded, and Reina scowled. (*TickTickTickTick*—) "It was *your* projection. That wasn't Parisa's doing," he snarled, tossing a hand toward the center of the circle to where Reina's initiation ritual had been. "It was *you. You're* the one who chose a knife, so what are you trying to—"

"They don't know, mate," Callum cut in calmly. So calmly that Tristan mentally collapsed into yet another montage of improvised violence. Kicking the chair out from under Callum and sending it sprawling across the fucking Edwardian floors. No, yanking him *up* from the chair, *then* winding up and—

"They weren't there," Callum said. "They don't know."

It fell on Tristan like a guillotine. Reina frowned. Parisa looked at him with obvious embarrassment, or possibly concern.

"Know about what?" said Nico loudly.

"Okay," Tristan snapped, rounding on him, "and as for *you*—"

He caught a flash of Atlas's watchful eyes before something iron overcame him.

"I told you to sit," said Dalton, whose hand was suddenly on the back of Tristan's neck.

In the next instant Tristan stumbled forward, blinking back white light.

"Hello, Tristan."

It took a while for Tristan's vision to clear. He had the feeling he'd lost his balance, toppling his equilibrium, sending him blindly forward. He heard the voice, recognized it, and then thought, oh.

Oh, no.

The image of her swam before him, gradually increasing in clarity. The shade of her hair. The shape of her lips. He knew it was being pulled from his own memory somehow, drawn out from him like from a tap, but that was the amazing bit—more amazing than the possibility that it ever might have been the real her.

He hadn't realized how clearly he still saw her.

How inescapably he still imagined things like the bones of her wrists.

The divot of her throat.

The bowstring of her clavicle.

That immaculate look of disapproval, as always sewn into her furrowed brow.

"Rhodes," Tristan said slowly. And then, "You look well."

The corners of her lips tilted upward, and in that moment, he wondered if he might be granted something. Absolution. However false it might have been. Couldn't he have chosen that for himself? A moment of peace.

But no, of course not. Dalton had called it a game, hadn't he? Perhaps it was, for everyone else. But this was Tristan's head. This was the prison his mind had made for him, and nothing in here was ever so forgiving.

"Fuck you too," Libby told him flatly, and expelled a burst of flame from the center of her outstretched palm.

· PARISA ·

Tristan, bless him, ducked.

"Bloody *Christ*," he swore aloud, stumbling to dodge the ire of Libby Rhodes that he seemed to have invented for himself—as if his own stumble with morality had somehow divinely necessitated her absence. If Parisa had been paying less attention to the ritual at hand, she might have found Tristan's absurd deduction of survivor's guilt to be funny. But something told her that whatever was going on was not very funny at all.

She glanced at Reina, whose forehead had appeared unceasingly creased in thought since she'd woken from her initiation rite. Was "woken" the right word? Had it felt like a dream? Parisa reached around a bit with her magic, creeping in like light through a crack.

But Reina glanced at her instantly, recognizing the traces of Parisa's magic in her mind. *Nice try,* Reina offered from her head, giving Parisa a gesture that could only be called uncouth, and promptly shut down.

Well. This was precisely why Parisa never spent too much time with anyone. Inevitably, one could learn how another person thought. In other versions of the same situation, that could be called intimacy, or friendship. In this one it was a nuisance.

From the corner of her eye, she could see the tiny quirk of Atlas's mouth. *I take it you think this is funny?* she asked him.

He did not respond, either telepathically or with any visible indication of having heard her. Since he had entered the room, he had been particularly stoic, even going so far as to position himself cryptically in the shadow of a bookcase. She considered poking around in his thoughts as well but could tell that her efforts would be wasted. He was especially well-armored today, and had been ever since Libby's disappearance.

(Which was something to be suspicious about, obviously. But there was a time and a place for such things.)

Parisa turned her attention back to Reina, who was sulking. Presumably Reina was feeling self-conscious about the fact that she'd conjured up Parisa, though that was a waste of time. Firstly, it wasn't like Parisa had never seen herself naked before. Partially because some of her inamoratas enjoyed filming themselves in various clandestine states, but, also, because contrary to what she told people—or rather, contrary to what she allowed them to believe—Parisa had actually made the majority of her expendable income as an art model during her university years. She had long ago embraced her value as an object of beauty, not unlike a flower or a statue. She had learned how to position herself for the best angles, the most expressive looks, all for the sake of bettering other people's perception of her.

Seeing herself reflected in the eyes of others did not bother her at all. If anything, it gave her more material to work with. There had been many artists and students during that time, some bolder than others, who had approached her for the purpose of showing her what they themselves had seen in her. Here was the light in her eyes, and here was the shading on her breasts. Here was the mystery in her Mona Lisa half smile, and here was the hourglass shape of her waist. For them the purpose seemed to be *here, I have perfectly encapsulated your beauty,* but after several versions of noticing some divergent detail or another, one thing Parisa had come to learn was that other people's view of her said far more about them than it ever did about her.

She was very accustomed to seeing herself through someone else's eyes—unlike Reina, who had clearly been overcome with discomfort at viewing herself through Nico's. Had Reina really never imagined how others perceived her before? Likely not, and for that, Parisa was very nearly amused.

Reina was a bit of an interesting case, in Parisa's opinion, in that she observed the truth of people quite easily, albeit simplistically. Reina saw people as a matter of their most basic descriptors: manipulative (Parisa), narcissistic (Callum), insecure (Tristan), or loyal to something other than her (Nico). Reina saw them all clearly, but without truly understanding the heart of things—the *how* or *why*—and therefore she expected them to act rationally, according to her own code of reason.

This was her downfall, of course. Reina Mori had not yet realized that people had a maddening tendency to be precisely what they were in the most unpredictable, erratic way possible.

Part of Parisa lamented that Libby Rhodes was not here to experience this particular ritual, if only because Libby would have been delightfully mortified by anything she saw. Libby did not understand people, not really. It was why she trusted Parisa against every indication she should not, and why she was wary of Tristan despite the reality that Tristan was the only person who would have never acted against her. It was funny, then, that for all Libby Rhodes did not know or did not understand, she was still closer to being right about all of them than Reina would ever be.

At the reminder of Libby's absence, Parisa felt a sharp prick of internal discomfort. Even after a month, Libby's absence was unpleasant to recall. As a general rule, Parisa did not like to deal with loss. She lacked any proficiency with sadness and so usually felt frustration instead, agitation, like a muscle cramp in her legs. That others succumbed to sadness was a detestable show of weakness in Parisa's view, but unfortunately it came with the territory of being human. She recognized the presence of malaise in herself but did not allow herself to actually feel it, being at least clever enough to know that if she let sorrow sink in even once, she would never rise out of it again. Even Callum had been smart enough to know that about her.

From within the bubble of Tristan's initiation rite, projection-Libby was obviously getting the better of him. It was clear he blamed himself in some way for her absence, which was a foolish waste of time. Though, to be fair, Tristan had been engaging in foolish wastes of time quite a lot recently.

Aptly, Callum glanced at Parisa, gesturing to where projection-Libby had nearly taken out Tristan's eye. "Bit sad, this."

Parisa slid a glance to him in return, then reconsidered the scene in front of them in silence. Tristan had attempted a bit of physical magic, which had gone about as averagely as one could expect given that his opponent was one half of the most gifted physicists of her generation. The projection of Libby shot some sort of silly firecracker thing at Tristan, who managed to dissipate the little ball of flame while dropping with one hand to the ground.

Always dexterous, Tristan. Parisa quite appreciated that about him.

She turned back to Callum, considering his blithe expression while observing Tristan's mild attempts to duel. It was obvious that Tristan was feeling far too much conflict about Libby to manage anything remotely near a fatal blow, and in that sense yes, it was a bit sad. But then again, Callum had been having quite a lot of fantasies recently, and most of them were far sadder than the very plausible prospect of being burnt to a crisp by Libby Rhodes.

Specifically, Callum had been dreaming. More specifically, he had been dreaming about Tristan's death. In Callum's dreams, Tristan always died under the same circumstances. It was a bit like being trapped in a nightmare, or a time loop, with the dining room for a stage. Callum attempted different scenarios in his dreams, testing a variety of weapons. Bludgeoning Tristan with a candelabra one night, smothering him with the upholstered cushion of the dining room chair the next. Strangling, of course. Always a bit sexual, that. Poisoning his soup, which was ridiculous. They all knew Tristan had some kind of persisting aversion to broth. Methodology aside, though, what wasn't clear was whether Callum understood *why* he was having these fantasies. Parisa guessed not. Probably Callum thought he was feeling something very male and powerful, like anger or betrayal. In reality he was childlike and lonely, and alone.

"Very sad," Parisa finally agreed.

Callum gave her a quizzical look, then wisely turned away.

Tristan was still dueling Libby's projection. Nico was bent forward, forearms resting on his knees like he intended to recap the match. His eyes followed the projection of Libby as she parried, attacked, spat fire—the usual, pervasive brooding that had overtaken him this last month, then.

Reina, the only interesting one left, was still blocking her thoughts, which was annoying.

Don't you think it's odd, Parisa sent casually her way, *that there's no requirement we win? This really isn't a game. It's just . . . a simulation. So what is the purpose of it, then?*

Reina offered an obscene motion of her hand again and Parisa sighed internally, giving up. She turned instead to Dalton, who was already watching her.

I can see you plotting from here, he thought, telegraphing it in her direction. It was rare that he addressed her directly when the others were present. She could not, in fact, think of a time he'd ever done so before, especially given Atlas's presence in the room. Though, come to think of it, that might have been precisely why he'd done it.

I never plot, Parisa casually assured him, aware that Atlas could very well be listening in. *Nor do I scheme. Though I do on occasion conspire.*

It's nothing, Dalton told her, gesturing with the tiniest motion to where Tristan had conjured up some sort of thin defensive shield, which fractured on impact. *Just another ritual.*

She looked at Atlas, who wasn't paying attention to her or simply appeared not to be. *Surely you don't actually believe that.*

It's not about what I believe, Dalton replied. *It's what I know.*

Then he, too, wiped his mind clean.

Parisa sighed again. With Libby gone, the balance of everything was so disrupted. Tristan was the anxious one and now, apparently, Parisa was paranoid. Already things were fraying between Nico and Reina, though in true Nico fashion, only one of them seemed aware of it. And was there something odd going on between Tristan and Nico, too? Perhaps it was the lingering awkwardness of having once agreed with each other. Which, fair. Parisa hadn't predicted it either.

She thought back to their discovery of Libby Rhodes's "body," which had not been a body according to Tristan, though of course no one else could see what he saw. Except for Parisa, who technically could, but in this case seeing was quite a different thing from understanding. It was the first time she'd ever been aware of what it was like to view the world from Tristan's perspective. Ordinarily she liked the whimsical little forays from Tristan's observation, like seeing Callum's actual hair color (blond only as a technicality) or his real hairline (genetics would strike quite soon, perhaps in his early thirties). What had been unsettling was the sheer potential of his perception, and how completely oblivious he was to it.

The sad truth was that while Tristan radiated a powerful hunger, power itself always seemed distinctly out of his reach. For example, look at him now! Not even the real Libby Rhodes and he could hardly stand to harm a hair on her head. He was practically cowering with the shame and guilt of her. But, in the room as they had looked upon her body one month prior, Parisa had seen inside his head. To Tristan, it was not a body at all—not, as the others saw, a gruesome murder scene, covered in blood—but rather something intangible, unreal, a cluster of lights, like the auroras. Observing the "body" of Libby Rhodes through Tristan's eyes was like looking through a telescope to follow the pathways of a thousand falling stars.

It was Dalton who had told Parisa that the thing, the body—the collection of stars—was an animation. Callum had confirmed her suspicions: that animations appeared like an illusion, but contained more . . . substance. Something that bore a spark of life. A typical animator's work was often clunky, like a mortal animatronic device, with no chance of being mistaken for a living, breathing human, but the fundamental concept still remained. Animations were not simply magical, but magic itself.

The question of Libby's animation—and the proficiency of its creator—aside, this was what disturbed Parisa. If Tristan could see magic in some kind of molecular form, then what *else* could he see?

Parisa knew something had existed between Tristan and Libby long before she interfered with them. They had shared something that couldn't be undone—something that had followed them around, joining them even in their absences from each other. History did that to people. Proximity. Love in some cases, hatred in others. The specific kind of intimacy that meant that every enemy was once a friend.

What was it about the day they'd found the body of Libby Rhodes that Parisa kept coming back to, exactly? Something was nagging her thoughts, sending them chasing their tails. Too much time with the same people, the same minds and their increasing defenses against her, was lessening the effects of her magic, dulling her edge. She felt like Callum in his indefatigable time loop of dreams. What was the snag, the catch? History, molecules, Tristan and Libby, Tristan spotting Libby's body on the ground—

Just then, it occurred to her.

What Tristan had seen in Libby's bedroom had not been from his own perspective.

He wasn't the audience to the projection. He was the stage. That was the trick to everything, wasn't it? That was what drove Parisa to madness now, the fact that they were performing for an audience they couldn't see. Earlier, Nico had conjured a false Reina, Reina had conjured a false Parisa, now Tristan and his false Libby . . . but why? These projections they were creating of each other would teach them nothing about their real competitors—if they were indeed still competitors. Their opinions about each other were no more authentic than Reina's inaccurate conjuring of Parisa's breasts.

But it *was* valuable information. Not about the projection, but about the person conjuring them up. What Nico considered easily defeated in Reina revealed something about himself, his own processes, his magic. He had shown his hand, as had Reina as soon as the projection of Parisa disrobed. Each initiate revealed their own biases, their imperfect knowledge of the others, and if they were still competing to the death—which, *were* they? allegedly not, but still—these would be obvious weaknesses. Fractures to unmake the whole. But since there were no further eliminations necessary, this was not an exercise for the benefit of the other four.

So then this ritual was being performed for *someone*—which should not, perhaps, have been a surprise. After all, the same Society that would take a life could very easily commandeer a mind. Parisa let her eyes flicker briefly to Atlas, who appeared unmoved.

If the five initiates were now revealing themselves to be simply patterns of habit, a series of trackable behaviors observable by each of the others, then perhaps that was the purpose, the true game. Maybe it was not about whether they could be defeated by one another, but how well they could be predicted.

But by whom, and for what?

Parisa returned her attention uneasily to Tristan, frowning as he dove behind a conjured wisp of smoke. His projection of Libby looked more powerful than Parisa would ever imagine her, and Tristan, poor thing, looked panicked. He was attempting to do something, then. Something even he didn't fully understand, by the looks of concentration and dread in his eyes. Maybe the Society would get nothing from him aside from his bizarre sense of chivalry and his enduring self-doubt.

Projection-Libby threw another fireball, this time grazing Tristan's bicep. Parisa leaned forward, frowning, as Tristan swore aloud and smothered his sleeve with one hand, yelping again. So the flames were real, or at least real enough to be perceived. Interesting.

"What are the fucking rules?" Tristan snarled, staring around from within the bubble of his projection. It was unclear whether he could see beyond the simulation he was participating in, but in his desperation, he seemed to have equated performing for an audience with having the right to be heard. Dalton, who apparently did not find this important, scribbled something down in the margin of his notebook.

"It's a fair question," Callum observed in a low voice.

Nico angled around to look at Atlas, who merely shook his head, gesturing as if to remind them that he was a mere third-party observer and it was Dalton who was in charge.

"I gave you the rules," Dalton replied without looking up. "There are none."

"A game with no winners, no losers, *and* no rules?" said Parisa doubtfully, wondering if Atlas would contradict her.

He didn't.

"Not a competition, then," Dalton amended. "Just a ritual." He aimed a wary glance in her direction just as Tristan gave up on receiving an answer, apparently deciding it was time to stop faffing about and actually do something for the first time in the twenty minutes since his ritual had begun.

It was by far the longest compared to Reina's and Nico's respective rituals, which was also very interesting. So the simulation would not end, then, until something of significance happened—and apparently Tristan singeing his sleeve did not count.

You're sure he can't die? Parisa asked Dalton silently.

He looked unfazed in response.

I'm sure, he said. *Only one of the participants in the projection is real.*

So only one person was actually using magic, then.

Projection-Libby continued her pyrotechnics, the glare of the simulation's magic bathing the painted room in glows of amber and red. Tristan dodged the blast from her palm, fumbling for cover beneath the table from the hailstorm of shrapnel overhead. His version of Libby was vengeful, it seemed. Destructive. She upended the table with one hand, sweeping Tristan from the floor in a stunning reversal of gravity. He, the chairs, the books on the shelves, they were all sent floating upward on a collision course with the ceiling.

Tristan managed to free himself from the hold of her magic, which clearly caused him substantial strain. Sweat was trickling from his brow, saturating the fabric clinging to his chest. In delivering himself from Libby Rhodes's fury, he sank hard to the ground, landing near her feet.

"Rhodes—" he started, but she wouldn't hear it, no matter how pathetic he sounded. Only a quick roll toward the floating bookcase saved him from another merciless blast, but his options for escape were limited. The drapes were in flames by then, the upholstery visibly smoking. Projection-Libby took a step toward him and Tristan rolled again, this time colliding hard with her ankles. She stumbled, but only just.

A swipe from Tristan's leg pulled Libby the rest of the way down, relinquishing her hold on the forces in the room. The table landed hard, splintering around the antique feet, and Tristan, who had rolled onto his stomach, shot upright just before a chair crashed down around the approximate location of his head. Projection-Libby flipped onto her back and aimed something at his spine that looked like a translucent wave.

It appeared she hit her target. Tristan let out a yell of something equally anguished and furious, rounding on her precisely like a man who'd recently been betrayed. She rose to her feet and lifted a hand while Tristan, suddenly reckless, stormed forward to tackle her backward to the ground.

The room shifted—or appeared to shift. It was projection-Libby taking liberties again with the forces in the room, altering the very energy inside it to her advantage. Tristan was knocked aside like a rag doll until he rose again to his feet, conjuring something unfinished that managed, at least, to limit her opportunity to return. The room was dark now with smoke, mere glimpses of limbs visible to the rest of them through heavily parting cumuli as Tristan, ignoring his magical limitations, took advantage of projection-Libby's pause to shove her into the now-toppling bookcase. The impact of his body meeting hers was almost poetic with familiarity; as if he remembered the shape of her down to the inch.

Projection-Libby's hand shot out to close around Tristan's neck. He let out a strangled laugh in return, deranged, and tore at her hand so hard she stumbled to the side, doubling over near his waist. She pummeled into his chest, a sheen of effort giving her a feverish look as it glazed the slickness of her skin. Her hair was matted down, soaked with sweat and grimy with ash, and the real Libby Rhodes would have been exhausted by now. But this was Tristan's version of her, and in his mind, she was tireless in defiance of her own limitations. So perhaps he deserved, then, to fly through the air concave, like the shape of a crescent moon.

His landing was hard, a crash through the windows of the apse, and when he stumbled upright, it was with shards of glass embedded in his shoulders. He spat to the side, blood trickling from the corner of his mouth.

"Good girl, Rhodes," he rasped. "Well done."

She answered that as Parisa would have done—with a flamethrower to his chest. Tristan backhanded it away, the impact searing the skin of his knuckles with a hiss of steam. He summoned up a shard of glass, threw it, and missed. Projection-Libby disintegrated the shard midair, the pieces scattering to dust that flew into Tristan's eyes, temporarily blinding him. He swore aloud, eyes red when he forced them open, and conjured something weak and sparking. Projection-Libby batted it away, then countered with a blast that was its astronomical equivalent. Tristan stumbled backward, shot down as if by cannon fire. As Libby slowly approached the outer edges of the apse, tiny flakes of painted ceiling drifted down to form a halo around her head.

Night was falling quickly now. There was an eerie, perfect silence from within the ritual's projection. Stars had begun to blink in the sky, indistinguishable from the falling flecks of ash. Tristan had the usual two choices: fight or flight. Okay, one choice, given how severely he was outgunned. He could run. Would the simulation follow him if he did? Parisa doubted he planned to find out. The only motion from the simulation was the slow stalk of Libby's stride and the haggard rise and fall of Tristan's bloody chest.

Projection-Libby loomed above Tristan—who surely was capable of more in real life, just as Libby would be capable of less. In the world of the ritual's simulation, reality was irrelevant. All that existed here was Tristan's own torment, his pain and his guilt. Parisa braced for a gruesome impact (worse than anything that happened in Tristan's head would surely be Callum's simulation, which would no doubt involve him bullying projection-Tristan into the same outcome Callum always produced when facing any emotional incapacitation) and she nearly looked away when projection-Libby bent down, reaching for a shard of glass the length and width of her forearm.

Something rasped from Tristan's throat. *Sorry*, possibly, or *save me*—and then he closed his eyes. Parisa winced, bracing, as Libby brought down the shard. Tristan, eyes still closed, let out a retch of something, the beginnings of a howl, and—

There was a blink in the projection. Like a glitch in the simulation. The image of Tristan dissolved, and—

As Parisa leaned forward, squinting, Tristan gasped awake inside his body, which remained on the floor where he'd collapsed at the start of his ritual. He was panting with effort, and from within the simulation, projection-Libby shot to her feet, peering through the wreckage as if somewhere, somehow, the rest of him could be found.

It took a moment for Tristan to rise to standing. He looked brutalized and sore, though none of the actual injuries sustained in the ritual appeared on his corporeal form.

There was something odd about it, thought Parisa with a frown. The way the simulation had ended. Nico's ended in a draw, Reina's ended with—presumably—Parisa's death, but Tristan's simulation was still continuing without him.

She glanced at Atlas, who had shifted ever so noticeably forward.

"Why is Rhodes still there if she killed Tristan?" Nico finally voiced aloud.

In the moments of silence, Dalton had risen to his feet, rapidly concealing what looked like a confused glance in Atlas's direction. "Nothing meaningful," he said, waving away their window to the ritual's projection. "Just a lag, that's all."

Lie. Parisa knew him well enough to see it. Reina glanced sideways at Parisa for confirmation, which she concealed. Mostly to annoy Reina, in retribution.

"Rhodes didn't kill Tristan," said Callum.

"We didn't see Reina kill Parisa," Nico pointed out. "But the simulation must have ended because she intended to, right?"

Reina gave him a withering look.

"Rhodes is the projection in this case, not the projector," said Callum.

"Yes," said Dalton quickly. Too quickly. "Yes, precisely."

"Oh," said Nico, looking only partially convinced. "But—"

"Mr. Nova," said Dalton, turning to Callum. "Are you ready?"

What did you do? Parisa asked Tristan, who glanced at her with a look of hollow resentment.

As always, the inside of Tristan's head was a blur of percussive rage, thunderous with the usual mix of spite and pain and umbrage. There was something else, though. A texture Parisa didn't recognize. A spark of something, closer to a flicker than a flame, the frustration preceding a climax. She saw something ordered, gridlike, accessible to him only in desperation. Scene one, Libby Rhodes's body on the floor of her bedroom. Scene two, the glint of Libby Rhodes from the length of a falling shard of glass.

It was as if, in Tristan's head, the image of Libby could suddenly shift into fractures, granularities that followed a familiar path. Parisa could feel the inauthenticity of projected Libby, the pretense of it, from Tristan's point of view. These were replications, approximations, waves. They had the same markers as every other blemish Tristan could see: the little warps of magic they each used to hide their imperfections. The energy that burst from Nico. The waves that dazzled off Callum.

Tristan could see magic in use; that much Parisa had already understood. But this—what he saw right before his imminent projection-death—was different. Almost a portal of some kind, a tunnel, as if when he'd closed his eyes the room around him had shifted, rearranged. It lost its definable characteristics, its colors and lines and basic solidity, but Tristan had . . . *done* something. *Moved* something.

He had *fallen through* something.

Time, Parisa thought with a sudden, ringing clarity.

Then she blinked, realizing she had been staring at him.

"What?" Tristan muttered gruffly.

What an omnipotent little idiot. She hadn't been the only one staring—Atlas's gaze was fixed on Tristan, a fragment of a thought slipping momentarily through the cracks of his careful preservation. It was something like desperation, only more flavorful, more dangerous. Barbed, so as not to be moved. Light at the end of a dismal tunnel. Something insidiously like hope.

In the same moment she clocked it, Atlas shook himself free, shooting Parisa a glance like he knew she'd seen it. So there *was* something to see, then. Some terrible misfortune had befallen their Caretaker, and Tristan was the answer. Or at the very least a sign.

"Nothing," Parisa said, turning to watch Callum's shoulders slump forward, his projection about to begin. "Everything is fine."

· CALLUM ·

He had braced for Tristan, assuming the game—*ritual*—to be emotional manipulation. Part of him wanted it to be Tristan. He felt prepared for it in some way, having by then mentally relived the day when his only ally—friend? a pointless thought experiment now—had determined him to be expendable, or at the very least, better off dead. Every night since then had been whiled away in endless philosophical rehearsal, so what might Callum do this time around, given the chance? He could be noble, lofty. The bigger person. No, Tristan, I could *never*. Harm *you*? I'd rather *die*. How could you even dream of it? The audacity. Et cetera. That would be fun in a dull sort of way. Comfortingly, it would contribute to Tristan's ongoing battle with his own inadequacy, which served him right. Tristan's feelings were all clouded now, and not in a good way. Tristan had walked away from their encounter in the dining room and said nothing, collapsing inward, choosing to sit alone on a throne of self-righteous entitlement that made Callum the sole villain in all of this.

As if Tristan's resolution to kill Callum was less of a betrayal purely because he'd changed his mind. As if everything that Callum had ever shared with Tristan—every intimate thought, every private confession—had been a falsehood—or if not a falsehood, then so very paltry that it could be unimagined, rescinded, undone.

Worst case, Callum thought, would be having to face Nico in the ritual. Callum had very little control over physicalities and could not compete with any sort of seismic activity, and worse, Nico had no emotional trauma to exploit. There was the absence of Libby, but that was hardly something to have a meltdown over. Nico was also delusionally certain that she still existed somewhere, which for purposes of leverage was unhelpful. Reina at least clung to something darker; something from her past she'd carefully built a cage around and preserved on ice. Nico was entirely bright futures, a horizon that glittered as it neared.

So Callum braced for either the annoying or the agitating as the projection folded out around him. He waited a long time, seemingly, to find out.

So long that he poured himself a drink, settling onto the projection of the painted room's sofa.

"So," came a voice behind him. "Are you going to tell them, or shall I?"

Callum choked at the familiar voice, the scotch in his throat fuming somewhere around his eyes. It was a tone he heard constantly from the confines of his head, insistent and grating. A snide, pretentious drawl.

"I'll make this quick," said the projection. From Callum's periphery, he caught sight of sage cashmere.

His mother's favorite.

She thought the color brought out his eyes.

"So," said the projection of himself, having poured an additional glass and settled himself opposite Callum. "Let's be honest with ourselves, shall we?"

There was a long pause as his projection waited expectantly.

His projection snorted. "Do I have to say it, then? Fine. No one thinks you ought to exist. Least of all you."

The scotch stung the back of Callum's throat as he came face-to-face with the *actual* worst-case scenario, which he had not heretofore considered: himself. The expected illusions were all present and accounted for, though they seemed more imperfect than usual. The augmentations to his face were insufficient, so obviously false that anyone could see it wasn't real. They approximated beauty without actually reaching it, much like Callum's face typically looked to himself.

He remembered that Atlas Blakely was watching and thought, *Ah.*

What doesn't kill me will inevitably try the next best thing.

"The thing is," his projected self continued, crossing one leg over another, "they're right, you know. You shouldn't exist. There's something very wrong with you, and to your credit, at least you've always known it." The projection paused for a sip, then considered Callum's silence. "Are you going to stop me? If you don't," he cautioned, "they'll all discover you're a fraud. Not that it matters. They hate you anyway."

He laughed Callum's odious laugh, downing the rest of his glass. It sounded even worse outside of his head.

"The trouble with you, Callum, is exactly what Atlas Blakely said. You have no imagination," Callum's projection informed him, rising abruptly to his feet. "Every punishment you've ever subjected anyone to? You do it to yourself every day. Every minute. *Your* pain is chronic. *Your* existence is pointless. When your consciousness blinks out—which it will," he added with an irreverent wink and a toast of his empty glass, "it will be as if you never existed at all.

There will be no lovers, no family or friends to think fondly of you the moment your hold over them collapses. No memories for anyone to treasure but the ones you manufactured, which will dissolve into nothing the very moment you come to an end. You'll be forgotten immediately, and this, the immensity of your power—the magnitude of your abilities," he clarified with a smirk, as if he took particular pleasure digging in this particular knife, "which is no small thing—it will be eclipsed by the utter fucking *enormity* of your pointlessness. When you no longer exist, you will have left nothing behind."

Projection-Callum made a face of repulsion, letting the empty glass drop carelessly from his hand. Rather than shatter, it came apart bit by bit, disintegrating as it would on a breeze.

"Everyone who casts a glance at you is witnessing the outcome of a tragedy," Callum's projection scoffed. "And yet not a single person will feel sad."

The real Callum considered his own glass for a moment. "You seem to be laboring under the impression that any of this is news to me."

"Laboring? No, this all comes very easily to me," replied his projection. Classically droll, as Callum himself most often was.

"So what do you want, then?" mused Callum. "For me to destroy myself?"

"Of course not," his other self replied. "Don't you understand? I don't *care* what you do to yourself. Nobody does. I don't care if you live or die. Isn't that obvious?"

"So then how do I win?" asked Callum neutrally.

"You don't win. This isn't a game. This isn't a test. This is just your life." His alternate self strode restlessly from the sofa to the fireplace, fingering the edge of the clock on the mantel. "There are no winners, Callum. No losers. You understand this better than anyone. Everything dies." He glanced over his shoulder. "Everything, eventually, ends."

"I must be terribly fun at parties," Callum remarked dryly.

"Oh, you are," his projection-self confirmed, turning to face him again. "In fact that's all you are. Fun at parties. You're effortless, so casually zeitgeisty with your malaise and your boredom and your indiscriminate spite—and isn't it terribly funny?" his projection mocked. "Your detachment, your observations of the world . . . it's all very *amusing*, isn't it? Oh, people are terrible," he mimicked, draping a pale hand across his falsely blond brow. Even though the projection was Callum, he affected a petulant, nasally voice. "They're weak and flawed and interesting only because they're so terribly chaotic, and we *hate* them—but not because they're dull or predictable." That smile, which was surely Callum's own, reeked of insincerity. His voice dropped and he looked Callum in the eye, going in for the kill. "It's because as small as they are, and as horribly unremarkable and as miserable and simplistic and stupid—even then, they do not spare an ounce of love for you despite how badly you wish they would."

Idly, Callum took a sip, parched.

"But of course they don't love you," laughed his other self. "And even if they did, how could you ever be sure that you had not been the one to put those feelings there?"

To that, Callum folded his hands in his lap. At this rate, Parisa was going to have a field day with him. On the bright side, perhaps this would liven things up for Tristan's ongoing adventures in existential decay.

"Tell them how it works," his projection suggested, a glint of something reckless in his too-blue eye. "Tell them how much it hurts. This is your chance, after all." His expression fluoresced with malevolence. "Or you could tell them the truth. How you know everything about them. How the library gave you their secrets, their ghosts and trivialities. Tell them what you told Tristan, for as well as that went." Another harsh laugh. "You may as well try something honest, Callum, for once. If they're ever going to listen, it has to be now."

This was, of course, a trap of some kind. Callum understood in a deeply disinterested way that the others did not think much of his capabilities, believing him limited when it came to physical magic. But everything was at least partially physical, was it not? They were physical beings, not amorphous blobs. To be beholden to the demands of a body or the laws of physics was a matter of transcendence, and to transcend naturally implied some baseline limitation. It was all very simple, really, that one could not create something out of nothing—and likewise, one could not create nothing out of something.

Even when others witnessed Callum at work, they could not know what they were witnessing. For a year they only saw the effects—Libby's skittishness, Parisa's destruction, Tristan's hatred, these were the only things that proved Callum had any magic at all. The rest was simply a story that was told to them, circumstantially. In order to reduce Libby's anxiety, Callum took it on himself. To ease or alter Tristan's pain, Callum had had to find the strength to hold it. And as for Parisa . . .

Actually, Parisa had not been all that difficult to work with when they had faced each other last year. She was not so different from him after all, and what the others could not see in their sparring was how little Callum had to push her in order to find her breaking point. The others had thought they were witnessing his influence when, in fact, they were actually seeing the stripped-back version of her truth—the kind of truth that no one could live with, if not for repression of the most stubborn and proficient kind.

The point was that Callum's magic was not without its costs. To build the vacuum of space necessary to protect the house's magic, for example, Callum had been the one to empty himself out. To create the fluid membrane within the Society's wards alone had meant absorbing everything that had occupied it beforehand. Terror, anguish, longing, isolation, envy, pride. The cost of that kind of magic radiated through his ribs into the bars of his container, and whatever else Callum Nova was or wasn't, he could only regenerate at a mortal rate. He could only repair himself slowly over time.

It was Callum who had been in pieces, not that anyone else would ever know or care. And not that he expected them to find out. He preferred hatred over pity, distrust over charity. The latter was an insubstantial gauze, like being wrapped in a thin film of cotton. A slow asphyxiation over time.

Sensing Callum's unwise surge of feeling, his projection-self postured on. "Do you think they know what it really means to love?" his projection-self mused aloud to him. "That it isn't the simple joy of fondness, I mean. In fact it's violent, destructive. It means to cut the heart out of your chest and give it to someone else." He slid a sidelong glance to Callum, who didn't look up. "To care at all about anyone or anything means inevitably to suffer. After all, what is compassion?" Callum's projection posed, pausing for the punch line. As if it were a joke, which it was, in some capacity. "To feel the feelings of someone else is to exhaust yourself with double the pain," he finished blithely, like a garden party toast. "All those insignificant little *feelings*, the annoyances of coexistence you claim to hate so much. When you alter them, they must go somewhere, isn't that right?"

"Somewhere," Callum echoed conversationally. Merely to be polite.

"Oh, and it is a burden, of course," his projection-self assured him. "The regular pains of ordinariness and existence. Wanting things you cannot have, assigning yourself a destiny that you'll never be able to fulfill, et cetera, et cetera. It's all obedience to our collective mindset, some atavistic pattern in our blood. Like whale migration," he mused, "or that silly compulsion we have from time to time to mate."

Callum eyed his glass, contemplating another. "I see that being this full of shit doesn't seem to tax us overmuch," he commented blandly.

"Not as such," his projection-self agreed, and then stopped. "Are you trying to influence me?"

"Am I?" Callum flexed his fingers outward, adjusting himself within the discomfort of their cramping. As with any chronic condition, his survival was a matter of becoming more comfortable, not some elusive unreality of being wholly pain-free. The trick was managing it until it no longer bit so angrily or stung.

"It won't work," his projection-self told him with an insufferable look of condescension.

"Well." Callum summoned the bottle of whisky toward him, doing away with the laughable insubstantiality of his glass. "You have to admit, it was worth a try."

His projected self offered a mirthless smile. "Have you told them how you learned to use it?"

"Use what?" Callum asked rhetorically, approximating a safe degree of ignorance. (He was long accustomed to employing a bit of pretense for the normies.)

"Your magic." His projected self smiled scornfully. "Your . . . abilities."

"Empathy is widely taught," Callum said. "Sharing is caring and what have you."

His other self tutted impatiently. "You're wasting your time."

"Am I?" Callum gestured around the projection with the bottle in his hand. "It seems to me I have so much of it."

"You know what I mean."

"Yes, I do. I always know what everyone means." Callum took a long pull from the bottle, closing his eyes. "Just as Parisa always knows what every man is thinking when he looks at her, regardless of what lie he chooses to tell. You know, I really quite admire her," he added with a bit of genuine adamancy. She was listening, after all. "To know what people really are and not destroy them is savagely remarkable. She has exceptional restraint." Though, by that standard, he probably ought to celebrate Reina just as equally. Of the five of them, she alone seemed actually capable of disregard.

"You know what people are," his projection-self observed. "Don't you?"

It was another rhetorical question and probably a trap, but Callum answered anyway. Why not, at this point? "To think as another person thinks and to feel as another person feels are disparate activities. Recreationally speaking, it's a different sort of challenge."

"Because feeling is less powerful than thinking?" mocked his alternate self. "So you don't even have that leg to stand on."

"No. Because feeling is more human than thinking," Callum corrected, closing his eyes and exhaling. "And the more human something is," he murmured, "the weaker it is."

Silence. After a moment or two to luxuriate in the tedium of the exercise, Callum's eyes fluttered open.

His projected self was watching him. Waiting.

"I take it you want me to confess my constraints to the audience? They're very simple," Callum said neutrally. "They're the same as the constraints on a computer, overloading any system with too many applications to run. Too much and the whole thing crashes, it fails, it dies." He sank lower into the cushions, taking another pull from the bottle. "The limits of my magic are the same as the limits on my body," Callum said, making what he considered to be a laudable effort at explaining himself. "It's a matter of choosing between feeling power and staying alive."

"But you have never really used your power," his projected self reminded him. "Perhaps you forget," he added, "that beneath your natural talent lies someone very, very uninspired."

Callum glanced down at his knuckles again, contemplating the soreness he still felt from time to time. Particularly since his experiment that night in the dining room with Tristan, when admittedly he'd overreached a bit for the sake of argument, impractically making a point. In subjecting Tristan to the best (and worst) of his abilities, Callum had magnified a lifetime's enormity of pain and then precariously dragged it back.

Occasionally he became arthritic in the aftermath of such an output, though more often he developed an immune deficiency. The clever thing to do was usually to isolate for at least a few days, possibly a week or two. Which was very doable now that nobody could stand to face him.

Funnily enough, Rhodes (and presumably Varona) would understand better than the rest of them what Callum was faced with whenever his magic was overused. Libby would grasp the nature of imposing this much force, which was to create order out of chaos. She would know, therefore, the prescriptive exertion required for that degree of thermodynamic implausibility, had she ever considered it in those terms. The amount of entropy reversed by Callum in order to create an emotion that did not otherwise exist was physical enough—it was energy sent outward, chaos accepted in.

Still, to claim the sophistication of a human battering ram was not exactly elegant. Certainly not to win some unwinnable battle for the sympathy of four idiots who didn't care if he lived or died.

"Make your point," invited Callum. "I can see what you're getting at."

"Make it yourself," said his projection.

Callum closed his eyes again, chuckling. "Really, and end this delightful exchange?"

"No," his other self said. "It will never end. I will disappear for the rest of them, true, but—"

With his eyes closed, Callum felt his projection kneel down at his feet.

"I will never disappear for you," said Callum's own voice in his ear.

So melodramatic. Callum's throat was dry, so he took another sip.

"Say it," the projection said.

Callum sighed with exhaustion. How tiresome this all was. No wonder people couldn't bear to listen to him. "I don't suppose you poisoned this?" he asked, gesturing to the little remaining in the bottle.

"Say it," his projection said again.

What an absolute farce of a ritual. What was the point of this, aside from public humiliation? There was no winning, no losing. There wasn't even any magic. There was only the image of himself and the knowledge that no, he did not care to have himself for company, how terribly amusing to know for sure. As if anyone would ever willingly choose to spend any time with themselves. (That, too, was surely something Libby Rhodes would understand.)

Callum took another long swig, waiting for some blissful end to the monotony. Would it be so difficult to simply expire right here? He waited for a quick count of three, wondering if he could will himself into nonexistence.

In that moment, he caught a glimpse of something. A flash before his eyes, like a sudden streak of starlight. Fate that intervened in a familiar form on his behalf. Finally, a favor.

Callum glanced at the knife that lay innocently upon the table. Ah, so this was the choice, then. Speak now or end it all, a truly theatrical scene. How very typical of him to ensure his only escape would be a comedy of errors and exquisite pain.

He leaned forward, picking up the knife by the handle and observing his reflection in the blade. In the dancing firelight he drew the pad of his thumb along its edge, admiring the impression it would make against his skin.

His other self looked smug. Knowing. "It won't last," he said.

No, it wouldn't. It seemed there was only one way to make this end.

"It hurts," Callum finally confessed aloud. The humiliation was acrid, spiked with his other self's glee. "I," he clarified, letting his eyes shut again so as not to see his own vacantness. The falseness in his own face. "I hurt."

His eyes remained closed when he heard his projection-self shift upright, rising to his feet. The projection took the knife from Callum's hand, then the bottle, audibly taking a swig before settling himself on Callum's right. Twin saboteurs and squanderers.

"Nobody cares," he told himself, neither cruelly nor kindly.

And then, finally, Callum woke up.

III

ORIGINS

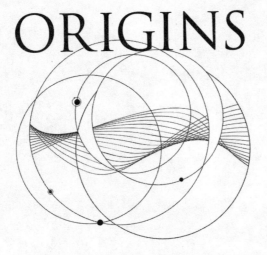

· NICO ·

I t was uncanny how quickly long hours could stretch exhaustingly into days, then into rapidly accumulating weeks. After Libby's disappearance, time that had so long stretched and yawned like a recalcitrant cat now seemed to have raced willfully by, vanishing at some point when Nico wasn't looking. Which was also relatively feline, come to think of it.

With the exception of yesterday's initiation ritual, Nico slept, he woke, he ate, he read. It was nothing and yet the days were dwindling, the discovery of Libby's disappearance growing increasingly microscopic in the rearview. At first he had hounded the others about it, then made polite requests, then academic suggestions, all abandoned once it was clear that no one could be of any help. After years of her bounding after him with insults and tedious corrections, he now found himself wishing to turn a corner and see her stooped with her horrible posture over a ratty book. What he wouldn't give to interrupt her reading session with a snide comment, or throw his feet upon her study table just to see her reaction. "Rhodes," he could almost feel himself saying, "this is too much volatility for one morning. Think of the ozone layer. Or the trees."

But, she was nowhere. Or at least nowhere they could find. And so there was nothing to say. Perhaps there would never be anything to say again.

It was as Nico began to wonder whether there was anything more to be discovered that Gideon, ever the cleverest prince in school, showed up again in his dreams.

"Well," said Nico, after a moment or two on the subject of how he was doing. (How was he? How *was* he? Answering left him winded.) "You've kept me in suspense long enough now, Gideon, don't you think?"

"Only because it's so very amusing for me," said Gideon, tapping the bars of Nico's usual dreamscape cell. From where Nico stood on the other side of the bars Gideon seemed very nearly refreshed, as if the possibility of sinister hijinks on behalf of his most reckless friend had improved his complexion overall.

"That," Gideon added, "or because you've been ranting for the last ten minutes about someone I take to be one of the other Society initiates. Who's Tristan again, by the way?"

Only the most unnecessarily surly dickhead to walk the earth. For weeks now, Nico had been attempting to sort out how exactly to begin a conversation with Tristan that did not end with the unmistakable implication (transmitted via Aggressive Glaring) that Nico should deposit himself immediately into the nearest crevasse. Was it really so *unreasonable* that Nico should try to establish a rapport between them, given that Tristan seemed the most natural ally in the wake of Libby's disappearance? But of course no, Nico you fool, obviously the only reasonable response was for Tristan to repeatedly and without explanation bite the hand that had done nothing but helpfully (!) agree with him. Not that that was remotely the point.

"You're not supposed to know about any of that," Nico sighed, realizing once again that Gideon always listened to his rambling at least ten times more carefully than any normal person should.

"What, the fact that you know someone named Tristan, or that you're all initiated now?" Gideon asked neutrally. (The menace.)

"None of the above," grumbled Nico, flicking a glance to the security camera mounted in the cell's upper corner. Even in dreamscape form, the surveillance served the Society's larger telepathic wards, which were presumably monitored by someone. (Parisa? Nico couldn't help but think that unlikely. Then again, maybe she had a lot more time than he knew about. Or just a penchant for voyeurism, which wasn't entirely out of the question.)

"What did you have to do for your initiation ceremony?" asked Gideon. "Ritualized human sacrifice?"

Not this time. "Just some kind of simulated game."

"A game?" One of Gideon's eyebrows shot up in an obvious display of skepticism, and Nico, who frankly did not deserve such treatment (today), gave a heaving sigh.

"Are you really so suspicious of me, Sandman?"

"Of you? No, Nicky, never." Figured, thought Nico, who according to Parisa was "incapable of guile" or some other vaguely insulting reassurance of his disgusting human fragility. "I do, however, have some ongoing reservations about your Society," Gideon clarified. "Has anything about this process led you to believe that the qualifications for membership can hinge so casually on a game?"

"Well, there was other stuff before that," Nico attempted.

"Oh," Gideon posed neutrally, "you mean the murder game? *For the six to become one,*" he dramatically intoned, "*one must—*" And here, a theatrical pause. "*Die?*"

"*Arrête,*" said Nico.

"*Nunca*," Gideon replied.

"It wasn't," Nico sighed, "a *murder game*—"

"I'm not here to judge your hobbies," commented Gideon, who was mercilessly smug.

"The point is—" Nico stopped. "Sorry, what was the point?"

"Your point? I haven't the slightest idea," said Gideon. "*My* point was that whatever it is you had to do for initiation yesterday, it must have meant something more to the Society itself."

"I doubt it," said Nico, shrugging. "Just seemed like a test to me."

"A test of what?"

"I—" Nico glanced at the security camera again, then decided to promptly give up caring. "Look," he muttered, "if you *must* know, it was a simulation. Us versus a projection of some other member of our initiation class."

Gideon's brow twitched knowingly. "And it was you versus Tristan?"

"What? No." Actually, it was Parisa who had faced the projection of Tristan in the final round. Which had been a very anticlimactic end to the day, considering that once Parisa had entered the simulation for her initiation ritual, she had simply curled her legs beneath her on the floor of the painted room and begun to meditate. Her version of Tristan did . . . something. Something that was very unclear to Nico, and that had obviously been of equal or greater confusion to Tristan. But Parisa, who was the projector, did nothing but meditate, and after a few minutes the simulation ended without any indication that she had performed any magic at all.

"It was me versus . . . a friend," Nico said, narrowly managing to not give away Reina's name that time. "My sparring partner, actually."

"And you . . . sparred?"

"Yes." It was fairly normal, all things considered. "And everything was fine."

"Was it?" Gideon asked, again with a rich dollop of skepticism.

"Why must you persist in accusing me? It *was* fine," Nico insisted. "And then afterward we were told to put together some sort of presentation for our independent research—"

"And then they kissed you on the forehead and tucked each of you in for the night," Gideon concluded.

"Yes, basically," Nico confirmed.

"Right," Gideon said. "Well, I'm sure it was all exactly as playful as you imagine and not at all some kind of ongoing experiment to indoctrinate you into their cult of homicidal academia."

"Yes, thank you, I agree," said Nico. "And anyway, Reina was perfectly fine afterward, so—" Ah, fuck.

"Reina," Gideon echoed, observing Nico's look of *balls almighty, did it again* and deciding that was an opportune time to appear as innocent as possible. "Noted."

Nico sighed, hopeless. Now that Gideon knew about the Society at large, Nico was continuously forgetting to have any secrets from him whatsoever. Next thing he knew he'd be confessing to having eaten the last of the Nutella that one time during finals their junior year. (Ha, never. He would die first.) But his options were to tell Gideon things and let him help with finding Libby, or . . .

"Well, forget I said anything," Nico reminded him, as Gideon gave a subtle shrug of *already forgotten, carry on.* "I'm obviously delirious from my full-time job as a homicidal academic."

"Oh, obviously." Gideon considered him a moment in silence. "You know, I suppose I never asked you. Who would you have killed, if you'd been the one put in a position to do it?"

"So you're just assuming I wasn't the one to do the murdering?" asked Nico, mock-affronted.

"Feel free to assume it to be an assumption," Gideon permitted. "I, however, will call it absolute certainty of fact."

"I could kill someone," Nico insisted. He'd done it before. In this house, even.

"Someone you actually *knew*?" Gideon peered at him.

This was all very insulting, probably. Unclear how, but it seemed like it probably was. "I mean, I *could*—"

"But you didn't," Gideon observed.

"I—" Honestly. "Look, for what it's worth, I didn't have an issue killing the person we were supposed to kill," said Nico, who had never been a fan of Callum. "Though if I'd known he'd wind up still being alive—oh, *balls,*" Nico hissed belatedly, having once again given away a critical piece of proprietary information.

"Interesting," said Gideon, whose continued look of smuggery now battled a smile of disgusting fondness. "So he's still alive? Continue."

"Okay, let's say for the sake of argument that he's not *not* alive," attempted Nico optimistically, to which Gideon replied with a shrug of *naturally, yes.* "I wouldn't necessarily mind his . . . continuing to be not not alive."

"That doesn't sound like the same thing as choosing him to die," noted Gideon.

"Well . . ." Fine, so Nico had been fairly certain that if all of this was a matter of who *deserved* to be part of the Society—which, in fairness, had seemed at first to be the point—then for a while there, one person in partic- ular had not seemed to possess much of a useful talent at all, and it wasn't Callum. "Never mind," Nico said conclusively, shoving Tristan Caine's un- believable unpleasantness (and ongoing mysteriousness) out of his head for the time being. Tristan was not only alive, he was also more useful than Nico had anticipated (or less, depending on whether one considered seeing the truth in Libby's dead body to be useful if the person in question then proceeded to do absolutely nothing about it) and so it didn't even matter.

"The point is," Nico said, "now I get to study whatever I want."

"Which is?" asked Gideon.

"You, *idiota*."

Gideon arched a brow. "You're going to present me to the rest of the class?"

"Well, not entirely. Not in so many words." It was actually Reina who'd suggested that Nico look into evolutionary biology. She'd first brought it up a week or so after they'd run their little experiment in creating a spark of life, which reminded Nico that he needed to press her further on what exactly she meant. It hadn't seemed like the *natural* follow-up to what they'd done—wouldn't she find it more interesting to study dark matter or some- thing? something she could actually *use*?—but then again, Reina was very cerebral by nature. Nico had wanted to discuss it with her since the initiation ritual, but she had seemed fairly distant and distracted recently, like there was somewhere else she needed to be.

"Well, anyway," Nico said, clearing his throat and changing the subject to the one they'd intended to discuss all along. "You said you've almost found her? Rhodes?"

It took a moment. Gideon was considering whether to push the topic of the Society, obviously. Nico held his breath until finally, Gideon relented.

"I think so," Gideon allowed, nodding. "I don't know the outside shape."

"Oh." The dream realms were formless, for the most part. Gideon had tried to explain this before—that dreams were a function of a collective consciousness, blahblahblah—Nico never made it through the entire expla- nation without suddenly recalling he was hungry—which reminded him, he'd been having the oddest craving for Portuguese egg tarts at the bakery he typically attended with Gideon and Max on Wednesdays (he'd read some- where about the excess of egg yolks at some sort of monastery and as a result, Wednesdays always seemed an oddly holy day), but the point was . . . hm. "Wait, what?"

"I can tell it's Libby's consciousness," Gideon clarified. "But I don't know where she is. If," he added, "it's even a question of where."

"Oh. Well, that's . . . something, at least." And it was, considering Parisa had been so convinced there was no trace of Libby Rhodes to be found. "So, what's the plan from here?" asked Nico, feeling a little thrill at the possibility of action. "Are you just going to hijack her dreams or something?"

Gideon tilted his head, probably gauging whether it was worth offering Nico the full explanation.

"It's not really that simple," Gideon eventually said. "Can't just pop in and tell her we're looking for her without any warning. Might startle her."

"But wouldn't it be reassuring?" Nico countered. "Knowing someone's got an eye out for her?"

Gideon shook his head. "She's not her conscious self in a dream," he reminded Nico, who probably knew that already in some inactive way, but shrugged. "She doesn't have practice being in her subconscious the way you do. And there's no telling if she's actually *aware* that she's been, you know . . ." Gideon hesitated.

"Abducted?" Nico suggested for the sake of terminology. "Kidnapping feels juvenile."

"Sure." Gideon shrugged. "So yeah, the situation calls for subtlety, I think."

Right. That was rather not Nico's expertise. "Subtlety how?"

"I'd rather not . . . you know." Another shrug. "Break her brain."

"Oh. Right." That did seem a distinct possibility. Hardy though Libby Rhodes tended to be as a medeian, she was something of a lost cause in the arena of needless concern. (And this degree of concern was possibly quite merited.)

"How do you know it's her, then?" Nico asked.

"Tricks of the trade, mostly." That was Gideon's usual shorthand for *my magic isn't entirely human and therefore can't be explained, please stop asking thanks ever so.* "It might take me a bit more time to get through to her."

"Why?" Nico asked. "Difficulty?"

"Not exactly." Another pause for consideration. "She just has to . . . accept me."

"Accept you?"

"Yes, accept me as a possibility. In her dream."

"But that's—" Nico withered. "Impossible."

"Of course it's not impossible, Nicolás," Gideon said. "You forget I'm very talented."

"I never forget that, *mon ami*," Nico replied spiritedly. "I meant it's impossible because Rhodes is a neurotic train wreck who never believes anything."

"Oh. Yes, then that's a good point." Briefly, Gideon looked troubled. "I suppose it may take me more than a bit, then. Depending how often she dreams."

"Well, at least it'll keep you busy," said Nico, doing his best not to give in to the sinking feeling of doom that lived slightly behind his left ventricle. "I'd hate to think you're just sitting around aimless and weird without me there. . . ."

He trailed off after he said it, feeling unexpectedly caught. Unwillingly *perceived,* actually, was the better word for it. It was a bit too close to the truth of the matter, which was that Nico was aimless and weird without Gideon, and had been particularly off since Libby had gone. Nico felt isolated now, and for a person who studiously avoided being lonely, Nico was the closest he had ever been to being alone. Something about Libby's absence had ripped a hole in the fabric of Nico's reality, allowing little unforeseen vulnerabilities to spill out.

He and Gideon both seemed to acknowledge the unsaid in the same moment, a look of softness coming over Gideon's features—which was unbearable in the way that Gideon's gentleness was usually unbearable.

Which was why, in a desperate effort to restore balance to the universe, Nico asked, "Have you spoken to your mother?"

He had meant it as a joke, though it was worth noting. After all, Gideon had contacted Eilif, his criminal of a mermaid (in retrospect, the term "mother" seemed unearned) in order to find out where Nico had gone, so despite Gideon's assurances that it had not cost him unduly, it was an ongoing possibility that the information had not come for free. Given Eilif's association with the kind of criminals willing to kill for Gideon's access to the dream realms, a favor from her was the kind of gift horse one couldn't look in the mouth without a nasty, unavoidable bite.

"I'm back within your wards now," said Gideon carefully. Too carefully. "She can't reach me."

That was fastidiously worded, in Nico's opinion, and it didn't do enough to rule out the possibility that someone very foolish (Gideon) could still choose to do something equally foolish (call his mom). "That's not an answer, Gideon."

"Close enough" was Gideon's uncharacteristically standoffish reply.

That was unexpected. For the first time since he'd been gone, Nico had the sense that perhaps his year of withholding the entire truth from Gideon had offset something fundamentally transactional between them. True, there were the occasional half-truths (or no-truths) they exchanged as a matter of chasing their collective bliss, but this oversight felt particularly earned. Negative connotation. Nico had not told Gideon about the Society, and now that Libby was gone, it was clear to Nico that the stakes he'd left out (including but not limited to: the possibility of his death, dismemberment, and/or disappearance) had been too big a secret. Nico had thought it was a small thing—a large necessity, which was in its own way a small thing—but maybe that was too much to hope for. Maybe too much stood between them now that Gideon knew exactly how much he hadn't been told.

"*Je suis désolé,*" Nico attempted. He suddenly wished, feverishly, for the opportunity to brush his shoulder against Gideon's, or to nudge him with his knee. What was that they said, about people who had lived through extraordinary loss missing the ordinary? The little things, the trifling reassurances that made up their primary language. The culture of their own tiny nation, which had recently withstood some bombs.

"You don't need to be sorry," Gideon said. "I know why you did it. Why you kept the truth of the Society to yourself. It wasn't your secret to tell."

Nico winced. So many secrets hadn't been his to share, and yet he'd parted with them anyway. "Knowing why isn't the same as forgiving me."

"Who says you need my forgiveness?"

Nico expressed every manner of offense he could conjure into a single glance and Gideon sighed, shaking his head.

"It's not a matter of forgiveness," Gideon said tactfully. "It's more . . . resolution."

"What can I resolve?"

"Not you, me. And there isn't much to say about my mother," he added. "She's pushing me to do the job I told you about, and I already told you. I said that I would."

"But you didn't mean that, right?" Nico said, and then, as Gideon seemed reluctant to answer, he frowned. "You won't actually *do* it, will you?"

Gideon hesitated. "Well—"

"Gideon," Nico said, reaching every register of disappointment in the span of three syllables.

"It's quite a bit different from anything she's wanted me to do before," Gideon admitted. "I'm not stealing anything. Or putting anything where it doesn't belong. Nothing like that."

"But how much do you know about the . . . you know. Job? Since we know your mother isn't telling you everything," Nico rushed to point out.

"I know. And honestly, I haven't decided yet whether I will." To his credit, Gideon did look immensely undecided. "It's just . . . it doesn't seem like it could be a *bad* thing, does it? Breaking someone out who's trapped in their own consciousness? I find it difficult to believe that's something that happened by choice."

"That's only what Eilif told you," Nico reminded him. "Which isn't necessarily the truth."

"Right, yeah, I know. Of course. It's just—" Gideon stopped. "It would be . . . interesting."

Oh no. "Gideon."

"I mean, only after I found Libby first, obviously—"

"Gideon, I don't think—"

"I promised I'd help you find her and I will, that's my top priority, but since you'll still be locked away with your Society—"

"Oh, fuck you," Nico heartily retorted, bristling at the possibility (reality) that this was predominantly his fault. "You and I both know that you've got a problem with boredom, with or without me." Which wasn't true, obviously, because it was *impossible* to be bored with Nico. Even he knew that, and Gideon's look in return proved as much. "Oh, I see," Nico tutted with a sickening realization of guilt. "So you're still punishing me for leaving, for keeping something to myself for once, is that it?"

"Aren't *you* punishing *me*?" Gideon countered. "You're the one treating me like some kind of Fabergé egg, Nicky. I'm not going to break just because you're not here to fuss over me."

They were dangerously close to something Nico would call a reasonable disagreement and Max would call a lovers' quarrel. "I came here," Nico said with a drum-kick of frustration, "to keep you *safe*."

Gideon leveled a glance at him impassively. "Did you?"

The implication that he might have done otherwise was briefly and acutely enraging. "*Yes—*"

"Fine," Gideon said, with Gideon's usual infuriating way of backing down before things got too heated. "Fine. Assuming that's true—"

Nico gaped at him. "*Assuming* that's true?"

"—then what exactly is the point of staying safe if you're not even here?" Gideon snapped.

They eyed each other for a second.

Then, gradually, Nico saw Gideon swallow heavily with remorse.

Not that remorse was owed. Nico shook himself, willing himself to be better, to be less . . . him, and more Gideon. "If this is a cry for attention," Nico managed, "I'm going to really resent you for stealing my move."

The tension dissipated between them, Gideon's shoulders slumping with feigned exhaustion. Or real exhaustion. (With Gideon, who could tell?)

"I promise," Gideon sighed, "that I won't get myself hurt, killed, or otherwise maimed."

"No psychological damage either," Nico warned. "Takes forever to get trauma out of the drapes."

"*Te odio.*" *I hate you* (affectionate).

"*Con razón.*" *Rightfully so.* "*Moi aussi.*"

They looked at each other again, this time less combatively. But with something, Nico thought. Something sad, like a window of opportunity, had come and gone.

It had happened before, Nico told himself. It would happen again.

"I'll let you know when I've reached Libby," Gideon said.

"You could come before then," Nico offered. Something in his chest felt heavy, like loss.

Gideon looked sympathetic. "Get your rest, Nicky," he replied, and snapped his fingers, leaving Nico to wake in his bed with a gasp.

Nico turned hastily in the dark to his phone. The light was too bright, blinding. He typed so quickly he misspelled things twice. *Are we okay?*

It buzzed within seconds. *Always, Nicolás, always.*

Nico let his hand fall, eyes closing.

It took a moment to slow his pulse. That had been happening lately; something critical to his existence was being overworked. It took him longer to calm down, or wake up. Even the initiation simulation had tested him more physically than usual, which was terrible news for his magic and worse news for his mind. He curled a fist, feeling his knuckles crack and give way to pressure he wished he did not feel.

He wondered if the others could see it, or if they felt some version of it. This . . . weakness. Something Nico wasn't accustomed to feeling and could barely even identify as something to feel. He'd thought for a while that Tristan had noticed, or that something similar was happening *to* Tristan. That since Libby was gone, taken, that had meant something psychologically debilitating for both of them. Slightly different things, but something nonetheless.

Naturally, though, Tristan was a fucking pill under the best of circumstances, so it didn't matter. Nico turned onto his side, staring at the blank wall, and waited for his heart to stop racing.

He was nearly asleep again when a knock sounded at the door, crisp and precise, no-nonsense. Nico contemplated ignoring it in favor of inching further toward the precipice of rest, but then rose to his feet with a groan. His ankles popped beneath him, an odd pinch somewhere near the lower discs of his spine.

He pulled open the door, ready to tell Reina that six in the morning was *not*, contrary to popular opinion, a good time to spar, and would she please come back later when they were no longer in a race with the sun?

But, hugely unpredictably, it was not Reina after all.

"I need you to help me die," said Tristan Caine.

Which was when Nico decided he was probably done sleeping for the day.

· REINA ·

Parisa was alone in the reading room when Reina arrived to request a manuscript from the archives. What exactly Parisa was doing there was unclear, because she did not have any books. She simply stood alone in the center of the room, eyeing the pneumatic tubes that were responsible for delivering the books and manuscripts requested from the archives.

"Are you making a habit of this?" asked Reina.

Parisa looked disgruntled at having to pause her very important task of staring into nothing. She scanned Reina with a dissecting look before deigning to answer. "Am I making a habit of *what*?"

"This." Reina gestured to her. To the empty tubes. "Inactivity. Are you losing your mind?"

"Yes," Parisa replied with a roll of her eyes. "I'm succumbing to madness, thanks. And you?"

"Making progress."

Parisa smirked in response, the subsequent moment tight with repulsive acknowledgment that they'd been very nearly cordial to each other.

"I don't suppose you're licking your wounds from the ritual," Reina remarked quickly, before anyone made the mistake of thinking them companionable.

"*My* wounds?" Parisa echoed, tension helpfully resurging. "You're the one avoiding Nico."

"I'm not avoiding him."

"Oh?" Parisa arched a brow. "You're just . . . suddenly very busy, are you?"

"Aren't *you*?" Reina countered, knowing that Parisa had been all but invisible for at least the last twenty-four hours. "I would assume you're refining your topic for independent study, but I'm guessing it's something a bit more—" Reina threw in a little flick of disinterest, like the cherry on top of an apathy sundae. "Extracurricular."

"Ha *ha*," replied Parisa, tossing her mane of dark hair over one shoulder in what appeared to be an escalation of annoyance. "You do realize this is not an effective method to hurt me, yes? I've been called much worse by people who mattered far more," she muttered with a glare.

"Not trying to hurt you," Reina said, shrugging. "Just pointing out the obvious."

"As am I." Parisa folded her arms over her chest, turning to face Reina with an impatient sigh. "He's not exactly worth your enmity, you know."

"Who?"

"Who else? Varona." A shrug. "Given the quality of people here, you could really do a lot worse."

"I don't feel any enmity toward him," said Reina. "I don't feel anything about him."

"Mm." Parisa's lips pursed. "If only that were true."

Parisa turned then, as if to leave the room, but Reina was getting a bit tired of her always hogging the last word. "Why didn't you do anything?" Reina asked, pausing Parisa mid-pivot. "During your initiation ritual. When you were paired with Tristan." It had been Parisa versus a projection of Tristan, which by all accounts should have been an easy win. Reina had not taken Parisa for the merciful type, but for some reason, she had not lifted a finger in her defense. The disruption of Parisa's character had been bothering Reina since it happened, though she concealed it now by mentally reciting Homer.

"Paired with, hm?" Parisa looked amused. "Is that what you thought you were doing with me? Pairing off?"

"No, I—" Fucking English. "When you *faced* him, then. Fought him or whatever."

The little curl of mockery to Parisa's perfect mouth only deepened. "So you think you were *fighting* me? How thoroughly depressing."

Reina regretted ever opening her mouth. "Never mind, I was just—"

"No, no, tell me," Parisa urged, half laughing. "Were you concerned for me, Reina? How charming. I didn't think you were the type."

"No, I was just—" Okay, to hell with it. "You should have beaten him soundly," Reina said, which obviously took Parisa by surprise, because she blinked. "We were all paired off that way for a reason, weren't we? Against someone we should have destroyed but didn't."

"Is that how you see it?" Parisa's voice was oddly contemplative. Sincere, even. Or at least not nearly mocking enough. Infuriatingly, it had the effect of magnifying her prettiness, or whatever it was that made her face look like that. "Interesting."

"Well—" Reina stopped. "What else is there to see? Nico should have beaten me, I should have—"

"Slept with me?" Parisa guessed.

"Stabbed you harder," Reina muttered, much to Parisa's apparent delight. "Tristan should have been able to kill Rhodes, and Callum—" That was an anomaly that none of them were able to make heads or tails of. "Whatever the deal was with Callum, but then *you*—"

"Interesting," Parisa repeated, her attention drifting beyond Reina and back to the archives again. She seemed to actually mean it—that Reina's point was *of interest* to her—which was . . . momentarily disarming.

"Why?" Reina said with a frown. "What did you think the purpose of pairing us that way was supposed to be?"

"Oh, I don't care about that," Parisa replied flippantly. "It seemed perfectly random to me."

Reina was astounded. "You think it was *random*?"

Parisa shrugged. "Why not? You don't feel any differently about me than any of the others, do you?" Reina blinked, wondering if it was a trap, though mercifully Parisa had already lost interest and added, "I don't feel any differently about Tristan."

That seemed fundamentally untrue, but admitting it felt like losing a completely different argument than the one they were having. "So then what did you think the arrangements were for?"

"That seems like a Callum question," said Parisa, transferring a look of disinterest to Reina. "I don't really care who or what arranged us that way. I just didn't want to be involved in it regardless."

Something was off about her phrasing. "Who or *what*?" Reina repeated, frowning. "What does that mean?"

Parisa's eyes flicked to the side briefly. Something rose to the surface of Reina's thoughts, though she couldn't identify what. Nothing, really. Nothing concrete. A familiar glimpse of the archives, though it was paired with the sudden impulse to grit her teeth—not unlike the way Reina had felt while watching Nico's projection.

Was Parisa trying to summon Reina's thoughts about . . . the archives themselves? Reina's eyes flicked to the pneumatic tubes again. Their emptiness, and Parisa's watchfulness.

"Nothing," Parisa said eventually, turning away. "Hyperbole."

"No it wasn't," Reina said, suddenly frustrated. "What do you mean *what*? You think it was something other than Atlas or Dalton?"

"Of course not," said Parisa evenly.

"But then why—"

Behind them, someone lightly cleared their throat. Both women turned to the reading room doors, Reina startled, Parisa unsurprised.

"Miss Kamali," said Atlas. "A moment?"

He was dressed more casually than usual. Gone was yesterday's pristine suit, and in its place were a pair of uncharacteristically rumpled slacks, a loosely fitted shirt. Even stranger than the absence of any formality was the pair of loafers on his feet that more closely resembled slippers, and the cup in his hand suggesting he'd taken his tea on the run. It was such a jarring change that Reina thought, firstly, that she'd been right to suspect him of hiding something. And then secondly, to immediately destroy that first thought.

"Fine," said Parisa, giving Reina a look of annoyance, as if Reina had been the one to summon him here. "As you were," Parisa added over her shoulder, sashaying past Reina and joining Atlas at the door.

He stepped aside, allowing her to pass into the corridor, and paused to address Reina before following. "Enjoy your research, Miss Mori," Atlas said in his usual hospitable tones, as if he were not currently in A) his pajamas and therefore B) a state of obvious distress. "Everything is fine."

"Reassuring," said Reina dryly.

Atlas was at least able to take her doubtfulness in stride, giving Reina some equivalent of a smirk.

"I'm on holiday," he replied, offering a curt nod and disappearing into the hall.

Reina stared after them for a moment, lamenting briefly the absence of plants in the reading room. It felt strange being the only witness to what was an incredibly bizarre interaction—not that the painted room's fern would likely offer any sort of consolation. Ultimately she shrugged it off, submitting her request to the archives.

She had very carefully made a list of the subjects she had in mind. First was another batch of creation myths—the origins of humanity according to "insert ancient culture here," that sort of thing. She had begun with the obvious—the classics, Greco-Roman mythology and of course Egyptian mythology, the Old Testament, the Taoist legends of creation—and had begun now to backtrack to the cradle of humanity, summoning Sumerian myths and ancient epics.

She supposed that in her way, she was conducting research on cosmology. "In the beginning there was only dark," et cetera, only without the Nico-Libby of it all that made everything feel so mathematically inaccessible. She wanted to understand life from within her naturalist perspective—with the understanding that it was a form of energy, some flame from within, not some great mysterious architectural schematic of molecules and vacant space.

Since their initiation ritual, they had yet to come to any sort of meaningful conclusion on Viviana Absalon, the mortal-cum-medeian whose autopsy had revealed a twenty-one-year-old's internal organs where a forty-five-year-old's should have been, suggesting a medeian-level gift for longevity. A foundation for their studies on death, Viviana Absalon left them without a meaningful conclusion, merely providing an experimental point of argument—could she have lived forever, had fate not intervened? Dalton's introduction to the subject—with the implication that perhaps the untimely death of a medeian whose gift for life was somehow an inevitable or predestined outcome—had triggered something in Reina; some idea she couldn't name.

His theory implied, to her, that the universe was ironic in some way, or that catastrophes were earned. It seemed a small and ultimately mortal (in the "destined to end" sort of way) method of looking at the world. There was an egoism to it, too: the concept of a grand plan where they were not grains of sand or a billion atoms in a trench coat, but each of great and irreplaceable significance instead.

(Reina was of the opinion that there was no chance this was true. And if there *was* a god—a God, that is—she respected Him less for having the time, capacity, or interest to personally fuck with her.)

In the end, all that their unit on longevity and death had produced for Reina was the same thing she'd tried to re-create with Nico: the concept, untested and half formed, that life was something that could be spontaneously created and therefore randomly destroyed. (Previously, Reina's slightly different hypothesis was that Viviana Absalon was a person whose life had ended not because she was born with a fated magical consequence, but because she was born at all and such things sometimes happen.) Reina's interest in pursuing the creation myths came from some fundamental suspicion that if life was *not* random, then humans, whatever else they were, were excellent note-takers. The universe predated humanity, true, but when had *life* come to mean what it did? Someone must have witnessed what it meant for the world as they knew it to begin, and if such a thing had any sort of design, Reina needed exceptional hindsight to find it.

The books were deposited in front of her in order. *Gilgamesh and the Netherworld*. *The Enuma Elish*. The myth of Adapa. Reina already knew each of these works to contain similar themes: humans granted immortality by the gods for their greatness. (A reflection of a general, species-long aversion to the unknown abyss beyond death.) There was an element of generational divinity, too. Old gods and new. This was the aspect that intrigued Reina most. The rise of the Anthropocene meant the supernaturalism of geoengineering, the indelible mark of humankind without interference from the divine. (Unless, by chance, someone had failed to mention James Wessex's mother being inseminated by a shower of gold coins.)

Reina sifted through the titles gently, the waxy undersides of the protective film brushing her fingertips like leaves. She reached the bottom of the pile sooner than she expected, and was trying to remember whether she'd left anything off her list when another piece of parchment fluttered from the archival delivery system.

CERTAIN REQUESTS DENIED.

Reina blinked, turning the slip of paper over to see if the archives had specified which titles were rejected. It had not, and her list was now gone. What had the library not given her? She could have sworn they were all essentially within the same category of mythology. Also, she was initiated now. What else would be kept from her at this point?

"Oh, hey," said Nico, peering over her shoulder and startling Reina into a brief hiss of surprise. "Sorry," he added with a smile, as if nothing between them could conceivably be wrong. "New loot?"

"What?" Reina blinked, and Nico glanced pointedly down at her pile of books. "Oh. Right, yes."

"Looks long," he observed, gesturing to the *Gilgamesh*. "Though I guess it's not called an epic for nothing, right?"

He seemed to be desperate for her to laugh. Probably his method of seeking forgiveness, which made sense. Why, in Nico's world, would anyone go to the trouble of admitting their wrongs when they could simply dimple with pleasure and spill a bit of sunshine from the tips of their unruly hair?

"What are you here for?" Reina asked him instead, because to give in to yet another of Nico de Varona's whims seemed an unbearable indignity for the moment. (Not that she was angry, obviously. Nothing about the initiation ritual had been real, and so it was a waste of her time to feel any particular way about it.)

"Well, um. Kind of a long story," said Nico. "Do you know much about Schopenhauer?"

"The German philosopher?" Of course Reina knew nothing about philosophy, which for a number of reasons struck her as largely a waste of time. Could Nico not have guessed this by now? Also, she had suggested that he study evolutionary biology for his independent research, but that was apparently not the advice he planned to take. "Isn't he one of the ones who says life is all about suffering?"

"Is he? Festive," said Nico cheerfully, filling out his request form and submitting it to the archives. "Can't wait."

"Is this for . . . you know. Your friend?" Reina asked.

"Oh, god no. No, not even a little bit." Nico made a face, then produced an apple from somewhere and took a bite. The sound ricocheted from the high ceilings of the reading room and reverberated somewhere deeper for Reina, who tensed. "You wouldn't believe me if I told you, honestly," Nico added, rolling his eyes.

"Oh. Right." Wonderful, thought Reina. What a productive use of both their time this conversation was. "Well, I should probably—" She gestured over her shoulder, motioning to leave, though Nico turned to face her before she could slip away, doing his usual thing where he vibrated at far too high a frequency in the limited distance between them.

"Hey, so which books did it reject?" was apparently the question he couldn't resist asking. Then he took another maddeningly loud bite of his apple and chewed through the words, "I didn't think that would still happen."

She hadn't either, though that wasn't the point that settled in her mind.

"It," Reina echoed.

"Yeah, it. Or they, I guess. Whatever." Nico gestured to the archival tubes, fluttering his fingers. "The divine delivery system and its little messengers."

"Oh." Nico was merely being facetious, then. Still, something about the word "it" struck Reina in a way that lingered on the tip of her tongue, like a half-remembered dream. "Nothing important," she said. "Just some creation myths I requested for research."

"That's it?" he asked. Reina shrugged in ambiguous confirmation. "And it wouldn't give them to you? Weird," said Nico. "You think it's afraid you're going to try to become a god or something?"

"Ha," said Reina dutifully, turning away. "So anyway, I have to . . ."

"Right, sorry." He gave her a salute. "Enjoy. Spar in the garden later?"

Oh. "Maybe." If she couldn't find a way around it. "Lots of work to do, but—"

"Right, right. Well, if it works out." The archives completed Nico's request with precisely the kind of thick, bound tome that he typically hated, and if Reina had been feeling slightly more conciliatory, she would have laughed at the way he clearly died inside. "See you."

Reina, who had intended to read inside the reading room, left with her pile of manuscripts in something of a somber mood, drifting toward the painted room (unless someone else was in there, in which case she would just call the day a lost cause and eat bonbons in bed). Someone needed to water the philodendrons. It was hot outside and the dogwoods shifted toward the sun. *Mother! Over here! Mother looklooklook bless us with your bountiful eyes Mother, praise us Mother helloooooooo—*

Reina stopped short, her mind belatedly capitulating with an answer just as she passed by Atlas's locked office.

Parisa had said *what*. As if the outcome of their initiation ritual had not been determined by a person, but a thing.

Nico had called the archives *it*.

Dalton, in discussing Viviana Absalon, had referred to magic almost as a god unto itself.

Atlas spoke of the initiation requirement as a sacrifice before the altar of knowledge, knowledge that was sentient, a sentience that undeniably filled this house.

But maybe magic—or the library itself—was less cerebral than that.

Reina hardly knew where she was going until she arrived in the dining room, pausing on the threshold until Callum, who stood in the corner, registered her presence with a fleeting, disinterested glance.

He was lingering by the bar, fixing himself a drink. It was nine in the morning.

"Your disapproval is noted," Callum said without looking up, appearing to pour even more liquid in his glass in retribution for her silence. "It is also discarded."

"Tell me something," Reina said. "Your initiation ritual—"

"Yes, I'm fucked up, it's pathetic, the end," Callum said, lifting the glass to drain it.

"No," said Reina, to which Callum paused mid-sip. "Well, yes. But also, I meant . . ." She swallowed. "You said something. You as in the other you. Something about knowing everything about us."

Callum looked sideways at her, then proceeded to finish his drink, remaining nose-deep in his glass for what seemed to Reina an age.

"Yes," he said eventually.

"Yes?" Reina echoed.

"Yes," he repeated.

"Care to elaborate?"

"Fine." He turned back to the bottles, pouring himself more of whatever that smoky scotch was that he preferred. "Are you drinking?"

Reina shook her head. "No."

"You are now. Indulge me."

"You could've just influenced me into taking one," Reina pointed out.

Callum looked over his shoulder at her, then proceeded to pour a second glass.

"Listen," he said. He put the stopper back in the bottle, then carried the two glasses over to where she stood beside the table, setting one down none-too-gently beside the head chair. "I don't give a fuck what happens to any of you beyond this. If you've got some kind of Rhodesian moral obligation to uncover what the archives choose to show me, fine. Whatever. I don't really have the time to waste on reassuring you of my intenti—"

"So it was the archives," Reina cut in, nodding. "They gave you information about us?"

He shrugged, lifting his glass. "A toast," he suggested. "To life being fucking pointless."

A little too dramatic for Reina's taste. "I'm just trying to ask if—"

"Drink," said Callum. When Reina opened her mouth, he repeated, "Driiiiiiiiiiink," which suggested to Reina that perhaps this was not his first indiscretion of the day. She raised the glass to her lips and choked immediately on the fumes, opting not to move until after Callum had finished his glass.

"Okay," Callum said, slamming down his empty glass. "You have thirty seconds. What the fuck do you want?"

"Can you influence the archives?" asked Reina.

"No," said Callum bitterly. "The library's sentient, sure, but at that magnitude—"

"Then I want you to use me," Reina said.

Callum blinked.

"I want you to use my magic," Reina clarified, "to influence the archives so they'll give me the books that I want."

Callum stared at her.

"I think that was thirty seconds," Reina said. "Which is honestly more than enough time for me, so—"

"Wait," said Callum, pausing her as she moved to turn away. "Wait. Wait. Are you . . . ? Are you serious, or—?"

This was ridiculous. She didn't have all day. It was really a very simple question and she had the very pressing matter of a lot of interesting books to attend to in the time it was taking for his neurons to fire.

This, she thought irritably. This was why she didn't drink.

"Get sober," Reina suggested over her shoulder, Callum still staring vacantly after her by the time she reached the door. "Then come find me when you're done."

I need you to help me die," Tristan said to Nico. Because in his mind, that was the fix.

It was actually a very simple solution. Tristan's process of deduction had begun during his initiation ritual. In the moment when Libby had been about to kill him—not the *real* Libby, obviously, though he wouldn't put it past her if she ever decided to try—he had suddenly been able to conjure up the use of magic that he had only thus far managed via long periods of staring blankly into space and completely disassociating from himself. Which was hard, honestly. A lot of work. And annoying. And a waste of Tristan's precious time.

But then, when Libby had been about to kill him, his perspective on the situation shifted. Suddenly he could see everything, which in practice meant that he could see one thing very clearly. He saw the magic constraining the simulation, and once he saw that—shifting, as it had done when he first saw the animation of Libby (again not the real Libby, albeit a second unreal Libby—that was going to get confusing, wasn't it? all these fake Libbys piling up in his mental storage, which was clearly logical albeit possibly unwell) lying dead on the floor. Blink once, it's Libby Rhodes! Dead! The horror! Blink twice and it's energy changing direction, suddenly following an orderly path.

In the painted room as he faced the wrath of Libby Rhodes, with death on the line, Tristan's vision had kaleidoscoped again, as it had last time, to enhance his other senses. He could taste the impending peril and it had gifted him clarity, ridding him of the usual fucking obtuseness he shouldered at any given time. His imagination was too small when he was just sitting there, perfectly safe, fretting about things like his father's opinion of him or whether his soul would still exist after he was dead. No, the trick was to *clear his mind*, or possibly abandon it altogether.

When Tristan woke from his projection, Atlas Blakely's eyes had been the first ones he met, and he doubted the spare degrees that had shifted in Atlas's posture were a matter of mere coincidence.

Hence, "I need you to help me die," which was not exactly met with enthusiasm.

"What," Nico had said, "the actual fuck."

"I know," said Tristan.

"I knew you were a masochist but that's taking it a little far, even for you," Nico added.

"Sure," Tristan amicably agreed. "But I wouldn't ask if I didn't think it would work, magically speaking."

"Why me?" Nico asked. Which was a fair question that Tristan had already asked himself several times in the seconds between knocking on Nico's door and being faced with the rumpled physicist.

"Because, unfortunately for all of us, I like myself just enough to not actually *want* to die," Tristan began.

"Oh." Nico blinked. "That's great news, honestly—"

"—which means I can't do it myself," Tristan sourly continued. "And since you're the only one with the magical capacity to try what I have in mind, you're also the only person I can ask."

He left out the obvious other factors: Because he couldn't ask Callum. Because Parisa would laugh. Because Reina couldn't be budged from her books, and anyway, Tristan wasn't convinced she wasn't a total psychopath. If there had been anyone else he would have gone to them instead, but there wasn't and so he hadn't. He wasn't even that convinced he should be here now, but again, the solution seemed to him very simple. So simple that for an impulsive moment it had outweighed other things, like his general dislike of the man standing shirtless in the doorway.

Nico sucked in one cheek, chewing it in thought, or possibly suspicion. "And what if I don't feel like helping you?"

Then just as I suspected, you're useless to me was what Tristan very cleverly did not say.

Instead, he shrugged. "Sad. Not world-ending sad. Just inconvenient." He turned away, having already devoted more time than he'd intended when he first knocked on Nico's door, but Nico stopped him with a long-suffering sigh.

"Fine," Nico said. "Tell me what you mean."

"Schopenhauer's will to live," Tristan said.

"Okay, use better words," Nico suggested, folding his arms over his bare chest. It wasn't unusual for him to be indiscreetly half-dressed, but for the first time he seemed aware of it in a self-conscious way. "Or, like, more of them."

There was a thin sheen of perspiration on Nico's chest that suddenly struck Tristan as abnormal. In pondering it for the briefest instant (humans occasionally sweated, after all), he realized that it was because he had never seen Nico or Libby have to regulate their temperature before. While the others adjusted their behaviors and wardrobes to the weather, Nico often did not. And Libby, who seemed enamored with knitwear in a mostly aesthetic way, only looked physically altered when she had recently performed a significant amount of magic—a degree of strain that, for better or worse, Tristan intimately understood.

"You look sweaty," Tristan observed, before immediately regretting it when Nico's expression naturally contorted into something of a smirk.

What had Atlas called Tristan once? A savant? So much for that.

"My eyes are up here," said Nico, in a voice altogether more irritating than Tristan had time for.

"I was just—Never mind." Tristan glared at him. Not for any particular reason, really. Just because it seemed like he should express his opinion on the matter of their interaction before either of them got confused. "Schopenhauer's will to live states that there is something innate in each of us. Something like self-preservation, which essentially comes to fruition in moments of impending death."

"Okay." Nico frowned, shifting against his doorframe. "So you think you'll be able to access something in the moments just before death?"

"I don't think it. I know it." After all, he'd very recently experienced it, and unless he was very much mistaken, Atlas had seen it too. Atlas's silence on the matter was, if anything, more telling than Tristan's personal suspicions. "I just need something to speed up the process."

"Process of what?"

"Of . . . seeing it. Things. I don't know." This was going rapidly downhill. "I have something," Tristan said irritably. "Some ability that I don't understand. But I can't use it unless things are very—"

"Dire?" Nico guessed.

"Yes." Tristan had a feeling they had finally managed a moment of synchronicity: both were envisioning Libby Rhodes's dead body on the floor of her bedroom, which was also the moment both men had realized there was something in her absence that they alone understood. "I've used it a handful of times before," Tristan added. "I think . . . I think there's something I can access. Something that changes the way I see reality. But—" he said, and stopped.

Nico waited.

"But I can't do it fast enough," Tristan confessed with a grumble. "Not unless my survival is on the line. And since you've died before—"

"I'm sorry, what?" said Nico, before Tristan recalled that the dossier on the others that Callum had shared with him—the information that Callum had secured from the library's archives, which had included the detail that Nico de Varona's magic had once resurrected him in a moment of intense strain—was not exactly common knowledge.

"Sorry, slip of the tongue, I just—" Great. Sweat and now tongues. "The point is, you do a lot of stupid things very regularly," Tristan clarified gruffly.

"Oh, right. True." Nico's brow furrowed in concentration. "Though I don't usually try to kill people."

"How wonderful for you." That came spitefully without effort. "I suppose you may have noticed that when I try, I have a tendency to fail."

Nico at least seemed to recognize the misstep. "I didn't mean—"

"I don't care what you meant," Tristan said, which was true, or probably true. "But I want to start experimenting soon. Like now."

"*Now?*" Nico blinked at him, then glowered. "What am I supposed to do, fetch the shotgun and take you out back?"

"That seems like it would involve a lot of excess cosmetics," Tristan said. "Try and keep the face pretty, if you please."

"Oh, so there's vanity involved now, great." But Nico was clearly contemplating the possibilities. "Are you thinking . . . electrocution? Asphyxiation? Suffocation?"

"Exactly how much time have you spent imagining my death?" asked Tristan.

"Not any more than anyone else, I'm sure." Nico's fingers tapped idly at the side of his thigh. He also seemed to have cooled a bit, not that Tristan was noticing. "Okay. Okay, fine." He nodded. "I'm going to look up Schopenhauer, though."

Tristan tried very hard and fruitlessly not to grumble. "Fine."

"And I want to . . . think about it. Ways to do it, I mean." Nico looked sincere, and very nearly earnest. "Because if something goes wrong—"

"You're a physicist," said Tristan shortly. "If something goes wrong, you'd better fucking fix it." The words, like most of his words lately, came out sharper than he intended.

"Nothing you can do about it if I can't," Nico tossed at him, equally charged.

They both tensed, Nico leaning against the opposite side of the doorframe while Tristan shifted his weight from left leg to right.

"Look," Nico said, running a hand through his unruly hair and appearing to fish around for an olive branch. "Rhodes trusted you. I know that."

That, if anything, was precisely the reason Tristan had come to Nico. "Yes."

"And you . . . whatever you can do." Nico contemplated him in silence. "It's obviously something worth exploring."

"Yes." Clearly. "I think it might be—"

But then Tristan stopped, because he did not want to be wrong. "I just think I could understand it better if I could get the timing right," he said, choosing his words carefully.

Nico considered him another moment.

"Fine," Nico said. "But don't wake me up this early again."

I'll do what I please, Tristan thought testily, though after a moment's indignity he decided that was probably a fair request. He had a habit of losing track of time in this abyss of a house. "Whatever. Fine."

"And let's do it when Parisa's asleep," Nico added as an afterthought. "I don't want anyone reading my mind and shouting at me over it."

"Fine." That was also a valid point. Not that Parisa would shout at him, but she *would* very definitely mock them both. Assuming Tristan survived it to begin with. "Later tonight, then."

"Great. Bye." Nico stepped back from the door and shut it firmly, leaving Tristan to linger in the hall.

Before he could turn toward his own room, a door opened to his right.

"Well," came a voice from his periphery, and Tristan tensed.

He turned slowly to Callum, who was eyeing him with something that might have been amusement.

"Making new friends?" Callum asked. He was sipping from a mug, which was presumably not filled with chamomile. Though, who could say? Callum was not looking any more or less troubled than usual. Perhaps he slept like a baby. Or the dead.

"I think I'm done with friends," Tristan replied tightly.

Callum's face broke into a wide, derisive smile. "Understandable." He shifted to return to the interior of his room, then paused. "I—" Callum began, and then stopped again, shrugging. "Well, you might want to consider dealing with all of this," he said, gesturing vaguely to Tristan. "Ideally in a healthier way than concocting perilous schemes with a hyperactive child."

Tristan felt another surge of directionless rage. "I take it you have notes?"

"Friendly suggestions, perhaps? I for one find yoga to be wonderfully refreshing." Callum raised his cup to his lips, eyes locked on Tristan's. "But I wouldn't presume to offer notes."

Wonderful. "Is that all?"

"Quite." Callum turned away from the corridor. "Night, then."

"It's morning," Tristan pointed out.

"Only for the unimaginative," Callum replied over his shoulder, and slipped from the threshold back into his room.

It was lucky for Tristan that he had more pressing matters to contend with. He made his way to his room, contemplating a nap, then gave up on the preposterousness of such a concept and decided to make his way out to the edge of the grounds instead. Under his arm was the notebook he'd been scribbling in since the conclusion of their initiation ritual, which was ostensibly meant to contain research for his topic of independent study (their syllabus for their second year in the Society archives was a ludicrously sparse page—"initiates will each contribute a treatise of significance to the archives, the topic of which is open to their choosing"—followed by a single line that Tristan, alleged scholar and possessor of words, still could not satisfactorily complete) and which instead contained incomprehensible diagrams of nothing.

Well, not nothing. Tristan understood a few critical things, here and there. One: he knew that he could see time. That was proven; Rhodes-ified, even. Two: he knew that he could see the shape and form of magic, which looked to him like granulated waves of energy. This was a matter of discussion to be had with a physicist, though he could not imagine consulting Nico on any subject of intellectual merit quite yet. One thing at a time. Murder first and then scholarly pursuits.

He snorted with laughter at himself, disgusted. Was this what he'd become, then? Some sort of reckless buffoon enamored with danger? He could feel it like the glint of a knife, the way something inside him had changed. He'd always been angry, but it had been the kind of anger that had no release, because it was with the intangibles: Life. Fate. Circumstance. He was angry at what he'd been born to, who he was. But now, fantastic news, it was all much more concrete! He was angry at Callum, who had essentially threatened to kill him and also, for fun, seemed to have *strongly implied* that Tristan was weak and small and kind of an idiot.

Which he was. Hence the anger.

But now, increasingly, it was different. Fruitful. The anger was becoming productive. Because Tristan had told himself that Callum did not have ownership of Tristan's value—did not have ownership of *him*—and that he, Tristan, was valuable innately, self-fulfillingly, because he could see, feel, *do* things the others could not. And now was his chance to prove it true.

In the moments before the projection of Libby Rhodes had killed him,

Tristan had been able to create an exit strategy. He had seen his doom and, in doing so, shifted his understanding of reality. Again. Because he was coming to understand that reality was not objective, and in fact it never had been. *Objective* reality stated that if a medeian used an illusion to magically conceal their true appearance, then the effects of the magic should stand. Callum's eyes should probably look punishingly azure to Tristan, but they were not; they were merely a normal, human shade of blue. There was something to be said about this, about relativity, and the relationship between the observer and the observed, but theory could only go so far. Tristan did not see what others called reality, but he did see something more useful. His definition of reality meant identifying the structures of time and space, but his experience of the world was consistently obstructing his ability to access it. Only in the moments where he felt his consciousness at risk of fracture or expiration was he able to dissociate from it, opening some other eye to a higher, truer truth.

He stood at the edge of the grounds, beyond the dogwoods, remembering the time he'd managed to access some other plane. The other man, the traveler—Ezra, if he remembered his name correctly—had met him here, and Tristan closed his eyes, attempting to reach the same degree of . . . Could one call it nirvana? Perhaps if one wanted to be completely fucking pretentious, yes. But it didn't matter, because something in the wards at the edge of the grounds had changed.

Tristan opened his eyes again, disappointed. The coarse-grain pattern in the wards seemed tighter, or perhaps it was that the little slivers of permission he'd wandered through previously were gone. Windows of fluidity had been sucked up through a vacuum, though presumably that was owing to some flaw they hadn't foreseen. The wards that someone had broken, which nobody was ever supposed to break, had been fixed. Which meant Tristan could no longer maneuver within them, no matter how minuscule his maneuverings were.

Tristan wondered if he should speak with Parisa about any of this. She had clearly observed something about his magic, and as far as he could tell, she had done it accurately. As a result, her projection of him during her ritual wasn't powerless—in fact, her projection of him had seen something. A wave pattern, a progression of energy. It was the exact thing that the real him had seen before, which he had not realized Parisa also knew. But what was bothering him was not that Parisa had seen it, but that she had chosen not to engage with it. In a simulation where only the two of them could accurately see what was happening, she had decided to disengage entirely.

Was that a reflection of her thoughts on him, Tristan wondered, in that she did not consider it important?

"Oi," came a voice behind him, and Tristan opened his eyes to the inky deep of fallen dusk.

That, and Nico de Varona.

"Been looking for you," Nico said, and tossed a book to Tristan, who caught it. It was a collection of Schopenhauer's notes on transcendentalism.

Tristan glanced at the book, then away. He already knew exactly as much about transcendentalism as he needed to, hence the theory. "And?"

"And the concept is sound." Nico flopped onto the ground beside Tristan. "What's supposed to happen if I agree?"

"I told you. You kill me, but not all the way." These were really not difficult instructions and Tristan was beginning to wonder if he had already maxed out Nico's capacity for intelligent thought.

"No, I mean what's supposed to happen in the moment before you die." Nico turned to look at him. "That's the part I don't understand. So, okay, something happens. Adrenaline or something. Magic?" he asked, and Tristan shrugged. "So what exactly do you see?"

That was the question, wasn't it? The one he had wasted an entire day asking himself. Which was the purpose of this exercise, because at this point precious time in the Society was slipping away, and he didn't have entire days to waste.

Tristan was tired of asking himself questions. Tired of being around people who already understood their limits, or lack thereof. He had lost a year of his life so far to confusion when he was promised greatness—was promised, unequivocally, that *he* was great. He had only one remaining year to prove to himself that Atlas Blakely, and by extension Tristan himself, had not been wrong to believe that there was something singular about him. That here in this house, living alongside the greatest medeians of a generation, if not an age—he belonged.

"I see everything," Tristan said. "And I think," he added, clearing his throat, "that I can use it, too. That when I was faced with Rhodes in that simulation, I—"

He could feel Nico looking at him and fixed his gaze straight ahead, on the slowly receding horizon.

"I used time," Tristan said. "It was like I expanded beyond myself. I don't know how to explain it," he added, "but it was like . . . in that moment, I went from being myself, from having a finite beginning and end, to folding in on myself, over and over. Both existing *within* myself and *outside* myself, continuously replicating. It was like being able to move through another—"

"Dimension," Nico murmured.

"Yes." Tristan kept his eyes locked on to the vacancy of night.

"What's funny," Tristan continued, "is that I'd seen it before. My dad—" He sucked in a breath, reflexively. He did not like to discuss this much. Nico, helpfully, said nothing.

"He's not a patient person," Tristan finally said. "Violent by nature, too. He used to have these things, these episodes. Explosions, my mum and I called them. She used to have this sixth sense—this way of knowing when to tiptoe around him, what to say to calm him down. But then she died." Tristan swallowed. "I still don't know how. I wasn't very old. I asked my dad and he hit me so hard I swear to fucking god I tasted stars."

Nico said nothing, and Tristan felt the usual mix of bitterness and disloyalty when he spoke of his father. The duality of their relationship meant that his love could not exist without rage, and his hatred was equally ineffective because it was brittle and porous with longing.

"I used to be scared of water," Tristan said. "Don't know why. Well, not water, depths. Then he held me by the neck over the Thames."

Silence.

It got easier to talk, having started. "The strange thing is he's calmed down a bit since then. I got bigger, I guess. Or he got tired. Or maybe he fucking saw God, I don't know. He's still a nasty piece of work, don't get me wrong," Tristan added with a laugh. "Still a dickhead for sure, and I can't think anyone would disagree. But he hid it so well, the other parts. The darkness. The way it was so . . . unusual, like something took him over. Demon possession or some shit.

"And now he's older," Tristan said after a second. "Softer. Doesn't raise his voice so much. Thinks he's too wise for that, that he's seen too much, knows too much. And he's right, yeah? He's gotten better as time's gone on, that's true. Not just better. He's gotten more respected, more thoughtful. Speaks slower. He's fair," Tristan said with a laugh. "Makes me wonder if any of it was even real, if maybe I dreamed it, because it couldn't be as bad as I thought it was. Because if it was really that bad," he added, "if it was really *so bad* that I saw through fucking time when I was seven years old fighting for my life above the river Thames, then someone else should have seen it, yeah? Someone else should have known. But nobody did, and so maybe it was just a dream."

Tristan's mouth felt dry. "Maybe some weird nightmare. He always said I had an imagination, that I saw things the way I did because I was making it up. And it's wild, isn't it, that I believe him? Because I do, I believe him,"

Tristan said, "and that's the shittiest part, that when I was supposed to be learning how to see the world, how to be part of it, he taught me to be scared all the time. I'm so fucking afraid that I can't see things clearly unless I go back there, to feeling like maybe I could die. And in the moment where I have to think yes, all right then, I'll do it—in *that* moment"—Tristan exhaled— "the hardest moment, the one that until coming here, I have done absolutely *everything* in my power never to face again—in that moment I have to see the impossible, the unbelievable, and then somehow find the energy to say no, I won't. I won't fall, I won't drown, I won't break, and I *won't*—"

A breath.

"I won't fucking forgive him," Tristan said. "And I won't forgive anyone else who makes me ask myself if I deserve to live."

He realized after several seconds of silence that maybe Nico had not asked, did not care. Because everyone had their personal tragedies, and who the fuck knew if Nico de Varona understood that kind of pain? That kind of *doubt*? And after another few seconds of silence Tristan wanted to take it all back, because he couldn't stand the idea of Nico's pity. He couldn't bear to see it, the look in Nico's eyes that said he was sorry. That Tristan was exactly what Callum said—a victim. If Nico offered one word of kindness, Tristan was positive he would punch Nico square in the mouth.

Beside him, Tristan felt rather than saw Nico's mouth open, and he tensed apprehensively. Anything, he thought, even a word, even a *breath* of apology, and—

"I think we should try giving you a heart attack," said Nico placidly. "Keep that pretty face of yours intact."

It was so unlikely, and so startlingly the only thing worth hearing, that for a moment, Tristan nearly threw up.

"Yeah." Tristan exhaled in a thin, slow stream of relief. "Yeah, all right then. But you can't warn me," he added, turning to face Nico, "because if I know it's coming—"

Then Nico's knuckles met Tristan's chest just before everything went black.

It was no surprise to her that Atlas would appear for the first time in weeks simply to fetch her from the reading room. She'd caught the slip of his mask after Tristan's initiation ritual and they both knew it, so why shouldn't he choose now, an arbitrary Tuesday, to inconveniently interrupt her unless she was finally on to something?

"Miss Kamali," said Atlas, whose unwelcome presence on such occasions was growing all too predictable. "A moment?"

Fucking Reina. Parisa would have glared at her if she felt the ennui would have been worth the trouble. She could only hope that Atlas had not heard Reina's last question, though if he had, that was entirely Parisa's fault. She had been so busy paying attention to her telepathic blocks that she had forgotten not to say idiotic things *out loud*.

Presumably Atlas had something to say about Parisa's perusal of the archives' sentience. (Or as Reina called it, "staring into nothing." Idiot. Slap a nose ring and some willful obstinacy on a hot girl with knife proficiency and suddenly the possibility for attraction went up in smoke.) That, or Atlas was finally ready to do away with Parisa, which seemed more inevitably forgone with each passing day.

Will I need witnesses? Parisa asked him dryly in silence.

I always love our little chats was Atlas's reply.

Reina was being useless as usual (staring, Parisa noted, at Atlas's apparent loungewear), so Parisa consented to do as she was told. Atlas, at least, waited for Parisa to slip out of the reading room, gesturing her down the corridor, before assaulting her with his usual parade of niceties.

"Are you well, Miss Kamali?"

"Depends on where we're going," she muttered. She felt around in the wards to see where everyone else was in the house. Callum was moving toward the dining room. Tristan was sitting outside, where he'd been for several hours already. Nico was restlessly prowling toward them on his path to the reading room, which was at least an improvement over having spent the morning restlessly in bed.

Atlas seemed to have performed the same investigatory sweep. He directed her through one of the doors to the garden, intentionally preventing them from running into Nico. "I'd rather not have to explain," he provided in answer to Parisa's questioning glance, gesturing down to his general state of unruliness.

Parisa glanced over his clothing; the wrinkled slacks, the slippers. "Having a self-care day?"

"I need your help," Atlas said, curtly disregarding her sardonic tone and gesturing her back into the house once their path and Nico's had failed to cross. "And I've made the rather flattering decision to choose urgency for your expertise over any sartorial formality, if that's all right with you."

"My expertise?" Parisa arched a brow. She'd been comfortably certain that there was something plaguing the Caretaker. She had not, however, expected him to share it with her.

"Is that so unlikely?" He led her to his office in the south hall, gesturing her inside and then closing the door securely behind them. "You are troublingly good at your specialty, as I'm sure we both recall."

Parisa gave a derisive snort. "If you're trying to reverse-psychology your way into my good graces—"

"I am not. Your graces can remain fettered if you wish. Sit," Atlas said, gesturing her into the chair behind his desk. "Make yourself comfortable."

His chair? She glanced at him for confirmation, waiting for the drop. He shrugged in apparent nonanswer.

"I don't like this at all," Parisa warned at a mutter, though she warily complied. She sank into the Caretaker's chair, frowning as Atlas remained standing in the center of the room. *Tell me the truth,* she directed at him. *Why are we here?*

It was difficult to lie telepathically. He could, if he wanted, but it would be harder.

I need your help, he said again. *And I swear, that is the truth.*

"Fine." He seemed to mean it. "What do you need?"

"There's a hole in the wards," Atlas said.

"A telepathic one? No, there isn't," Parisa replied. She would know.

"No, not a telepathic one." Atlas scratched at his chin, which Parisa noted had not been shaven. Curiouser and curiouser. She had always thought of him as relatively vain, or at least tactically devoted to appearances.

"What kind, then?" *And get to the point,* she added. *I have things to do.*

You mean a sentient library to question? I do not expect you will receive any meaningful answers today.

He wasn't wrong. All she had to go on was a general sense of decay from

Reina (and, unless she was very much mistaken, from Nico) and Dalton's ominous warning—*Parisa, knowledge is carnage, you can't have it without sacrifice*—ringing inconclusively in her head. The question was, now that they weren't expected to murder one of their own, what would they sacrifice this time?

There's always tomorrow, she replied.

He gave her a glance of mild impatience, but could see they were at an impasse. "It's a physical ward," he admitted.

Parisa shot him a narrowed glance. "Then get a physicist. You do still have one, as you might recall."

"Mr. de Varona cannot know about this." A reasonable conclusion by most stretches of the imagination, albeit still unclear as applied to this specific instance. Atlas seated himself in the chair opposite hers—where she ought to have been, had the hierarchy of the conversation been as expected. "Nor can anyone else," he warned.

Interesting. Not that she planned to spoil her fun by obligingly pointing it out.

"Does Dalton know?" asked Parisa mildly.

"Mr. Ellery does not," Atlas replied. "He is a researcher here. This is not under his purview."

"But you'd place it under mine?"

"Only because I can see no other way." Again, he seemed to mean it. The necessity of coming to her clearly afforded him no pleasure, which she could see because he had taken no care to hide it.

"What if I tell someone?" Parisa asked.

He rubbed a thumb absently over his knuckles. "Then you tell someone."

"Is your career on the line?"

"I suppose." He sounded tired.

"Does this put you in my debt?" Parisa decided to ask, shifting to place both ankles, delicately crossed, atop his desk.

Atlas followed the motion with a grimace. Beatifically, Parisa smiled.

"No," Atlas said. "I am not in your debt. It is simply a favor I am asking, which you can comply with or not as you please. And then we will return to our usual roles as Caretaker and researcher."

"You seem to take quite an *active* role with Dalton," Parisa challenged.

"Miss Kamali," Atlas said. A warning. "Is there a hole in the wards or not?"

She sighed, lamenting that he'd tired of the game so quickly. She'd been having such a marvelous time. "Fine." She closed her eyes, tending to the sentience of the house and its wards. It soothed under her touch like a kitten. "What am I looking for?"

"Something about six feet tall."

She cracked one eye. "What shape?"

"Man-shaped." Atlas leaned forward, bracing his elbows on his knees. "Presumably you are familiar with those dimensions," he murmured, and Parisa considered being grievously offended until she decided to be delighted instead.

"Is that a joke, Mr. Blakely? How shockingly upbeat." She closed her eyes, sifting through the textures of the house's magic, asking it for a favor. Call it neighborhood watch for the medeian arts.

"Nothing," she determined after a moment. "Bulletproof."

"Good." Atlas exhaled with what seemed like genuine relief. "Thank you." He rose to his feet. "Now get out of my chair."

"You patched it up, then?" Parisa guessed. She was in no hurry to vacate his position of authority, particularly when there was so much personal turmoil in the air. To Atlas's warning glance, she innocently added, "What did you need me for, if you'd already figured it out yourself?"

"Peer review." *Up, Miss Kamali. I have work to do.*

I'm sure you do. There was obviously more to this than he was saying. "That bad, is it? Someone," she remarked with dry solemnity, "must have made a terrible mistake."

"Someone," Atlas agreed, "certainly did."

They eyed each other for another long moment before Parisa, growing bored with the stalemate, allowed a sigh. She rose to her feet, gesturing to the chair. "All yours."

"Quite." Atlas paused beside the desk, waiting.

As did Parisa.

"So," she said. "I imagine you must have heard what Reina and I were—"

"You're looking for something to be wrong," Atlas said, rubbing a crease into his temple. "Or for some kind of sinister agenda. I cannot dream of why."

"Call it my nature," Parisa suggested. "Or the fact that everyone has an agenda and there is always something wrong. Who can say?"

Perhaps realizing that she was in no hurry to leave, Atlas took his seat behind his desk, awakening the thin screen of his computer and returning to his correspondence. Parisa realized that she had never seen him use a computer before, but clearly his work was more logistically ordinary than she'd imagined.

"Are you tracking us?" she asked.

"No," Atlas replied without looking up.

"But something is, isn't it?" *Knowledge is carnage. Dalton said that for a reason.*

I haven't the faintest idea what you're talking about. "Good day, Miss Kamali."

"That simulation. The ritual ceremony that was . . . What did Dalton call it? *Not* a test." She abandoned her efforts at subtlety and stepped in front of his desk, casting her shadow over it. "That wasn't for our benefit. We've already earned our place here, as you said—so learning each other's weaknesses is no longer useful." He did not argue. "Unless something else was trying to learn something from us. To observe us." Something, or perhaps someone.

Atlas pointedly tapped a period before glancing at her. "And what do you imagine this elusive *thing* would want to know?"

"Our patterns," Parisa replied instantly. "Our behaviors."

"What for?" Atlas asked. "Do you really find yourself so interesting that everything you do is worth analysis?"

She did, yes. And more to the point, he was being intentionally difficult. "Is this what I get for helping you?" she asked with a sigh of disappointment.

"Yes." He leaned back in his chair. "I'm afraid my stores of eternal gratitude require some replenishment."

She felt the bubble of a laugh in her throat, which was an astonishing change of pace. The volleying, which was so unusual from him, managed to be almost enjoyable.

"You know, I like you like this," she commented aloud. "The lack of fucks is so refreshing."

"I'm very likable, Miss Kamali." *Or how else do you think I got here?*

Valid point. "So," she said. "Is this about Libby Rhodes, then? You calling me here; the hole in the wards?"

This time he looked at her squarely. *What makes you say that?*

It was a catastrophic error, Rhodes disappearing as she did without your knowledge, she replied. *And only a catastrophe would drive you to me.*

He held her gaze for a few more seconds. The small clock on the wall ticked down to the hour, both of them intently still.

"Where do you think she is?" asked Parisa.

"I don't know."

She considered the tone of his response. *But you do know who took her.*

"I have my guesses," he said, pointedly ambivalent. How tiring.

Answer me here, she dared him.

His mouth tightened with impatience. *Yes. I know who took her.*

That was obvious enough. *A man about six feet tall?*

Yes.

A physicist?

Of sorts.

And you're not telling the others?

The others do not need to know.

Parisa begged to differ. *But you think she's alive?*

One hopes.

You realize that Varona will keep looking, perhaps even Tristan will—

And I hope they find her, Atlas said. *Because I cannot.*

That much seemed truthful, if not entirely honest.

Where do you think she is? asked Parisa again.

I don't know, he said again.

But it was different this time. From his head, the answer was amorphous. He didn't know the answer concretely, but he knew something, and what he did know was a betrayal of such high magnitude that even he, Atlas Blakely, Caretaker of the Alexandrian Society, was rendered small and human for knowing it. The effort at sealing the wards had cost him gravely—not just physically. Something inside him was forever altered, forever wretched, eternally forgone.

Atlas Blakely had lost something—Parisa understood that much. Something close to his purpose in life, which was not quite unbound enough to be passion, but higher, more dense and more pure than happiness or joy.

Where Libby Rhodes had gone was a small question, tiny, dwarfed by a larger question of the things he now knew. *Everything* he knew, in fact. His was a world thrown out of orbit, out of balance.

This was why it had taken Tristan—or something Tristan had done—to return him to stasis. Because where Atlas had been helpless, Tristan was the answer. Now Atlas had potential again. Momentum. He had come to Parisa because he had lost something—something that had once defined his entire being, his whole self. It now no longer mattered what she knew or what she saw, because Atlas had Tristan. His orbit had changed.

Somewhere in the enormity of Atlas's swirling thoughts was precisely what Parisa had come for. There were whispers of conversations in his mind, fragments. Where was Libby Rhodes? Lost to the sins of Atlas Blakely. Parisa caught the pieces of a thought, splinters of memory fluttering like errant wings or unraveling threads. She found the frayed edges and did what she did best.

She pulled.

—damn books—

—dead, long live the Society—
—it done?—
—knows how to starve—
—you and me, let's—
—solutely must have both—
—dies, nature makes a new one—
—Society is dead—
—mean you found something? I thought—
—'s make a new one—
—Atlas, you are not a—
—and me, let's take over, let's—
—be gods.

Parisa inhaled sharply, jerking back from Atlas with a step. This answer, which Parisa had stolen from him, was a violation. She knew it, and so did he.

"I take it our brief détente is over now," Parisa murmured. An apology of sorts.

"Goodbye, Miss Kamali," said Atlas, which was not forgiveness.

She slipped out of his office, knowing he hadn't bothered looking up.

Still, a smile crept across Parisa's lips, surprisingly victorious.

"I have a feeling we'll see you soon, Rhodes," she remarked into nothing, shaking her head to wander blithely down the hall.

· LIBBY ·

Recently, Libby Rhodes had taken to sleeping in a way she had never slept before. What had changed? Perhaps it was the environment. The cool sheets, the enticement of rest, the lack of anything to do but succumb to a cavernous dark. Or perhaps it was the fact that her ex-boyfriend had abducted her, betrayed her, and left her for all-but-dead. In the end, really, who could say.

She slept like an addict: mouth wetting for another opportunity to curl up on her side, to be buried in blankets, swaddled in the misery of being lost. The process of maintaining her existence had become so exhausting that the only option was to succumb to eternal nothingness, drifting to the bottom of some unexplorable deep. When she was awake she prowled the room that had become her cage, dully monstrous, coaxing smoke into flame only to feel the air suction closer around her, like she'd been packed into a fluid sort of noose.

It wasn't as if she'd given up.

It was more like all the sleep she was doing was unraveling some half-formed idea that her conscious mind couldn't understand because she was—as she had always been—too anxious, too taken with the exquisite panic of hypo-thetical escapes. Libby had always been unbearable when she was awake—ask Nico de Varona or Reina Mori; ask Tristan Caine or Parisa Kamali; try asking Callum Nova, assuming he was even still alive—and now that she was left alone with herself, she could agree: she was the worst person she had ever known, and the least enjoyable to be trapped in a single room with.

For purposes of setting the scene, the ingredients to her captivity were as follows:

A box with one window. The window was illusioned, so for all intents and purposes nothing existed outside of it. Observation suggested to Libby, who had previously existed in the universe at one point, that this was a terrible studio apartment or a room at a cheap motel. Most likely Ezra, her ex-boyfriend whom she had not considered sadistic in any recognizable way until quite recently, could not afford to expend the magic on a more livable habitation. Though, perhaps it was purely economical. His habits suggested that he did not live here, and who could afford two rents in this economy, anyway?

There was a door, warded shut, upstage. Stage right contained a small bathroom that she resented having to use. Being dragged from the precious incubation of her meditative, pickling sleep in order to entertain her body's willful reliance on consciousness was among her least favorite things. She spent very little time there and rarely opened her eyes when she did.

Stage left was the bed, and admittedly this wasn't a prison. Aha! A glimpse of affection or perhaps simply humanity from the man who'd once been so accommodating in allowing Libby to come and go as she pleased. Nice sheets, jersey cotton, soft and luxurious while still comforting and unpretentious. Ezra had, after all, slept in her bed for nearly three years. The sheets smelled like peonies and lavender, a ripe bloom paired with the sultry-soft reassurance of her grandmother's arthritic hand cream. Such marvelous attention to detail he had, filling her little cage as if she were a troubled, anxious pet. For days she had not been eating any of the food, wondering if he might try to dose her with something. Eventually she realized he wasn't dangerous, not actually, and that in fact if she died he would be very upset with himself. He wanted her to stay here, out of the way of whatever exorbitant tyranny he now suspected her of contributing to, or of being complicit in. Elizabeth Rhodes, destroyer of worlds. The thought alone made her crave a doughnut, or perhaps some sort of custardy pie.

Not to lose track of the thread, but she often thought of Tristan in a similar way. She thought of all of them, the other five to whom she had only recently belonged, but each one seemed to accompany her thoughts in a different way. Nico was relentless, always pestering her. *Rhodes wake up, Rhodes you're a wildfire, Rhodes just let it burn.* She wanted him to go away because he exhausted her in a different way than everything else. He kept her from sleep, but what was she supposed to do? She had already felt around for magic she could use to escape, but this room, its wards, had all been designed for her, against her. Every element of magic at use in this room was her enemy, primed and curated specifically to prevent her from stepping out of line.

Reina was a wonderful presence in her thoughts, very quiet, undisturbing, occasionally giving Libby a glance from over the top of her book that suggested *you, Libby Rhodes, are a fool, and nobody ever misses a fool.*

Rhodes, you're being so tiresome, I would have guessed you'd make a terrible victim. (That was Parisa's input.) Sometimes she was whispering it in Libby's ear, lasciviously. Other times she was sighing it, bored, while flashing just a hint of calf below her dress. *Oh Rhodes, you make such a pitiful lump of despair, make it stop or I'll have to find something else to amuse myself.*

Look at the pieces, Rhodes.

That was Tristan. Libby allowed herself to shape those interactions more than the others, to play them like projections from where she lay in her floral-scented bedding, her cottony cocoon. He'd prowl over to her, eyes heavy-lidded and gluttonous, annihilatory with patience. *Look at the pieces, Rhodes, that's the only way to see the whole.* Traditionally these mental forays went wildly off track and she would crave a hit of something, a dose of fantasy. She played games with herself, allowing a taste of her imagination's reckless projections and then reversing them when they came too close to pleasure, playing the doldrums back in slow motion so as not to waste the bittersweetness of the build.

Inevitably, though, Callum would interrupt. *Nobody likes a martyr, Rhodes,* he'd say, tutting while examining his fingernails. *I'd help you if you asked.*

Not to actually *be* helpful, of course. *Only because your anxiety is giving me a headache,* he'd point out.

At that point, Libby would remind herself that Callum was probably dead now—that surely even if Tristan had failed, then one of the others, Parisa maybe, would have taken it upon themselves to remedy the situation—and she'd feel better for a time, but Callum was always harder to shake than the others.

You're ignoring the important bits, he'd say.

To which she would point out the obvious. Wards. Something in here was counteracting the magic that usually came so easily to her. There was something kinetic, making her drowsy, sluggish, slow to respond, like a toxin in the air. She knew it was there and she knew what it was and what she did *not* know was what would await her if she left.

Where had Ezra Fowler, a man with whom she had once speculated in private to her mother that she might reasonably spend the rest of her life, decided to put her?

There we go, Rhodes, now you're thinking. Not everything is a matter of vast physicalities. More often everything comes down to the fundamental weakness of a single human being. Do you even know how many fractures a person can contain? Look at your own faults and don't be stupid. You're not special because you're flawed, everyone has broken pieces. Everyone has something to hide.

At this point Callum would rise to his feet and stretch out his long legs, giving her surroundings a look of aristocratic disdain. *Did you know that most of our behaviors come from our adolescence? Tastes evolve, but there's a particular slice of youth that never leaves us. They're called our formative years for a reason. Because we always return to them in some form.*

With Callum it was always about people, about the frailty of humans, as if he were some other species, and maybe he was. He always talked with an arm's length of distance, as if he were simply the audience for a comedy unfolding on the stage.

And it was always comedy for Callum, who was never invested, never involved. Libby wondered if it had been hilarious to him, hysterical, the idea that out of everyone that he considered so thoroughly useless it was him they'd decided to kill. She couldn't help assuming he found the betrayal diverting in the purest sense—absurd to the point of amusement.

She tried to see it from Callum's perspective, taking Tristan's advice and looking at the parts that made up the whole, because evidence seemed to suggest that Ezra Fowler was ardently convinced that by containing Libby, he was actually, genuinely saving the world. And if anything needed closer inspection, it was probably the idea that Libby mattered incidentally, even a little bit, even remotely at all.

Not that she ever came up with anything, but thinking like Callum did lend everything a slightly more interesting flavor. How else could one possibly face the prospect of being one-sixth of a dystopian nuclear code if not to simply laugh and go back to sleep? Which was what Libby did, persistently, except that now she was starting to dream. The chronic drowsiness she felt was enough to render her body numb and empty, but her brain, previously busied with academia beyond that of any mortal scholar's dream, could not be content with such a disaffecting stasis.

I bet his music taste is awful, Callum would say, unsurprisingly disdainful in his presumption that any paramour of Libby's would be painfully banal. *He wouldn't be able to fight his attachment to whatever he listened to at fifteen, sixteen. And what would that even be?*

Well, Ezra was close in age to Atlas, according to him. He thought of himself as accentless but that was impossible; his particular speech must by necessity belong to one unique part of the world. Ezra himself had only ever specified Los Angeles, which was a big place that Libby had only seen on a family vacation visiting some child-friendly pier that had been closed at the time due to the dangerously rising tides. Ezra said that he was raised by his mother, that he had no siblings, had not spoken to anyone from his home in several years. She had assumed the two were simply estranged until he corrected her one night, half a bottle into some cheap champagne on New

Year's: Actually, she was dead. Had been dead for some time. Had died when he was a kid.

Well, that's where the heroism comes from, Callum said mockingly. *Survivor's guilt and all that. The weight of responsibility.* Libby had known that about Ezra, the way he tended to want to save her from her anxieties instead of simply listening when she spoke. He wanted her to *want* to be rescued, and she had thought the occasional decision to indulge him was just something people did in relationships. Male ego or whatever. Things good girlfriends did in order to keep the peace.

Ego is a funny thing, Callum commented, still dropping in uninvited to interrupt her sexual fantasies or mock her persistently blooming malaise. *Supposedly the ego is the true self, did you know that, Rhodes? Rhodes, you aren't listening. Not many people actually understand what they really are, haven't you sorted that by now?*

A previous Libby would argue that of course she understood herself, she *was* herself, but given the nature of recent events she felt she had no choice but to circle back and reconsider. She understood very clearly that she was *not* herself at the present time, which seemed close enough to understanding for now.

We can't help clinging to our origins, Callum said. *The past always seems more ordered, Rhodes. It always seems clearer, more straightforward, easier to understand. We have a craving for it, that sense of simplicity, but only an idiot would ever chase the past, because our perception of it is false—it was never that the world was simple. Just that in retrospect it could be known, and therefore understood.*

. . . Conceivably, that is, Callum would qualify, *though, as you know, the world is highly populated by idiots.* Then he would offer her a humorless laugh, suddenly raising the glass he invariably held in his hand.

Which is how Libby would realize she was in a dream, because she'd look down and see that she had a glass as well, and that outside the walls of the painted room the sky was burning with Ezra's foretelling of how the world would end. The destruction that Atlas Blakely would foist upon them, raining it down like tears of blood. Ezra never actually described it, whatever it was he'd seen when he followed the outcomes of Atlas's plan, but there were certain things Libby felt they'd been designed as a species to predict. The end of days always looked crucially the same, no matter the hand that had written it. All of humanity shared a single, dismal imagination: fires and floods, locusts and plagues. The Earth casting us out from her rotten, despoiled Eden.

Mass extinction is a hoax, Callum reminded her. *It's an idea populated by small minds, conspiracy theorists. Of course there are no dinosaurs, there are lizards and birds. This Ezra of yours can't possibly know what he saw, and even if he did, who's to call it anything less than survival?*

The fact that she could hear Callum speaking to her in full sentences lent a lot of credibility to the idea that naysaying had far more tendency to stick than positivity. She had been listening so closely to his criticisms that she could now call them to mind more easily than even Nico's huffing reassurances or Tristan's muttered corrections.

Libby had half a mind to tell Callum he was dead and therefore wholly inconsequential, but then she'd registered where she was and realized again that she was dreaming. This, now, was the hallway of her freshman dorm at NYUMA, poorly lit and with carpeting expressly cast to show no evidence of wear—though, that sort of spellwork had rendered it distinctly institutional. (Sort of like how mortal carpeting in dorms was so often the color of whatever revolting habitation it was chosen to obscure.)

She moved mechanically, perfunctorily, as if all of this had been rehearsed, and knocked on the door of a room that she vaguely knew to be somehow incorrect. Later, when she woke, she would place it. (Her unconscious mind had taken details from the Society's manor house and melted them down with her fourth-grade class trip to the Museum of Natural History.)

"Gideon Drake?" called Libby. "It's Libby Rhodes. I'm your notetaker from NYUMA disability services."

The man who opened the door looked like a cross between Tristan and someone else that Libby would not initially recognize as a priest that she'd mortifyingly thought was hot when she bumped into him on Seventh Avenue last summer—but she knew he was "Gideon" in the same way she always knew who people were supposed to be in dreams.

She was dreaming of the first time she met Gideon, so of course that's who she was talking to.

"Libby," said Gideon with Priest-Tristan's face. "Can you hear me?"

The lights flickered in the hallway and she spun, suddenly feeling threatened.

"Should've asked Parisa to teach you about lucid dreaming," remarked Callum, who had not been there a moment before, but was now standing next to her again.

"Myth," said Libby, but then Callum was gone.

"Libby." It was Gideon again, though his face hadn't changed. "Try to do something. Change something."

Ugh, but she was so *tired*. And this wasn't how it went, anyway. It should have begun with her and Gideon chatting about narcolepsy before he asked her why she was working for disability services (this would be weeks, if not months, before she accidentally slipped and told Nico about her futile practice of taking diligent notes in school, something she'd done for her sister Katherine during the interminable length of her sickness) and it would end with Libby realizing that Gideon Drake was roommates with the asshole who sat behind her in Physical Magics 101. She would decide at that very moment to hate Gideon by association, though of course she would not bring herself to do it in actuality. (Not because he was narcoleptic, although that was a factor, but because he was Gideon, and Gideon was impossible to hate.)

But this was a dream, and everything Libby knew about dreams suggested that she was somewhere in the midst of a REM cycle lasting no more than twenty minutes. Shortly, a deeper, less occupied sleep would begin and she would finally get some well-deserved rest.

"You know," said Callum, who had apparently not left, "it's a bit stuffy in here."

"I can't change the *air*," said Libby crossly. "Just deal with it."

"Actually, you can," said Gideon as Priest-Tristan. "And honestly, you probably should."

She looked at Callum and then away, exhausted. Why couldn't she have dreamt about Mira? She missed Mira, her roommate from NYUMA. Or couldn't she dream about Katherine, which in this context she imagined would feel like an affectionate haunting instead of the recurring dream where she was late and Katherine was somewhere waiting, just out of sight and impossible to reach. If Libby was going to talk to a dead person, Katherine was the only dead person she'd ever really liked. (Libby hadn't known her grandfather all that well, and being faintly aware that he had played tennis until the ripe old age of ninety wasn't really a substitute for actually having *known* a person.)

"I know you don't want to," said Priest-Tristan, frowning in concentration. "You're somewhere very distant, I can see that, but—"

"The future is so *messy*," remarked Callum. "So disordered. So many outcomes. Entropy only moves in one direction, have you ever thought about that? Like heat." He bounced a small rubber ball three times, watching it disappear. "Did you see that? Of course you didn't."

"Libby?" asked Priest-Tristan, turning to Callum. "Is that you?"

"No, that's not me," said Libby, though the momentary consideration left her to wonder if Callum didn't, in fact, look the slightest bit odd. He was doing all the usual Callum things, but he wasn't dressed entirely correctly. He was wearing one of Tristan's blazers.

Suddenly she felt an absurd pulse of opposition. Why was Callum always mixed into her thoughts of Tristan? Even inside her head she was jealous of him, still seeing them as interwoven parts. Stupid.

Change something. Okay, fine.

Libby stared at the blazer and burned a hole through it. Then, watching the little wisp of smoke that curdled outward, she set the whole thing aflame and giggled to herself.

(Blazer. Get it?)

"Well, that's a start," said Callum, who was not Callum anymore, but Libby herself. She could tell because it looked like her and sounded like her and had mousy overgrown bangs that still weren't quite normal length yet, like hers. Yep, this was her, all right: the flames had cooled and now Libby herself rose up from the ashes like a diffident, unsexy Venus.

"Balls," said Libby to herself. "Everyone knows you're useless."

"Libby," said Priest-Tristan, whose face had warped slightly. "Can you change where we are?"

Both Libbys glanced at him. "Change it into what?"

"Anywhere. Anything."

"How?"

"The same way you do it when you're awake."

"Why aren't I awake now?"

"Your body's sleeping. But your mind's awake."

"Is it?"

"Not fully. But yes, nearly."

"Are you Gideon?" Libby asked Priest-Tristan.

"Yes." He sounded surprised and pleased. "Can you see me?"

She blinked and she could. There he was, all sandy hair and bruised shadows. He had such rounded edges to his shoulders from slouching. Constant exhaustion. The narcolepsy, she thought, or rather remembered. She remembered, also, that she had never actually learned what his specialty was. (Some people were so ridiculously secretive. What, after all, was the point?)

"How do I know it's really you?" she asked suspiciously, and above them, the ceiling rumbled. She glanced up and noticed the apse in the painted room, marveling a little at how soft and golden the light was.

"You're waking up now, Libby, so you'll just have to trust me. Do you know where you are?" asked Gideon.

"Mm, no," said Libby, before thinking about what Callum—Libby—had said about Ezra and serial killers. No, not serial killers. Adolescents. *Adolescence.* Origin stories, only Ezra wasn't a villain. Was he? No, she was the villain, no Atlas was, no it was Ezra, kidnapping people was rude. Something about forms. Ladies, let's get in formation. No no, formidable, *fromage,* formative. "Formative years," she murmured.

"What?" asked Gideon, plainly bewildered.

Ugh, this was exhausting. She just wanted to *sleep.* It figured that she would sink into some sort of pseudo-coma when someone tried to harm her. If it were Parisa, the world would be razed to the ground by now. Nico would look at Ezra and he would be dead, just like that. Splat. Death, death is what makes us what we are, which is alive. Mortality, those clever little brackets. Births and deaths, beginnings and ends.

"Time," said Libby.

"Are you in the future?"

"No, of course not, stupid," said Libby, feeling suddenly crabby and overwhelmed. Infinite possibilities. Statistical dissonance. Diverging paths. Entropy only moved in one direction. Order was important for abductions. Crime required neatness. "How would he find me?"

"Who?"

"You *know,*" said Libby, who was beginning to feel aware of something. Her bladder, the cursed thing. Curses. Luck and unluck. Intention. What was his intention? Disruption. Hilarious to think how shortsighted this must be. What was he going to do with her? He'd have to kill her, probably. Not yet, he'd work his way up to it, but eventually he'd realize he couldn't put her back and he couldn't hide her and right now it was simple, it was easy, because she was sleepy and she didn't want to cause any damage because she was more interested in fighting her own cerebral dissonance, but eventually her muscles would atrophy and her magic would spasm and she would have fits of explosivity and Ezra would think oh nooooo I forgot I kidnapped a magic girl, and then he'd have to kill her and sure, they'd all feel bad about it, but eventually he'd dismiss the guilt because he *intended* for her to be out of the way, and there was really only one way to ensure it.

"Breakups, am I right?" she said to Gideon, growing foggily aware of herself where she lay in the blankets, and Gideon was saying something, but she couldn't hear him because she was aware of herself, aware of her physical form, aware of someone else in the room, someone waking her from her precious, sacred slumber.

"Libs." Ezra's voice was gentle and sorry, familiar and soft. "Are you hungry?"

Later, Libby's reasoning would be that she wasn't even fully awake when her hand shot out to close around her ex-boyfriend's throat.

"Yeah," she said hoarsely. "Starved."

IV

ENTROPY

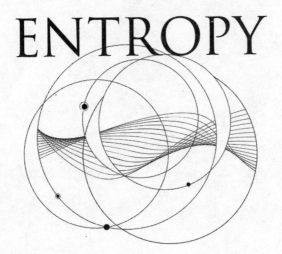

· LIBBY ·

Libby stumbled out of the wreckage, coughing up paint chips and kernels of popcorn ceiling. The sun outside the small apartment building (or was it a motel? it must have been a motel, and a sordid one at that) was bright, putrid, blinding. She could see heat wafting above the asphalt, blurring her vision of the cracked sidewalks lined with dilapidated cars. Wherever she was, it was clearly an industrial street, full of auto repair shops. By the sounds of it, she was very near a highway. Gusts of hot desert air went by along with the sound of receding car horns. Smog hovered where the horizon should have been, a smoky gray haze rising up toward a white-bright sky.

The street was narrow, barely enough for two lanes. She shivered despite the heat, the wave of rasping flames behind her like a furnace at her back. Which way to go? Libby glanced left, then right, then decided it was probably a wash. She hurried quickly away from the smoldering motel room and chose a direction at random, following the path of the street.

"Hey," called a male voice from behind her, emerging from one of the nearby garages as she passed. "Did you just come from the fire over there?"

Libby's heart flipped in her chest as the man, who was wearing a mechanic's greased-up coveralls, came toward her. He had a tool in his hands, a wrench or something, which she tried not to think of as a weapon (paranoia?) but couldn't quite put out of her mind. "Hm? Oh, yeah. I was just walking by," she said, aiming for acute but distant concern, as if she didn't personally have any idea what might have happened and, more importantly, was not individually responsible for any property damage or severe bodily harm therein.

She forced her breathing to slow, wrestling with her sense of foreboding. She was usually very good at this, but was recently out of practice. "I think there might be people in there," she said, pointedly chewing her lip. Would it be best to appear more feminine? Would that make her appear vulnerable to him, and if so, would it be in a good way or a dangerous one? There was never any knowing who was safe and who was a risk. Though, she remembered at the last second, seeing as she had recently blown up part of a building while only half-conscious, perhaps these were not very central concerns.

Could she have hurt someone, some innocent bystander? She hoped not. It took everything she possessed not to look over her shoulder again. Last she'd checked, only part of the building had been decimated. And the only person she'd intended to injure was very firmly still alive—though that didn't guarantee that nobody was injured.

"Can you call for help?" she asked.

"Already did when I heard the explosion." The mechanic was frowning at her. "Thought it was a car backfiring at first. You were just . . . walking by?"

Admittedly, not a great lie. The neighborhood, if one could call it that, was hardly picturesque, and Libby Rhodes, a twenty-something female of the delicate (okay, academic) persuasion, was precisely the demographic to avoid this kind of setting. "I heard the explosion and wanted to check that everything was okay," she lied. "Do you have a phone?" she asked, though she doubted she'd have time to use it before someone became aware that there was another person left inside the building.

Worse, she wasn't sure who she'd call.

"Ambulance is already on its way." The mechanic was still frowning at her; specifically, at something on her face. Following his gaze, Libby reached up, realizing in the same moment that there was a slow trickle of wetness dripping from her forehead. She wiped it away as nonchalantly as possible, noticing the telltale smear of blood that must have been in the process of saturating her now extremely awkward bangs.

So the mechanic was a risk, then. Just in a completely different way than she suspected.

"If you saw what happened—" he began.

"Oh, I didn't, sorry." All her instincts told her: *Run.* "But I'll go see if I can get some water or something. In case anyone is trapped inside."

By the look on his face, the mechanic definitely suspected her of something. "It's probably better if you just stay," he said, eyes narrowed. "The police might have questions, so if you saw something—"

"I'll be back!" Libby called, and turned and kept walking, faster and faster as a second explosion went off from the motel behind her. Probably a gas line. She shivered a little, hoping once again that there had been no one else inside.

Even without looking over her shoulder, it was difficult to unsee the place in her mind's eye where Ezra lay unconscious on the ground, his chest shallowly rising and falling. He had been breathing when she left—would probably be found before long—but still.

Libby turned her guilty thoughts away from Ezra, walking as fast as she could in the direction of what she hoped might be something to orient her as to where she was. There was a gas station, a small one. They might have a phone. She felt a sudden relief to at least have daylight on her side, grateful she hadn't accidentally blown half a structure to smithereens at midnight or some other, more dangerous time.

What exactly had happened? The whole thing remained unclear to her. She had only the faintest sensation of memory, like something from a dream. Something, some thought or concept or song lyric had earwormed into her brain. Something about having fewer limits than she suspected?

And then, of course, she had blown everything up.

Ha.

Well. If there was ever a time to be limitless, this was probably it.

Libby kept up her brisk pace as she approached the gas station, which had an odd look to it. She hadn't thought she was somewhere remote, but maybe she was? Or not. Her head pounded, the throb of her stride across pavement ricocheting in her brain. Being awake was increasingly oppressive to her. Everything seemed so much more offensive, from the fumes of cars and paint nearby to the solubility of the wards she'd left behind.

Where was she? Surely a good distance from the Society's manor house. Ezra might have been a motherfucking traitor and an absolute sham of a man, but he was unfortunately not an idiot. He was also considerably less mediocre a medeian than Nico had always speculated, which annoyed Libby all over again. Because of course Nico would pop up in her thoughts now, in her hour of need, purely to be unhelpful.

Her throat was dry, her lips cracked. She was almost certainly dehydrated. She hadn't been eating much, or well, or even at all. This whole thing was an excellent plan by Ezra, that stupid not-idiot, who clearly knew or at least suspected that she would have a hand in her own destruction if she ever tried to break out of his cage. She should have been reserving her strength for something of this magnitude—if she'd known she was capable of it, she would have—but no, of course she hadn't. She had done half his work for him, letting her own foundation collapse over time.

Furious, she chewed at the flaky skin of her lower lip. She knew better than this. And she was angrier about this whole thing than ever before. Wherever she was, it had not been her decision—and worse, she had been tricked. This was what came of having feelings, of seeing goodness in people, of letting her guard down and being real, being honest, and therefore being weak. Someday she'd have to examine that particular thread in therapy, but today, she let it drive her. She let it consume her. Under most circumstances that would be unwise, possibly even dangerous, but Nico de Varona would do it. And so what if she had done the equivalent of sticking her finger in an electrical socket? She had pressed a hand against the self-destruct button and pushed—something she might not have done if not for the distant, inexplicable reminder that actually, *she* was the one in control. The result was positively explosive.

Her pulse was rising again, steadily. Her breath quickened and, increasingly, she smelled smoke. It was coming off her palms, rising from her shoulders. She hoped that whoever owned the hellscape she'd just left behind had insurance that covered spontaneous explosions. Most insurance plans accounted for magical accidents, right?

She shook herself, remembering that this was Ezra's fault. She hadn't chosen to kidnap herself. Everything that followed from here was *his* responsibility. What she did in the name of her own survival was the result of his ridiculous fucking choices, and she would just have to be long gone before he could chase her down again.

Libby took another stabilizing breath before pushing through the doors of the gas station's mini-mart; one of those twenty-four-hour places that must have been for truckers passing through. The cashier didn't look up at her entry, being engrossed in some transaction with a large man in an old baseball cap, so Libby ducked quickly into the bathroom. An OUT OF ORDER sign hung on the door to the women's restroom, but she pushed inside anyway, pausing beside the mirror.

Well. Her hair was bad. No surprise there. Her face looked swollen and amorphous somehow, her eyes sunken like deep wells into her skull. Not that this was the time for vanity. How long had she been gone? She would have to find out the date, figure out where she was. Would it make sense to buy a map, a newspaper? Did people still sell those things? Would she be out of place for making such a strange purchase? She wished she had her phone so she could look up where she was and how to get back to the archives. Plus, if someone was going to hunt her down over the explosion she'd left behind, wouldn't she be too memorable? A girl walking around alone, buying things nobody ever used with smeared blood on her forehead (she scrubbed it away, bits of wet paper towel clinging to a greasy lock of hair), and of course she was dressed in—

She looked down, realizing she was dressed in the same baggy sweats she usually wore, so not great. But also not ostentatious.

She shook herself. Okay. No point worrying about things she couldn't control.

She pushed out of the bathroom and fanned herself, pretending to have gone in to cool down. "Hot out there," she remarked to the cashier, before remembering that normal people did not make conversation with cashiers, and that she was already doing a catastrophic job of blending in. The cashier was luckily an older woman, uninterested in her. Good. Excellent. Libby walked over to the limited refrigerated selection, pulling out a bottle of Coke that looked like it hadn't been touched in half a century.

"I'll take this, and—" Wait. Did she have money? She rummaged around in her pockets, realizing that ugh, these were Ezra's sweatpants—why did men always get the functional pockets?—and then sorting out that no, of course Ezra had not also slipped a wallet in there to make her life easier. She grimaced, reaching slowly for the fridge door and replacing the soda bottle where she'd pulled it out. The cashier arched a brow.

"One of those days," Libby offered in flustered explanation, wondering if maybe the woman thought she was a vagrant. Which technically, she supposed she was. Her nose felt dry and runny simultaneously, and she sniffed. The sound was off-puttingly loud. "Could I use your phone?"

"Pay phone's outside," said the woman, gathering the pages of her newspaper to turn promptly to the back pages. At the motion, Libby suddenly recalled her father saying something about his geriatric fondness for "the funnies," as in the funny pages. Such a nostalgic thing—an *old* thing—to read the comics out of a newspaper. Almost as ridiculous as being told to use the pay phone outside.

"Ha," said Libby, who assumed that was a joke. She was quickly proven wrong when the woman's attention slid disinterestedly away. "Oh. Right." She sniffed again, swiping at her nostrils. She supposed that if she *were* a vagrant, she certainly couldn't be expected to be lent someone's personal phone. "Well, I would, but I don't have, um—" Jesus, did pay phones still take coins? Which she obviously didn't have. Not that she had any way of using a credit card, either. "Well, okay, never mind. Thanks."

Libby turned to step outside, wondering if there was some magical way to make a phone connect a call (there probably was, not that she'd ever had to use one) before the cashier whipped the pages of the newspaper upright, the motion catching Libby's eye from the register. The cashier peeled away the excess pages and set them on the counter, ostensibly unread.

"Wait—can I see that?" asked Libby, reaching for the newspaper the cashier had been reading. Presumably this would tell her where she was, which from the visible letters—NGELES TIMES—she guessed to be Los Angeles.

That explained the heat. And probably the irritation in her nose. Ezra had always told her the air quality in L.A. had improved a lot in recent times, but a childhood trip to Palm Springs had left Libby with the faint impression that it was still essentially a desert. She used to tease Ezra about it, referring to his home city as a place filled with annoying amounts of veganism and dry heat.

"Forty cents," said the cashier without looking up, which did not sound right to Libby, though she hadn't actually bought a newspaper in . . . god, ever. She sniffed again, then surreptitiously wiped her nose with her sleeve. She should have grabbed some paper towels.

"I don't have any, um—"

The cashier shifted disinterestedly, crossing her ankle over one leg and accidentally kicking one of the newspaper's pages aside.

Finally, a clear view. It *was* the *Los Angeles Times,* unsurprisingly. It made sense, what with Ezra being from somewhere in L.A., though he'd never taken her "home," insisting that he hadn't had one. The headline on the front page was something about local politics, the names unfamiliar. The date was right there, just in view. AUGUST 13, 1989.

Wait. Nineteen eighty-nine?

"Fuck," said Libby, who hoped she was still dreaming. "Is that . . . is that *today's* paper, or . . . ?"

The cashier lowered the funny pages as if she planned to make some kind of snarky comment in response, but stopped. She frowned, something catching her eye. In the same moment, Libby lifted a hand unconsciously to her nose, noticing for the first time that her sleeve was smeared with blood.

"Something wrong with you?" the cashier asked, scrutinizing Libby closely for the first time.

Outside, an ambulance went by, heading straight for the mess Libby had left behind. Someone was going to come for her soon, she realized.

If Ezra didn't chase after her first.

"My boyfriend." Libby's mouth felt dry, but maybe this one truth would behoove her. "My ex, he's—"

"Oh." That much the woman understood. Her expression became at once stony and soft, chin tilting in the direction behind her. "Go out the back way."

Was there time to offer her something, to explain . . . ? Not likely. Libby felt torn, but it was a small, necessary win after a streak of Ezra-related misfortune.

"Thanks," Libby said, hurrying toward the gas station's delivery entrance.

"Wait—"

Libby turned, then lifted a hand, reflexively catching the Coke bottle the cashier had thrown at her from the fridge closest to the register.

"Good luck," the woman said, seeming to mean it.

Libby nodded, already feeling guilty. She wondered how long it would be before the cashier started to question what kind of person she'd helped.

"Thanks," Libby said again. She slid out the gas station's rear exit, trying her hardest not to run.

· CALLUM ·

I t was a Tuesday or a Saturday or something when Callum groggily lifted his head from the painted room's sofa to find Reina standing over him.

"Substance abuse," Reina remarked impassively. "Your imagination really is small."

She, from what Callum cared to observe, was draped in a long sweatshirt, the color a utilitarian shade of gray that Callum's family typically marketed to a certain brand of punishingly dull androgynists, and she was clutching a pile of books that seemed to suddenly overwhelm her frame.

He nudged her away with a finger to her kneecap, gradually strong-arming her backward and struggling to force himself upright. It took several seconds to rise completely perpendicular to the floor, which felt very wrong and much too soon, so Callum abandoned the effort. He leaned forward to rest his forehead on the coffee table instead.

"It's not abuse," he said, mouth dry, "if you both enjoy it."

He turned his head to see that one of Reina's brows was arched. "It definitely still is," she muttered, "but okay."

"Shut up." His head pounded and he couldn't think. He could feel something from her, something vibrating too high, much too annoyingly. Not like Libby, more like excitement, but still, he didn't appreciate it. He raised a hand to alleviate the pain behind his temples, which in turn prompted a seizure near his calf. "Ouch. *Ouch,* son of a *bitch*—" The muscle cramped, tightening first and then aching, and Callum pressed a hand to the catastrophizing knot, untangling the waves of pain. Immediately, the pulse in his head returned. "*Fuck—*"

"So," Reina continued. "About our previous discussion."

"Can you—" The sharpness in Callum's head was searing, pinpricks of discomfort settling into a fabric of misery like a thin layer of gauze over his eyeballs. "Can you not?"

"I know I said for you to come find me," Reina said, replying as if he'd said nothing. "But obviously you're going to need further persuading, so. Fine." She scrutinized him for a second before taking a seat on the sofa beside him, apparently content to ignore the ongoing agony that was forcing him to double over in a cold sweat. "So," she said. "I think I've narrowed down what the archives are refusing to give me."

Callum gritted his teeth, starting to shiver. "What?"

"The archives," she repeated, louder, as if her volume were the problem and not the ongoing state of her being in his space. "They aren't giving me books about the origins of gods."

"What?"

"The library will give me mythology," Reina said. "And stories. But the more I try to find the origin stories of gods—anything beyond the primordial," she said, "like Zeus and the Olympians against Cronus and the Titans, or—"

"Get to the point," said Callum, who did not have time for a recap of Greek mythology. Narrative personification of earth and sky always gave way to human indulgence, to wine and warfare. No surprise there. After law and order inevitably came indecency and art.

"Anyway, the archives reject me," Reina blandly concluded, "and I'm thinking it's because I might be one."

That he did not expect. "What?"

"I think I might be a god," she repeated. "I mean, not an *actual* god," she added carefully, "because I don't have your ego. And I'm pretty sure I'm not immortal, although who knows."

He was definitely shivering now. He reached over her for one of the cushions, attempting to shelter himself behind it. "I do not think you are a god, Reina Mori."

Obscenely, she found this an unremarkable argument when really it should have been fact. "Why not? I can produce life," she said. "And as far as I can tell, the Anthropocene is following the right pattern."

He bristled. Could this not end? "The what?"

"Anthropocene," she recited. "It's our current geological age. Means that there are no natural ecosystems anymore that aren't affected by humans."

"I know what Anthropocene means. I meant—"

"Oh, you mean the pattern? Right, well, in pretty much every culture there are . . ." She paused to find the word. "Generations of gods. Eras, epochs. The first ones always precede civilization." She turned to him, tucking one leg under her. "The first gods are essentially time and the elements. Earth, the sun, the darkness, storms and volcanoes. They create the code by which everyone else survives. Then they give birth to the later batch of gods, who represent culture. Wisdom, and mercy, and . . . play. Egyptian gods were born from the primordial abyss, then from the Hemsut, from fate and creation. And even the Judeo-Christian god had a son."

She checked to see if Callum was listening, which by all accounts it should have appeared that he was not. He was focusing on numbing the pain that was creeping down from the back of his neck to his shoulders.

But he was also listening. So fine. "Understood. Go on."

"It's time for new gods," Reina replied simply. "We've progressed to another new generation, one where humans are no longer at the whims of the elements, but the shapers of them, the determiners." A pause. "Which is why I think the archives won't give me the books. Because the library thinks I'm looking for instructions."

"And are you?" This was madness, probably. Who knew anymore. Who cared.

"I wasn't." She chewed the inside of her cheek. "But I might be persuaded."

Ah, and wasn't that an interesting choice of words. "Speaking of persuasion." Callum dragged his gaze up to look at her. "You're not even remotely concerned that I might be influencing you to want this?"

"You're falling apart," she said without derision. Pure fact. "I'm not terribly concerned about what you might be doing to me."

"Fair." He stretched out his legs, rolling out his neck, the whole of him resisting like a broken accordion. "So what do you want from me?"

She shrugged. "I told you. I want you to use me to help you influence the archives."

Callum had a feeling he should care about this. Find it interesting or something. He didn't.

"Okay, so you're a god," he summarized. "Then what? What's the plan?"

"I don't have one yet," Reina said bluntly.

"Yet?"

"I'm still in the early stages of research." She sounded perfectly serious, which was preposterous, and if Callum were not severely in pain he would have laughed.

"What was it you said?" he asked. "About creating life."

"I can create life" was Reina's revelatory answer.

"Okay, so do it," Callum suggested, leaning back and gesturing to the empty space between them. "Go ahead. Dazzle me."

"I can't do it alone." She looked genuinely disgruntled for the first time. "But I *can* do it."

How convenient that she couldn't prove it. "What do you need in order to do it?"

"I—" She looked away, and at that, Callum finally felt something from her that was not the throb of his own head. "It doesn't matter. The point is—"

"You're feeling small," Callum realized, fighting amusement. "Don't tell me Varona actually got to you?"

She still wouldn't meet his eye. "Of course not. He's a child."

"Oh no, no. False." This was delicious. If the rest of him weren't in excruciating pain, he might actually savor it. "You don't think he's a child," Callum corrected with a stitch of opportunistic pleasure. Not that he cared, but it had been *so long* since someone had been noteworthily delusional. "You never have before."

"Does it matter?" Reina looked irritated, as if she really couldn't imagine why he might find the obvious trauma in her psyche to be of relevance to this positively unhinged conversation. "Why would I lie about this?"

"I don't know," he replied. "Why does anyone lie about anything? Because lies are convenient," he answered for her, "and truths are stupid, and doing anything for any reason is based on a random series of choices built on a self-serving morality that ensures that the species survives." Okay, even he knew that was a rant. "The point is I don't care whether you're lying or not," he concluded. "I just don't understand how you go from needing Varona's help to suddenly deciding you must somehow be God."

"I don't think I'm *the* god," Reina said impatiently, like this was perfectly obvious and he should have intuited as much from the beginning. "I think the world has changed and there's a new definition for gods. At the very least it's been established that there *are* generations. Did you know," she added brusquely, in the tone of voice that preceded a losing argument, "that there was a matriarchal god for millennia before the last six thousand years of Abrahamic patriarchy? Neolithic female cults predated the male god—"

"Something-something not all men," muttered Callum, who couldn't be bothered to defend his Y chromosome at the moment.

"I'm not making a comment about gender," Reina snapped impatiently. "I'm making a comment about deification and change. Gods *change*. Generations are born. That implies there can be new ones."

"For a god," Callum said drolly, "you're not doing much to convince me."

"Fine." She rose to her feet, obviously furious with him (no, more likely herself, though he was certainly not helping) and unable, despite apparent effort, to hide it. "Is anything about this interesting to you?"

"I like the idea of the archives having a brain that can be influenced." Callum closed his eyes and slumped lower on the sofa, sensing the conversation would at last coast to a blissful stop. "It does appeal slightly."

"Slightly?"

In that it would be a convenient excuse for Callum's casual suspicion that parts of him were dissolving into putrescence and despair. "Well, just think how fun it will be if we're all just slaves to some bloodthirsty, sentient thing. I don't suppose the archives are gods too, are they?" he mused, and Reina gave a short, irritated sigh.

"You're mocking me."

He cracked one eye. "Of course I'm mocking you. You're being an idiot." She glanced witheringly at him. "What if this had been Tristan's idea?"

He felt a jab of something. Like a sleeping limb on pins and needles.

"Tristan," Callum mumbled, "doesn't *have* his own ideas. It's what I like about him."

He meant to say *liked,* but it obviously didn't matter. Luckily Reina had gone by then, and so Callum did not have to defend his incredibly stupid use of present tense. Besides, maybe she would consider it a poor translation.

The following day was when they were supposed to have identified their topic of independent study, two weeks or so from the date they were assigned their so-called syllabus, which of course Callum had lent absolutely no thought to. He was initiated, wasn't he? So what would happen if he said no thank you, I'm simply done with books? He just had to live here for another year. Nobody was going to *fail* him if he didn't produce some kind of academic thesis. Wasn't he contributing to the magic of the house simply by existing in it? He'd contributed to the wards. It was feeding off his magic now, obviously. In fact, if Reina was right about the archives being sentient, it was probably feeding off him all the time. He felt like shit most of the time regardless, and it was fairly obvious to anyone looking that Nico was newly under strain. He had coughed the other day, loudly, then looked surprised. He was probably accustomed to having a certain degree of control over his bodily functions. He probably did not often, if ever, get sick.

Which did leave Callum with an odd little niggling of something he might have called intrigue, because if the archives—or perhaps not the archives, but definitely some source of magic in the house—were feeding off of them, tracking them, then that would explain both the statistical dossiers Callum had discovered and the initiation ritual that had seemed to be nothing more than humiliation dealt their way by Atlas Blakely. That had been Callum's assumption—that Atlas, who had always been very clear about hating Callum, had chosen to punish him by forcing him to spend time with himself.

Joke's on him, Callum thought. Nobody knew better than Callum how terrible it was to spend time with Callum—except possibly for Tristan, who had been willing to kill him. So there was that.

So it would be fun, then—fun! that was certainly the word—if in fact it was *not* Atlas Blakely at the helm but something bigger, more sinister. If perhaps they had submitted themselves for scientific observation and not the other way around. After all, *they* were magic—*they* were the ones who kept the wards powered, the lights on—and if the library was sentient, why wouldn't it want what they had? Perhaps, in that sense, they *were* gods. Which was something Callum himself had compared them to, yes, but mostly for rhetoric's sake. He had never bothered to wonder whether he actually was one.

At some point, Callum fell asleep on the sofa. Sometime around two in the morning he rose to his feet and dragged himself upstairs. Then he fell asleep in his bed and slept through that morning's meeting about what their independent study topics were going to be. Then, feeling peckish, he stumbled to the dining room, sat in one of the ornate chairs, and opened a package of soup crackers.

At which point he felt a tap on his shoulder and turned to find Reina, again.

"So, I asked Dalton if he would explain how the archives worked," she said.

"Okay." Callum was thirsty now. "And?"

"And he's right here," Reina said, stepping aside to gesture to where Dalton Ellery stood beside her, looking uncomfortable. Or ill. Or perhaps that was just how Dalton Ellery always looked and Callum had not cared to pay attention before today.

"Yes?" Callum said.

Dalton gave him a look of clinical concern, as if perhaps he was aware that Callum was not entirely in top form. Though of course, Callum couldn't imagine what could possibly have given Dalton that impression.

"The archives don't offer every title to every person," Dalton said. "I don't know that there's any codified reason as to why. But there is some implication of the contents being earned, which we told you all before you were initiated."

"Cool," Callum said. "Question answered, then. Good luck."

He turned away, suddenly feeling a desperate craving for his mother's biryani. She didn't cook it herself, obviously. But she rang for it and he ate it beside her, usually. If she was in a good mood that day, which wasn't always. She was a moody creature, and not in the derogatory way, in the sense that her moods took oppressive turns. They did. But sometimes they turned for the wonderful, and when they did, Callum ate biryani.

"No," Reina said. "No. That's—No. I have more questions."

"Mr. Nova," Dalton said, "as to your topic of independent study—"

"Miss Mori has questions," Callum said without looking, gesturing over his shoulder to Reina.

"Yes. Why does it reject certain requests?" pressed Reina. "What are the specifications for approval or denial?"

"As I said, it's not exactly codified," Dalton said stiffly. "If there are any sort of concrete rules about accessing the archives, we didn't make them."

"Who is 'we'?" Reina's voice was at its most unintentionally bullying. "You and Atlas?"

"Any of us," Dalton said. "We are only the library's stewards, not its rulers."

"What can you not access?" asked Reina.

"My research is highly specific. I'm sure there are any variety of subjects I can't access that I would never know about, because I haven't tried."

"But—"

"Maybe the library is like nature," Callum posed neutrally, toying with the pitcher of cream that had been set out hours earlier for tea. "It's just rolling the dice."

"But the library's *not* random." Reina sounded so annoyed that Callum half suspected she might punch him. "That's the point. And if it were, that would be one thing," she argued, "but it's not, it's specific. It *specifically* does not let us access certain things. So why?"

It occurred to Callum in an odd, splicing sort of way that a previous version of himself had once found it interesting that Libby Rhodes could not access any information about degenerative diseases.

"Because they're dangerous," Callum murmured. That information could have killed Libby. Not actually, of course. But in some life-changing, destructive way, possession of an answer would have killed the spark of her that kept her going, moved her forward. Knowing for certain whether her sister should have lived would have been an anchor, plummeting her to an existential standstill either way. She was only truly alive for not knowing the answer—for knowing there could be no answer. Perhaps the library was testing her, forcing her to come farther before it would give her what she needed. Or perhaps it was merely protecting her, knowing she never would.

Callum felt suddenly very aware of Dalton watching him.

"What?" demanded Reina.

"Nothing," Callum said, backing his chair away from the table and rising to his feet. "So," he added to Dalton. "Are you and Parisa still fucking?"

Dalton blinked at him.

"Sorry," Callum offered insincerely. "Are you and Parisa still making love?"

There was a tiny line of tension between Dalton's dark brows, though it must have occurred to him that shock was precisely what Callum had been hoping for. Callum, who had not felt much of anything these past few days, was hoping to jump-start something interesting in Dalton.

But Dalton was not much of a team player, it seemed. "I'm afraid you may have been more accurate the first time."

"Right." Callum felt a sickening wave of envy at the thought of having someone. Or being so slavishly beholden to them that you allowed a substance-abusing empath to batter you with his derision and let that make no difference, no significant impact on the rest of your day. "Right, well, enjoy."

"Wait," said Reina, leaving Dalton behind to follow Callum up the stairs. "Wait," she said, breathless by the time she caught up to his purposefully elongated stride. "Don't you care what *Dalton* researches?"

"No," said Callum, who considered going to the kitchen. He could probably figure out biryani if he really tried. Or he could just drink from the tap and curl up in one of the corners until Reina finally left him alone.

"He basically said nothing is denied to him," Reina said, and repeated urgently, "*Nothing.*"

How exhausting. "Yes, and . . . ?"

"That's an anomaly." She was thinking very hard. He found it borderline offensive. Couldn't she see he was going through something? Of course not. She was too busy trying to solve a nonexistent mystery.

"Okay, so it's an anomaly," Callum said mildly. "Are you done?"

"No, think about it." She began chewing the nail of her thumb. An oddly Libby gesture, but then again, who among them had not picked up some oddity of Libby's by then? Callum had clearly decided to lean into her habit of existentially decaying.

"All of us are denied something," Reina said. "We all naturally want to research things that we shouldn't, right? But he's able to see *everything he requests.*" She glanced up at him triumphantly. "Have you ever wondered what Parisa sees in him?"

God, no, never. "She spent too long in France," Callum said. "He's just her type."

"No. Wrong." Reina shook her head. "Parisa doesn't *like* people."

"Nor do I," said Callum.

"Right," Reina agreed. "But you picked Tristan. Why?"

"Because he's a masochist. And I'm a sadist." On another day he would have congratulated himself for that remarkable succinctness.

"No, you picked him because he was *interesting* to you." Reina, on the other hand, was sounding increasingly pleased with herself, though Callum couldn't imagine why. "And what's interesting about Dalton?"

"Nothing," said Callum.

"Exactly." The light leaking from Reina's face was too much. The rays of victory hurt Callum's eyes. "Don't you see? There's something wrong with him."

"Don't you mean there's something wrong with *her*?" Not that it mattered. There was something wrong with all of them. That was the whole point. Callum had told Tristan that they were gods born with pain built in, and they were. That's what kept them weak. Too weak to be the new Olympus, regardless of what Reina Mori thought.

"No. No, don't you see . . . ?" She stopped walking, but Callum continued. Eventually he had left her behind in the corridor, so he went into the kitchen and stole a jar of Marmite. Then he went to his room and slept.

The next morning Callum received an envelope under the door.

> *Mr Nova,*
>
> *It has come to my attention that you have not picked a topic for independent study. Please submit a drafted proposal before the end of the week.*

It was signed with an *A*, for Atlas presumably, or for Asshole, whichever worked. Callum crumpled the page into a ball and tossed it into the bathtub before returning to his bed.

It was dark when he heard a knock at the door. He cracked one eye, waiting.

Silence.

Good.

He closed his eyes again and the knocking started again.

He opened one eye.

Silence.

He closed his eyes.

Silence.

Good.

And then the knocking started again and he burst out of bed, infuriated.

"What?" he snapped, yanking the door open.

It was Nico, which made Callum want to drop-kick him into the next county. "Yeah, hi," said Nico. "Any idea where Reina is?"

"Why are you asking me?" Sickened, Callum suddenly remembered the visual of Tristan murmuring to Nico in hushed tones from the corridor.

Not that he—

Not that *they*—

It wasn't as if Callum suspected anything between them, friendly or otherwise.

"Well, I can't find Parisa," said Nico, frowning, "or I'd ask her." He didn't mention Tristan, which meant he had either already asked Tristan or Tristan was the reason he was asking, which made Callum suddenly incandescent with rage.

"And I'm supposed to be Reina's keeper?" Callum grunted.

"No, I just . . . I mean, I assumed you could like, sense her. Or whatever." Nico looked increasingly flustered, which was at least very gratifying to Callum.

"Is that what you think my magic is? That I'm some kind of metal detector for your individual feelings?" He was, actually. Not that he'd ever admit it, but each of them had an emotional signature, and if he wanted to be helpful—which he didn't—he would know exactly what to focus on to find Reina.

"Right. Sorry." Nico turned away, agitated, without waiting for a response, and Callum shut the door.

He returned to his bed before realizing he was no longer tired. The exhaustion that had driven him back to sleep was suddenly overtaken by a sharper sensation: curiosity.

"Damn," said Callum to nothing.

He rose to his feet and grabbed a robe, trotting into the corridor and bypassing the drawing room. He considered going downstairs, figuring the obvious rooms were obvious, before he remembered that he knew only two things about Reina. One, she was very into books and privacy. Two, plants annoyed her. They interrupted her thoughts and she resented them for it. That was what her energy felt like—the constant exasperation of a tethered thing.

He made his way across the gallery balustrades to the east wing of the upper floor, padding toward the chapel. The doors were parted slightly and he pushed one open, spotting Reina on the floor below the stained-glass triptych. She sat bathed in the light of the scales for justice, directly beneath the torch for knowledge.

She looked up, spotting Callum, who realized he was wearing a dressing gown and was presently shoeless. Then she looked down again in disinterest, flipping a page in her book.

"The truth is I'm fucking furious," she said without looking up. She hadn't said it in English, but it was familiar enough a sensation that he easily grasped the point. "And it's terrible. It's so much worse to be angry," she said, for him to understand that time, "because I'm not supposed to care."

Callum considered telling her that the world was essentially a stupid place and they were all basically flawed in the same ways. There were variations here and there, but functionally they were all idiots.

Instead he sighed and walked forward, sitting beside her on the cold wood.

"If you're a god," he offered indulgently, "does that mean you're immortal?"

"How should I know? And regardless, gods die," she said. Her tone was guarded, waiting for him to contradict her. "They die all the time."

He shrugged. "So then what makes them gods?"

"People to worship them, I guess." She flipped the page again, then looked up. "What did it say about me? Whatever it was you read from the archives."

"Stuff about your family." He leaned his head against the wall, though for once he didn't feel pain, or tiredness. Perhaps he'd finally slept it away. "How you have more power than anyone but you'll never be able to use it."

He had told Tristan once that they all had the exact curses they deserved. He understood his own, that he felt everything because he wanted terribly, with all of his being, to feel nothing. Because to feel nothing would be to finally no longer feel pain.

"There's a quote," Reina said. "From Einstein. About how God doesn't roll the dice." She paused. "It doesn't mean god like *God*. It means nothing in the universe is random."

"Mm," said Callum, closing his eyes.

"But I used to not believe that," Reina continued. "I believed the universe was completely random, and that's what eluded us. Because we all want to believe we are fundamental in some way. We are our own myths, our own legends. *We* give things reason. We are reasonable creatures and so everything must have its place, its purpose—but we are also egotistical creatures, and so we give ourselves reasons that don't exist."

Callum considered a world where nothing was justified or earned. It just *was*.

"But then, do I have this power because something happened randomly in the universe?" Reina said. "Does entropy, chaos—does that actually make *more* sense? That all of this, it isn't irony just to punish us, it's randomness? We're just things, trinkets bouncing around in space, trying to make sense of it? Maybe it does, maybe it doesn't. But nature is not completely random—ask a physicist," she said wryly, or as wry as Reina ever got. "It has constants, discretion. Consistent rules that are always true and never change."

"So then your theory is that the alternative to a random universe is . . . we're gods," Callum deduced slowly.

"We are in all the ways that matter," said Reina, shrugging. "The power is real. The magic we have creates order. Doesn't it? So, everything may look perfectly random," she said, staring contemplatively ahead, "but in fact it's not to us."

It made an odd sort of sense. Or at least managed to ease something painful. It was probably still nonsense, but it wasn't the worst nonsense Callum had ever heard. He'd suffered far worse inside his head.

"So," Callum said. "What now?"

"We see what the archives are hiding from me," Reina said.

"Couldn't I just request it for you?"

"Maybe." She shrugged. "But isn't it more interesting to experiment this way?"

Valid point. Their day jobs were scholarly, after all. "And then?"

"Then we find out what it's giving to Dalton."

She sounded certain. Not quite cold, but something metallic.

Iron. That's what it was.

He could respect that. And it was better than stale crackers. Possibly more interesting than substance abuse. Or at the very least, a certain degree less cliché. Not that he planned to admit that she was right about that, or anything.

"You're not trying to save me, are you?" Callum said. The idea repulsed him.

"No," Reina replied. "Not to feed into your whole 'nobody cares' thing, but I really don't give a shit about you."

Perfect.

"So should we test it? The influencing? We could try it on a person first," he said.

He watched something beautifully sinister alight around the edges of Reina's mouth.

"I know just the person," she said.

So Callum closed his eyes, temporarily satisfied.

· NICO ·

Tristan's chest had not moved in several seconds.

From where he crouched over Tristan's body on the floor of the painted room, Nico glanced up at the clock on the mantel, watching it tick and counting silently to himself.

Sixteen, seventeen, eighteen—

Okay, fuck it. The lunacy of this experiment certainly wasn't going to get better with lasting brain damage. Nico took a brief inhale and aimed a jolt of force into Tristan's heart, jump-starting it like a faulty engine. The effect was immediate and perhaps overdone—Nico stumbled backward when Tristan shot upright with a gasp, his forehead only narrowly avoiding an impact with Nico's front teeth.

"Fuck," Tristan gritted out, panting, as Nico slammed an ankle (again) into the Victorian end table that was consistently in the way. Nico felt another little tremor of metal in his mouth, a radioactive aftertaste from the effort of reviving Tristan. He stalled for time, breathing deeply, until the aftershocks had passed, then looked up to find Tristan propped up on his elbows, legs rag-dolling out while he caught his breath.

"Should we try again?" asked Tristan, which was so like Nico himself he wasn't sure which one of them to strangle. (Not Tristan, they'd already tried that.)

"Why, so you can just die slower over time?" Nico reminded him, irritated at having to be the voice of reason, a role he did not fill naturally and should not have been forced into.

But Tristan was starting to look a little gray around the edges, which meant someone would have to do it. He was like a bad animation of himself, and Nico wasn't doing much better. Not that he wanted to discuss it.

"This was supposed to be straightforward," muttered Nico to himself. Additionally, it was supposed to be more of a one-time thing, not a third strike for the evening on a night that was already the third strike that week. "Are you really not seeing anything different?" he asked Tristan, regrettably using a tone he felt certain would elicit an irrational response, which of course it did.

"Maybe it's your fault," Tristan shot at him, which was clearly a no. "How hard is it to almost kill someone?"

"I don't know, Tristan, you tell me," Nico snapped, at which Tristan's mouth tightened, irritated.

Great. So things were going well.

Not much had changed since the first time Nico had tried to kill Tristan, which was well over a month ago now. Then, like now, Tristan had simply hovered in the wake of death instead of miraculously shifting his vision to perceive time and space as he claimed he was meant to do. Each time had been slightly different, but always ultimately the same: whether Tristan meditated first or listened to heavy metal first or slept first or kept himself awake all night, the outcome was that Tristan's body loved dying and clearly wanted to do it more than Tristan's brain thought he should.

"Maybe we need a bigger gamble," Nico said. "Bigger risk." That was Nico's modus operandi, after all. If things weren't working, make them worse.

Tristan rubbed the back of his neck. "Like what?"

"I don't know. I'll have to think about it." Nico wanted to discuss it with Reina, but Tristan had made it clear that he didn't want other people to know about this. Probably because it sounded insane, which it very definitely was. "But whatever your magic is, it obviously doesn't want to be disturbed unless it has to be."

"Maybe the problem is that I don't believe I'm actually dying." Tristan's natural expression of resting asshole face was starting to bother Nico less, but only marginally. At the moment he wanted badly to punch Tristan in the mouth.

"So you want me to be a more convincing murderer?" Nico snapped.

"Maybe I do." Tristan shook his head, glaring at Nico—who was obviously at fault, why not. "I should have asked Parisa to do this," Tristan muttered to himself. "I have absolutely no doubt that she'd kill me given half a chance."

"She also wouldn't save you. Which honestly sounds ideal to me at this point." Nico let his head fall back against the floor, staring at the ceiling.

He had been wondering what to make of Tristan since the confession of his upbringing, clearly shared to soothe something blistering between them. Nico had thought, idiotically, that knowing something about what made up the parts of Tristan Caine would make him more sympathetic to Tristan overall, or more patient in the aggregate. But patience was not something Nico excelled at in general, and no matter how tragic Tristan's background, this was all getting hugely out of hand.

"Look," Nico said. "I don't know how much more of this I have in me."
He heard Tristan's breath falter, the motion of his chest hitching. "Oh."

"I want to help you," Nico added. "But maybe you're right, maybe I can't."
Tristan didn't say anything.

"Because for this to work," Nico continued, "you have to find the exact right conditions of believing you're about to die. And if you think I'm too soft to kill you, or too weak, or—"

"I don't." Tristan's voice cut through the silence of the room. "I think—"
He stopped.

"I think you're probably quite a good person," Tristan muttered.

Nico said nothing, assuming it to be an insult.

"Which is ultimately the same problem," Tristan finished gruffly. "Because if you're that good, then yeah, I can't possibly believe you'll let me die. Or that I'm actually in danger."

"Great," Nico said glumly, staring into the flames of the painted room's hearth. "So I've just wasted a month of my life, then."

"Yes." Tristan struggled upright, pausing for a moment before rising completely to his feet. "Which I appreciate," he added with aggressive distaste as he stood over Nico.

Nico wondered for a moment if Tristan might offer a hand to help him up from the floor. He hoped not. Something about this whole situation was starting to mess with him. Maybe it was that he and Tristan shared some kind of fundamental devastation, some advancing degree of decay that neither wanted to confess aloud, but which both knew to share one name. And that name was Libby Rhodes.

Helping each other only seemed to make the devastation worse.

"Night," said Nico, pointedly closing his eyes. He would live here now, on the floor of the painted room, if that's what it took.

"Night." Tristan paused for a moment, but not much longer than that. Then he padded out of the room, his footsteps receding down the corridor as Nico gradually opened his eyes again, staring into the fireplace.

He wondered what Gideon was doing. Wondered if Gideon had found Libby, obviously, but also if Gideon had laughed that day or pondered something stupid that only Nico would understand. Nico was starting to miss the little things, the painful ordinariness of existing in Gideon's periphery. The things he sent to Nico throughout the day that contributed to some shared language—some thread of stupid, easy amusement that bound them both so tightly that even while apart, Nico knew exactly what made Gideon laugh and Gideon, too, knew that Nico did not like his eggs flipped or his competency questioned. The way he knew that Gideon would say, *Nicolás, you said that you would help him.* Or *I know you, Nicky, and the one thing you are not is a liar or a quitter. Even if you are also the dumbest idiot I've ever known.*

Something in Nico ached and he curled up on his side, facing away from the hearth. He stayed there for a second, listening to the clock tick. The crackle of flame gradually fell away until the shadows crept up from the floor, the room filling with darkness.

Then Nico rose to his feet, making his way up the stairs.

From a physicist's perspective, everything Tristan had explained about his powers made sense and should work. That was the maddening part, that theoretically Tristan had every reason to be right. His description of his own magic, the melding of space and time into space-time, seemed consistent with a fourth dimension that only Tristan could see. And Tristan's explanation for the look of it, the way particles moved, sounded consistent with Brownian motion: that the movements that seemed random were not actually random, but ordered relative to something that Tristan could apparently understand.

"If I could figure out its motions," Tristan had said, "I could control it." And what Nico had not confessed was that if Tristan could control it, then he could do more than Nico. More than Libby, too.

Because if Tristan could control the motion of things down to their quanta—down to the fundamental particles of their energy—then he was more than a physicist. He was not limited by the physical world or bound by the properties of force. He could also alter the chemical. He could travel through time. He could identify the materials of the universe, and if he could find them, he could move them. *Create* them. He could reverse entropy, master chaos. In fact, there would be no such thing as chaos anymore—no randomness, no spontaneity. It was no longer a world made up of things, but of events, systems, paths of a larger design that the rest of them, ignorant as they were, mistook for something human: A will. Fate. A plan. The universe through Tristan's eyes would be orderly—and that, more than anything, was the closest thing Nico could imagine to omnipotence. It was as close to divine as anything could possibly be.

And Tristan couldn't access it, all because Nico did not actually want Tristan to die.

There was something very ridiculous about that.

"Have you chosen your topic of study?" Dalton had asked Nico earlier that day, coming upon him in the reading room. Nico was holding a book in his hands, something he had not been intending to read. His goal, he reminded himself, was to understand *Gideon*. To have answers *for* Gideon.

There was still nothing more important, and ultimately no other reason for Nico's continued presence in this house.

But there was also something calling to him. Some awakening of his own sense of wonder that he blamed on Tristan Caine. Because nothing about Nico's magic had been sufficiently interesting before—neither his abilities nor his limitations—until he finally understood that there was more of it to be had. Gideon had said that if his theory was right, then someone who could travel in time did not necessarily have to be more powerful than Nico—that perhaps that skill could be very narrow, very limited—but if *Tristan* was right, then that did not have to be true. And so, for the first time, Nico de Varona had asked for a book from the archives that was not about creatures, not about evolution or classification or genetics, but about life.

Aviditas. Appetite. *Aviditas vitae,* the wanting to live. The hunger for it, which drove everything. Nico knew it to exist because he had seen Reina create it. He knew it to be powerful because he believed Tristan to be correct. He now believed the desire to live to be more than philosophy, more than psychology, but rather, a primordial principle of physics.

That things would unravel given half a chance was part of an intricate infrastructure. Entropy was law—the Second Law of Thermodynamics, to be precise—and therefore written into the codification of existence. Some human animus, some fundamental consciousness, was still an element of naturalism, and therefore of the physical world, but perhaps to master entropy was to master more than just some formless rule of chaos. Perhaps what it meant was the possibility of control over the cosmology of life itself.

What would it mean to create that spark of life? To have mastery over it? To birth it or destroy it at will? What mysteries of the universe could they uncover if they stopped associating all forms of danger with the inevitability of death?

Which was why it was a simple matter to silently dismantle the lock on Tristan's bedroom. To step quietly across the floor and hold his breath, waiting to determine the motion of Tristan's chest. To tell himself that if Tristan was in fact wrong, if Tristan's calculations of being doomed to failure were even remotely incorrect, then there was a lesson there worth knowing, a certainty worth defying. Because this—Nico being here, alive, breathing, in existence at the same time as Tristan Caine, despite all the versions of their lives in which they did not meet—this confluence of events was not, could not be randomness. This was relativity at work, wasn't it? That Nico existed relative to Tristan, and as a result, their research was fundamentally intertwined. Their experiences were shared. Caring for Gideon had driven Nico here, and existing beside Libby had pushed him, and pushed Tristan, and everything that had led to her loss could not be random. It wasn't chance. It was by design, and if Nico could *see* the design, then somehow he could change it. He could change the ending and start again.

Tristan slept on his back, restless. Nico put out a hand, letting it hover above Tristan's chest.

And then he slammed it down, applying the maximum force to Tristan's heart just after Tristan's eyes shot open, the instinctive reflex of terror waking him up with a strangled gasp.

Something pushed against Nico's magic, warping it. It neither ricocheted nor reversed itself, but bent, shooting lethally toward the window at an angle, like a reflection off the mirror of Tristan's chest. The glass shattered, obliterated particles glittering from the corner of his eye, and the sudden shift in momentum sent Nico stumbling forward to land face-first in Tristan's bed.

Which was empty.

Nico tried to lift his chin, the effort piercing the twinge in his neck. He would have to do something about that. He raised a hand to massage it, then looked up to find Tristan standing by the window.

Which was whole.

Nico blinked. "The window, it's—"

"I know." Tristan stared down at his hand, which remained outstretched in the direction that the force of Nico's magic had gone.

The window had not been broken. Nico's magic must have gone somewhere else, dissolving outward. He could feel the settling of the house's frame, as if the direction of force had been scattered on the wind.

Nico sat up slowly. "Did you . . . ?"

"Stop it? Yes." Tristan inspected the bones of his hand like he was shocked it hadn't broken, curling a fist and then stretching his fingers out again, unharmed.

"So then—" Nico frowned, rising to his feet. "It worked?"

Tristan looked different. The expression on his face wasn't its usual stiffness, nor was it lost. Nico knew the distinction, the shift. He had cut his teeth on that feeling. It was a surge, notch by notch up his spine, of resiliency. Determination. It was the grit of a man who had learned he could take a punch and rise up swinging.

"You motherfucker," said Tristan in disbelief, or possibly awe. "You tried to kill me."

"Yeah," said Nico.

Tristan's brow twitched with bemusement or wonder, his hand falling to his side.

"Why?" he asked.

Nico tried to think of something to say that Gideon might find productive. Then he changed his mind, opting for something that would make Gideon roll his eyes.

"Because I could, Tristan," said Nico de Varona truthfully, feeling a renewed surge of satisfaction at the reminder of what ran through his veins, which did not exist by chance. He was born this way for a reason, and suddenly it had become important—no, critical—no, *paramount*—to fulfill those obligations. Because what he was had not been seen before and could not be replicated.

With one exception.

"And," Nico said, "because I'm now holding you personally responsible for finding a way to get Rhodes back."

· EZRA ·

Ezra was dying.

Of boredom.

Which was, it turned out, a far slower death than asphyxiation, or smoke inhalation. Not that he had any concerns there, having had at least sufficient magic to remove himself from the wreckage of Libby Rhodes's explosion. The fire was an outcome he had done his best to prevent but had known, like red sky at morning, was inevitably on its way. As she took him by the throat, it had occurred to him with a flash of something, possibly relief or comeuppance, that Libby might even kill him; might even want to watch him die under her thumb. Ultimately, though, she had cast him aside, leaving him for dead as the room burned, which was not the same thing as cold-blooded murder. Not that it was much better.

In any case, Ezra Fowler was now traveling again. Something he did often these days, attending meeting after meeting. Ezra had never been to Budapest, or to anywhere, really, in what he was starting to think of as the before times. He had not really been much for travel, given that it was easier for him to visit the distant future than it was to procure a passport and haul his carbon footprint off to France.

He supposed it was a good thing, all this travel. Or more accurately, what the need for travel represented, which was the effectiveness of his plan. And it *was* an effective plan, as plans went, because it was simple. When he had presented it to the others, it was very apparent that he had chosen his co-conspirators correctly, because he required very few words to make it a simple matter to them, too.

Ezra's chosen six were Nothazai, who infamously represented the Forum; James Wessex, who was infamously James Wessex; Julian Rivera Pérez, the CIA technomancer whose work was notoriously unmentionable and publicly unmentioned; Sef Hassan, the mineral naturalist who represented the magical interests of the MENA region; a medeian from the Beijing operation that was easier to seek out than to actually name; and a professor, Dr. Araña, whose government contracts were likewise of extreme and remarkable confidentiality.

Unlike the six chosen for the Society, Ezra's coalition were selected not to destroy themselves for the sake of some elusive, exclusive prize, but to share a common outcome. A common goal. The same goal, in fact, that Ezra and Atlas had shared over two decades ago: to bring down the Society and replace it with something more widely distributed; something less full of bullshit and secrets and cloak-and-dagger pretension that served only to conceal the fact that below the dignified mask of righteousness was merely another clan of despots seeking to rule the world.

"I happen to know for a fact that each of you has a stake in wanting the Society exposed," Ezra had announced to the group on the fateful evening he first gathered them. For half of them their purpose was ideological, philosophical. Nothazai and the Forum wanted the Society's carefully protected—or maliciously hoarded—knowledge in the open. Hassan wanted the colonized and therefore stolen knowledge back where it belonged. The professor, a mostly retired activist, wanted to use the archives academically, in her lab or in her classroom. For the others it was more a matter of profit, but philanthropy alone didn't pay the bills or destroy a secret society of homicidal medeians. What was significant here was less the means than the ends.

"I have accessed the contents of the archives myself," Ezra said, carefully revealing his ace. The others were too adept to show their surprise openly, but not nearly disinterested enough to conceal it completely, either. "And I know firsthand that what each of you longs for, regardless of your intentions, is contained within it." After all, Ezra had once been willing to give up everything to possess it. To rule it, and to do so with Atlas, which had been his mistake. He hadn't done the calculations properly enough to foresee that by the time Atlas got his foothold into the Society, he would no longer need Ezra at all.

It was a familiar offer, as temptingly unspecific as the Society's own. The looks on the faces around the table proved each of them was filling in their respective blanks, populating their own treasures. Only the professor seemed mostly unaffected, and James Wessex, who appeared cautiously restrained.

The billionaire was surprisingly soft-spoken. The moment he opened his mouth, the others instinctively leaned forward, straining to listen. "Are we to believe the Society allowed you to wander in and back out again alive? Assuming," Wessex murmured, "that the library even exists beyond some collective delusion."

That earned a shared glance of amusement around the table. Everyone knew the Society's archives existed. How else to explain it, the very nature and topography of power, or the way that certain medeians seemed faultlessly marked for success?

The question was what the archives contained, and, more relevantly, how to prove it—and Ezra was the first who ever could. So he continued.

"Prior to today, all anyone has ever had to confirm the existence of the Alexandrian Society was its shadow. The medeians who never returned, or the ones who did so with unprecedented power. Until now it has been a matter of speculation, of deduction from the outside." Ezra paused to lock eyes with Nothazai, who was peering back at him intently. "But I can confirm for you the names of the most recent class of initiates as well as their specialties. I know their education, their upbringings, their pasts. I know their families, their allies, and their enemies. And I also know which of the candidates remain."

There was a moment of pause.

"So then your plan is to . . . hunt them?" asked Nothazai placidly.

"No," said Ezra, though it was, in a sense. "The Forum already has its methods for hunting, and I believe it's fair to say they are ineffective." He gave Nothazai a blunt look at that.

Nothazai folded his arms thoughtfully over his chest but did not argue. He, more than anyone, would know that the Society's most effective weapon was its secrecy. What could not be proven could not be held against them. Every accusation leveraged by the Forum against the Society had exactly the consistency of dissipating smoke.

"My plan," Ezra clarified, "is to apprehend the Society's newest initiates, officially." In the past, without evidence of wrongdoing, the Society was able to bury its secrets as effectively as they had buried Ezra himself, erasing his existence and thus crafting their own doom. They routinely expunged their own sins, trusting that death or their promises of glory could buy them silence. Unfortunately for them, one of their number was a liar. Which meant that thanks to Atlas Blakely, Ezra was both alive and gloriously pissed off. "We'll be able to treat the Society's candidates as the criminals they are," Ezra pointed out, tacitly referencing the murder clause at the heart of the Society's contract, "and use them to lead us in. From there, taking the Society down will be only a matter of exposing its most illicit secrets. Of which there are many." At least one every ten years since the ancient libraries began.

Pérez drummed his fingers on the table. "You only need one of the initiates for that. Not all five." Beside him, the Beijing medeian's mouth quirked just enough to indicate agreement.

"Four," Ezra corrected, because as Libby had helpfully informed him, one of them was dead. And the other was safe. "And would one be enough," he posed neutrally, "should the Society allow one of their number to drown alone rather than risk revealing its secrets?"

Meaning: the Society would undoubtedly martyr one medeian for the cause. They did so every ten years as it was. Only the full collection would be appropriately persuasive.

Pérez was immediately assuaged. "Point taken."

"You'll still need a lot more resources. More than just ours." Nothazai's fingers were steepled at his mouth. "Their systems are impenetrable. Their Caretaker alone is a formidable opponent." Ezra tried not to bristle at the mention of Atlas. "And more importantly, the Society will not crumble just because one class of medeians opens their mouths. The library has stood far too long for such a simple weakness."

"Their system isn't perfect," countered Ezra, who, at the time, had slid through a vacancy in their supposedly impenetrable wards just that evening. "And there are fractures among the remaining initiates. It will not be difficult to find the cracks in the Society's foundation."

It was clear that his confidence was beginning to impact the others, who all looked as though they had been handed a rare and valuable prize.

Well, all but one. Ezra's attention snagged on the professor, who remained perfectly still while the other heads began nodding.

"What happens to the library after you apprehend the initiates?" asked Nothazai.

"Make it available," said Ezra with a shrug. "Circulate it."

"Not everything in that library is meant for public consumption," said Pérez. He paused to glance at the medeian from Beijing, who did not look at him, and James Wessex, who brazenly did.

But Ezra had heard that argument before. They all had. "Better dangerous out in the open than in the hands of some secret elite," he said. Pérez could not disagree, nor could any of the others.

From there, it became obvious to all of them that the resources Nothazai alluded to—institutional power, intelligence operations, and, of course, money—would be a critical piece of the plan. Their influence would need to span the width of the globe, to unite their disparate aims, however reluctantly, against one common enemy—and on top of all that, the clock was ticking. Upon release from their obligations to the archives, the remaining four of Atlas's pawns would no doubt secure a foothold in the world, making themselves above reproach as every Society member had done in the past. For now they were contained, but out of reach. In another year, they could be virtually untouchable. For a brief window of time, though, Ezra would get one shot. Just one. If he missed, he reminded himself, the consequences would be dire, unsurvivable for more than just his conscience. Hence the sudden need to be everywhere at once.

But seeing the vast, cerebral forest of saving the world still consisted primarily of accounting for dull, monotonous trees. Ezra was learning very quickly that travel was kind of a headache, even when he used the most efficient medeian channels afforded by his new group of associates. The transport passages owned and operated by the Wessex Corporation—which worked like Ezra's doors between points in time, but between private wards in major cities—were about as convenient as anything could be, but still. The logistics of setting traps for the most dangerous medeians to ever live was not actually enough to captivate the imagination for every moment of the day, and the time differences were a real drag.

"You get used to it," said Eden, who was James Wessex's secretary or something. Maybe his assistant. (Ezra, unlike Atlas, did not have a good memory for names or occupations or other trivialities.) She had met Ezra at the hotel where Nothazai had suggested he stay, which had an ostentatious name and looked like some kind of palace. "Unfortunately we haven't evolved beyond circadian rhythms."

"Right." It wasn't the first time Ezra had spoken with Eden, but he never knew what to say to her. She had a very lofty quality, like she was judging everyone silently inside her head, which she probably was. She was willowy and quite tall for a woman, nearing his height. She had glossy, chestnut hair and starbursts of amber in her green eyes, and there was something about her that was very intimidating. Like she'd killed her last mate and eaten him for sustenance.

"Anyway, Nothazai is meeting you at the brasserie," she said. "I'll be there myself later this evening. Just have to take care of some personal business first."

Ezra wasn't sure whether he was meant to comment on said personal business. "Oh?"

"Meetings," she said vaguely. "We're sourcing a deal here. Can't tell you or I'll have to kill you," she added with a sidelong smile. She reminded Ezra of a fox. Something about the arrangement of her features, he supposed. Or the way her eyes moved very quickly over his face. "Anyway, do you need anything?" she asked, pausing beside the suite that was reserved for him.

"Um. A key?" said Ezra.

Her smile flickered.

"It's a retina scan," she explained after a moment to reset her forced expression, gesturing to the scanner beside the door. "No keys anymore. Terribly old-fashioned."

"Oh." Well.

"Coincidentally, my ex sourced the technology," she said, this time reserving an element of distaste for the ex in question. "Such a pity he'll be dead soon."

Again, Ezra wasn't sure if he'd missed something. "Oh?"

She let out a bark of a laugh. "He's Tristan Caine," she explained. "You know. One of the six."

"Oh, right." Ezra bristled, stiffly reminded of the loose thread in his best laid plans before processing what she'd said. "Not dead, though," he corrected. "Apprehended."

"Figure of speech," she blithely agreed. "Though he has it coming."

"Did you . . . work together?" Ezra asked, choosing to find the mention of the elusive Tristan Caine to be auspicious rather than belittling. He wondered how well Eden had known him aside from romantically. Would she have any further insight about his magical specialty than his professors, or his boss?

"Ha. No." She gestured Ezra closer to the scanner, which flashed scarlet before the door automatically unlatched. "Anyway, enjoy your afternoon," said Eden, departing the way she'd come.

"Right, thank you." Ezra stepped further into the hotel suite, taking stock of the bar to his left. The open apartment feel of the layout was a fanciful echo of the art nouveau lobby below, though the highlight of the décor was without question the view. The drapes had been thrown open, Buda Castle on glorious display across the Danube. It was so beautiful it made Ezra's throat a little dry, and he coughed into his closed fist.

Reflexively, he lowered his hand to his throat, fingering the slow-fading bruises. A parting gift in the shape of Libby's familiar fingers.

Then he shook himself, depositing his things beside the sofa and heading out for the brasserie down the street, preparing for his meeting with the representatives from the Forum. In practice, the Forum was a global nonprofit, public-facing in every way that the Society was not and running counter to the Society's foundational purpose. That, however, was approximately where the distinctions ended (give or take a murder clause). The Forum was no less formal than the Society, no less bureaucratic as far as he could see, nor were they any less driven by structure and hierarchy. Each time they met with

Ezra, he became more aware of how resoundingly he failed to hold up to their status markers. Not in terms of wealth, but something . . . else. Something Ezra had always lacked. It was the same inauthenticity he smelled on Atlas; that sense of not only belonging, but *commanding*. It was an aura of certainty, the kind that typically came with privilege, which Ezra had never known how to replicate. An eau de institution that Ezra supposed made them feel dignified, or right.

Good for them. As long as they shared a desire for the same end, that was okay by him.

The inside of the brasserie was lush with foliage that sprouted overhead, the mirrored bar reflecting pops of forest green from the upholstered bistro chairs. It was all very soothing, or would have been, until he scanned the room's populace and saw two things.

First, the presence of Nothazai, who was deep in conversation with one of the other Forum heads. He was tucked into the corner of the room, camouflaged behind the presence of a large fern.

The other was Atlas Blakely, who sat at a table by the bar.

Hello, manifested in Ezra's head. *You missed our last appointment.*

Ezra looked over at Nothazai, who was still in clandestine conversation, and then at Atlas, who sat alone at his table in his usual tartan-lined sport coat. A cup of tea sat before him, also as usual. Sitting in front of the vacant chair was a cup of American coffee, black. Ezra did not need to try it to confirm it. He wasn't sure how Atlas had found him, or whether Atlas suspected him of any duplicity beyond his failure to stay in touch—but then, Ezra hadn't put himself through torment over the threats of an amateur.

And anyway, it would be undignified to ask.

He shifted to take the seat across from Atlas. "I only have a minute," he said.

"I only need one," Atlas replied. "You said everything you needed to when you left the body of Elizabeth Rhodes behind."

Ezra kept his mind carefully blank, as thoroughly wiped as he could make it, despite the lurch in his chest and the sudden impulsive need to touch his throat again—to put his hands where hers had been.

There was no way Atlas could know it was him. Certainly no way for him to prove it. Ezra eyed the cup in front of him, twisting it to finger the handle and willing himself to channel surprise, or better yet disbelief. "Libby's dead?"

"You already know she is not." Atlas fixed him with a look that Ezra chose not to interpret. Similarly, Atlas said, "I'm not going to bother asking where you put her, as I know you won't tell me. And I'm already quite sure it wouldn't matter if you did."

"I don't know what you're talking about," Ezra said. His neck suddenly itched, unavoidably.

"You must have known you could not hold her for long," said Atlas.

Ezra gave the cup of coffee a swirl. "I really don't know what you're getting at." He wondered if Atlas had changed the wards yet. Even if Atlas had already come to suspect there was a flaw built into the house's security, it was doubtful that he could repair it alone. Ezra was more physicist than Atlas, who would struggle with the physical nature of the Society's wards. He would manage it, probably—eventually—but it would hurt.

Good.

"You won't find your way in a second time, you know." Atlas took a sip of tea. "And I imagine you're already aware that this will not end well for you."

Ezra tried to stop an embittered laugh. "Is that supposed to be some kind of threat?" he guessed dryly. "You'll find me wherever I go, that sort of thing?"

"I *can* find you wherever you go, yes," Atlas said. "But I don't need to. Whatever enemy you think I've become, I do not feel the same way."

Another bitter laugh. "So, we can still be friends, is that it?" Ezra asked.

Atlas placed a few hundred forints on the table, sipping the last of his tea and rising to his feet.

"No, Ezra, we are not friends," he said. "And you will pay for what you've done. But you are of no consequence to me."

There was a flame in Ezra's chest, slow-burning.

"Then why find me?" he asked, forcing restraint. "Why follow me here, if I really mean so little?"

Atlas, who had already been turning to leave, shifted back toward Ezra, his gaze falling lower to the prints of Libby's fingers on his throat.

"I wanted to see what she'd done to you," Atlas said, and nodded in farewell. "Enjoy the coffee," he added, nudging the cup's handle. "I know how much you like a piece of home."

Ezra bit his tongue on something both childish and profane. "Fine. You've made your point."

"Have I?" Atlas paused to consider him. "You know," he began, indulging his favorite hobby of dispensing unsolicited advice, "you're much too close to this. I hope it's not too late before you realize you've tied yourself inextricably to something that can only fail."

Ezra said nothing, having given Atlas more than enough of his attention already. He inspected the grain of the table, thinking only that there was nothing left that Atlas could say or do that mattered. His mind was fixed, immovable, whatever Atlas might try to dig up inside it. It was Ezra who had witnessed the world's impending destruction at Atlas's hands, and Ezra who was prepared to save it. There was nothing more to discuss.

Atlas looked at him with pity. "Your problem, Ezra," he began, as Ezra scoffed and turned scornfully away. "Your problem, whether you realize it or not, is that you're still there in that room while the bullets fly, choosing life and hating yourself for it."

Behind Ezra's eyes was an explosion of memory, a flash of pain. The temple. His mother. The doors. The shooter's empty eyes; the mental trigger that only Atlas could pull. It was the one thing Ezra was not prepared to ignore and Atlas, the bastard, knew it. Atlas turned away in the second it took for Ezra to blink free from his temporary paralysis, leaving him behind.

Ezra stared after Atlas's retreating back long after it had disappeared into the crowd.

"Ezra?"

It took a moment for Ezra to realize someone was speaking to him.

"It *is* Ezra, isn't it?" came the voice again, as Ezra blinked, remembering himself, and looked up. It was the woman, the professor, one of Ezra's chosen six: Dr. J. Araña, the *J* standing pretentiously for something Ezra could not recall. She was a diminutive dark-haired chemist in her fifties—with, every now and then, a ghost of prettiness, despite a face that was now predominantly sunken eyes and puckered cheeks—who specialized in geoengineering, and who ran a notoriously private government-funded university lab. She had been a guerrilla activist in her youth, her work and protests decrying the nature of the Society, though as time went on Ezra was beginning to doubt her usefulness. She seemed a touch too passive, too quiet. Alone of Ezra's chosen six, the professor never spoke or offered resources. She did, however, insist on attending these sorts of meetings, perhaps because of her academic association with Nothazai and the Forum. Whatever the nature of her motivations, Ezra had yet to puzzle her out. Her curiosity seemed at once ambiguous and undeniable.

As for Nothazai, a biomancer whose specialty revolved around the diagnostics of the human body, his magic was secondary to the political nature of his work, or (more flatteringly) the philosophical. His role as the functioning head of the Forum was, to Ezra, exceedingly opaque. He was, at first glance, a consummate networker—the Forum, unlike the Society, was reliant on fundraising, grants, institutional connections, that sort of thing, and it seemed to be Nothazai's first instinct to collect his resources like trinkets, filing all of his ducks in an orderly line. He was like a magpie that way, which Ezra tried not to be unnerved by. He didn't always manage it.

For Ezra, the problem with the Forum's broad reach wasn't Nothazai so much as the possibility of all sorts of crumbs falling through the cracks. Already the plan was extending beyond Ezra's control, the circle of his trusted associates growing wider and more expansive, and therefore less trustworthy. This was not the Society. By definition, these people did not keep secrets. Fine, so be it, understood—but this couldn't get messy, Ezra reminded himself. Atlas was never messy, and Atlas had the resources of the Society, which meant that any loose ends Ezra left behind would need to be tied up.

Including the one who'd recently escaped him.

"Right, sorry," he said to the professor quickly, rushing to his feet upon jarring himself from his thoughts. "I'm so glad you were able to join us," he added, leading the professor to the back of the restaurant where the rest of his plan was waiting.

He had done this for a reason, Ezra reminded himself. If he had not felt it worth the costs, he would not have done it to begin with. The truth of his convictions remained. If Atlas wanted to destroy him, he would have to do more than conjure a cup of coffee and make vague threats in a Hungarian café. And as for Libby . . .

No, there was no point thinking about that now. She wouldn't be able to get herself here, which meant she was safe, and therefore so was he. So were their plans. He would simply have to keep an eye on her, and until then—

"Ezra," Nothazai greeted him warmly, glancing at his watch. "And only ten minutes late? Impressive." He turned to the man beside him, the Hungarian who had been their reason for meeting. He was some kind of intelligence specialist who specialized in cryptography, which, magically speaking, was no small feat. But Ezra was growing increasingly concerned that in virtually guaranteeing the success of his plan, he had undersold the sophistication of their enemy.

Which was not Atlas Blakely, of course. Atlas was merely an arm of the Alexandrian Society, or perhaps a sleeve or a glove. Whether his personal destruction came about as a result of their plans was of no consequence to Ezra.

Though it would be a necessity either way.

"—rest of the world's caught up to the tracking technology of the Society by now, of course," Nothazai was saying, to which the Hungarian agreed. "And given the output of a transport from within the Society's wards—"

"It must be astronomical," the Hungarian pronounced firmly.

"Yes, yes, absolutely—"

Across the table the professor was watching Ezra with an odd expression on her face. He met her eye by accident and quickly looked away, fixing his attention elsewhere in the café. He did not understand Nothazai's comfort in public like this, where anyone could overhear. It was almost as if he *wanted* to be heard—as if things were more righteous when they were done in the light, for anyone to see them.

"It was Ezra's idea, of course. Granted, we don't actually expect the new initiates to leave until the year concludes, but there is always the small possibility that one or two of them may venture out from captivity. The point is that we know the details of Blakely's weapons now, unlike in the past," Nothazai added to the Hungarian, who nodded, "which means we can be better prepared upon their arrival. Tea?" asked Nothazai, turning to the professor.

"No, thank you," she said as Ezra eyed the small copper sugar bowl, watching his reflection warp along its mottled surface.

"This was your idea?" asked the Hungarian, addressing Ezra and startling him into looking up.

"Sorry?" said Ezra. He realized belatedly that the Hungarian was referring to the tracking of magical outputs that Nothazai had mentioned, which naturally *would* occur to Ezra, who understood how the Society did its recruiting and also how his own method of traveling worked.

"The amount of magic generated by instantaneous transportation is exceptionally large," the Hungarian offered approvingly, perhaps even in a congratulatory way, as someone might speak of a prized ficus. He wasn't wrong that it was clever, but more importantly, it was *informed*. Anyone leaving the Society's wards via its medeian transports would be leaving a bomb's worth of energy traces upon arrival—to someone who knew what to look for, that is. "It is so very obvious now, though I would not have thought of it myself."

Ezra nodded, but said nothing. Obviously no one else had thought of it or the Society would not be the Society, but that did not feel appropriate to mention. The professor glanced at him again and Ezra fixed his attention squarely on the Hungarian, whose slightly bulbous forehead was beading quite noticeably with sweat amid the warmth of the café. Again, not the location Ezra would have chosen. They were clustered around a tiny table, in a tiny dining room, full of other not-so-tiny parties. His own shirt felt damp, the small of his back increasingly slick. The Hungarian followed Ezra's gaze and offered an amicable shrug, mopping the thin chandelier of perspiration discreetly away.

"Young Mr. Fowler here is something of an eccentric," Nothazai offered to the Hungarian before turning back to Ezra, giving him another glance of *kidding, I'm only kidding.* Ezra did not care for him. Nor, by the looks of it, did the professor, whose first name he still could not remember. He tried to recall the specifics of her recent research (he had chosen her based on her renown, and her substantially less demure academic past) but couldn't.

There was a crash of dishes behind Ezra, who jumped. Old habits. He disliked crowded places, loud noises. Particularly sounds that mimicked gunshots. He recalled that Libby had intuited that, known it somehow. She had always been very diligent about picking quiet restaurants whenever they'd gone out to eat.

Last he had checked, she wasn't far away. She was easy to find and even easier to follow. She did not understand, perhaps, how well he had once known her. He could feel her decisions like nostalgia, following the tracks and patterns of her thoughts, having lived beside them for years. What else was intimacy if not the memorization of her thoughts, her dreams, her fears? And he had almost had a life with her. That meant something.

That had to mean something.

Right?

"Are you quite well, Mr. Fowler?" asked the Hungarian.

Ezra made a noncommittal sound in confirmation, and then, realizing that was not quite sufficient, attempted a little shrug of nonchalance. He could tell by the face of the professor beside him that he had not effectively obscured the awkwardness of the moment. "Apologies," he said. "Just a bit jumpy, I suppose."

This was another reason it had been Atlas to stay behind, Ezra thought grimly. Atlas was better suited to traversing the slow-moving present while Ezra removed himself from time for the benefit of their plans. Atlas tended the bureaucracy of things, giving Ezra space to disappear, which to him had once been necessary. It had been an easy choice to make, to leave while Atlas stayed, because Atlas was the charismatic one. Atlas remembered names. He remembered birthdays and celebrated achievements and deftly minimized flaws. He was the one who determined the energy in the room, shifting it to suit him. His likability was never bland or generic. It was a gift, and by contrast Ezra was an eternal outsider. Ezra had the gauche psychological trappings of a man who'd borne witness to the destruction of everyone he'd ever loved. Until recently, when Ezra had begun taking a more active role in their demise.

"So," said Nothazai, beckoning Ezra into the circle of his confidence. "How goes the master plan?"

The professor shifted in her seat quietly, dark eyes falling on Ezra with obvious expectation. Ezra exhaled, plastering a smile on his face. If destruction was what was needed, then destruction he could provide.

"Every day a little closer, my friends," he replied, sitting up straighter in his seat at the head of the table and trying to look as if he belonged there, or at the table in general, or anywhere at all. "Every day a little closer to the Society's inevitable end."

· PARISA ·

"You're back," said Dalton. Not the *real* Dalton, of course, who saw her every day.

The other one. The one inside his head, hidden away within the castle—the telepathic fortress—of some other medeian's design.

His . . . animation.

The face of Dalton's younger self came into view above Parisa's head, floating there in midair as she felt herself drop onto the hard stone of the castle floor. She was once again struck by the quality of this particular astral plane when her back was met with cold, the abruptness of the impact prompting a shiver.

This version of Dalton continued to stare down at Parisa, expectant, while she struggled to sit upright. He was, as ever, a sprightlier version of himself, albeit less . . . whole. Less complex. Like a slightly pixelated version.

"Do you keep track of my comings and goings?" she asked him.

He gave her a mirthful little smile. "You're testing me," he observed.

She supposed there was no point denying it. "Yes."

"What are you testing?"

"You have sentience," Parisa said. "So now I want to know if you have memory." If he could remember her in detail from visit to visit, then it would prove this wasn't simply some projection of his subconscious.

Dalton looked amused. "You think I'm a time loop?"

That was a deduction, and a complex one at that. She added it to the list: this version of him could think independently of his corporeal self. "*Could* you be a time loop?"

"No," he said with a sly shake of his head, like he knew she was making a list and he felt it banal, or otherwise worth dismissing. "I remember you."

"Well, it was worth a try." She allowed him to help her to her feet, noticing again that he was slightly less real than his environment. He moved in flickers and bursts, which even their projections during the initiation ritual had not done.

Convincing Dalton to let her inside his mind again had been . . . something of an unexpected difficulty. And also, technically, ineffective, which came as a great surprise to Parisa.

Over two months ago, Dalton had told Parisa—Parisa and *no one else*—that the corpse that had been left behind in place of Libby Rhodes was not, as they had thought, an illusion, but rather an *animation*, and one so singularly effective that the only possible creator could have been Dalton himself. As Dalton had put it, that was an impossibility—after all, how could he have performed such substantial magic without his own knowledge?—and yet he seemed to have no doubt that it was his handiwork. In the weeks that followed, slowly bleeding into months, Parisa had thought the circumstances of Libby's disappearance would make Dalton more inclined to let Parisa continue with her experimentation in his subconscious, given what now seemed a matter of dire and unavoidable importance. In actuality, though, the loss of Libby had had the opposite effect, rendering Dalton more avoidant than ever.

No, Parisa corrected herself. No, it wasn't the loss of Libby that had caused the distance. The haunting of the house's other occupants by the ghost of Libby Rhodes (the careful avoidance of her name, the collective reflex to stiffen whenever they intuited the absence of her living habits or moral concerns) did not seem to have affected Dalton to any noticeable degree, but something clearly had. *Something* had set him on edge, forcing distance between him and Parisa, who sensed the something in question was likely more related to the Caretaker who'd very recently fucked up.

In short: Dalton had been very reticent about allowing her back into his head, which Parisa found absurd and blamed on Atlas. Ultimately, though, Parisa could be highly resourceful when she set her mind to something. She had the sense that at this very moment, Dalton's corporeal form was sleeping quite well indeed, having been expertly satisfied.

"So," she continued to Dalton's younger self. "You have some form of memory." That paired with his reasoning skills meant animations could think, to some extent. Some cognitive activity was occurring beyond simple programming or biological instinct. "Do you remember anything aside from me?"

"I remember waking up here," said Dalton. He suddenly looked listless, as if he had only just remembered his constraints.

"When was that?" Parisa asked.

"This is boring." He wasn't looking at her. He had crossed the room to the bars on the tower window, observing them as if they had not been there before. "All of this is so very boring. Did you know that I have surveillance now?" he asked in the same breath. He flicked the iron of the bars. "Someone is watching me."

Parisa had never thought to check the specifics of the view outside the castle window. "Wasn't someone always watching you?" she asked, inching toward it. She saw only forest, the outlines of a maze, glimpses of various bends within the labyrinth below. Dense foliage and heavy fog, but nothing of magical significance.

"This is different." Dalton's animation turned around with a deep sigh of impatience. "Are you going to get me out?"

"I'm trying," Parisa said.

"Good. But I'll need help," he said. "So that he doesn't win again this time."

"Who, Atlas?"

"That's the part he doesn't understand," Dalton continued, which was neither confirmation nor denial. Just the ego of a man not paying close attention to the conversation at hand. "He can't always win, you know. He barely managed it before. The likelihood of doing it twice is even smaller now. Smaller every day, every minute. And you," he added with a shrug of recognition. "You're changing things."

"Yes," Parisa said. She felt quite certain that was true.

"So he won't win again. And he knows it. You'd think he'd be more careful." It remained unclear whether he was speaking of Atlas, but she never got the chance to press the point. The smile on Dalton's face went brilliant, almost blinding, when he turned it on her. "People are never careful when it comes to you, are they?"

"Not even remotely," Parisa confirmed.

Which was true, as she had not, strictly speaking, been invited in for this particular visit.

Actually, the evening had begun with Dalton (the corporeal version) cornering her in the reading room about her topic of independent study.

"I don't understand," he said without preamble, showing her the page she'd submitted as her official proposal.

"What's not to understand?" Parisa countered, glancing at the page. "I wrote it in big letters and everything."

The sheet of paper contained one word: FATE.

"Parisa," said Dalton in a voice that sounded a bit like *please don't embarrass me at work*, "is there perhaps something less . . . cerebral, that you might consider in terms of a proposal?"

"First of all, I *am* cerebral," she told him. "By definition. And secondly, I meant it in terms of Jung's blueprint." Meaning psychoanalyst Carl Jung, who believed that humanity contained some atavistic properties as a collective. "The idea that everyone is born with access to some larger, interconnected subconscious. Something we share as a species, instead of something determined for us as individuals."

Dalton obviously did not believe her, though she couldn't imagine why. She was always so very forthright. Hardly ever worth suspecting.

"I know you've been trying to understand the sentience of the archives," Dalton said. (So okay, she did have her moments.)

"Tell Atlas snitches get stitches," Parisa replied. "It's colloquial but he'll know what it means."

"It wasn't Atlas," Dalton sighed, before catching himself. "And what I meant was—"

"Wait. It *wasn't* Atlas?" That left Reina as the most likely option, which was almost impressive. So Reina had taken a moment to notice that things were happening on earth? How deliciously out of character for her. "Since when is Reina confiding in you?"

"She isn't," said Dalton, who was unfortunately keeping things very tightly sealed. Not that it wasn't possible to slip into his thoughts if Parisa really wanted to, but the effort of uncovering what she already knew felt too taxing for the moment. "But if you're trying to manipulate the archives in order to see how they work—"

"I was under the impression that the archives couldn't be manipulated," Parisa said.

"Of course not, but—"

"So why would I even try?" she added innocently, batting her eyes for effect. "And anyway, the blueprint concept seems perfectly scholarly to me." The truth? She *was* trying to understand the sentience of the archives. Unlike animations, which Dalton had previously hinted (and Callum had confirmed) were alive but not fully sentient, the archives appeared to be sentient but not fully alive. Parisa herself had made use of the primordial consciousness within the house, following patterns that felt to her like thought. Was the library not simply a lifeless vault of knowledge, then, but to some extent a brain?

She had been considering it ever since the implication from Callum's projection-self during his ritual that the archives were tracking them in some way. What need would the Society, via the archives, have to track its occupants? There was nothing meaningful to glean from the data points of their behavior unless the goal was ultimately to model them, predicting what they might do next. Which, if that was the case, could only mean either villainy or proof of concept. If it was the Society, then that was uninspired and dull. It made them no better than Web 2.0. But if the archives were actually *learning* the behaviors of its initiates—if the task of nurturing the archives, making them grow was not, in fact, a metaphorical assignment—then that was a tick in the column for atavistic blueprints after all.

If Parisa's class of initiates could each be predicted by something that did not technically qualify as alive, then wouldn't that affirm, in some way, the concept of a collective conscience, a predestined fate? Either that or it would simply prove the Society's unlawful surveillance, which would be predictable as far as sinister plans went, but still worth knowing. Whatever the outcome, Parisa felt an answer worth divining before she left the confines of this house and never looked back.

But Dalton still did not look convinced, and so she remembered that a bit of intimacy would be called for here. Sharing was caring, to put it another colloquial way. Or in this case, the reverse.

"I have been thinking," Parisa remarked, "about dreams."

"Dreams," echoed Dalton. This time he sounded more curious than patronizingly disappointed. While Parisa resented being pressured into telling him the truth, she couldn't deny it was occasionally effective.

"Yes, dreams." Nico, by virtue of disclosing the nature of his dream-traversing friend, had given her the idea that dreams were the intersect of time and thought. "They occur on a shared astral plane. Potentially in the fourth dimension."

"Mm," said Dalton, thinking.

"And when I enter *your* dreams," she added carefully, "I encounter the same thing. Almost as if a piece of you lives there permanently." Almost as if. *Exactly* as if. "Don't you think that's interesting?"

But she seemed to have crossed back into problematic territory, because the light in his eyes was snuffed out as quickly as it appeared. "Parisa—"

"You were the one who brought it up," she reminded him. "That it was you who made that animation of Rhodes's dead body." They were very nearly arguing, which as a rule Parisa didn't do. Certainly not with a lover, which was a waste of everyone's time when better, more satisfying things could always be done in the name of conflict resolution. A person had to care about the outcome of a fight in order to pick one, and Parisa never did. "Am I supposed to forget about that now?"

Dalton shook his head. "It's impossible for me to have made that animation. I have no explanation for it."

"No," Parisa corrected. "You have no explanation for it, and *therefore* you suspect it to be impossible. But I *know* you," she reminded him. "I know your mind."

That had been his error. He had let her in, and now she knew him. He had let himself be known—which Parisa would be the first to say was a critical mistake.

"I know," she continued, "that you recognized your own magic the moment you saw it. I know that you know that to be true, whether it's possible or not. *You* made that animation," she accused him, and he flinched. "Your methodology is the only thing up for debate. So trying to persuade me not to ask you how or why is never going to work."

They were facing each other head-on, his arms folded over his chest, hers combatively on her hips. There they were, a portrait of conflict. For all her usual rules, for all her better judgment, she had still managed to walk into a trap.

Dalton would not like this, the sudden abandonment of subtlety simply because she'd gotten frustrated, lost her patience, spelled things out. It was close to a demand, which wasn't sexy, and certainly wasn't seductive. This was as domestic a disagreement as anything Parisa had ever allowed. *You're wrong, no I'm right.* Amateur hour. Why had she even bothered with any of this? Two years in one place was two years too many. That, or as she suspected, the library was draining something from her. In this case, her better judgment. She couldn't help feeling her thoughts had begun to chase themselves in circles, overworking until all that remained was nonsense and rot.

She was still in the process of tacitly sulking when Dalton's hand snaked out to her waist, his palm brushing over her hip. "Let's not fight," he said. Which was terrible in its way, because he acknowledged they were fighting and evidently did not mind.

Intimacy. Disgusting. It was invasive and repellent, which Parisa shoved aside to avoid worsening things, or deepening them. "What do you propose instead?"

"I've missed you." He leaned in, skating his lips along the side of her neck in a way that might make a softer woman sigh. "You've been very intent on destruction these days."

"Not destruction." She didn't want to destroy the archives. Just to understand them. Though if they were revealed to be completely repugnant in any way, then yes, fine. She could burn that bridge when she got to it. "Though I suppose it has left a bit of tension in my back," she mused, glancing up at him through her lashes.

"Let me fix that for you" was Dalton's suggestion. Things progressed and she had enjoyed their usual talent for escalation. Slipping into his thoughts was no trouble from there, almost the work of an open invitation. Fairly simple, all things considered.

Hm.

Too simple, perhaps?

There it was again, the bombardment of thought. Parisa was unaccustomed to fighting with her lovers, true, but in retrospect, something seemed to have disrupted the usual sequence. It was one thing for Dalton to back down from a fight, but quite another to have left his mind so open. It was a careless, untroubled slip of routine that now seemed out of place against the backdrop of Dalton's faultless control. Because after all, she knew him. For another man, the error of leaving the front door unlocked was commonplace and occasionally expected. Dalton Ellery was an ordinary man in many ways, but not this.

Suddenly Parisa was sure, painfully certain. There was no chance her access to his head on this specific night had been an accident—or worse, something romantic, some rose-tinted trick of the light as she might have otherwise believed it to be.

Something was wrong.

Convincing Dalton to do something he usually wanted to do with her was no noteworthy feat on its face, but a door left ajar on the same occasion? That could only mean the presence of an intruder come and gone, the imprint of an idea left behind like fingerprints in their wake.

The sudden sense of vulnerability abruptly woke her from a trance. Hypothetically, of course, not actually—because in actuality, she was still inside Dalton's subconscious, visiting with the fragment of his other self.

Parisa looked again at the image of younger Dalton, surveying the walls of his mental fortress, and wondered how she had not thought about this before. Dalton usually *was* careful around her, so what was the explanation for any of this?

"Do you see what he does?" she asked his younger self, the animation. "Your host. Do you keep track of him?"

"I know what he does." His younger self was irked, borderline infantile. "He reads. And reads and reads and reads and reads and—"

"Right." Well, fuck. She must have missed something, then, and the more she considered what it might have been, the more concerned she got. "I've got to go."

"Wait." Dalton's fragment flickered again, reappearing next to her. "Are you coming back? I told you, there's someone watching me."

"I'm sure he's watching you all the time," she said, only half listening. After all, Atlas seemed to always know when she'd been in Dalton's head too long. Come to think of it, why hadn't he pulled her out already? Curiouser and curiouser once again, only more annoying and worse. "I just have to do someth—"

"Wait." Dalton's face was suddenly close to hers when he stopped her again, closing his fingers insistently around her wrist. "Parisa."

She felt a shiver that she hadn't anticipated at his proximity. Like the real Dalton—or whatever one could call the version of him that she currently suspected of having been tampered with—this Dalton had a beautiful simplicity to his construction. Clean lines, hard angles. Parisa, who was herself a work of art, appreciated the sophistication of his minimalism. His proximity was powerful, enlivening.

"You know, don't you?" he said in a low voice. "Why you keep coming back."

An involuntary shudder climbed the notches of her spine. "Of course," she breezily assured him. "I love a good mystery."

"That's not what this is." His hand loosened around her wrist, becoming tender. "You know me. You recognize me."

Of course she recognized him, she had another version of him accessible to her whenever she liked—this, or something equally coy and weightless, was what she meant to reply. An answer unaffected by him or his closeness lingered on her tongue, waiting, though she knew what he meant. That something in him was not only recognizable, but shared. Something about him called to her.

She said nothing. His eyes were liquid with something, dark pools of suggestion that should have had no effect on her. She knew how chemistry worked far too well to let herself be swayed by biological pinpricks of desire. She had slept with him tonight already, would sleep with him again, probably many more times without much effort.

And yet when he leaned closer, she couldn't quite summon a reason to pull away.

"You're not real," she commented. Even now, he was too false to be mistaken for corporeal; too unformed to be the distraction he so strangely was. He was at best an idea, or a question. It was like having a sexual attraction to a flavor or a state of mind.

"Aren't I real enough?" She could feel his smirk against her mouth. "I'm real for you. I'm undeniable to you in at least one sense."

"Which is?" It suddenly felt unwise to exhale.

He seemed to know it. There was trouble alighting on his lips.

"I'm what you've been waiting for," he said.

Parisa woke up with a gasp, tearing free from his astral hold to find herself beside his sleeping form. In a flash, the gloom of the castle tower became the dark of the Society manor house, one abyss traded for another. She took a moment to place herself, mouth dry and thoughts disoriented. The familiarity of Dalton's sheets gradually drew her back, as did the house's sentience stirring around her.

After a moment she turned her head, contemplating Dalton in his sleep. He was twitching a little. Presumably she had felt like a bad dream, which she tried not to feel too guilty about. After all, she had other things to do.

She gathered her clothes, dressing quickly in the dark, and padded across the gallery to their residences in the west wing. The rooms were empty, which was disconcerting. She placed her hand on the wall and shook her head with sudden fury, forcing her scattered thoughts to reconfigure themselves before she turned angrily to the stairs.

She hadn't the faintest idea where Tristan and Nico were, but the moment she sensed Callum and Reina sitting together in the painted room, Parisa understood exactly what must have transpired. At this time of night it was too odd a pairing, the confluence of two strange bedfellows who ought to have killed each other rather than share a proverbial (and certainly not literal) bed—unless something else was at stake. Reina had always had a strange obsession with Dalton, and surely Callum would know how to capitalize on an opportunity, however pointless it was.

Parisa had known she was looking for an intruder. She'd forgotten that she already knew exactly where to find one.

"How'd it go?" asked Callum, toasting her with a glass.

Parisa remembered for a moment with a sudden, sharp sensation of unfettered rage that she probably should have killed Callum. Months ago, last year, yesterday. Never mind about not having a reason to; never mind that he was nothing, hardly even worth it. It turned out that the reason was that she simply did not like him, and that was reason enough for her.

Callum could clearly feel her resentment. He smiled, taking a sip from his wine, a Bordeaux that caught the light insidiously. "I do hope the good Mr. Ellery was at least as attentive as normal," he assured her. "In the end it wasn't as if it was something he didn't want to do, anyway."

"That couldn't have been easy," Parisa said through gritted teeth. Dalton was a lot of things, but easily influenced was never one of them. Even for her, the effort to persuade him of anything was a strain.

"Depends who you ask," Callum replied. He was obviously riding the high of whatever he'd just accomplished, so Parisa turned to Reina, who watched her through expressionless eyes.

"You can do better," Parisa said tightly, gesturing with a flick of a glare to Callum.

Reina shrugged, eyeing the glass in Callum's hand and turning back to Parisa with a fleeting look of boredom. No—bitterness.

"Actually, I've done just fine," Reina said.

Which was when it occurred to Parisa, belatedly and with a sense of utter idiocy, that she must have been mistaken. It wasn't Callum she hated after all. She'd been right the first time: he was nothing. Worse than nothing. He'd been walking around in a stupor for weeks, if not months, because for once in his life things had not gone his way. He was easy, so easy to destroy. Even easier than Parisa had been at his hands, and wasn't that ironic? Wasn't that the sad, pathetic truth, that he used others as his weapons so as to continuously destroy something that was fundamentally rotten about himself? He believed himself inconsequential and small and he was right, and people who were right about things like that did not suddenly come into their own power.

Callum was not the mastermind here.

"What did you want from Dalton?" Parisa forced out, trying not to choke on resentment. Or the burn of having been successfully played.

"The same thing you want from him," Reina replied.

Not sex. Not affection. Not loyalty. Those were the things Parisa had, but could easily do without.

No, it was the mystery. The puzzle. Damn her, Parisa thought, and then, less flatteringly, redirected the thought at herself. Because when had she ever had something for herself without others deciding that they wanted it too? All she had ever done was increase Dalton's value by choosing him. Call it desire by proxy.

Reina drummed her fingers atop a book, drawing Parisa's attention to it.

Genesis. The same book she had seen Dalton carry. The subject of Dalton's research.

"I think you're wrong about the archives," Reina said.

Something inside Parisa ignited at that, white-hot. It was atypical for her, this kind of violence of feeling. Generally speaking, Parisa was measured. Calm. Practical. Focused. She respected a talented adversary. She respected Reina more for this.

But only in a way that made her want to take Reina by the throat.

"Careful," Callum warned Reina with a laugh, his eyes cutting to Parisa's. "You'll make an enemy of her."

Reina shrugged, rising to her feet with the book in hand. She headed for the corridor, pausing before the doors to stand beside Parisa.

"Don't envy me, Parisa," Reina suggested mockingly in her ear. "Fear me."

The hairs on Parisa's arms rose, the sudden taste on her tongue coppery sweet. It was an echo of Parisa herself, a moment of perfect symmetry. Very well executed, if only Reina knew what she'd gotten herself into by throwing down a gauntlet she hardly knew how to wield. This was one trick play, not a war won.

And anyway, it was not lost on Parisa that both of them were breathing hard.

What do you think it means, Parisa replied, *that you've been letting me live in your head this long?*

The look of loathing was fleeting on Reina's face, but not unsatisfying. She left without another word, and in her absence Parisa turned to Callum, who was chuckling into his glass.

"So," Parisa said, arching a brow while he drained the remainder of his wine. "You went from someone who couldn't love you well to someone who can't love you at all." She folded her arms across her chest, watching him summon the bottle up from the floor where it sat discarded at his feet. "How does it feel?"

"The same as it always feels," replied Callum, pouring another precarious glass and closing his eyes. "Now either sit and have a drink," he beckoned, taking a sip, "or leave me the fuck alone."

It occurred to Parisa to be repulsed.

Then again, Callum had chosen an excellent vintage.

She snatched the bottle from his hand, settling herself beside him on the sofa.

"Just so you know," she said. "I let you get away with using your powers on me once. But if you ever influence me without my knowledge," she warned, "I will do everything in my not-inconsiderable power to make you regret it, painfully, for the rest of your very short life."

She raised the bottle to her lips, taking a long sip.

"I actually believe that," Callum remarked when she swallowed, toasting her with his glass. "*Salud.*"

She lifted the bottle. "Cheers."

They both heard someone's footsteps lingering outside the doorway and exchanged a glance, shrugging, the moment they recognized who it was.

"Any idea what he's been up to?" Parisa asked, gesturing to the quietly receding presence of Tristan Caine.

"None," Callum said, "by choice. You?"

"No."

They contemplated this in silence, each taking a long drink.

"Well," Callum said eventually, rising to his feet. "I'm for bed. Start again tomorrow?"

Meaning their brief détente was over. It was Parisa's turn now, should she wish to exact her revenge.

Exhausting. As if having to teach Reina a lesson wasn't bad enough.

"No," Parisa said. "Do whatever you want. Leave me out of it."

He looked unsurprised. "You're sure?"

"Yes."

"No matter how nefarious?"

She scoffed. "You want to destroy the world? Enjoy," she assured him. "I doubt it will bring you much satisfaction."

"*Destroy* it? No," Callum said with a shake of his head. "What would become of me without the existence of other people? I'm not entirely self-loathing."

They both smiled grimly at the joke.

"Have the world, then, if you want it. Drain it if that's what you prefer." Parisa shrugged. "Maybe Rhodes will come back and stop you."

"Ha." Callum barked a laugh. "God, think how dull that would be." He set down his glass, shaking his head. "Good night, Parisa."

She let him leave. She watched the dying embers leaping in the hearth.

"*Santé,*" Parisa murmured under her breath. A drink to his health.

And to it never outlasting her own.

V

DUALITY

· LIBBY ·

Libby woke up facedown on a checkered linoleum floor. Blocks of garish turquoise came into view, and an ashy white that was now mostly gray. Her cheek was throbbing, which was no surprise considering the angle at which she must have met the ground. Her mouth and throat were painfully dry, her lymph nodes swollen.

"Elizabeth," called a feminine voice. "Is everything all right in there?"

So it hadn't worked, then. Not that she'd really expected it to. Libby looked glumly up at the analog clock on the wall, which read 8:13 P.M.

Great. Wonderful. She'd been passed out for ten minutes, which explained why the librarian sounded reasonably frantic. Presumably Libby was not the first person to abuse library resources, although she doubted anyone had tried anything this implausible before.

"I'm—" Libby's voice was hoarse. "I'm fine."

She sat up slowly, tensely. Her joints were aching, her head pounding, and her stomach growled in protest. She had sweated through her clothing—assuming perspiration was all her oversized sweatpants were soaked with.

This, she thought, surveying the mess of herself in silence, was what she got for the deeply Varona decision to attempt something she knew perfectly well she could not do on her own. Given the degree of risk, it was a miracle she hadn't done worse. She could have just as easily blinded herself, or set the entire building on fire, or not woken up at all.

Idiot, she thought, cursing herself. The archive room had been cluttered to begin with, and now the files were in disarray, boxes overturned and scattered in pieces across the floor. There was a scorch mark on the linoleum. That couldn't be removed even if she had the proper fortitude to do it. The desk—atop which had sat her now-useless calculations—was, much like Libby herself, in pieces. Despite the math (a clear "no" from the universe), she had still thought it could be simple; not *easy*, of course, but intuitive in some way, not unlike the explosion she'd half-consciously caused to escape the puzzle of Ezra's wards. There was always the possibility, however distant, that it would be only a matter of grasping at the spark inside her—the fury that thundered in her chest, the anger that had crackled like open flame. But the enormity of her chaos, the omnipotence of her rage was getting harder to access. It was receding, her reach was shrinking, and the brightness, the garish intensity of who she'd been within the Society's walls was faltering more erratically the farther she got from the house and its archives. The power she'd once found, raw and wild and uncontained, was buckling to the circumstances of her condition. The dampeners of hunger and sleeplessness, anxiety and fear, were reshaping her limits once again.

Which reminded her that she would have to leave here. Whether Ezra or the police came for her first, the strange young woman who was first seen fleeing an explosion at a motel only to blow up a public library within the same city would not be difficult to track down.

She wished someone else could do this part for her. Recklessness was Nico's domain. Even Parisa would have been a welcome voice in her head. Something other than the constant refrain of doubt. She needed someone's help, but whose?

Not the librarian's, that was for sure.

"We thought we heard something break," the librarian called as Libby struggled to stand, which had to be an understatement. They would have heard something shatter, or possibly explode. "Did something fall, or . . . ?"

"Oh, um—" Every single bookcase in the room had collapsed. Great. Wonderful. "Just dropped something, that's all." Libby forced an upbeat hint of something closer to infantile ineptitude rather than, say, purposeful vandalism. "Tricky shelves!" she sang.

"Well, do let us know if you need anything!" the librarian replied, in a passive-aggressively warm suggestion that Libby had better stop doing whatever sort of nonsense she was getting into, which was fair. More than fair, really. Generally speaking, Libby assumed most library patrons were not trying to open wormholes through time on government property. Though they could potentially be doing worse.

"I'm just cleaning up in here," Libby replied, "and then I'll be out!"

"Oh, don't worry dear, take your time!" Translation: *Good.*

Libby breathed in heavily, then out. Attending to the bookshelves magically was her best option. The rest could be explained away, maybe, or at least hidden away until she was long gone. And she *would* leave, too, at the soonest possible opportunity. She would just . . . need a minute, that's all. To center herself. And rest.

And to stomach her disappointment.

Not that she had any right to be disappointed. She had known the implausible physical requirements for magic of this magnitude before she started, having once successfully created the very same thing in miniature within the walls of the Society's manor house. To create a wormhole to the kitchen, which Nico used to fetch himself hummus, both of them—all three of them, counting Reina—had expended so much combined energy it left them sore and depleted for weeks. To create a wormhole to *the future*, Libby needed access to power she simply did not have.

It had been Tristan who figured it out all those months ago; nearly a year by now. "What you'd need," he'd told them with a crease of concentration between his solemn brows, "is to cause a pure fusion reaction."

Pure fusion would be comparable to a supernova, the spontaneous release of energy by *actual stars*. "Impossible," Libby retorted at the same time that Nico, who had been eating, said through a scalding mouthful of soup, "What? Fuck, sorry, burned my tongue—"

"It's impossible to create a wormhole *for now*," Tristan clarified shortly to Libby, "because it's currently impossible to generate a sufficient release of energy. An atomic bomb is fission," he said, mimicking the splitting of an atom, "which then creates the energy necessary for fusion. Which is the part that makes things go boom." Another motion, this time to combine them, which ended with Tristan slamming a hand into the table and upending Nico's too-hot soup. "Sorry," Tristan said, with an impressive lack of sincerity. "But more to the point—stellar energy is not only theoretically possible," he said with a glance of scathing disapproval, which was what all his glances looked like to Libby at the time, "you're not even the only ones trying to do it. Wessex Corp is, too, along with about a dozen government organizations." A shrug. "Not that I have ever been invited into those particular rooms."

Nico pursed his lips, returning his soup bowl to its original state, as Libby hummed, "So then the two of us would need to cause a fusion reaction in order to . . . create *more* fusion?" So, harnessing the power of the sun. Give or take a nuclear bomb. Fission was hard enough, but fusion was another matter. It was the difference between shattering a marble into smaller pieces and shoving two marbles together to make a bigger marble. One was doable. The other boggled the mind.

Nico, who was now somewhat more interested in the theory at hand, had been the one to point out the obvious: "We'll need a lot more than just us."

A problem that they had later solved with Reina. So, essentially, Libby had needed Tristan to do the math, Nico to channel their respective powers into something effectively streamlined, and Reina to give them the jolt of naturalism they could not conjure from anywhere else. A four-man job—and at the time Libby had been rested, and fed, appropriately bathed, and not in fear for her life.

None of which was true now.

It took Libby another half an hour to repair the damage to the library's archive room, at which point the librarian returned to tell her in very restrained tones that they were closing, thanks, and could she kindly fuck off (implied), which Libby replied in overtly cheerful tones that she would, thanks very much for the very good idea. Where she would go next remained a mystery, but she was slowly but surely sopping up the dregs of the Los Angeles Public Library system's hospitality. It was time to get herself somewhere that might—*might*—have some degree of the impossibility she was missing. Short of uncovering 1) another physicist of her caliber, 2) the most powerful naturalist yet to be born, and, well, 3) Tristan Caine, some other power source would have to suffice. Again, give or take a nuclear bomb.

Though, ideally, *not* a nuclear bomb. Assuming she didn't kill anyone—which was a very big if—that energy still had to go somewhere. Libby wasn't especially interested in leaving traces of radioactivity all the way to Canada, or in rupturing some kind of time-space paradox that meant she was never born. Even if a bomb would work, damage was inevitable. Consequences would range from lasting and unavoidable to catastrophic and unfixable.

Within a couple of hours Libby was nodding off on the bus. She was less likely to cause significant damage to any public works here, although it was unfortunately still an option given the state of her exhaustion. She'd conjured a shield around herself but kept losing track of it each time her attention wandered. She was going on thirty-six straight hours without any sleep (minus ten minutes of unconsciousness, which surely didn't count), and still had very little as far as a plan. She wasn't exactly cut out for life on the run, but she didn't know what else to do, either. So this was just going to be what it was.

After she'd left the gas station beside the highway, she'd gone to the local hospital first, pretending to be there for a patient—even with the displacement in time, it was easy enough to blend in, minus her lack of shoulder pads or unfashionable jeans. Libby had spent enough time in hospitals waiting for her sister to get better, so sartorial details aside, she knew very well what it looked like to brace for bad news. Specifically, she knew how to look so that people wouldn't ask questions, understanding that the answers would be traumatic to hear. She stayed there for a few hours, cleaned herself up in the bathroom, then waited to see if Ezra would turn up. He hadn't. Neither had anyone else.

She wasn't sure how Ezra had done it, but he had definitely trapped her somewhere else in time. She kept trying to prove herself wrong, to find evidence that she had been tricked somehow, or mistaken, but every source she could find within the hospital filing system said the same thing. The day she had broken free of him had been Sunday, August 13, 1989. Libby had been born nine years later.

So there was no going home.

She could try to find someone who was alive in 1989, of course. Her parents. One of her professors. Atlas Blakely, though even he wouldn't be more than eleven or twelve. Why had Ezra brought her here? How had he done it, and how could it be undone?

She nearly nodded off again, her neck snapping beneath the effort of holding her head upright. She jumped, snorting awake, and someone several aisles ahead looked over at her. She shivered and secured the invisible shield she'd conjured around herself. It was probably a waste of her effort for the time being, but it seemed safer than going around with no armor at all.

So anyway, her parents. They were probably too young and unmagical to help even if she knew where they were at this point in their lives (so much for eye-rolling through their rambling oral histories). And wasn't there something about messing with time? Rules about not interfering? Libby was no expert on the butterfly effect, but she was pretty sure she shouldn't try to talk to anyone she knew. Plus, how could they help?

From a theoretical standpoint, she and Nico had proven that wormholes could be created, and she and Tristan had proven there were ways to use time. Sure, she had no idea how to *traverse* time, exactly, but what she needed was to find a source of energy with a powerful enough magnitude to plausibly work. What that looked like, she had no idea. She also did not know if such a power source existed in her own time, much less in 1989. But she was comfortably certain that someone would be working on it, which was why she was now on her way to the Los Angeles Regional College of Medeian Arts.

It was difficult to dig it up. Not because the institution or its medeians were trying to hide, but because *everything* was difficult to dig up. The first library she'd gone to hadn't even had a computer. A different library had one, but it wasn't connected to the internet. Libby tried going through the journalism archives instead. She was relieved, at least, that magical technology was being openly developed in the 1980s, which for all her rapt attention to medeian history (that was sarcasm, she hadn't bothered with much of that, being already several years behind in her magical specialty by the time she set foot on NYUMA's campus) she might not have guessed it would be. In perusing old newspapers, she found an article from the early sixties about schools opening across the country in order to facilitate the growth of magic as an alternative energy source, which was the most substantial source of relief she'd found since arriving in 1989. She wouldn't have to hide what she was completely. Now she would just have to find a university research team that could help.

Which led her to LARCMA. NYUMA was out of the question, given the distance. She wasn't sure how successfully she could get access to LARCMA, but at least it was only a bus ride away.

Her eyelids drooped again, sinking heavily as the bus made its way southwest. Headlights came and went, beams from oncoming traffic lulling her rhythmically to sleep. Streetlights winked overhead. Her head felt like it was warping from the inside, swirling and melting behind her eyes. She was so tired she felt drunk, the bus floor rising up to meet her where she sat with her legs pulled up to her chest. The lull of the bus's motion was so soothing, the buzz of white noise intoxicating. She felt drowsy and hungry and warm, though she focused on maintaining the schematics of her little shield. So long as she stayed within her bubble, she would—

"There you are," said Gideon Drake, his hair flashing gold as he suddenly sprinted up the bus aisle to reach her. Startled, Libby jerked upright, snapping sharply awake.

The aisle was empty. The person a few rows ahead—a middle-aged woman—glanced at her again, dully. Libby's pulse was in her throat, panic gradually subsiding. Had she imagined it, or . . . ?

She blinked. Kept blinking. Her head swam.

The drowsiness was like a blanket, settling over her once again.

"—op *doing* that," said Gideon, who looked very stern. This time he was dressed as a doctor, and Libby realized she had been running. She was wearing Katherine's favorite sweatshirt and she was crying, and Gideon was here but not here, and she was so fucking tired, and *fuck*.

Katherine was dead. Libby had lost that sweatshirt on the subway three years ago and cried for days.

This was a dream.

"Fuck," Libby gasped, but Gideon's hand shot out, holding her still.

"You're okay." His expression had changed and so had his medical scrubs. He was wearing a regular gray T-shirt now and looked normal. He had a black dog sitting beside him who seemed to be undressing Libby with his eyes, but that was probably just part of the dream. "You're okay, Libby. Take a breath, okay? Just . . . kind of, um." Gideon looked puzzled and sheepish at the same time. Two expressions that never crossed Nico's face. "Just kind of . . . *give in*, okay?"

The dog looked doubtfully up at Gideon. "Shut up," Gideon said to the dog, fixing his attention on Libby's face. "Are you okay? Where are we?"

"Um—" She looked around to find that now, they were in the painted room. Overhead was the usual apse, and for a moment she felt calmer, safer. Like maybe all that would happen now was that Parisa would decide a sexual awakening was at hand, which was not so cataclysmic an outcome in retrospect. "We're at the Society."

"Okay. Okay." Gideon nodded, then nudged away the dog, who appeared to be arguing with him. "Stop it. Hey, Libby, can you tell me where you are? Or like . . . when?"

"What?" She blinked at him and he receded for a moment, but he held on, securing her with one hand on her wrist.

"In real life. Outside of this dream." He looked insistent. "You don't have a lot of practice here, so you don't have much time. Try to give me as much information as you can as quickly as you can, okay?"

"Here?" Libby echoed groggily. The flames in the painted room's hearth were rising, warming her cheeks. She became aware of motion, the smoothness of a road, wheels turning and turning and churning along, rhythmic and—

"Libby. Hey." Gideon snapped his fingers in front of her face. "Indulge me, because I've got a theory. Do you know what year it is?"

"It's—" Gideon's face was fading again. "I don't . . . Gideon, I'm not—"

There was a loud sound of pistons firing to open the bus doors. Libby jerked upright, realizing she'd fallen asleep again. The shield around her was gone, so she put it back up.

The middle-aged woman had disembarked at some point. In her place was a teenager with his hood up, a pair of thin wired headphones over his ears. Libby swallowed thickly, checking the bus map she'd stolen from the library. One more stop. She wiped a thin layer of drool from her cheek and tried to remember what she'd been dreaming about. Her sister? She vaguely remembered dreaming about the hospital, or maybe that was just because she'd recently been in a hospital.

The bus reached the next stop: Union Station. The railway station was an art deco, Spanish mission–style design with rounded arches, white walls, and a fleet of palm trees that swayed on a dry bloom of wind. Libby got out quickly, scouring the outside of the train station before hurrying through the main doors.

The interior had terra-cotta floors, travertine marble, high ceilings with exposed wooden beams. She walked up to the information services desk adjacent to the ticket booths, suddenly feeling jittery as her footsteps echoed amid relative silence. "Quickest way to the college?" she asked, fighting the ongoing urge to yawn.

The man at the desk didn't look up. "You want the dash."

"What?"

He pointed wordlessly down at the small pile of transit maps in front of him.

Libby picked it up, reading the acronym DASH. It was a short bus line that traversed downtown Los Angeles.

"Great, thanks. Can I . . . ?" She motioned to the map.

He waved a hand to indicate sure, fine, whatever and Libby took the map, venturing out of the station again and shivering a little upon emergence. It got colder here at night than she expected, or possibly she was just still overheated from sitting on the last bus she'd been on. She wasn't sure if they were using magical technology yet on buses. Trains, maybe. Why was she thinking about this? Her brain was exhausted, her thoughts frantic. She felt tremors beneath her feet and thought oh shit, earthquake, and then thought oh fuck, is that Varona? And then eventually she remembered it was neither and that she was disintegrating slowly, desperate for sleep.

She popped back into the information services area, realizing she needed more than a bus. "Are there any hostels or anything? Something, um." She glanced down at her sweats and the bus ticket she'd stolen. "Affordable?"

This time the man looked at her warily.

"You could try Skid Row," he said. "They're cracking down, but at this hour you'd be fine."

"Skid Row?" She realized with a jolt that he assumed she was homeless. Which, again, she very much was. "Right. Um. Is that—" She felt a sudden wave of horror at not actually knowing what resources were available to her. "Is there some kind of a shelter, or . . . ?"

"Picky, are we?" The man looked repulsed.

"I—" Right. This was pointless. "Sorry. Thanks." At least it was close. She ducked her head and hurried outside, traversing the few unfamiliar blocks and trying to decide where to go now. Outside, there were a few people, some empty cabs. She spotted a vacant bench and sat down, unfolding the map to look again until she spotted the LARCMA campus.

She realized it wasn't a campus at all. Just one single building, and most likely the man at the information desk had assumed she meant the mortal university nearby, which would have dorms and student services. Could she go *there*? Yes, maybe—she could pass as a college student still—but it wasn't walkable. She leaned her head back against the bench, trying to calm herself. She wished she'd thought to get here when it was still early, when maybe there was somewhere to go. She wished she'd killed Ezra, or at least used him. Why hadn't she thought to do that? Surely she could have . . . *forced* him to put her back, somehow?

No, she thought with a sigh. Even at her worst, she didn't think she could follow through on the kind of threat she would have needed to make that happen. And who knows? Maybe he would have rather killed her or died himself than help her. He did say he had a plan.

She felt another shiver of fear, of wondering whether the man she'd loved was actually that diabolical. God, she was exhausted. Maybe she should have stayed back there in that motel room. She could have swayed Ezra eventually, maybe. Assuming she could have stomached it, she could have convinced him. Could have reminded him why they were good together.

They *were* good together, weren't they? Had it always been pretense? She didn't think so. She hoped not. There was something so dual-sided about her memories of him now, the forgotten good and unseen bad that now reached her simultaneously, disorienting her like whiplash. She used to think of Ezra as funny and easily misunderstood, the way he was so charmingly awkward. She had been so protective of him, once. It was so easy for Nico to take shots at him, because Nico was charismatic and impossible to truly hate, so there was an element of bullying there, or so Libby had always thought. Even Gideon had always been kind to Ezra—although that wasn't saying much, because Gideon was always kind.

"Listen to me," Gideon was saying, because he was here somehow, in the wavering light of the street, following her around in her thoughts like a little storm cloud overhead. Was she asleep? "The year, Libby. Just tell me the year." He glanced over his shoulder, like someone was following him, or maybe watching him. "Or give me a hint. Is it—"

"Nineteen eighty-nine," said Libby.

"Oh." Gideon blinked. "Is that . . . really? Okay. Okay." He seemed frazzled, stressed. Behind him Libby caught a glimpse of someone blue, or blue-veined. There was a little dazzle before her eyes and she blinked it away. "Nineteen eighty-nine?" Gideon asked. "Do you know why that year, or—? Actually, never mind," he said hastily, "that's enough to go by."

The person behind him made a sound that cut through Libby's head like a guillotine.

"Stop, I *told* you I'd be right there—Libby. Libby, listen to me. We're going to help you, okay? We're going to find out how to bring you back, I promise. Ouch. Ouch, *stop*—" He said something in another language, something that sounded unintelligible to Libby. "Stop, I told you, let *go* of me—"

"Hey." Something slammed down like a whip beside Libby, jolting her awake with a gasp. "You can't sleep here."

"Sorry, sorry." She wiped her hand across her mouth. Drool again. Always drool. She leapt to her feet, nodding to the police officer or security guard or whoever it was that looked significantly less than pleased to see her. *They're cracking down,* the information desk man had said. Could she get arrested for this? "Sorry, I'm going—"

She hurried to her feet, then glanced down at the map again.

LARCMA wasn't that far. She just had to cross over the highway, then go a few more blocks. Yes it was late, but she'd been a student at a medeian university once, and surely things hadn't changed that much in thirty years. Someone had to be burning the midnight oil, right?

So she set out into the night, shivering a little as she went.

· TRISTAN ·

He was brushing his teeth when he felt rather than heard the door creaking open behind him. Mouth foamed with toothpaste, Tristan caught the flash of silver from the mirror and whipped around just in time to face the thin blade aimed at his back.

There was still a lag, a hitch in his lungs. Not hesitation, exactly, but the hairline fracture between knowing death was coming for him and summoning the means to stop it. The knife stayed a knife for just a sliver longer than he would have liked, but eventually matter stopped fighting him. The bathroom curved outward; the knife transformed, glittering, to smaller and smaller particles, the energy behind the movement extended outward. The knife's flight was now constrained and shifted inward at Tristan's command. This was the key, when he could see it—changing the energy of the knife's pieces, then using that to transform it into something else, anything he liked.

"Seriously, again?" came Nico's voice as Tristan opened his eyes, toothbrush still in hand.

The knife was on the floor in pieces. Nico was standing in the doorway, shaking his head.

Tristan turned and spat into the sink, then looked up at his own redrimmed eyes. He hadn't been sleeping all that well. He knew he wasn't going to die during any of Nico's random infiltrations—he had proven that often enough over the past couple of months—but try telling that to the rest of his body. His eyes were bloodshot and wide, his chest pounding. Adrenaline was a hell of a drug.

"You've got to start playing offense, not just defense," Nico was saying. "I just tried to fucking stab you in the back and all you can do each time is destroy the weapon? What if I had *two* knives, Tristan, what then?" he demanded.

Tristan aimed a heavy, irritated sigh into the sink.

"I mean honestly," Nico ranted, "if all you can bring to a knife fight is a bunch of *smaller pieces of knife*—"

"I get it, Varona, you've made your point clear." Tristan reached for the hand towel beside the sink, wiping away the excess toothpaste from his mouth. "But for the record, this is the fourth time today," he pointed out, turning to face Nico. "I'm concerned you're getting a little too much enjoyment out of plotting to kill me."

"I'd hardly say this rises to the level of *plotting*," Nico said. His eyes were wild, too. He seemed to have regained some element of hyperactivity that Tristan hadn't seen since the beginnings of their preinitiation year, when they had been studying the intricacies of space. "You're extremely predictable, you know," Nico muttered in accusation. "You even layer your scone the same way every time—"

"It's pronounced 'scone,'" said Tristan gruffly, "and *obviously* I do it the same way every time, because I'm not an animal—"

"The point is," Nico interrupted, "you've got to consider doing something *else*. Something besides just breaking things. Like, who is going to clean this up, hm?"

He gestured to the pile of knife shards on the floor. Tristan arched a brow, and Nico sighed.

"Fine." In a blink, the knife was once again a knife, and it was also in the palm of Nico's hand. Tristan, who still found Nico's abilities uncanny, gave an unintended shiver.

"Oh, get used to it." Nico shot him another impatient glance. "You realize that you're a physicist too, right? A weird one," he amended with a shrug, "but still—"

"I don't do what you do," Tristan retorted, which was true. Tristan's specialty, whatever it was, was not the same as redirecting force or altering gravity or whatever it was that Nico was always using to make things happen. Tristan could tell, even now, that it wasn't the same as what he had felt from Libby. The memory of her magic still flooded him from time to time, the beat of her heart below his hand. It was different, the feel of her, the push from inside his veins that belonged unequivocally to her.

What he could do wasn't nothing, but still. There was no point being inaccurate.

"Still." Nico stifled a yawn, raising a hand to his mouth. There was a slight sheen of perspiration on his arms and Tristan frowned, briefly considering saying something.

He didn't. "How is your friend doing?" he asked instead, turning back to the mirror and running a hand along the edge of his jaw. He should really shave.

"Friend?" asked Nico evasively.

"The one who's helping you find Rhodes." He didn't fully buy into Nico's theory—that Libby Rhodes was lost in time—but unfortunately, he couldn't discount it either, for lack of a better one. He wanted her to be alive. If she was lost in time, fine. At least then it would make sense why Parisa couldn't sense her anywhere on the planet.

Tristan reached for the shaver. The prickle of stubble along the bone of his cheek felt rough, like sandpaper. No point putting it off, even if Nico insisted on lecturing him while he did it.

"Oh. Yeah. That friend." Nico looked elsewhere. "I haven't really seen him."

Tristan paused, then determined that Nico probably wouldn't respond well to any measure of kindness. Tristan certainly wouldn't. Though, he didn't consider it a *kindness,* really, to ask. And as none of the rest of them were getting any closer to finding Libby, it wasn't avoidable, either.

He turned the shaver on, leaning toward the mirror. "Think he's given up, then?"

"No." Nico's voice was adamant, even passionate. "He wouldn't give up. It's not that. He's just . . . busy."

Tristan ran the blades beneath his sideburns carefully. "Got ghosted, did you?"

"Fuck you." Nico rubbed his neck. Sore muscles, Tristan observed. Not a good sign for an omnipotent physicist who should have had every reason to sleep well. It wasn't as if their independent research was all that demanding—most of their days were filled with books and nothing else. Aside from casually showing up to murder Tristan throughout the day, Nico should have nothing else on his mind but research.

"Gideon's just—" Nico's eyes cut sideways. "He has other things going on. Or it's taking a long time to find her, I don't know. It's not like the dream realms are easy to navigate."

It didn't take a deranged empath to know he was lying. (Though Tristan did know where to find one, should the need arise.)

"Look," Tristan said. "Not that I care about whatever the fuck is going on with you. But."

"Noted," said Nico, looking rightfully revolted. They locked eyes in the mirror and seemed to share the same shudder of resentment over the possibility of bonding.

"You're obviously falling apart" was Tristan's final ruling before he returned his attention to dutifully shaving his face. "Something's draining you."

"Something," Nico muttered in agreement, his eyes traveling distractedly over the moldings of the bathroom walls. His fingers were tapping at his thighs, a symphony of agitation. "Hey," he added after a moment of aimless fidgeting. "What's your topic for independent study?"

Right. That. "Oh." As if Tristan hadn't been hassled about it enough already. Just that afternoon Dalton had accosted him over it in the reading room.

"Atlas," Dalton had begun with a look of pained suppression, "would like me to speak with you about your independent study."

"Great. He can speak to me himself." Tristan flipped a page in his book and then realized that Dalton was still standing there, and it did not appear that he would be leaving anytime soon. "Yes?" Tristan prompted with a sigh.

"The subject of time is—" Dalton cleared his throat. "Broad. Well-traveled."

"Yes, and?" At that very moment, Tristan was reading about quantum gravity, which was a subject the archives seemed delighted to hand to him. Most of what he found was authorless handwritten notes, all tightly scripted.

"Perhaps you might consider something a bit more practical," said Dalton.

Speaking with Dalton was increasingly like pulling teeth. Part of that might have been Tristan's personal resentment, since his feelings about Parisa had not been positive of late, and they were bleeding into his opinion of her paramour. Though, it could have also been Dalton's supreme inability to make a point. "Such as?"

Dalton took a seat at Tristan's table. "You worked at Wessex Corp," he said.

Oh good, so now they were trading bits of obvious tedium. "Yes," Tristan said slowly, as he would to a small child.

Dalton didn't seem to take offense. "And you are of course aware from your previous employment that James Wessex began his career in fission technology."

"Yes. Obviously." That much was on the James Wessex Wikipedia page. Medeian companies funded by the original Wessex foundation, which had preceded James's involvement, had once been instrumental in stabilizing the climate crisis, which naturally gave way to alternative energy. The return on the Wessex investment had been the equivalent of utter financial lunacy. James was a billionaire several times over, and the vast majority of his work was so private it was speculated about rather than released.

"I only worked for him in venture capital," Tristan reminded Dalton. "Mostly in medeian technomancy." Most of the technology Tristan sourced had never exceeded luxury products or consumer-based software, and even then, he had always passed it off to higher-ups for approval without seeing the end result.

And besides, what did Atlas Blakely care about the specifics of Tristan's pre-Society work?

Tristan's mood abruptly darkened. "Are you trying to tell me that Atlas Blakely wants me to compete with Wessex Corp?"

"No, no." Dalton looked horrified. "The Society does not endorse any sort of material gain and would *never* pursue any kind of competition with—"

"Yes, yes, academic purity, integrity of thought, understood." Tristan was feeling bullish and impatient, and potentially a bit used. "So then what's the point of bringing it up?"

"James Wessex's research in nuclear power . . . Well." A tiny, demure throat-clearing sound. "Atlas believes—" Another pause. "We have reason to believe," he amended, "that perhaps you have made some progress in expanding the use of your abilities."

Tristan was relieved that Dalton, unlike Parisa, could not see the various images of Nico de Varona—giving Tristan a heart attack, attempting to strangle him, dropping heavy objects overhead—wandering idly through his mind. "In a sense, yes."

"There is something to be said for widening the scope of your consideration," said Dalton.

Fine. Deeply patronizing, but sure, fine. "And what does James Wessex have to do with my research?"

"I only meant to bring him up as an example of a . . ." Dalton trailed off. "Well, an expansive thinker."

Alas, Tristan thought. Foiled again by his tiny, tiny brain.

"I can see I've chosen a poor entry point to this conversation," Dalton rushed to say, cleverly reading Tristan's silence as the contempt that it was. "James Wessex is obviously no significant medeian. But *you* are, and I suppose I thought—"

"You want me to study something bigger than time," Tristan summarized for him.

"Yes. Well, no." Dalton looked supremely uncomfortable. "Not bigger, per se. Not necessarily."

"Right," Tristan said darkly. "Just more interesting, then."

"I just feel—" Dalton halted again. "I just sense that perhaps you might be quite an important piece, Mr. Caine, to the kind of research this particular group of initiates could provide."

Tristan frowned. "I thought our research was independent."

"Yes, of course—but still, each group of candidates is selected for a reason." Dalton rose to his feet, obviously reaching the end of what he could stand to offer by way of human interaction. "You and Mr. de Varona have found common ground," he said in a vaguely congratulatory tone. "Mr. de Varona has done the same with Miss Mori, and with Miss Kamali—"

"What?" asked Tristan, frowning. He had expected Libby's name, but not Parisa's.

"Though there is, of course, a bit of a snag," added Dalton.

Tristan's interest soured. "Meaning Callum."

"Meaning that there is a chance the group's interests may . . . diverge," Dalton equivocated. "Mr. Nova has yet to choose a topic of study. And Miss Mori is . . ." He hesitated again. "On the precipice, I suppose one might say."

"So because I failed to kill the empath," Tristan again provided succinctly, "we're all researching the wrong things?"

"Not all of you." It seemed to be a joke, based on the smile Dalton tried to conjure. Amusement was not something that came easily to him, Tristan supposed. "But perhaps there might be something that you specifically would find more stimulating. Given that the archives make their return on the strength of your sacrifice, which was—" A pause. "Fractional, one might say—"

"Again, many apologies for my little *oversight*," Tristan muttered.

"—you may wish to reconsider your topic," Dalton finished, which seemed to be the entire point of their conversation.

So. Given every subject matter available to him in the entire world, Tristan had picked a boring topic. How predictable of him.

"Is this the ruling on high?" Tristan asked Dalton derisively. "Official command from Atlas?"

"By all means, study whatever you wish." Dalton shrugged. "No one will interfere. I'm simply passing along the message."

He had left Tristan alone after that. Tristan had put it out of his mind over dinner. Then Nico had tried to stake him through the heart with one of the balustrades. Now he was in the bathroom having once again reduced a knife to shards, but only barely. And in his head was the constant, abusive refrain: Think bigger.

Be smarter.

Do *more*.

"Uh, hello?" said Nico, who was evidently still standing in the bathroom doorway waiting for an answer. Tristan realized he had been letting the shaver run for almost a minute without making any contact with his face.

"Right, sorry." He traced the underside of his cheek. "I'm thinking of shifting gears a bit."

"Are you?" Nico sounded carefully uninterested, which meant he was deeply interested.

"Why?" Tristan sighed. "Did you have notes?"

Nico's nod in response was borderline manic. "One or two," he said in a rush, as Tristan returned his attention to his half-shaved face. "Have you given any thought to MWI?"

The blades of the shaver lightly skimmed Tristan's jaw. "What?"

"Many-worlds interpretation." Nico was off and rambling. "You realize you've essentially proven that quantum physics is philosophically correct, which means you can also prove some of the other long-standing theories. Like whether there are parallel worlds. Or hidden variables. Or, like, the actual *structure* of space. The formation of galaxies. If you can keep breaking things down into smaller and smaller pieces," Nico added excitedly, "what do you find when you keep going? What is emptiness? Is *anything* emptiness? What's dark matter? If everything just exists in relation to everything else—"

"Fuck," said Tristan, who had shaved too close to the skin of his throat. "Listen, Varona—"

But when he looked in the mirror for Nico, he was gone. Tristan blinked.

"Varona, I—"

The lights went out.

In the next moment there was another flash from his periphery, the glint of a knife from the faint glow of moonlight, a sliver through the window. It happened again, the pounding of Tristan's heart in his ears, the throbbing in his veins, the fear he never quite got used to, like never fully catching his breath. The hairline delay, and then the sudden shift in time and space. The curving of the world to cradle him inside it.

There were tiny fragments of light that Tristan compiled, arranging them so he could see where Nico held the knife to Tristan's throat. The blade was a breath's distance away from his Adam's apple, not a hair more. Tristan was the taller man, but Nico had used his relationship with force to his advantage. A former version of Tristan would have been dead already, throat cleanly slit, but *this* version of Tristan had seen the precipice of death and spun it. He took the knife and rearranged it.

When at last things had calmed inside his head, Tristan opened his eyes. In his right hand was a fistful of Nico's T-shirt. In his left hand was the shard of a broken knife, aimed at Nico's chest. The rest of it was in pebbled fragments that had spilled across the bathroom sink.

Tristan stared down at Nico, whose chest rose and fell against the hold of Tristan's fist.

"Stop breaking knives," Nico panted.

Tristan released him gruffly, leaving Nico to collapse against the sink. "You said to play offense."

"Not like *that, idiota*" was Nico's reply. "Don't fight *me*. What a fucking waste of time."

"Why," Tristan scoffed, "because it would have taken me another minute to beat you?"

"No, because you're wasting it," Nico snapped. "Your energy, your talent—you're fucking *wasting* it." He turned away, one hand skating through the dark curls of his hair. Then he exhaled, planting both hands atop his head in apparent defeat before turning back to Tristan.

"It's not a knife," Nico said.

"Because I broke it," muttered Tristan.

"No. Listen to me." Nico took another step toward him. "It's not a knife. It's just an arrangement of atoms, electrons, quanta, whatever you want to call it. It's just a knife because your brain is telling you it's a knife, because in this order, it is one. Other people see a knife and it's just that, a knife, because that's reality for them. But *you*." Nico gave him a look so scalding Tristan nearly felt it. "You don't have to see it the way anyone else sees it. You could take this—" He held up what remained of the handle. "You could make this a fucking pony. An ice cream cone. An atomic bomb. You can see *time,* you can *use* it, I mean for *fuck's sake,* Tristan, do you even—? I mean seriously, are you—?"

Nico seemed to run out of steam, the air collapsing beneath his monologue.

"Fuck it, whatever. Good night." Nico turned and walked out of the bathroom, letting the door slam behind him.

Tristan stood beside the sink for another long moment.

Then he finished shaving.

Then he carefully toweled off his face, gathered the knife shards, and abandoned them in the bin before making his way downstairs to the office beside the morning room.

He knocked on the open door of Atlas Blakely's office, unsurprised to find it occupied.

Atlas looked up as if he'd been expecting him. "Mr. Caine," Atlas acknowledged, leaning back in his chair.

Tristan shut the door behind him, taking the seat opposite Atlas's desk. Whatever was about to pass between them had been a long time coming; perhaps since the very day that Tristan accepted the Society's offer to become something more.

"We should talk," Tristan said. By which he meant: *Don't send your fucking lackey to tell me what you ought to have said from day one.* Because clearly, Tristan was special. He was powerful. But he was also deeply limited. And on top of that, he was an idiot, too, which meant it was time for Atlas to stop fucking about and tell him the truth that Tristan could not see on his own.

"Yes," Atlas replied carefully. "I rather think we should."

· REINA ·

S he wasn't a megalomaniac. This was not a god complex.

"It isn't *not* a god complex," said Callum.

Mother! trilled a distant upstairs fern. *Eat him alive MotherMother eeeEEEeeee!*

"It's a purely philosophical matter, not religious," corrected Reina shortly. "Again, I am not a god in the sense that I need to be worshipped."

"But you are a god nonetheless?" Callum drawled.

"By the terms of my theory, so are you." Unfortunately. "And so is everyone else in this house." He was still being willfully obtuse about it, not that Reina was surprised. This was what came of choosing a depressed psychopath for a partner. Though again, her choices were limited.

"Don't tell Varona," Callum said. "Not sure he'd take all that elegantly to omnipotence."

"Mocking people will not make this go faster," Reina pointed out, and gestured to the reading room's archival delivery system. "Now. Try it again."

Callum looked at her with such violence of exasperation that for a moment, she nearly respected him again. "Just because that's where the archives deliver requests doesn't mean that *is* the archives," he said impatiently. "They aren't just sitting there waiting for your call."

"Well, whatever." This foundational personality clash would surely *not* grow tiresome, Reina sourly thought. "It's not my job to understand the house's sentience."

"Oh, so omnipotence you want," Callum said, "but omniscience is off the table?"

She could have said: For the last time, I do not think I am holy. I am not divine. What I am is the kind of powerful that could rewrite cultures, restructure societies. This is what it means to be a god: to enforce a new era of change. Not to create empires, but to shape a new generation. Do you know how many times society has already collapsed? It will happen again and rebuild itself, but *how* will it rebuild? Think about it. The old gods are dead, no one believes in them, so what is left now but a broken, faithless world? Give me seven days and I'll make light, I'll make the heavens and the earth. Not literally, because I'm not insane. But I have power and talent and it was given to me for a reason. Because if I can make life, then I am obligated in some way to do so.

But all of that seemed wasted on Callum, so instead Reina said, "Yes."

Callum gave her a scrutinizing look and appeared to cast off any remaining reservations. "Fine." He angled his head up, speaking to the ceiling. "O cherished archives, beloved minions of the Library on High, blessed by the Goddess Herself—"

"Stop," gritted Reina through her teeth.

"Fine." He slid her a look of amusement and beckoned to her with a tilt of his chin. "Hand, please. Or whichever appendage you prefer."

Disgusting. Reina slapped a hand onto his shoulder. "I'm still not sure this kind of proximity is necessary."

"It worked before, it'll work now." He meant that it had worked to influence Dalton Ellery, which according to Callum was not nearly as difficult as he expected it to be. *Not that it wasn't hard,* he had clarified, *because he's using every emotional block known to man. But still, there was something missing.*

Reina hadn't bothered asking what was missing, because she did not care for or understand whatever it was about the human psyche's construction that Callum trafficked in. The only thing that mattered to Reina was how effectively he did it, and their initial exploration of what her enhancement of his powers could accomplish was unequivocally successful, so there. It also had the added bonus of pissing off Parisa, though that was more theatrical than anything of actual use.

So now Reina knew what Dalton was studying. Genesis. Cosmic inflation. Cosmological order. The primordial universe. But all of that was meaningless to her, and worse, a sinking part of her felt sure that it would not be so meaningless to Parisa, who was cleverer than she was hot and therefore twice as irritating to Reina as she was to anyone too busy drooling over her to notice. Reina had hoped that Callum might express some understanding of the subject, but instead he was hung up on something else about Dalton *specifically,* when this was obviously not an issue of who Dalton was at all. What did it matter what kind of person Dalton was, or if he could feel his emotions with the full range of everyone else? These were irrelevancies, trivialities at best. The trouble with people being guided by their own specialties was that Callum felt people were the only true mysteries. Reina, who had known plenty of people who weren't mysterious in the slightest, vehemently disagreed.

In any case, they were stepping up their game now, or trying to. It had taken some time for them to agree on what to summon from the archives, but in the end it was Callum who held the cards, which Reina greatly resented. For as many days as it had taken to convince him to see her point, it was now taking weeks to get him to actually follow up on it. In the end she'd had no choice but to agree with the experiment he suggested, which she found pointless. But he was immovable, so there they were.

"What happened last time you tried?" she asked gruffly, wanting to adjust the placement of her hand on Callum's shoulder. She felt acutely aware of his warmth below her palm in a way that agitated her. She could feel him sapping her of something, power or energy or whatever it was that was making its usual way through her. But unlike when Nico did it, or when she allowed any element of nature to take from her, it was spilling into Callum more thickly. "Oozing" was perhaps the better word.

"The same thing that always happens. My request was denied." He looked at her sideways, crossly. "I'm concentrating."

"Fine. Sorry." It hadn't looked like he was doing anything. His magic was admittedly very bewildering to her.

After a few seconds, Callum's breathing patterns shifted. A small trickle of sweat had formed on his brow, and then he shook her hand away. "There. That should have worked."

"How will we know?" She stared hard at the delivery system.

"It took a few minutes when I tried it alone before. It probably will again." He leaned his back against the reading room wall, eyeing her. "So what's the deal with your family?"

"What did *your* file say?" Reina countered loudly. "I assume you read it."

"Of course." He was watching her with a faint smile on his face. "You do know that my asking you is just a formality, right? I can already tell most of what I need to know without you saying a word."

"Good." She glared at him, then down at her shoes. "Don't you ever get bored of learning people's secrets?" Not that this was a secret, she reminded herself. She didn't keep her family a *secret,* because that would mean they mattered. She simply didn't speak of them, because they did not register for her with any importance. They were mortal. And irrelevant.

"Actually, no, I never get tired of it," Callum said. "Everyone has secrets. And they vary so widely from person to person."

She could feel him watching her, which she shook off like a tick. "I know you think everyone has a sob story, but I don't."

"True," he said. "You're no Parisa. Or Tristan."

"I'm nobody's victim," Reina said flatly.

"Neither were they. Not in that sense." Callum folded his arms over his chest. "But if you think about it, nobody asks for any of this. What they're born into. We just get what we get, and that's a tragedy in itself. Everybody's got one."

"My family is not my tragedy," Reina said.

Callum's mouth quirked. "So you admit that you have one, then."

She glared at him, and he laughed. "Fine, sorry. I'll leave you alone."

He probably wouldn't. That wasn't in his nature.

"It's cute," Callum added. "How badly you try to hate me. I should thank you, I think."

Oh good, this. She might as well have recruited Parisa.

(Once again, Reina decided she loathed nonphysical specialties.)

"It doesn't have to make you weaker, you know," Callum continued. "You're allowed to have human qualities. Which inherently means silly things like sadness and longings and flaws."

"You hate that in other people." She hadn't meant to answer him, much less acknowledge him, but it did seem worth bringing up.

"Not true," said Callum. "I don't actually hate people. I hate predictable things," he admitted. "I hate boring little anxieties, like Rhodes's. People who never exceed their shape because they're too busy wondering why people don't like them, or who they're meant to be, or why they aren't loved, or—"

"But isn't that exactly what you're doing?" Reina interrupted.

Callum's mouth stiffened in a way that suggested that what she'd said had genuinely bothered him.

But by then something had arrived from the archives in front of Reina, and Callum leaned quickly to his feet.

"Is it . . . ?" He looked greedily at the cover of the book—which, like the one Reina had seen Aiya Sato procure from the library the year prior, was blank. "Open it."

Reina folded the cover back, scanning the page.

ATLAS BLAKELY.

"This is it," she confirmed, handing it over her shoulder to Callum, who either couldn't conceal his hunger or hadn't bothered to try. "So now can we try my thing?"

His response was a strangled laugh. "I know you think my magic costs me nothing," he replied irritably, already burying his attention in the dossier he'd felt was so critical to his happiness, "but it's not as if I plan to attempt it twice in one day. These archives aren't the same thing as a person."

For fuck's sake, Reina thought. Exhausting.

"Wow," murmured Callum, rubbing his fingers below his chin. "This is both more and less interesting than I'd imagined."

"How wonderful for you," muttered Reina. Realizing they weren't going to get any further, she gave up, turning away to leave before suddenly remembering something. "Put it back," she said, and Callum looked up, traveling a long way in his thoughts to reach her. "As soon as you're done," she clarified. "Put it back."

He frowned. "Why?"

"Because he knows things. And I don't want him to know this." To be clear, she wasn't afraid of Atlas Blakely. However, she also didn't feel like antagonizing him.

This was the part that Callum didn't understand—he might have understood people, or the way their narratives took shape, but he underestimated the actions they might take, the things they might have lived through, the irrationalities they might be willing to pursue. He hadn't understood Tristan's emotions. He didn't understand Parisa's. And he clearly did not understand that a man in Atlas Blakely's position did not get there by being easy to take advantage of.

"Just put it back," she warned, and Callum shrugged, which she took to be a yes.

So she prowled out of the reading room, suddenly feeling the need to hit something.

Nico wasn't always easy to find these days. It wasn't entirely clear to Reina whether he was avoiding her of his own volition or if she had successfully given him the impression that she wanted him to go away. At first she had doubted it was the latter, assuming that Nico was unable to pick up on subtle signals like one-word answers and general antipathy, but she had forgotten that Nico was far more adept at emotional intelligence than people (cough, Callum) gave him credit for. Nico was eminently likable, had always been, and there was nothing more likable than a person who knew exactly when to become scarce.

Reina wandered the first floor, aimlessly checking Nico's usual hiding spots (the kitchen, or the wormhole he had left beside the kitchen) before wandering outside. The days were considerably cooler now, to the point where even Nico might consider putting on a shirt.

She found him beside the wilting roses, doing precisely what she wanted to do in that moment: punching things. In this case, a heavy bag of his own conjuring.

"Oh, hey." Nico wiped the sweat from his eyes as Reina approached and gave her an easy smile that made her instantly furious. "Didn't expect to see you today."

Of course not, as apparently he couldn't be bothered to go looking for her when he was doing the exact thing alone that they had spent all of last year doing in tandem. Which again was probably her fault, but still. If she'd been such a bitch to him that she'd successfully driven him away, then why was he so pleased to see her? Unforgivable.

"Yeah," she said, and his grin broadened.

"I've missed that wit." He beckoned her closer. "You in for a quick round?"

She tried to make it seem like she hadn't planned on it; had simply been wandering around and come upon him and decided yes, sure, why not, she could spare a few breaths of her one life for this ridiculous hobby of his. "Sure."

"Cool." He vanished the bag and put out a fist in offering. "I'm getting out of shape."

"Doubt it." She tapped her knuckles against his, initiating the round. He looked, quite frankly, delighted. Or possibly relieved. "Been busy lately?"

"Kind of." Nico threw a testing jab and she slipped it, whipping up her own cool breeze. The dogwoods chanted their approval from a distance. "Have I told you much about what Tristan's up to?"

"Not much." Nothing, in fact.

"Yeah, well—" He rolled fluidly beneath her hook. "It's kind of a long story, but basically we're trying to get him to manipulate quanta."

"Quanta?" Reina echoed. What she really meant was: *We?*

"Yeah." Nico danced around her, leading her clockwise before deftly switching his stance for a kick. He tapped playfully with his toe around the back of her knee, and once again she wanted to strangle him. In a fond way, which was even worse. "He can see through things, right? He can see the little particles of magic when we use them. But he's fucking hopeless."

"Oh." Figured. Reina had always personally categorized Tristan as hopeless.

"Yeah." She came in with her knee, which he lightly blocked. They were sparring at a fraction of their usual energy, so delicate with the placement of their motions that they barely touched. "Anyway. Saw you with Callum," Nico added.

She wondered if it was worth providing any defense and then decided that as usual, she didn't owe anything to anyone. "Yeah."

"I feel like he's been very . . ." Nico paused to throw a jab-hook combo. "Drunk."

"Oh. Yeah." At that she couldn't help a roll of her eyes, and Nico laughed.

"Are you his sponsor or something?"

"What?" She blocked his cross.

"Sponsor. You know, the person to get him back on track or whatever."

"No." If she was doing anything even remotely along those lines, it was only incidental. "He is also hopeless."

"We should have left them to each other." Nico slid away from her hook, nimbly out of reach. "I don't even think I've seen Parisa for a week."

Reina had a guess where Parisa might be. "You know she's sleeping with Dalton, right?"

"Wait, really?" Nico paused, only narrowly blocking Reina's jab. "Damn," he sighed, temporarily forlorn.

Against her will, Reina was amused. "You don't actually find that disappointing, do you?"

"I mean, he's just so . . ." Nico trailed off, making a face that generally summed up Reina's opinion of Dalton, pre-influencing. That Dalton had no obvious sense of humor, no evident ambitions. He was good-looking, maybe. Everything on his face seemed to be in the right place. But if Reina were someone angling for Parisa's attention—which Nico had made no secret of doing over the last year—then she felt pretty certain that Dalton's qualifications fell perilously shy of Parisa-worthy.

"I figured out what he researches," Reina said. She hadn't meant to tell Nico about any of that, but there was something about the mindlessness (or rather, mindfulness in a meditative kind of way) of sparring that left her feeling unwisely open, the door to her recent thoughts left ajar.

"Yeah?" Nico kicked with deliberate slowness at her head, laughing when she shoved him away and off-balance.

"It's something physical. Cosmology, I think." Nico jogged back a step and Reina came toward him, then ducked under his punch. "Any idea what cosmic inflation is?"

"What?" Nico, distracted, stayed upright instead of changing levels, meaning he got caught exactly in the middle of Reina's hook. "*Fuck*—"

Nico doubled over, his hand covering his face as Reina paused, somewhere between extremely proud of herself and also deeply sorry. "Are you okay?"

"Yeah, I—" When Nico looked up, his eyes were watering. There was a smear of blood on his hand when he swiped at his nose. "Oh fuck, seriously?"

He tried twice before the blood clotted. "Sorry—"

"Why are *you* sorry?" Reina stared at him. She had never seen him take so long to heal an injury. Not that it was long by mortal standards, but this was Nico de Varona, and mortal he was anything but.

"I just . . . got distracted, I don't know." Nico waved her away. "You don't know what cosmic inflation is?"

Well. There went her sympathy. "Obviously not."

"It's like . . ." He touched his nose, which looked swollen. "A spontaneous reaction. The universe expanding out at, you know. An inflated rate." He swore under his breath, rubbing his cheek briefly. It was red from taking the brunt of the impact of Reina's knuckles. "People think that's what happened after the big bang, that the universe expanded quicker than light. And then everything formed out of chaos."

"Oh." Reina wondered briefly if that was just another form of mythology. A belief system for scientists who'd decided that if it wasn't a god (or a God), then it was something just as ineffable. "Wait." Something about Nico's explanation was sticking out in her mind, unruly. "Spontaneous . . . life?"

"Well—" Nico's hand paused partway to his mouth. "Well yeah, I guess so. I was going to say spontaneous creation but yeah, I guess ultimately that means life, doesn't it?"

"But I can do that. Make that." Which abruptly reminded her of something. "I kind of thought that was going to be more interesting to you." She had, after all, been expecting him to pursue it further after she'd let him use her magic last year.

"Well—" Nico's brow furrowed. "It *is* interesting to me. But I told you, I can't do anything with it. Not without—" He hesitated before Libby's name. "Just . . . not any more than I've already done."

"But you haven't even tried." Distantly, Reina became aware that her temper was rising. She did not even think of herself as having a temper, but every now and then she saw bright spots of white and determined them to be anger. She saw one now.

"I didn't think you wanted me to try." Neither of them were sparring now, though they were still facing off, combative. "I've hardly even seen you for weeks."

"So I was supposed to come find you?"

"I've been—" Nico rubbed his forehead. "Busy. Tired."

"Seriously?" Reina prickled with annoyance. "We live in the same house."

"I know, but—"

"And since when are you so weak?" she asked, gesturing to his nose. Nico blinked, swallowing, then blinked again.

"I . . . Wow. I don't even know what to say to that."

It occurred to her that it might have been a problem of translation. (Or was it?) "I just meant that you don't usually get hurt."

"Right, well, I haven't exactly been myself. Not that you'd know that, because apparently neither have y—"

He stopped again.

"Whatever," he said eventually. "This is . . . Let's just not."

"Not what?"

"We don't really fight, you know? I like that." He shrugged. "Makes it easy."

Yes, Reina thought. Yes, I'm very easy to forget about. To ignore. Because everything is so very easy between us that whether I'm here or whether I'm not, it's all the same.

"I mean it's not like with Rhodes," he said. "Always bickering. Annoying," he offered with a grimace. "You know how that was."

Yes. She did know how that was. *Annoying.* That was Nico's word of choice for Libby Rhodes and their bizarre cosmic tango? Sure, yes, Rhodes was so very *annoying* to him. So annoying that in her absence Nico was *not himself.*

Suddenly Reina couldn't remember why she'd come to find him. She felt oddly humiliated by having been the one to do it at all.

"I should go," Reina said bluntly. "That was a long round."

"Oh, right." Nico looked genuinely apologetic, which made her either sorrier or angrier. At this point, there was no telling which. "I didn't mean to keep you. But hey, if you want to talk, or—"

He broke off. "That's probably dumb," he said. Mostly to himself.

Reina had the sudden sensation that she understood with perfect clarity what was wrong with Nico de Varona.

He was lonely.

Because of course he was. He was, in very simple terms, accustomed to being as antagonistic as he pleased while still managing to be adored. Libby Rhodes had served him perfectly, paying him exactly the kind of attention that made him rise up higher, to be more of himself. But she was gone, and Reina was still here, but apparently that didn't matter. Because again, Nico didn't see anything more in Reina than someone to feel neutral about. To assign the purest, least impactful sense of ambivalence. To simply allow to come and go as she pleased.

To that, Reina unwillingly caught a glimpse of Callum's smug face in her mind's eye. Human fragility, he might have said.

(Which meant very little from a perpetually intoxicated empath with no friends.)

"Good luck with Tristan," Reina said curtly, and Nico gave her a crooked half smile.

"Yeah. Same," he said. "With Nova."

"I'm not doing anything with him."

"Oh. Well yeah, I just meant—" He gave her a look of something wound tight. Irritation? Probably. Great. So much for not fighting. Not that she wanted to, either.

Kill him! sang the gleeful grass below her feet. *Maaaaaaaim him!*

Mother will make a soup from his boooooones!

"See you," Reina said.

"Yeah. Soon, right?"

"Yeah."

They were both lying, so Reina once again did him a favor. She turned around and ended the conversation, walking toward the house without another word.

· PARISA ·

Parisa was seated at the table in the painted room when Atlas found her. It was an odd thing, them intentionally seeking each other out—or rather, *him* intentionally seeking *her* out for the second time, and Parisa obligingly remaining in place because the house had informed her he was coming. Presumably he had also been informed that she would stay and listen to whatever he had to say, just by virtue of the thought entering her head, so. It was all very amicable and impressive of them.

"Are we friends now?" she asked, looking up from her book when he came into the room. "Or is it more like flatmates who've seen each other's dirty laundry," she amended with a shrug. "Because honestly, I only have the requisite attention for the latter."

Atlas had returned to the usual crisp shirts, the formal outerwear. He slid a chair back from the table, seating himself diagonally to her left.

"I would consider myself very privileged indeed to have any knowledge of your secrets, Miss Kamali." He looked quite comfortable for a person who was here to lecture her, or so she had initially assumed. She decided it must not have been that.

"Please," said Atlas, with a glance of weary admonition. "If you could consider staying out of my head for the span of one conversation?"

Parisa withdrew the tendrils of her magic, but only far enough to be ruled adequately sportsmanlike.

Atlas arched a brow. "I've brought a knife to a gunfight, I see," he said, "since I have no intention of doing anything more than delivering logistical details."

"Oh, don't sell yourself short," Parisa assured him. "More like you've brought a knife to a tournament of knife fights."

"Kind of you." Perhaps it was just her imagination, but something about his air had shifted in the months since they'd last spoken. He wasn't entirely unburdened, but there was something else; a distraction at hand. A light at the end of the tunnel. Whatever he had planned for Tristan must have been put in the oven to bake and would soon be turning out golden.

"I merely wanted to inform you," Atlas continued, "that as initiated members of the Society, you and your fellow cohort will be invited this year to attend the annual Alexandrian Society gala."

"The what?" asked Parisa, though she hardly needed to. The Alexandrian Society was obviously antiquated in every possible way aside from the progressive contents of its research. Presumably there were operating costs. Important people. Recreational pursuits. Of course there was some kind of bourgeoisie ball.

"Of course there is a ball," Atlas agreed, sharing a conspiratorial shrug with Parisa. "Most Alexandrians consider it an excellent means for networking."

"Okay." Parisa frowned. "And it takes place here?"

"Yes." A nod. "You may recall that last year we asked you to vacate the premises in order to accommodate the event."

"But you're not sending us away this time?"

"No." Atlas drummed his fingers on the table. "You are under no obligation to attend, of course. But you will be invited."

"Okay." She waited for there to be more, but when Atlas appeared to have reached the end of his planned remarks, she frowned. "Why are you telling me?" she demanded. "Because I'm a woman and therefore naturally adept at event planning?"

"I do not need your help throwing a party, Miss Kamali." Atlas gave her a look of long-suffering patience. "I am merely informing you because I know you'll interfere, and I'd rather you do it in the house where I can see it."

"Speaking of seeing things," Parisa said, changing the subject so as not to rise (or sink) to the implication that she was an unruly teenager who mutinied purely for the sake of rebellion. "Increasing your surveillance is a bit much, don't you think?"

"Surveillance?" Atlas echoed.

She wasn't sure if his expression of bemusement was real or not. *You're watching Dalton,* she clarified.

"Ah," he said. "Watching, no. Keeping an eye on, yes. With good reason," he pointed out. "Seeing as Miss Mori and Mr. Nova have recently chosen to make Mr. Ellery the subject of some very invasive experimentation."

"Have they?" asked Parisa innocently.

Atlas's expression remained carefully still. "Unless I am much mistaken," he said, "I would not have thought such a thing could escape your notice."

So here was the lecture, then. It was one thing for Parisa to interfere with Dalton—after a year's effort, Atlas seemed to have correctly ascertained that no amount of warning her away from Dalton would conceivably work—but now, evidently, Atlas believed she should *also* take responsibility for making sure nobody else did.

"Did I leave your favorite toy unattended?" Parisa asked. "Silly me."

"I'm not blaming you. Mr. Ellery's research is not a secret," Atlas replied tonelessly. "And his autonomy is his own to guard."

"How interesting that you should say that," Parisa scoffed. *As if you haven't pulled me out of his head multiple times.*

So you admit, remarked Atlas with another drum of his fingers, *that you're the one interfering with him in the first place?*

"Very funny." *I'm not interfering.*

Yet, she added.

"I must admit, I did think I'd find you a bit more concerned," Atlas said. "About what? Dalton?"

"Mr. Nova." The look on Atlas's face was the closest thing he had ever given her to a smirk. "Last I checked, the two of you were not entirely on good terms."

"Oh, you mean because he killed me on an astral plane? Bygones," said Parisa, waving a hand. *And in any case,* she added, *he has a dossier on you.*

She had been very nearly delighted to sense the presence of it in Callum's head. He was not very careful these days—if one could consider Callum Nova to have ever been careful, which he had not. But he was particularly unguarded about his enthusiasm for whatever he had recently learned about Atlas Blakely.

There is nothing interesting to be learned about me, said Atlas with a shrug. *I am not very interesting.*

You have six feet of a problem that suggests otherwise, replied Parisa.

He gave her a look that did not quite rise to contempt. (But didn't sink far below it, either.)

"The point is," Atlas said, "this event is an annual security risk."

It took her a moment to recall that he was talking about the so-called Alexandrian Ball. "Security risk? Why?" *Surely you know how to keep things to a respectable din.*

Atlas smiled thinly. "Because the Forum is invited."

That was genuinely surprising information. "What?" Parisa asked, by which she meant: *I respect the old adage about keeping your enemies closer, but in this case . . . ?*

"As I said." Atlas shrugged. "I prefer subterfuge to take place inside the house where I can see it."

Something about the way he expressed the sentiment—the ownership he seemed to have over the risk—left her with a hint of real surprise.

"This is . . . *your* idea?" she asked doubtfully.

A nod. "Yes. One of my signature implementations over the years as Caretaker."

"Years," she echoed. "Not terribly many, I expect."

"A sufficient amount," he replied, rising to his feet. "In any case, I would hope that while you're here, you will recall that you are an initiated Alexandrian and act accordingly."

Atlas turned to leave, nodding to Parisa in apparent farewell, but she stopped him, rising sharply to her feet in his wake.

"Was it them?" she asked. "That took Rhodes. Was it the Forum?"

Atlas looked as if he had hoped she might ask him that. "I don't think so. But I cannot be sure they're not working with the person who did."

"Then we should stay out of sight." Atlas blinked, not following, and Parisa clarified, "Or at least some of us. So they can't be sure whether a member has been killed. Or which one."

"Ah. Interesting." He faced her with what appeared to be genuine absorption. "How much have you gathered about the Forum? Since I assume you have tried," he added, which was not expressed in a flattering tone. (But also not unflattering.)

"*Mr. Ellery*," Parisa replied with mocking emphasis, "does not consider the Forum to be a valid threat, so that's as much as I've gathered."

"Ah, well." A shrug. "There he is mistaken. Physically they may not be threatening," Atlas explained, "but ideologically, they are the reminder that to every coin there are two sides."

"And that's dangerous?" Parisa asked, though she knew as much already. Because of course there was nothing more difficult to discard than a thought that was carefully planted. Certainly nothing more compelling than seeing both sides at once.

"Miss Kamali, I will admit that I have not always appreciated your insistence on behaving as you do," Atlas said, adding, *and perhaps, at times, I have not cared much for you in general.*

Darling, you flatter me, Parisa replied.

"But I also know that you are exceedingly pragmatic," Atlas continued. "I do not often worry about you running away with your worst suspicions. And besides," he added, "I'm sure you understand that a bit of sacred hospitality can go a long way."

Ah, so there it was: this was a détente, a temporary surrendering of weapons on all sides, including theirs. She had known there was strategy hidden beneath all his docility somewhere. "You're asking me to attend this gala so I can be your eyes and ears?" *You don't trust the others not to be persuaded, I take it. Is it Nico you're worried about?*

I worry about Mr. de Varona increasingly. Fair, given the state of him, which nobody paying attention could ignore. *But not in this sense.*

Parisa considered it. Tristan never trusted anything, much less attempted institutional subterfuge, which left two possibilities.

Well, one possibility. A unit. *Callum and Reina, then.*

Atlas gave her another shrug.

"You absolutely *despise* him, don't you?" Parisa couldn't help a smile. "You're aligning with me because you think that between the two of us, I'm the lesser evil."

"Either that or I find you the safer bet."

He was taunting her again. Delightful. In reply, Parisa gave him her most simpering smile.

"I'll be there," she promised. *And in exchange? Stay out of Dalton's head.*

Miss Kamali. To that, Atlas's expression was grim. *I assure you, I am not the antagonist you're looking for.*

She gauged his face for any trace of falsehood, then slipped as discreetly as possible into his thoughts.

He invited her in. *It's not me, Miss Kamali.* The tonality of the thought was reluctant with truth, perhaps wry with it. Something of a cosmic irony, a twist of a knife, that he would deny something that under other circumstances would have been true. *I promise you,* he added, *I am equally curious who might be watching Mr. Ellery's thoughts. Perhaps someone aside from you has reason to find him valuable, hm?*

He tipped his head at her, then turned decisively, departing through the painted room door.

Parisa stared after him, contemplative.

Then Callum waltzed in and Parisa sighed, instantly annoyed by his presence when he knew perfectly well she was here to be alone. "Do you mind?" she demanded, gesturing to her now-forgotten book while Callum, who had evidently chosen to forgo trousers (she would not have taken him as the type of man to wear boxers), rummaged around for a bottle he must have squirreled away behind a set of antique books of quotations.

"Me, mind? Never." He toasted her over his shoulder with a crystal decanter. "As you were."

"You have a problem," Parisa observed, arching a brow.

"Nonsense. I have a hobby," said Callum. "It's everyone else who has a problem."

Before she could answer, there was another set of footsteps bounding through the painted room door.

"Has anyone seen—Oh," said Tristan, falling to a halt as he registered first Callum, then Parisa. "It's you two."

"It's not '*us two*,'" said Parisa with disgust. Callum, who was nose-deep in a martini glass, gave her a thumbs-up. "And what are you looking for?" she asked, abruptly curious.

"Nothing. Just—nothing." Tristan scowled in typical Tristan fashion. "Are we all just going to avoid each other for the rest of the year, then?"

"Why not? We're handling it so beautifully," said Callum, falling into the seat beside Parisa's and plucking up her book. "Jung, really?" He retched into his glass. "How fucking European."

"Nobody is avoiding anyone," grumbled Parisa, who *was* very much avoiding Callum and also Reina and not technically Nico, but only because he seemed to have been devolving recently, and regrettably she suspected that she might actually start to care if she paid any attention. But Tristan she was not avoiding. Tristan she had many questions about. "You've just been mysteriously absent."

(And, if her observations were correct, he'd been experiencing life-altering scares several times a day. But if he wasn't going to bring that up, then she certainly wasn't.)

"You know, things are much more peaceful without the two of you trying to manipulate me," Tristan remarked, only barely able to suppress a grimace. "I sleep like a baby."

"Categorically false," commented Callum to the bottom of his glass.

"He's right," added Parisa, gesturing to Callum. Then, because she could not help herself, she added, "And just because *we're* not manipulating you, does that really mean *no one* is?"

"Zing," said Callum.

"Oh, fuck off," snarled Tristan, turning away to leave and clipping his shoulder against the doorframe. "Fuck," said Tristan, before disappearing.

In Tristan's absence, Parisa waited to see what Callum's reaction would be. More drinking? Less?

"He looked good," she offered experimentally. Which was true. Tristan was a very attractive man and he had been decaying at such a reasonable rate lately. Hardly any melting to be seen.

"It was never like that," Callum muttered, perching his bare feet atop the table beside her.

Parisa swatted them down, revolted. "Wasn't it, though?"

By then Callum was engrossed in Jung, or was at least reading Jung inside his head very loudly.

"Fine. It's not as if I need your confirmation to call things what they are." She turned to leave, then backstepped quickly. "By the way, what did you find out about Atlas?"

"Couldn't you pop in and find out?" Callum said, gesturing to his forehead without looking up from his glass.

"I could." And she probably would, too, later. She had things to conserve her energy for at the moment, and besides. It wasn't like Callum was going to forget it anytime soon. "Never mind."

"Ta," said Callum disinterestedly.

Someday she was going to have fix that little problem of his, Parisa thought.

Or not. She wasn't his mother. And he had killed her once, for fuck's sake. She would have very happily killed him, so by all accounts she shouldn't mind if he chose death by liver poisoning. But perhaps it was all their mutually assured destruction that was making her so very annoyed with his current state of affairs, because it was not fun at all to exist without a rival.

What was she supposed to do, focus on *Reina*?

Parisa wandered over to the reading room, feeling restless. Everyone was being extremely unhelpful by being wildly and unpredictably unpredictable. Atlas was being informative, Callum was being drunk, up was down, north was south. Either that, or she'd spent far too long in this house and no longer had any idea how anyone normal was supposed to behave. She quite relished the thought of having new blood, new enemies.

The Forum, for example. Not that they were necessarily *enemies,* though it would be a nice change of pace if they were. She doubted they were all that different from the Society in the end. People always craved power—that was a constant of humanity, a truer rule than any law of physics. If they weren't given power, they took it. And however lofty and moral their foundational creed, people historically did not choose to give it away.

But then, maybe there was someone more immediate to unpuzzle for the day.

She wandered to the reading room and found Dalton poring over his notes, as usual. He looked up, startled, when she approached. "Miss Kamali," he said in tones of pleasant surprise when she took hold of his face with both hands, tenderly brushing her thumbs over the bones of his cheeks. "Is this affection from you? How perfectly alarming."

He was smiling up at her, all quiet delight and delicate waves of contentment. She brushed her lips across his cheek, sweeping a kiss over it in answer. Then she touched her lips to his eyes, his nose. The little tired crease between his brows. She hovered over his mouth, letting him tilt his chin up in breathless anticipation.

She could do this subtly, of course.

Or.

Or.

She could just get this done.

"Brace yourself," she whispered, finding the hinge of his thoughts and prying it open.

Then she closed her eyes and dove in.

The castle was something of an eccentric touch, Gideon thought while squinting at the parapets. It was a bit too fairy-tale for his taste, though presumably Nico would find that funny. Not that Gideon was meant to be thinking of Nico at this moment, because being here was already challenging enough without inviting in all the other things that came with thinking of Nico. Regret, namely. But Gideon was—also regrettably—a man of his word, however unclever that happened to be, and he'd promised his mother he'd do her one favor. Just one.

Beside Gideon, Max whimpered.

(It had all seemed so innocent at the time.)

"Can't you make that thing be quiet?" said Eilif, who had not been invited along. Or so Gideon would tell Nico later when he inevitably asked why Gideon's mother had come at all. (Assuming that Gideon did not get killed inside the weird, haunted playground of somebody else's consciousness. Which was a definite if.)

"Max does what he likes. And be nice to my friends," Gideon said before adding perfunctorily, "Mum."

"I don't see why you've brought him," muttered Eilif, who had a general suspicion for mammals. She didn't care for warm blood. "I told you, this will all be much simpler if we do it alone."

"We," Gideon said, "are not doing anything. And it hasn't been simple." He had expected telepathic wards, but this was nearly the degree of difficulty that getting into the Society had always been. There was a labyrinth around the castle, full of bramble and shifting cypress trees, and the occasional intrusion from some sort of dream creature that had to have been born in a nightmare. If Gideon were not already accustomed to the sorts of things that lurked in the dream realms, he would not have gotten this far without damage. "You told me this was going to be easy."

His fault for believing his mother, he supposed. He wasn't sure how long he'd been stranded here, but he felt certain it had been weeks, if not months. This was not a dream. This was not any layer of subconscious, which Gideon had known but not understood when he accepted the task. Whoever had created the castle had left something behind that was functionally flypaper for Gideon, who could not free himself from its grip. Gideon had been trying to make his way out of the labyrinth and couldn't, so the only remaining option—aside from successfully breaking in, which seemed less likely every day—would be to force a return to his corporeal body and wake himself up, which he couldn't do because his mother would follow, and then he would be at her mercy in yet another dimension.

Again.

He sighed with another surge of self-hatred. Why had he done this, again? To make some sort of infantile point to Nico? He *had* been bored, but what had come of this? He had been so close to finding Libby, and now, because he had thought—*very idiotically*—that his mother might somehow speed things along, he had gotten himself trapped inside the errand that was only supposed to take a few minutes, at most.

"It *is* easy," Eilif insisted, flashing silvery blue in the refracting light from the gleaming castle stone. "I told you, the Prince simply sends me his messages, and then I—"

"That's not what we're doing here," Gideon interrupted, shading his eyes to look up at the castle. It was Gothic in style, all slim towers and sharp lines. "We're beyond messages at this point, Mother. Clearly we have to be invited in. But I thought the whole purpose of this was to break him out?"

"Of course it is," said Eilif, in a way that sounded very much like a lie. Then again, it was very difficult to tell, as Gideon did not have a strong handle on what it sounded like for her to tell the truth. It happened so rarely he was beginning to confuse it with the sound of something else, like choirs of angels or some divine chime of world peace.

"Maybe you could leave," Gideon suggested for the hundredth time, "and reach out to the Prince some other way, and then possibly you could tell him, you know, that we're at his door and would he mind very much *opening it—*"

"Nonsense, I'm fine here," Eilif said, before glancing sideways. "Minus that gruesome thing."

"His name is Max, and he is not a thing," corrected Gideon as Max made a low sound of annoyance. "And—"

There was a sudden flash from the castle. Like a strike of lightning.

"Did you see that?" said Gideon, frowning. In answer, Max barked.

"Oh, lovely," said Eilif. "Visitors."

She didn't sound concerned, which was twice as worrisome for Gideon. "Visitors?" he echoed. "You mean . . . other than us? But—"

The ground below him shook, sending Max tumbling into the backs of Gideon's knees and knocking both of them to what was very convincing hard-packed dirt. For a moment Gideon nearly forgot he was on an astral plane—it both looked and smelled like earth, fresh and sodden with petrichor, the distant memory of rain. Whoever had mimicked this knew dampness intimately, without flaw. The creator of this little mind prison was definitely from somewhere wet.

"Well," said Eilif, shading her eyes from the rapidly darkening sky. "Let me know when you sort all this out, hm?"

No, Gideon thought, panicked. No, she might have been a menace, but if she left, that was one less creature, which was also one less source of magical output in a realm he could only interpret, not control. If this storm was something serious, or more likely, someone who'd noticed his presence and come to hunt him down . . .

"Mum, please don't—*Eilif!*" Gideon shouted after her, but she was gone.

Naturally. Which, well. At least that meant that *he* could leave, too, if he could just—

He heard a loud bark, followed by a whimper. The clap of lightning overhead was blinding, the ground below them undulating wildly beneath their feet. The sudden tectonic shift left Gideon dazed and tumbling forward, landing hard on his hands and knees before scrambling up from the oscillating tides of dirt.

Who are you?

The voice rang out in Gideon's head, burrowing deeper the closer it came. The pressure seared behind his sinuses, his temples. It took a moment for his head to clear, and when he was finally able to lift his chin, it was only with bleary eyes, wet with strain and a sideways sheet of precipitation.

Yes. Whoever had created this prison certainly knew rain.

"I'm here for the Prince," Gideon said through gritted teeth, wincing from a throb of something inside his head. It was like a migraine, if a headache could reach a boiling point. His head was lava. It occurred to him that he did not know where Max was, that he could not feel lasting pain in the dream realms unless his corporeal form suffered a stroke, that if he died then he would do so without having said goodbye, which was generally unacceptable. Gideon lifted his chin in defiance and then recoiled, struck by a blow from somewhere he couldn't see.

Who sent you?

"The Prince," he said again, shouting it. Sound was doing something funny, swallowing itself up. "The Prince, he sent for me, I'm just—" The pressure cracked like a whip. Who could be doing this? Only a telepath. Presumably the telepath who put the Prince here, who trapped him on this astral plane, which meant that Gideon was fighting for his life—no, not his life; worse, his consciousness, his lucidity—against someone whose magic far outmatched his own.

He tried again to look up, to see who he was fighting. Not that it mattered. This was the problem with Gideon, whose main talent was his ability to survive. There were only one or two ways to kill him with any permanence, as far as he knew. They could hurt him badly enough in here to cause an aneurysm out there. Or traumatize him severely enough to depress his nervous system, which would mimic the symptoms of an overdose—shallow breathing, weak pulse, eventually seizures or a coma. Either way, his death was a high ask. But his pain wasn't. And if anyone could manage to kill him, without a doubt it was this particular telepath.

Who is the prince?

"He's in the tower! He's—" Gideon's hand, scrabbling in the dirt for the means to launch upright, found a tangle of thorns. The fact that pain was entirely in the mind was quite a sinister touch, all things considered. That he could not exist here physically and yet still feel that his skin was torn open was proof of some cosmic sense of humor. "Tell him, tell him I was sent here—"

By whom? The Forum?

They were getting nowhere with this. So Gideon, who couldn't take much more, focused inward. Pain isn't real, he reminded himself. It's a sensation. It's an illusion. It does not have to exist. This is a dream from which you cannot wake, yes. But there are no laws of physics here, no rules at all. You do not have to exist the way they made you.

You do not have to die this way.

He forced himself upright, stumbling through the punitive din of chaos in his mind, and thought of something, anything but the burn in his muscles, the ache in his head. Pie. Yes, pie. He enjoyed pie. As far as desserts went it was vastly underrated. What was better than breaking into a buttery crust? Nothing. He enjoyed Sundays. He did not feel dread about Mondays. He did not feel dread, dread was for people who wanted to suffer twice, suffer three times. Most people would assume Gideon was a pessimist because hello, look at the obvious (everything fucking sucked) but actually he wasn't, because he *enjoyed* being alive. He loved being awake. He *missed* being awake. He missed pancakes. He missed bad, cheap coffee. He missed Nico waking him up early, too early, before the sun was even out. He missed Nico's worst habits, the way Nico had never met a sentence he didn't want to interrupt. He missed the way it felt to look at Max and Nico and realize that they had left a space in their lives specifically for him, they had given him a place to belong. He missed places that weren't raining but also, he missed rain. *Real* rain. He missed missing the bus *because* it was raining. He missed the soggy, awful smell of the subway. He missed his first bike, which had obviously been stolen, and his second bike, which was also stolen. He missed walking with Nico because of his stolen bike. He missed talking to Nico. He missed suffering like this but doing it wholly by choice because of Nico, because Nico was on the other side. He missed Nico. He missed Nico. He missed—

There. It was fading now, the pain. Gideon could see again, he could feel something other than anguish. He looked at his hands and thought, fireballs, and then boom, a fireball. Magic! Dream magic! It made no sense and it did not need to. There was no science here, only vibes. He lobbed a fireball blindly and someone ducked, warping out of sight.

He caught the ripple of stylized black armor followed by the whip of long dark hair, like a vindictive Joan of Arc. Okay, so the telepath was a woman. That wouldn't have been his first guess but he supposed it was feminine, the voice in his head. Did he want to set her on fire? Not really. He wanted to do a job, which was to break into the castle. To break the Prince out of the tower.

And to get out of here, to see Nico again.

Gideon cleared a pathway through the bramble, parting the thorns like the sea. Why hadn't he done this ages ago? It was easier now, like a cloud had been lifted from his eyes. He was blind, but now he saw. It was so simple, honestly, the simplest possible thing. He caught the flash of black armor hovering in his periphery and thought, tornado hands, and then there it was, a gust of wind. The telepath, whoever she was, was racing him to the tower. Bullets rained from the sky, violent starlight. Combustible dewdrops. Beautiful dreamer, wake unto me!

Gideon slid along the stone pathway outside the castle, the telepath's armor glinting only half a step behind him while he skidded across cobbles and contemplated a way up. Okay, vines. Climbable vines. They propelled down from the tower window and Gideon leapt, launching himself higher to reach them. No gravity here, Nicolás!

An ax flew through the air, slicing the ivy of Gideon's creation. He tilted backward and dove, transforming castle stone to water, to marshmallow fluff. Yes, here, this was his domain now, because they were in a dream and Gideon was a dreamer. He was an optimist, an idiot prince. He saw the possibility of doom and said *not today, fucker!*, flipping off the whims of fate while diving backward into hell.

The telepath wasn't prepared for it. She was powerful and quick, but what exactly was one supposed to do with marshmallow fluff? It was, after all, very sticky. Gideon launched himself at the tower again, clinging to its stone-cobbled side like one of those gummy tree frogs. The telepath took apart the tower stone by stone, removing them from Gideon's path as he climbed, but he replaced them with toy bricks, with oversized beams, with pastel-colored gumdrops. If Nico were here, he would never let Gideon live this bullshit down.

He was nearly to the top of the tower when he felt the telepath gaining on him, grabbing the back of his heel, clinging to the Achilles of it all. He kicked her away, once, twice, but she was stronger than she looked, and apparently none of this magic had cost her much at all. She felt familiar to him in some way, like a sharp pain that he'd already lived through. Something about her felt distantly recognizable, like déjà vu, or like someone he'd met in a dream. He felt her fingers close around his calf, her body throwing him through the tower window, and he thought, Interesting. I'm pretty sure we've been here before.

She really was strong, or at least the version of her that took control on this astral plane was strong. She wrestled him onto his back, overpowering him easily, brutality on the brain, and delirious with pain, Gideon laughed. Was this it? Was this how the story ended, with a cautionary tale about calling his mom?

She had her hand on something. A sword hilt. Of course. The telepath was going to kill him—she knew how, he could tell her instincts for violence were draconian to the extreme—so now Nico's research was useless. Assuming Nico had any. Assuming he had not already forgotten Gideon was ever alive. *Gideon, you're my problem, you're mine,* that was easy for Nico to say. Too easy. Nico could feel fondly toward a gust of wind but not Gideon, who tended toward devotion. On the bright side, if Gideon died, Nico would be fine. Nico de Varona did not stay still for long.

"Gideon?" said the telepath, just as Gideon was mentally preparing to be over, to finally be done. He was relieved about it, maybe. Okay, so he would not get to say goodbye to Nico, but that was fine. At least if he did not exist, then Nico had no reason to run around doing dangerous things—said the dream walker who was currently busy being endangered, and for what? *Fun?*

God, he really was a dumb motherfuck.

"You're Gideon," the telepath said, releasing him and stepping away, and holy shit, she was absolutely beautiful. Was that part of the dream? Was this Death? Gideon had always wondered what Death would look like, should she exist, and now it was clear that she would look, you know, *like that.* Like the kind of thing you walked toward even when you did not remotely want to die. She was a beautiful, vengeful angel; a sweet and terrible release.

From the corner of his eye, though, Gideon caught sight of someone else. A boy. A man. Someone who looked like the kind of person whose nose Nico would enjoy breaking. Wait, the Prince! This was it! And Death, who was here for Gideon, was distracted. What luck! So much for not being a realist, he thought. Ha ha ha, Nicolás! I told you this would all pay off for me someday!

With the last reserves of his strength and the soggy dregs of his sanity, Gideon lunged for the ankle of the man, the Prince, and threw him over his own shoulder. The Prince was the taller man but too bad for him, Gideon was an optimist! He could do the impossible because he belieeeeeeeved! Behind him the telepath was swearing; she'd freed her sword from the scabbard now and was chasing them, but Gideon was quicker, impossibly quick. He took the Prince and dove out of the tower window, the ground rising fast to meet them, faster and faster and faster and—

Gideon woke with a gasp, sweating. His lungs strained with effort. The floor beneath him was dry.

"Holy fuck," said Max, who was naked as usual, looking down at Gideon from where he'd crouched beside him on the living room floor. "You haven't taken a breath in ages. I thought for sure you were dead."

"The Prince." Gideon sat up so quickly his head spun. "Did I get him out? Is it over?"

"You're awake." Max seemed to think Gideon was still dreaming. "Gideon, you're awake. You're in our apartment."

Their apartment. Right. The Mukherjee brothers were shouting downstairs. The Chihuahua was barking, someone outside was swearing. Home. He was home. He could almost taste the ropa vieja, the way it melted so tenderly on his tongue.

"Where's Nico?"

Max frowned, hesitating, and Gideon blinked.

"Wait. No. Sorry." Right. He was home. Nico was not.

Also, he was drooling. Whoops. Gideon wiped his chin. "Did it work?"

Max offered a sympathetic grimace. "I don't know."

"Oh. Okay." If he had finished the job, all would be well. Eilif would have her end of the deal, which meant he had no further obligations to her. If he *hadn't* managed it . . .

Gideon exhaled slowly, then closed his eyes. "Fuck, I'm tired."

To that, Max's smile was languid as usual.

"Cool," he said, flopping onto his back beside Gideon. "I could totally go for a nap."

VI

EGO

· NICO ·

H e was lying sleepless on his bed when he heard the knock at the door. He glanced at the clock, determining that it could not possibly be anything important, and promptly closed his eyes. "Go away, Tristan," he muttered.

Which was when he felt a sharp jab to his thoughts and a strange, intangible reflex that launched him to his feet. Like a tap against his knee or something, only it was his brain, and in response his entire body was strung tight like a bow.

"Holy balls," Nico said, opening his bedroom door to find Parisa waiting there. "I didn't even know you could *do* that—"

"Something just happened." She pushed past him, looking wild-eyed and frantic. She stumbled in her haste, which was unusual. Her dress was rumpled. One strap slipped down her shoulder. It occurred to Nico that he had never seen Parisa look anything less than perfectly composed.

"Are you okay?" he asked her, watching her pace in front of his fireplace. Gradually, the various elements of her appearance were beginning to compile into something more worrisome. Her hair looked oddly frizzy. There was a sheen of sweat on her dress, stained rings of condensation below her underarms. Her skin had a greenish tint, like she'd just gotten over a fever.

He was unfortunately still very attracted to her, which did not help.

"Your friend Gideon." Parisa paused to glare at Nico. "You didn't tell me he was such a powerful medeian."

It took Nico a moment to understand the implications of what she'd just said.

"You . . . saw Gideon?" he asked, bewildered. Or furious. Or deeply lethargic. Or in some kind of horrifying, indigestion-related pain.

"I thought you were worried about him." She paused her pacing to glare at Nico. "You're *always* worried about him. I thought he was some kind of invalid, for fuck's sake!"

"I don't understand what's happening right now," said Nico, and Parisa took off her shoes with a grumble in his direction, muttering under her breath in French about how he was a hopeless idiot. "Hey," Nico said. "That's a little uncalled for. It's true," he conceded with an inward sigh. "But still, I reserve the right to not hear about it in my own room. Or whatever."

"I've been here too long," Parisa snapped. "I've started to—" She paused to give Nico the most contemptuous glare that he had ever personally received from anyone, and perhaps the most contemptuous glare in the history of the world. "*Care*," she muttered.

"About . . . Gideon?" Nico could not imagine for the life of him how that could be a thing, and yet it seemed very much to be a thing. Parisa looked oddly small in front of his fireplace, which Nico couldn't help but notice. Unhelpfully. He'd always thought of her as sort of a larger-than-life kind of person, as likely to punch him in the face as any man he'd ever met.

"Yes. No. I don't know." She glared at Nico again for good measure, and it occurred to him—belatedly—that he should probably ask more questions.

"I'm sorry, are you trying to tell me that something's wrong with Gideon?" The prospect of harm befalling Gideon had crossed Nico's mind more times in recent weeks than he cared to admit. He'd rationalized it, choosing self-righteous annoyance over potential hysteria, but now, something in Nico's internal circuitry froze up with panic.

Was it possible that Gideon's silence meant he was—?

"No." Parisa scoffed. "The opposite. He's perfectly fine."

"Oh." Well, in that case, Nico strongly wasn't. "So then what's the problem?"

"Nothing. There's no problem." A valiant effort at indifference, though her appearance suggested otherwise. "I thought . . ."

She trailed off, and Nico arched a brow. "Yes?"

"Nothing." She turned away, frustrated, and Nico, who did not know what to do with his hands or his face or any of the rest of his limbs, sat down on the edge of his bed, waiting.

Parisa did not elaborate. With Gideon being unharmed (albeit potentially a bit of a fuckhead), Parisa's agitation became Nico's more immediate concern.

"Are you okay?" Nico asked her. "You look . . . shaken," he realized, determining the pulse of her stride in the room and then wondering, immediately, what someone else must have done to her. "Was it Callum? Dalton?"

"No. It was you." The look she gave him was venomous. "I nearly killed him. I was going to. I nearly did, and then—"

Her mouth tightened.

"What is he like?" she asked. "Gideon."

"A menace," Nico said instantly. "The best person you can imagine," he explained to the deepening furrow of her brow. "Which is exactly as bad as it sounds."

"Of course it is." She let out a sigh, then turned to fall backward, aligning herself beside him on the mattress. "You," she said witheringly, turning her head to look at him. "Something's wrong with you."

"Only the usual," Nico replied. He angled himself to look at her so that they were on equal latitudes.

"No, you're deteriorating," Parisa said, looking up to the ceiling instead. "Something's draining you."

"Nah." Yes. Definitely. He'd been having aches and pains everywhere. Tiny things. Normal things. The things that happened to other people as they aged or as they coped with stress. Things that did not happen to physical medeians of the highest caliber, which he was supposed to be. Things that had come easily for so long were no longer like blinking an eye. It was nothing to complain about, having to think about things before he did them—a second's delay, or a moment's—but it still felt like his body was not entirely his own. "I'm fine."

"Do you miss her?" Parisa asked quietly.

They didn't have to say her name aloud.

"Sometimes." He missed Libby Rhodes the way he would miss having electricity. Or his left hand. He did not know how to function without her.

"And you miss him," Parisa observed.

Again, no names. Which meant Parisa probably already knew that Nico missed Gideon like he would miss his conscience, or his ability to slip a punch. He did not know who he was when Gideon was gone.

"It's funny," Nico said. "This library. Everything we can have."

"Yes," said Parisa.

"It's everything until it's nothing," Nico said. By which he meant: Why had he given everything up when he could have stayed in one place and never known how much he didn't know?

"Yes," said Parisa again.

Nico turned on his side, curling up to face her. She mirrored him, the two of them staring at each other on his bed.

He had never been this close to her before. Their knees were touching. He had always had the feeling that she preferred him to keep his distance, and so he had. It was only now that he felt some kind of door had opened. Like Parisa Kamali had let down her walls in exchange for a moment of peace.

One of her long hairs tickled his forehead and he turned, scratching his head on the duvet before meeting her eye again.

She gave him a look as if she understood something stupid was coming. "What's wrong?"

What did he have to lose? "I kind of thought you'd smell like roses," he admitted, and to his surprise, she laughed, genuinely. It was surprisingly girlish and kind of sweet. Melodic in a way.

"What do I actually smell like?"

"Um." He sniffed her until she batted him away. "Sweat?"

"Stop."

"And, like . . . jasmine?"

"My shampoo." She made a face. "Don't tell anyone, but it's a Nova brand."

"I'm telling *everyone*," said Nico instantly. "I'm drafting a memo to the house as we speak."

"You're a child." She sighed.

"I'm not." He inched closer to her on the bed. Their knees knocked. "In case you were wondering."

"Oh, Nicolás." He took it as a win that she at least didn't laugh at that. "We've discussed this."

"I know. But I thought I'd bring it up to the top of your inbox, in case you were saving it for your quarterly review." He glanced down, eyeing her fingers. They were long and bare and still.

"Are you really married?" he asked, remembering what Callum had said when he and Parisa had done their little waltz of emotional trauma.

"Yes." She shrugged. "Not in any way that counts."

"Legally?"

"Okay, so one way that counts." She tucked her hands away, using them to prop up her head. He did the same. "But let's not talk about that."

If she wanted to stay, that was motivation enough for him to stop asking questions.

"Nicolás," she murmured warningly.

He sighed. "Sorry. Forgot you were in my head."

"You're the only one who ever does."

"Oh." Well, that was disappointing. He supposed it was a miracle he hadn't ended up murdered.

"No, it's cute." She smiled at him thinly. "You're cute."

He felt acutely, brutally injured. "Am I?"

"Yes."

He inched closer again. Perhaps two inches. "*How* cute, exactly?"

She nudged him back again.

"I know what I'm doing," she reminded him. Cautioning him, perhaps.

"Good. I would be happy to learn," he blithely replied.

She sighed. "You're much too troubled."

"Parisa." He lifted his head with one hand. "I don't need to read your mind to know you only came here tonight because something went terribly wrong."

"Ah yes, cute *and* clever. My downfall." She let her eyes flutter shut. "I'm fine."

"*Are* you?"

"Yes. But I—" She stopped. "I think perhaps I'm developing a weakness."

He hoped so.

"Stop," she said again.

"What? Can't I live aspirationally?"

"Some people can. But not you." She opened one eye and squinted at him. A very unsexy thing, and yet he was sure he'd never seen anything more sensual. "Tell me something vulnerable," she said, "so I can recall my usual repulsions."

"I'm not that close to my father," Nico told her cheerfully. "My mother signs my birthday cards from both of them."

"Oh, revolting. Tell me more about your mother," Parisa said at once.

"She's extremely particular. Always has things removed when we go to restaurants. I think it's a game for her. She always wants something changed just so she can establish her dominance over dinner."

"Terrible. Anything else?"

"She taught me to cook. And to dance."

"And to fight?"

"No, that was my uncle. I was small," he explained. "For my age. I had bullies."

"No," whispered Parisa. "Really?"

"I don't know. I don't remember them."

Her eyes had closed again. Her smile quirked. "Good for you."

"That's what Gideon says." His name slipped out unbidden. "He says my number one quality is my attention span and I should never let anyone tell me otherwise."

"He's right." Parisa seemed to be holding her breath, so Nico continued.

"I came here for him. To figure things out for him, to help him. But since I've been here—" He inhaled slowly, then exhaled. "I tried. But the library has nothing. It doesn't have answers for me. And there are so many other questions I have, so many things I want to know. The universe, it's so big—so massive—and somehow, studying it is also *for* Gideon in a way, because a universe this vast, it can't make mistakes." He swallowed. "It doesn't make mistakes. Gideon can't be some kind of statistical accident or some genetic roll of the dice. He can't be—he *isn't*—a mistake."

Parisa said nothing.

"If I'm being honest, I've been selfish," he said, clearing his throat. "Because I've been thinking . . . I've been thinking about this power. This, everything I am. If I'm being *really* honest, I want to use it. If Gideon is not a mistake and I am not a mistake, then there is a reason for this, a purpose. Why do I exist? Is it the same reason goldfish exist? Is it purely to be part of an ecosystem, to exist relative to everything else in nature, or is it . . . could it be something else?" He hesitated, then continued, "Because if I, if something I have—if that can make life. If it can make universes." Another pause. "If that is something I can do, then *should* I . . . ? I mean, do I have some kind of obligation t—"

"He thought of you," Parisa said softly. "Gideon. When he was dying. He thought of you."

"Oh," said Nico, exhaling.

He only realized he was staring blankly over Parisa's head when he saw her eyes float slowly open, landing gently on his face.

She touched a finger to his temple and he breathed out again, emptying. Weightless.

Charged.

He felt her lifting her head from the mattress, moving closer. He was embarrassingly willing, readily shifting onto his back to angle her hips above his own. Her hair fell around her shoulders like a curtain, dark ends lightly brushing his chest. He took one lock and curled it gently around his finger.

He was aware that his heart was thudding madly in his chest. It was something, the effect of her, the crush of everything that landed on him like a weight. The emptiness of this life, the way he had tried so hard to fill it with something, anything. Books. Power. *Just leave,* he had told himself so many times, *just leave,* but he couldn't. He knew he never would.

I have a theory, he wanted to say to her. A theory that we can open doors to other worlds, that we can make them. That we can open crevices in time and space. I think that I was given these gifts as a tool, that I was taught to wonder for a reason. I befriended a dreamer so that I, with all of my power, could dream for myself.

Instead he lifted his head recklessly to meet her kiss. She lowered her chin and kissed him back, and in that moment, he did not long for anything chemical or animal. He understood now what she had meant, that he would fuck her with his whole heart. Because it was sweetness and it was goodness and it was enough. This, whatever it was, was enough.

She pulled back and he stopped her with his fingers in her hair. "Am I making it unbearable for you?" he asked, a little bit of shame bleeding into his voice.

She stared at him for a long moment.

Several moments.

"No, actually," she said, and kissed him again.

Unsurprisingly, there was a sensuality to Parisa's kiss that Nico found intoxicating in the drowsiest sense. His fingertips trailed the risen hem of her dress slowly—lazily, as if he had nothing to do in that moment except account for every inch of her skin. Consciously, he cleared his mind of everything but the slow motion of her hips, the drip of fabric along the inside of his knee. He had always admired Parisa's use of textiles, the silk that met the valley of her waist. He traced a finger up the lining of her thigh, pressed his thumb into the dimples of her lower back, tilted his head back with a groan when she drew his mouth up with one hand. Beneath them the floor vibrated seismically, a low rumble to match the sound of pleasure from his throat.

His right hand found her left. A tangle of fingers, a pulse of pressure. She nipped at the base of his jaw and he *growled*, like, actually *growled*, and rolled his hips below hers, fitting them together on a deliberate, decadent tide. He didn't know how long they stayed like that, hands clasped, ebbing and flowing, neither making the choice to escalate but neither retreating, either. It was well and truly physical, and for the first time in months, Nico wasn't thinking of anything at all. He could feel something from her, something like an echo in himself, like their motions were in fluent conversation. A reflective desperation, or something quieter, still profound but more enduring. Like maybe he could ask her something silly and trifling, like if she'd ever looked at the moon and felt empty or if she knew how it felt to set foot in a country with a language she didn't speak, and she wouldn't have to tell him the answer, because he would just know it. He would just know.

His free hand wound up to the nape of her neck, gathering her hair and pulling her back for another kiss, another. Again. Again. Deeper, closer, more. His eyes were closed and her skin was warm, molten. Soporific. He sighed in her mouth, relinquishing each breath. He felt the bed give way beneath him, swallowing him up, cavernous with acquiescence while he mumbled things, embarrassing things, all inadvisable softness and forthcoming despair. *Querida mía. Quédate conmigo.* Stay, stay awhile with me.

The kisses got slower. Sweeter. Like the trickle of golden honey, slow drips of summer sun. Yes, yes, there. He had yet to release her hand. She was nothing like he had imagined—nothing that was *possible* to imagine—she was more like a dream. It crushed his chest with yearning, the stupor of infatuation, the idleness and opulence of a memory that had never existed. The velvet softness of her. He missed her already, like she was already gone.

He wondered what she saw inside his head. If it was empty, no thoughts, or if he was actually full of sensations. Bliss seemed like it probably took up space. He imagined the moment stretching out like bubble gum, like being carried away on a cloud. He felt boneless, legless beneath her, anchored safely by the grasp of her fingers in his.

The truth was it was taking something from him, this house. This ecosystem. This network of answers that only spawned more questions. The mysterious pattern repetition evaded him, as did all of those who had existed here before. He could feel himself becoming part of it, slowly, no longer able to tell the difference between which thoughts were his and which were the thoughts of the house. He used to be able to account for every spare atom of himself but now, now it was impossible to identify his edges, to find the places where the library's power swapped in for his, where his hunger ended and the archives began. There were bites taken out of him somewhere, he felt more human and less, so at least there was this. Touch. Taste. Pleasure. Something that could not be robbed from him. Something he could neither willingly nor unwillingly give up. From somewhere in his mind's periphery he caught the vestiges of a very Rhodesian sigh—*Varona, honestly,* like the proverbial chord that David played to annoy the Lord.

Yeah, he thought with an inward laugh, a hiccup of relief. Yeah, Rhodes, I know.

His words felt slurred, his eyelids heavy, his body gradually relaxing. His calves sinking into the mattress, his hips, his shoulders, his back. He pulled Parisa in tighter, closer, shuddering at the pleasantness of it all until it felt like she had merged with him, falling in deeper with him. Oh fuck, he thought belatedly, this was what she meant, my heart, my heart, the thud of it, the pulse, so rhythmic and calming and sure. The way it beat so familiarly. The ground shook and he thought, Cast me away. Go on, take me up.

When he looked around, he understood where he was. The light from the window, golden hour in a galley kitchen, coffee with cream, the old sense of safety. There was a glint from on high, sun from the corner of his eye, like a wave of sandy hair.

"Gideon," Nico said, and the light bent, and his heart went rapturous.

"No."

He felt Parisa's voice before he saw her. She was less panicked now. Probably because it was a dream. "Sorry," she said, leaning against the wall of Nico's apartment. "But I thought you could use the rest."

"Oh." He blinked. "Does that mean I—?"

"Fell asleep? Yes. You're welcome." She smirked at him. "But don't worry, I enjoyed it while it lasted."

It occurred to him, not for the first time, that things that seemed too good to be true very often were. "Was any of it real?"

"Who's to say what is and isn't real?" She shrugged.

Nico felt the odd sensation that he should thank her. Or possibly marry her.

She rolled her eyes. "Don't get carried away, Nicolás," she said, turning away. "Enjoy your convalescence."

It was only when she turned away that he realized it must have been real—had to have been. The important parts, anyway. There had been communion between them, something genuine and unmissable and shared. Not like a meal or a secret; more like the way grief is shared.

And it *was* grief. It was loss, though untraditional. The surrender of a future self, like parting from a lover he'd never get the chance to meet. Nico knew he was swallowed up by some enormity—knew he was trading more and more of his strength for the chance to finally know whatever there was to know—but with each passing day, he was surer and surer. There was no ceiling to his power or his misery. His emptiness marked him in a way she must have had more than just the fluency to read.

"Wait." He shot forward to catch Parisa's hand. "Don't you want to stay here with me?"

She seemed surprised. Or suspicious. Both looked equally good on her, so there was really no way to know. "What?"

"Well, since you tricked me into sleeping," he explained. "And you weren't in the best shape either, as I recall." She must have noticed that, having rearranged herself on this plane, or in his head, or whatever she was doing. Her dress was once again immaculate, her hair so polished it shone. "Though, I have to say, I thought I would remember things better," Nico commented, glancing around the apartment. "This plane really changes things, doesn't it?"

She watched him for a second in silence. "Like what?"

"Oh, just. I don't know. Things." He suddenly felt nostalgia for the creaky corner cabinet. A sharp, painful longing for the claw marks on the floor. All the things they would not be getting their security deposit back for. "It's just not quite right, that's all. I thought things would have been better in my head."

Parisa inhaled as if to speak, then stopped.

Then she said, "I told you to get a talisman."

"What? Why?"

Now she looked irritated. "Because you should know that we're not in your head."

"What?" Just when he had gotten used to the idea, too. "So where are we?"

Her mouth tightened. "Try not to get emotional about this."

He frowned. "What?"

"Just . . ." She exhaled impatiently. "We're in mine. My head."

"Your head." He parroted it back without much comprehension.

"Yes. Yours was . . ." She looked away. "It just seemed like you needed a break."

"Parisa Kamali." Nico wanted to gape at her. He wanted, actually, to laugh, though he sensed that that would be far worse, because the idea that she had let him into *her* head was closer to intimacy for a telepath than sex could ever be. "And here you told *me* not to fuck you with my whole heart—"

"That's enough. Enjoy your rest." She glared at him, but it wasn't so effective now. It wasn't effective at all, in fact.

"Why?" he asked. "And you might as well tell me," he added, "because if you don't, I'll just assume it's because you're a *nice person,* which I'm guessing is bad for the brand—"

"I was feeling philanthropic," she said. "And now you're annoying me, so lesson learned. Rhodes was right to hate you."

"Ah, see, you're bringing her up now to spite me, but it won't work," Nico said gleefully. "She and I despise each other, as you know."

"Yes. Of course. You have such a capacity for loathing." Parisa fixed him with a knowing glance. "Is there any limit to how many people you can '*hate*'?"

"Nope," said Nico.

She rolled her eyes at him. "Go to sleep," she said. "I'll be gone when you wake up."

"And yet the memory of this night will live on, Your Royal Softness," replied Nico.

Which he supposed he should not have done, because when he finally did awake—after close to ten hours, his body sluggish and restored—it was to find his favorite sweater stolen, a note left in its place.

Good cashmere can be so hard to find.

It would be a cold winter now. Oddly, Nico wasn't that fussed. He felt better than he had in a long time—which was why he pulled out his phone, suddenly overcome with the courage he'd so long been lacking.

I'm the dumbest boy in school, he typed.

Gideon's response was instant.

Can't argue with that, he said.

And then another buzz:

I've been away too long, Nicky.

I just have one more stop, and then I'll see you very soon.

R hodes is right," said the shorter postdoc, Farringer. He was ges-
ticulating wildly in a way that wasn't quite Nicoesque; more like
something Nico would imitate with stunning accuracy after class
to the delight of all their peers (minus Libby). "Quantum gravity makes
more sense, and—"

"Of course Rhodes is right," said the taller one, Mortimer. "But that's not
the point at issue."

"Then what *is* your point, Mort, because if you're going to go on like this
every time we raise the question of dynamic backgrounds and relativity—"

So this was what life would have been like without Nico de Varona, Libby
thought idly. If she had been the sole talented physicist at NYUMA, people
would just *agree* with her. They would say things like *of course* Rhodes is
right. And of course she was! She had always *been* right. The difference was
that she said things correctly without a set of dimples. Or with a pair of ova-
ries. Who could say, at this point.

She stifled a yawn, suddenly feeling the classroom was quite hot. It was
one of the basement labs where the physical doctoral specialists were essentially banished, and more was the pity for it, honestly. LARCMA was housed
in one of the most beautiful buildings that Libby had ever seen. From the
outside it was a brick-laden office building, perhaps Victorian in origin, and
the moment she'd first walked up to it she'd expected nothing but industrial
workspaces inside. She was partially correct, but also not even remotely. The
inside of the building featured exquisite wrought-iron stairways and original
wood floors, hollowed out as if hand-carved around the central courtyard.
The central atrium was glass, beautifully open to the night sky (at the time
she'd first seen it, of course), and featured a flawless mix of Mexican tile
and Italianate marble. Smooth reds blended with the industrial brick, and
several birdcage-shaped glass elevators were in constant motion against the
ever-changing shadows throughout the day.

When Libby had arrived in the middle of the night, she had been greeted
by the postdocs who had been observing the night sky through one of the
first medeian telescopes. She had been lucky, then, to spend her first twelve

hours at LARCMA beneath its incomparable skylights, observing the students like flakes in a snow globe down below.

It was a wonder to behold, but because medeian curricula had been around for only a handful of decades, the upper floors with their high ceilings and decorative landings were reserved for undergraduates with flashier specialties: illusionists who would contribute to the mortal economy, naturalists who would assist in the climate engineering that would eventually form the basis of Libby's version of the world. All the nights since her arrival had been relegated down to the labs, where Alan Farringer and Maxwell T. Mortimer (Fare and Mort to their grad students, the seven or so physical specialists who had carried on beyond their undergraduate degree) conducted research, wrote papers, and taught the occasional (*very* occasional, given so few students) class.

Unsurprisingly, Libby had been an oddity when she'd shown up. Not knowing how to explain herself—after all, how does one say things like "I'm from the future" when one already looks like an unstable vagrant?—she merely introduced herself as Elizabeth Rhodes, physicist and recent graduate of NYUMA, and allowed them to fill in the blanks from there. Evidently (and she wasn't proud of this, but it was what it was) things were hard enough for medeians that they did not probe into the state of her appearance. They simply saw a scholar in need and leapt to welcome her to their ranks, particularly after they saw what she could do for their research on gravitational fields. Until her, they said, everything had been merely philosophical. ("And to think you were in New York the whole time," marveled Mort, looking more annoyed than concerned at his oversight.)

For months now she'd been a fellow compatriot, hoping that in making herself useful to the team of postdocs, she might persuade them to do her a favor. For example: figure out a very impossible solution to the whole "being trapped in the wrong time" thing. Even if one considered space-time a simple fourth dimension that could be traveled at will—already a significant if—there was nothing beyond the theoretical to explain the science of getting from one point to another. In 1989 there was no research remotely close to what she had studied at NYUMA, much less the Society's archives. As far as anyone here knew, the Second Law of Thermodynamics—essentially, entropy, which made certain processes irreversible—prevented the possibility of traveling through time. Which was easy for them to say, because they, unlike her, had never actually seen a wormhole, and they, unlike her, did not possess approximately half (more or less) the energy it took to create one.

So, what were her options? Subject half the country to generations of nuclear fallout? Try to get recruited by the Society all over again? Or even if she did, what could she accomplish without Nico—who was, for better or worse (worse, definitely worse), her necessary other half?

Ugh, that smug bastard. She hoped he couldn't hear that particular thought from wherever he was, which she assumed was somewhere idyllic. Because of course he would be somewhere nice. He was Nico. He would never accidentally date someone who would trap him elsewhere in time.

Libby sighed loudly, a Varona-related reflex, and Fare—who had lately taken to wearing a boxy sport coat with his preppy salmon slacks to make him look more professional, a highly optimistic thought—looked up from what he was scribbling on the—and here, another sigh—overhead projector. "What, Liz? Problem?"

Liz. She hadn't bothered to correct that. She was mostly Rhodes, because there were no other female postdocs, but every now and then one of the others decided to be . . . *familiar.* The kind of familiar that people got when they expected to have to work together for a significant period of time. Which Libby shouldn't have minded, really, because they were nice, and they were trying very hard to include her in their limited social circles. She didn't mind them that much at all, except that they were also . . . you know. Thirty years behind all the relevant research in quantum theory, which was not something she felt she could bring up. Much like the subject of Fare's new loafers.

"No, no problem," she said, stifling a yawn. "Keep going. You were saying about dynamic backgrounds?" God, she missed Tristan. (Not because of *Tristan,* of course. Although she felt a certain nostalgia for his well-cut slacks.) The point was she missed working with someone who could see the things she couldn't. As it turned out, being the smartest person in the room was honestly kind of dull.

"Actually, we were discussing paradoxes," said Mort gently. The kind of gentle correction that suggested to Libby that he would very generously take her out for dinner, engage in some affectionate necking, and then saddle her with the task of raising his three obstinate children while he did Very Important Things at work. "It's apparently a subject of discussion over the state line."

"State line?" Libby echoed, wondering what Oregon (or Nevada) had to do with it.

"You know, over at the Wessex testing site," Fare explained, which Libby knew nothing about, other than the fact that apparently the other two coveted the chance to work there. She supposed the possibility of privatized research would be an academic's dream in any era of dismal university funding.

"What's your take on MWI?" Mort pressed her.

It took her a moment. "Many-worlds, you mean?"

"Yes, many-worlds interpretation. Do you think it has any value?" asked Mort, with the air of wanting to correct her the moment she produced a response.

"I don't like it," Fare helpfully cut in. "I think it's absurd. It gives us no answers."

"What kind of answers are you looking for?" asked an indignant Mort.

Vaguely, Libby decided they reminded her of something.

"Well, if *every* possibility is real, then doesn't that rob us of some kind of . . . of . . ." Fare was flustered, which was never a good sign. It meant Mort would become sure he was winning, which would lead to him becoming doubly insufferable. "Well, of some *exceptionalism,* don't you think? So then I never *make* choices," Fare argued, "I just . . . *am* one of an infinite collection of random outcomes?"

Not necessarily infinite, Libby thought. And then, oh.

Bert and Ernie. That was it.

"So? Isn't one of infinite random options preferable to predestination?" They were off and running, Libby once again unable to prevent a yawn. "At least you're autonomous in the moment you make the choice, are you not?"

"It's *just as bad,* Mort! All that says is that if fate doesn't trap you, the multiverse will—"

"Libby. Libby? Are you . . . Can you hear me?"

Libby looked down to find that Gideon was there again, and also that she was flying. Oh, rats, she thought. Evidently she had fallen asleep.

"Isn't it weird that I keep dreaming about you?" she mused to Gideon. "Not that I wouldn't like to see you, of course, but still. I don't know that it makes a lot of sense."

"Yeah, so, you're not technically dreaming *about* me," Gideon said hesitantly, and then appeared to toss the details aside. "Never mind. The point is I want to talk to you about how you're going to get back."

"Back down?" asked Libby, glancing below her at the ground, which was hidden well below several layers of cloud cover.

"No, I mean . . . *back.* To, you know." He hesitated again. "Your actual time?"

"Oh." This was quite a lucid dream Libby was having. Normally in dreams she wasn't so aware of things like being trapped in time. "Well, it's pretty near impossible to do it without the Society." By which she meant Nico, but would die before saying aloud.

"Is it?" Gideon asked. Libby realized that he had grown wings to keep up with her, but she did not herself have any. Was she flying if all she was doing was levitating? She had the faintest sensation that she had done this once. Her sister was there. Why was Katherine never in her dreams? Libby was only ever chasing the ghost of her, awake and asleep.

"The thing is," Gideon said, "I think if you could just find a sufficient power source . . ." He dodged something that seemed to be a calculus textbook and temporarily dropped out of sight. "I mean," he continued, struggling to reach her again, "all you need is the right amount of energy to allow you to travel between points of time."

"That's impossible," said Libby glumly.

"It's not, though," Gideon pointed out. "Because you are currently in the past."

"Well. That's an anomaly." She sighed. "And anyway, there's no energy source I can find that's powerful enough to manage it. Except—" Well, except Reina. Or rather, the combination of Libby herself *with* Reina and Nico. And whatever Ezra could apparently do. And maybe whatever Tristan could do, too, if he had even come close to figuring that out yet. And, like, a nuclear bomb. "The point is I—"

"Don't know how," Gideon finished for her, and then nodded very seriously. "Okay. Yeah, okay. Good talk."

"What?" She frowned at him, realizing his wings were now a parachute. "But wait, Gideon, I—"

Then something fell, and Libby snorted herself awake to find that she was back in the basement classroom, and had accidentally knocked her bottle of water off the desk. "Oh god, sorry—"

"Are we boring you, Liz?" drawled Fare, half seriously. He seemed to have taken the negging approach to achieving Mort's whole raising-his-three-children thing.

"Sorry, I just—" She blinked. Blinked again. The fog of sleep was clearing, but not the thought that was apparently sitting fully formed in her head. "On the subject of theoretical physics." Or whatever it was they'd been discussing, which was not in itself uninteresting—except to someone who had already met the five most powerful medeians she'd ever known. "Do you two have any idea what kind of energy source would be enough to create a wormhole through time?"

"What?"

Fare and Mort exchanged a glance, with Mort tacitly deciding to be the voice of reason. "There's no proof wormholes even exist, first of all—"

There was proof, actually. In a manor house thirty years into the future. Being used by a hyperactive Cuban with a prediabetic dependence on snacks.

"—and even if there was any way to prove it, what kind of energy source would that be?" Mort continued. "The equivalent of a nuclear bomb, if I had to guess—"

"Or a ley line," suggested someone near Libby's feet.

Libby jumped, not realizing that someone had very helpfully been cleaning up the spill she'd left unattended on the floor. "Oh my god," she said, scrambling to help, "I'm *so* sorry—"

"Not your fault," said the girl cheerily, waving Libby away. She was one of Mort's undergraduate students, if Libby recalled correctly. She had tawny skin and a cherubic face, nearly all cheek. Libby had guessed her to be Hispanic before listening to the girl speak to someone in something Libby was pretty sure was Tagalog, based only on her limited experience with a Filipino neighbor in her dorm at NYUMA. If not for the bits of Spanglish and culinary references mixed in, Libby might not have recognized it at all.

"Belen," said the girl, reading Libby's mind and helpfully providing her name. She wore a soft pink cardigan that looked more baby blanket than clothing item, and it seemed noticeably misplaced. Like she might have swapped it for leather the moment she left school grounds. "Sorry, I didn't mean to eavesdrop—"

Libby waved away her concern, reaching for the bottle she had dropped. "No, no, that's—"

"Ley lines are nonsense," interrupted Mort, who had a tendency to reveal his true personality when speaking to someone he considered beneath him. "Sacred geometry is a conspiracy theory at best."

"Only because nobody in academia studies them," Belen said. "And they're called dragon lines in China. They've been called that for centuries," Belen added to Libby, apparently choosing (quite wisely) to ignore her professor's derogatory tone. "There's a big one in Indonesia. And there are sacred places everywhere, really. My mother always said Mount Pulag was one."

Libby recalled that Reina had once read an enormous tome about creature magic. Secondary magic systems existed in the archives, which was plenty good enough for her. "I always thought of ley lines as more of a Stonehenge thing," remarked Libby, toying thoughtfully with the fallen bottle.

"It was just an idea," qualified the girl, Belen, quickly. "But I figured hey, if wormholes don't exist, cool. Ley lines don't either." She flashed Mort an irreverent sort of smile that reminded Libby of Parisa. Not in the seductive way, but in the way that Parisa occasionally permitted when she was being exceptionally clever and underhanded. "But anyway, I'll let you carry on, Professor Mortimer. I was just dropping off my take-home exam."

"A day late, Miss Jiménez," tutted Mort, as if he were a distinguished academic in his fifties rather than a twenty-something on a high horse.

"Yes," said Belen. "I had to work, I'm sorry—"

"Miss Jiménez," warned Mort, "this is not the first time—"

"That I've had to work? No, it's not, and sadly for both of us, it's unlikely to be the last, Professor." Belen's smile was plastered beatifically on her face. "I'm afraid my grandmother is in hospice back home in Luzon. My mother is her sole caregiver, and I—"

"If you are not prepared to take your studies seriously, Miss Jiménez, then I have to wonder what it is you're doing here," said Mort. "Perhaps the scholarship afforded to you by the college could be better apportioned elsewhere."

There was a flash of something in Belen's eyes. Not that Mort could see it, because Mort was unaccustomed to noticing flashes of things in women's eyes that weren't adoration (or at least what he perceived to be adoration). But he had levied a threat and Belen had responded to it, however fleetingly. Libby clocked a sudden chill in the air that was gone as quickly as it arrived.

"My apologies, Professor." Belen forced a placid smile. "I'll do my best to make sure it doesn't happen again."

Mort arched a brow. "Better do better than that, Miss Jiménez."

Belen slid a wary glance to Libby that made Libby suddenly aware of her position in the room. Specifically, her position of complicity. To Belen, or to any student at LARCMA, Libby was indistinguishable from the other doctoral students or postdocs. She was, after all, exclusively seen in the company of the faculty that she had expected to be furthest along in the relevant medeian research.

But Libby was wrong—and she was not, like the other two, a bully. Belen had turned loftily away, not quite respectfully enough for Mort's taste, and was already out the door by the time Libby finally realized she had cast her lot with the wrong crowd.

"Hold this," she said, thrusting the discarded water bottle into Fare's hands.

"Rhodes—?" came the distant call of bewilderment behind her, but Libby had already hurried out the door after Belen, speeding around the corner so sightlessly she collided with someone approaching from the other side.

"Sorry, I—" The words left her in a gasp, her heart leaping as she clocked the head of messy black hair, the familiar leanness. "I was," she began, and swallowed. Her racing pulse reached a perilous spike and then, after a moment's recognition, slowed.

"Yes?" asked the stranger. Thank god, a stranger. Just some other teenager with Ezra's hair, his height.

Libby shook herself. "Sorry, never mind, I was—Miss Jiménez!"

She spotted Belen as she was about to step into the basement elevator, pausing at the sound of her name. Libby shook herself of the not-Ezra undergraduate as politely as she could, then jogged after a waiting Belen, who stood holding the door to the birdcage elevator.

"Going up?" asked Belen.

"Sure," Libby said, because why not? She wasn't sure how else to broach the conversation of *Oh, sorry about the men, any further thoughts about enormous unprecedented energy sources? Just curious.* "Are you headed to class?"

"No, I've got a break for lunch." Belen hit the main floor. She glanced over Libby quickly, hopefully finding nothing too suspicious in Libby's secondhand jeans and oversized LARCMA crewneck she'd snagged from the lost and found. "You?"

"Ground floor too, please. And same." The elevator began going up, the courtyard-facing glass emerging from the basement floors to overlook the herds of students going by.

For a moment, they rode in silence, Libby contemplating what to say. They both directed their attention outward, orienting to the crowds coming into view as they rose.

There was one head in particular weaving through the flock at a slower pace than the others. More leisurely. In the wrong direction. A head of black hair, riotous. But it wasn't, Libby told herself with a heavy swallow. Of course it wasn't.

(And it wasn't. Plenty of young messy-haired men at LARCMA. Significantly fewer women, which was entirely the point of getting in this particular elevator.)

"You look like you've seen a ghost," commented Belen in her chipper sort of way, and Libby blinked.

"Hm? Oh, yes. Sorry." No point bringing up Ezra, much less anything else. Libby glanced at her, realizing Belen must have been a little older than she first thought. She had a sort of world-weariness beneath the youthfulness of her face. A prettiness, too, that Libby envied more the longer she looked. Belen had long lashes that complemented a set of arresting dark eyes. "I wondered if we could have coffee or something. Unless you have plans?"

"No, coffee sounds great." Belen sounded surprised, but pleased. The elevator reached the ground floor and Belen gestured Libby out first, in apparent deference. Odd, Libby thought with suppressed amusement. She'd been a big fish in a huge pond at NYUMA, then whatever she was at the Society. Now it appeared she was in a position of authority—at least for Belen.

"You're an undergraduate, aren't you?" Libby asked.

"A sophomore," said Belen, "though I'm a bit older than the others in my class."

"Are you?" Libby wondered if they were the same age. By the looks of it, probably close to it.

"I was supposed to study in Manila," Belen explained, removing her cardigan. "I had planned to. There's a new medeian university opening there, though they were still acquiring faculty by the time I was eligible to go. But then there was a program for me to be able to study here on a student visa . . ." She trailed off, perhaps anticipating Libby's boredom. "It just made more sense to come here instead. And besides, Lola insisted." Belen shoved the cardigan carelessly under her arm, fiddling with the pierced holes in her ears, which were empty. Her black T-shirt—which Belen wore tucked into worn black jeans that emphasized her waist instead of just bizarrely framing her pubic area (as the jeans of the era tended to do)—had a faded logo on it. A band name Libby half remembered from her father's beloved record collection.

"What's your specialty?" Libby asked, and Belen laughed. It took a moment before she realized that Libby wasn't joking.

"Oh, sorry. I just thought—Never mind. I'm here as part of the nuclear program," Belen explained. "I'm a chemist, but they expedited my visa for the scholarship because I can also work with heat conversion. Fission, specifically, is what they want me focused on."

"Oh?" A narrow but critical specialty, which would be on the verge of ubiquity within a handful of years. Without it there would be no network of medeian transports, no medeian power plants. No global medeian economy at all. "But you're actually a chemist?"

Belen shrugged. "Ocean alkalinity enhancement was my original specialty. You know, binding." Binding bicarbonate ions in acidic ocean water to reduce global carbon emissions, she meant. Which was yet another thing that had been solved well before Libby was born. "Me and everyone else they've brought in from the third world," Belen added jokingly.

They stepped out the doors into the concrete wave of unseasonable heat of downtown Los Angeles, Belen continuing to talk as Libby listened. "It's a smart program, really. Very focused. And I'm guaranteed employment here after graduation, so it's really for the best. Assuming Professor Mortimer doesn't fail me first." Belen barked out a helpless laugh.

"I'm sure he won't," Libby offered reassuringly, though she was pretty sure that wasn't true. She knew Mort and Fare had an unspoken competition for who could set the most difficult exams. They took pride in their students' failures, which they interpreted to mean that their standards were high and not that they were insufficient educators.

"Well, there's plenty I could do back home as a chemist." Belen shrugged, as if this was an argument she had had with someone before. Presumably her grandmother. "Things will be disproportionately worse for us, anyway. And Indonesia, and Thailand, and Vietnam . . . you know, us silly island nations with our little earthquakes and storms." She gave Libby a fleeting look of nonchalance. "If it weren't for Lola, I really wouldn't have bothered coming here. But you know, the chance to study in the U.S.," she said, ending the sentence there as if that explained everything.

"Right," said Libby. They paused at the corner, Belen again allowing Libby to choose where they went. "Listen," Libby said, taking a left turn, "I have my own research, actually, about the possibility of enhancing existing energy sources. Something to create higher volumes of energy more efficiently." Something to help her tear open the universe and fall through it to land . . . somewhere else.

Somewhere very, very specific.

"Some alternative to fission, you mean?" guessed Belen, looking interested. More so than the simpering look of toleration she'd given Mort, anyway. "You mean like stellar energy? Or fusion?"

"Pure fusion would be ideal," acknowledged Libby carefully. "Albeit impossible."

Belen's brow knitted in thought. "I don't know about impossible. But there would be a cost to that much magic, so it would certainly be unethical. Not to mention expensive. Professor Mortimer was right about a nuclear bomb, and those aren't what I'd call safe to play with." She and Libby exchanged a grimace. "Though," Belen added, "I assume you already know there's some kind of Wessex Corp grant that the college has Professor Mortimer applying for—that's why I'm in his elective, even though my curriculum is government sponsored," Belen explained before Libby had a chance to respond to the reference to James Wessex, noted Society villain, for the second time that day. "I don't know what it's about, exactly, so I couldn't say if he's gotten far. I figure that sort of thing's way above my pay grade, and anyway, Mortimer hates me. Are you writing for a specific organization?" Belen asked tangentially.

"Oh—" Libby realized with a belated kick of guilt that Belen obviously thought her so-called research was funded and not just a matter of personal interest. Which made sense, since she probably thought (equally mistakenly) that Libby was a doctoral student or rising faculty member as well, instead of just a liar who occasionally taught sections of Physics 101. "It's more of . . ." Again, the struggle of explaining. "Well, an alternative power source like the ley lines you were talking about would be beneficial to supplementing geoengineering," Libby said half truthfully. "Some alternative to carbon emissions?"

"It certainly would," Belen agreed. "And it would be a nice change if that kind of research actually got funding." Belen glanced over at Libby, looking oddly appreciative. "I was starting to think no one was concerned anymore with preventative measures."

There seemed to be something darker implied. "Oh?" asked Libby carefully.

"Well, it's just . . . nobody cares if my grandma's house winds up underwater, right? So long as people here don't have to change their lifestyles." Again, Belen barked a gloomy laugh. "I mean, sure, alkalinity tech here is outdated enough that they'll pay for my schooling to work on something else, but it still hasn't trickled down to anyone in the *developing* world, so . . ." She paused mid-rant to glance over at Libby, cheeks suddenly flushing. "Sorry. I'm getting too antiestablishment too soon, aren't I? Sorry, Professor, carry on—"

"No, no, you're right." Perhaps more than anyone, Libby understood that medeian technology would remain prohibitively expensive for at least the next few decades. Biomancy advances that might have saved her sister (if such advances even existed) would not have been reasonably priced on the other side of the new millennium, either.

Even in Libby's world, magic was more expensive than the individual—*any* individual—could reasonably afford. Only the affluent had the resources to make "ethical" decisions, which was to say nothing of other countries, much less other social classes or secondary species. If Belen thought the state of carbon emissions in 1989 was a crisis, she was fortunate not to know how little would actually be done to change things in the future.

Things were stable in Libby's world. Thanks to a joint effort by medeians and lobbyists, most large corporations now contributed to efforts at decarbonization that Belen's specialty had once been necessary to perform. But preventative measures? Most natural disasters were still regarded as isolated crises, not the result of global systemic decline. The American medical system was still for-profit. The Wessex Corporation was still the primary distributor of medeian technology in the world. Magic had definitely fixed things in

Libby's lifetime, but it still wasn't free, nor was it free from politics. Nothing was created or destroyed without some money changing hands.

So perhaps this meeting was fortuitous. More than. Not to romanticize her situation, but Libby had a feeling the alliance she'd just stumbled upon was too fruitful to be entirely random. What, after all, were the odds?

"How about this one?" Libby said, realizing that Belen was still waiting for her to choose a café. She indicated the coffee shop down the block, adding, "And I don't suppose you have any interest in helping me with my research, do you?"

A glint of wayward black hair caught Libby's eye from the reflective storefront beside the café, and in the rush of blood that followed, she didn't catch Belen's answer. She clocked the tones of enthusiasm, but found herself swallowing through another unexpected spike of adrenaline, a moment's panic washing her throat dry with fear.

"—happy to," finished Belen, who paused again to let Libby take the lead.

It was nothing, Libby reminded herself, stepping aside to let a wave of strangers pass. Not Ezra.

(Not this time.)

(Not yet.)

"Great," Libby managed, doing her best to slow her pulse as she reached for the café door, holding it open for the both of them. The face she'd seen, if she'd even seen it to begin with, was gone, or had never been there. "Sorry," she said, realizing Belen was glancing expectantly at her yet again. "So you're interested, then?" she confirmed, waving Belen inside. "Even if it's not your actual specialty?"

"Oh, absolutely, Professor—"

Libby frowned over her shoulder again, allowing Belen to enter first.

No one. Nothing. She had not seen Ezra. He had not found her. She was safe.

(For now.)

Libby inhaled deeply, then exhaled.

"Right," she said, turning to a waiting Belen and remembering only afterward to tell Belen to call her Libby, not Professor. "So. Tell me again about ley lines."

· CALLUM ·

Two things were becoming very clear to Callum. One was that Reina was actively insane. He considered bringing up the obvious: that the circumstances of her birth—being born into a family that fundamentally did not want her—were doing very strange things to her emotional processes. The thing is, Callum considered explaining to her, that actually childhood is very fragile, and you can't technically outgrow the fractures. You can't *undo* the damage, and pretending that the damage does not exist or trying to outgrow it somehow—to become larger, more invulnerable than the pain—was definitely not something that someone of Reina's emotional ineptitude should attempt on their own. Even worse would be for her to influence an ancient magical library into giving her things that she was clearly not equipped to have.

It's nothing personal, Callum thought about telling her. It's not like *you personally* are doing something astronomically stupid. Plenty of people suffer these kinds of inadequacies and you should really not take it as an insult when I tell you that this will not give you the love you never got when you were five. But unfortunately it all seemed like a drag to get into—and who had the time for that kind of vulnerability management?—so Callum decided to say nothing at all.

The second thing that became clear to Callum as the days got shorter and colder was that Atlas very much did not want Callum to attend the annual Society gala, and was attempting some sort of strange reverse psychology in order to secure Callum's compliance.

"You are welcome to attend" had been Atlas's exact words, which he addressed to Callum without preamble when Callum had lingered after one of their now quite rare gatherings in the painted room. Atlas had issued the invitation to all of them as a group before dismissing them. (It was difficult to say who was most displeased by this captivity. Each seemed to have their own sense of having somewhere better to be.)

"I believe Miss Kamali has already expressed her intention to join us," Atlas had clarified to Callum's unasked question, "so perhaps you might consult her as to her intended wardrobe."

No underhanded threats, no covert suggestions? "Am I supposed to have forgotten that you wanted me dead a few months ago? Don't try to deny it," Callum posed to Atlas conversationally, being of keen empathy and (arguably) sound mind. This all seemed incorrigibly decent to Callum and therefore implausible, and as requested, Atlas did not argue. "And now you want me to attend your party," Callum mocked, "as your . . . honored guest?"

"As a member of the Society," Atlas corrected. "Which you are, unrelated to my feelings about you." He fixed Callum with an expressionless glance. "It was never my decision whether you lived or died. You're alive, and therefore you're invited."

How incredibly civil, assuming that was true.

"So you want to keep an eye on me then, is that it?" asked Callum.

"I have my hands full keeping eyes on people as it is," replied Atlas. "Come or don't come. Enjoy the aperitifs or don't. It makes no difference to me."

He turned away in dismissal, reminding Callum of another moment entirely. "You once told me that I had a vacancy," Callum remarked to Atlas's back, pausing him as he sifted through paperwork. "A lack of something. Imagination, was it?"

"As I recall, what I said was that I admired your choices," Atlas said without looking up. "The things you had chosen not to do."

Ah yes, such lovely rhetoric between admirers. "But then you also—"

"Questioned why you had not done them, yes, I know." Atlas glanced over his shoulder to meet Callum's eye once he had finished gathering whatever logistical tedium seemed to be before him. "Are you questioning it now yourself?"

Of course not. Callum had no interest in . . . What was it Atlas had said? War. Existence. Survival of the species. Pointless magnanimity, in Callum's opinion. More often he concerned himself with smaller, sharper pains.

Retributive ones.

"I've chosen a topic for independent study," Callum announced, to which Atlas arched a brow, seemingly in amusement.

"Have you? I wondered whether you might recall the conditions of your initiation, Mr. Nova." Atlas's expression was tight, more impatient than grim. "You are beholden to the Society—"

"As it is beholden to me, yeah, I know. Quick question," said Callum. "How bad is it?"

Atlas was very pointedly trying not to tense. "How bad is . . . ?"

"This time of year," said Callum coolly, knowing that a telepath of Atlas's proficiency would not require clarification. "The change in temperature, the dreariness. Does that affect you much? Your magic, I mean," he amended, "not your state of mind. Though for you it's rather one and the same, isn't it? Cursed with clarity of thought when yours are so terribly dismal."

Callum was gratified to see that, as he had hoped would be the case, Atlas had to pause before responding. He had not expected Atlas to respond emotionally, of course. That wasn't the point. It didn't matter whether Atlas lost his temper or burst into tears, or if he suddenly decided to take Callum by the throat and toss him into the gardens outside.

What mattered was the split second of tension. The need to consider how to respond. What a beautiful strain of anguish. Like biting your tongue and then, just for an instant, tasting blood.

"What is your chosen subject matter?" Atlas asked. So genteel, so distinguished. So fucking civilized and dull.

"The effects of clinical depression on telepathic specialties," replied Callum cheerily. Like the burst of a cherry tomato. A sweet little pop.

"Ah." Atlas gave him a thin smile. "Well-trodden ground, I'm afraid."

"Well, I thought I might also consider some other factors. Post-traumatic stress. Survivor's guilt."

Atlas's restraint, his silence, was lovely and tense, like a window-glass of pulled taffy.

"I figured, well, I'm an empath, aren't I?" mused Callum. "Where is the separation between *mental* illness and the emotional reality? Surely there's some validity there. Some . . . untrodden ground, as you say."

What was Callum even talking about? He wasn't sure, really. Hadn't given any actual thought to the matter, though it did make sense. Parisa was reading motherfucking Jung, and how was any of that different, really, from influencing emotion? The more Callum considered it, the more his taunts were beginning to make an absurd sort of sense. Why *shouldn't* he study brain chemistry? After all, that was what he was really altering, wasn't he? What were feelings except for hormones and weakness, the falseness of the mind?

"A very good proposal, Mr. Nova," said Atlas. Unfortunately he had probably come to the same conclusion Callum had—that, or Callum, who had already had a glass of wine (well, more like a carafe), was not being careful enough to conceal his unintentional foray into the scholastic arts. "Though I would perhaps widen the scope," Atlas advised dryly, "from the telepathic specialties."

"Perhaps." Hm, how unfortunate that Callum was now genuinely intrigued by the topic when he'd meant only to prod at Atlas Blakely's past, waking his many ghosts. "Still," he said, not quite ready to give up the game. "I suppose you'd understand why I'd come to you for a test subject."

Atlas smiled curtly. "How flattering."

"Does it bother you, this time of year?" Callum asked again, gesturing outside to the snow that flecked the garden paths.

"I am susceptible to a certain disorderliness," Atlas replied, "as the seasons change. As many people tend to be."

"No," Callum said. "I mean the other thing."

Atlas paused.

"It's very interesting," Callum noted. "Your sense of responsibility."

Atlas said nothing.

"I wondered," Callum remarked at a meandering pace, "why anyone would be so devoted to something so remarkably callous."

Atlas was silent.

"Killing," Callum amended, leaning back against the table so as to better appraise Atlas with a glance. "Nobody seems to have asked me whether I would have done it. Murdered one of the others. They all simply assume that I would have."

"For good reason," murmured Atlas.

"Yes, true. This is why you despise me, my existence," Callum said. Atlas was likely referring to the outcome of the medeian dispatched by Callum during the attack on their first night of residency. Or possibly he meant to imply the results of Callum's battle of wits against Parisa the previous year. Or any number of things, really. It wasn't as if Callum had ever claimed to be innocent—but still, he could taste the supple Chardonnay of a righteous upper hand. "But, as I see it, the blood I have on my hands is nothing."

"Is that so, Mr. Nova?"

"At least," Callum added, "nothing compared to yours."

It seemed that at last Atlas would be willing to have it out with him. To finally offer some cruelty, some derision, which they both knew he felt. For a moment it seemed as if Atlas might actually indulge his baser impulses—his need to punish Callum, to put him in his place.

Callum found he welcomed it. How humiliating, that everything he had once said to Tristan was true about himself. Tristan was the one who *ought* to be punishing him, who ought to be so repulsed by him that he spent every moment plotting Callum's death. But Tristan was growing, he was thriving, he was unfurling in bright blooms of forward motion.

When had Tristan last glanced Callum's way, or last wished immensities of misfortune upon Callum's head, his bloodline? Weeks, maybe even months, and somehow, this was Atlas's fault. Or at least, Callum blamed him for it. Callum was sure that Atlas Blakely was owed a dose of suffering.

"To every villain an origin story," Atlas said, finally responding to Callum's taunt. "Does mine disappoint you?"

"Not in the slightest." That was even more unfortunate, as it was true. "Everything you've done has been hideously irrational. I can't think why you'd even still be alive."

"Nor can I," said Atlas, who then gathered his things and departed the room.

Perhaps if Callum had been soberer, he might have stopped him. But as he was not, he hadn't, and now it was time for the Society's gala, which despite Atlas's feigned ambivalence was an opportunity to do what Callum did best: be awfully fun at parties.

Just think, Callum considered as he dressed himself in his best suit, regarding his reflection in the mirror. Just *imagine* the things he could do with Atlas Blakely's emotions. Callum hadn't spoken of what he'd discovered from Atlas's file to anyone, having not found a partner in conspiracy that didn't make him want to throw himself headfirst into a lake. Parisa was too smug, Reina too flawed, Nico too Nico. But if anyone else knew what he knew? If any of the others could understand the true depths of the Caretaker's sins?

Callum folded his mother's silk scarf into the pocket of his jacket, shaking his head.

That kind of guilt would not even need an empath to interpret. There wasn't a chance that Atlas Blakely did not spend every day of his life in service to trauma, and what remained for Callum was to find out why.

Callum wandered out from his room, observing the closed doors, and wandered to the gallery. It was the mortal holiday season, though the Society house avoided the garishness of festivity for the sake of the gala, choosing instead its usual palette of gloom except with more interesting lighting.

From the balustrades, it was clear that the house was filling up quickly with a variety of the usual suspects. Politicians, philanthropists, prominent medeians of all kinds. It was unclear if they were all Society members—probably not, Callum reasoned—but the ones who did belong to the Society were obvious. They all avoided inspecting the house or lingering long to admire it, as if they suspected the beams of the floors of having an all too clear memory.

Callum disembarked from the residency wing of the house late, of course, as anyone reasonable would do, and found that Parisa had had the same idea. She was wearing yet another silky number, a figure-hugging dress that dripped from her like tears. Instead of her usual black, she wore a blazing, molten gold. He caught up to her where she had paused on the stairs, carefully timing her entrance. The others, if they intended to come at all, were already downstairs, or bound to be unfashionably late.

As Callum reached Parisa's side, she looked at him for a brief moment before disregarding whatever thought she'd had. Probably that he looked nice or should die. Or both, which was not unheard of.

"Shall we?" Callum said, offering her his arm.

She squinted at him.

"Fix your face," she advised.

Maybe not the nice-looking bit, then. "Fix it?"

She replied, nonplussed, "You're just so terribly noticeable. Have you ever actually tried blending in?"

"I could ask you the same," he said, gaze purposefully skimming the curve of her hip.

"People don't remember me unless I allow them to." She admonished him with a brow, as if he ought to know better.

"Who says I can't do the same?" But that sounded like too much work, so he let one of the illusions fall. "Better?"

Her eyes narrowed. "What did you do, recede your hairline?" She reached up and he ducked away, the tips of her fingers brushing the base of his inherited widow's peak.

"Get back to me when your hair starts turning gray," he said. She smirked, shrugging, and he offered her his arm again.

"You were meant to stay in your room," she commented, though she rested a hand on his arm this time as they descended the stairs. "You know he hates you, right?"

The derision in reference to Atlas seemed to have faded for her. Interesting. "Of course he hates me." As he should. "Is anyone else coming?" Callum asked her as they reached the ground floor, gesturing over his shoulder to the remaining bedrooms.

Parisa shrugged, then released him.

"Fair enough."

They walked in silence to the entry hall, merging with the sea of other attendees. They bypassed the velvet upholstery, the tapestries in shades of mahogany and wine. The expected trappings of finery were even more dazzling than usual, the familiar carved Greco-Roman arches and gleaming pillars now set off by jewels that winked from the subtle motion of the chandeliers. Everyone's eyes fell on Parisa, and then, just as she'd said, went through her, attention melting away.

"You're quiet," Callum remarked.

"Am I?" She didn't seem bothered or impressed by the observation. "I suppose I need a drink."

"Shall I fetch you one?"

"No." She looked at him with something close to bemusement. "You don't actually intend to follow me around all evening, do you?"

"No." He had no intentions whatsoever. He had no reason for doing anything anymore, or for *not* doing things. It was really very freeing. Or depressing, but then again, he was not the one depressed. "I just know he didn't want me here, so I'm here."

Parisa followed his line of sight to spot Atlas, who stood by the great hall doors and roared with laughter at something the Canadian prime minister had to say. "You learned something from his file, I take it?"

He didn't ask her how she knew about that. "Modest origins," Callum provided. "Humble background."

"Well, of course," scoffed Parisa. "People born to wealth are intolerable no matter what they do." She smirked pointedly at him.

"My mother was poor," Callum said.

"Good for her," replied Parisa, dark eyes catching opportunistically on a passing tray of champagne flutes. "She failed to pass along any industriousness to you, I take it," she murmured.

Callum shrugged. "It didn't take, I suppose."

"Evidently not." Parisa angled herself away from him, catching the eye of someone else as she reached for the champagne. "Put a pin in this weird moment you're having, would you?" she said, addressing him disinterestedly over her shoulder. "And don't drink any more, you're bound to get all morbid. And don't kill anyone," she added as an afterthought. "Or do. It's really none of my business."

"Have you ever been in love?" Callum asked her.

Parisa looked revolted. "Jesus Christ, never mind. Here," she said, shoving her glass of champagne into his hands. "You're embarrassing all of us."

"Right." He drained it, but by the time he was done, she was already gone.

Callum tossed the glass over his shoulder, where it dissolved somehow before it could shatter. Pity. He supposed there was all sorts of magic put in place, which Tristan would know how to see, but naturally Callum couldn't. Tristan could see lots of things that other people never would. Like how Callum was actually very, very nearsighted in a way that had given him a permanent squint. He had fixed it, obviously. Because he fixed things. He was a problem-solver, generally. At one point he had been in the business of fixing people but *ugh*, the whole thing was such a drain. And nobody ever stayed fixed. That was the fuckery of it, really. That people were so easily changeable, so readily changed. They loved you one day, didn't the next.

Callum had watched himself fade in significance from too many people's lives, and yes, okay, that was not an excuse for . . . what *was* it that Tristan had disliked about him, ultimately? Hard to say, really. He had so many wonderful flaws to choose from. Luckily nobody ever stuck around long enough for him to care.

Callum glanced around and spotted something. An absence. Atlas was gone, hm, interesting. Also, there was a woman winding through the crowd. Atlas, you dog! Callum reached for another champagne flute and missed, summoning it clumsily into his palm. He drained that one and then followed the woman to Atlas's office, quietly lingering in her path.

The door was conveniently left ajar. "Professor J. Araña," Atlas's voice was saying. "Your reputation precedes you. Tell me, the *J* is for . . . ? Ah yes, Jiménez," he observed, sitting down at his desk. "Are you married now, or just pseudonymous?"

"It's my grandmother's maiden name." The voice in response was measured, mature. She sounded older even than Atlas. Her emotions, as far as Callum could sense, were mostly a mix of repulsion and rage. She wanted very badly to divest Atlas of his limbs but was unfortunately holding herself back for some reason.

"I see. And what can I do for you, Professor?"

"Die," she said. "Slowly. Painfully."

"Understandable," said Atlas.

"In fact, I only came here to kill you," she said, at which point Callum was about to interrupt, to say something along the lines of oh noooo no no that's what he waaaaaants, don't do it, señora—but then she kept talking. "But the truth is, it's not about you. If you die, someone else will just replace you. Like the hydra's heads."

"True," said Atlas.

"The poison is institutional. It's bigger than you."

"It always is," Atlas replied, sounding sympathetic. "I regret not being able to offer you more, Belen."

"Right." The woman, the professor, suddenly seemed drained. As if the veil of a life's purpose was falling away. Uh-oh, thought Callum. That's not good, that's never good. Watch out for that. "Well, so much for the party, then."

"I'll take a sock to the jaw if it helps," said Atlas, which Callum thought was not very sporting of him. The woman was depressed enough. She didn't need condescension.

"Very patronizing, thanks," she replied, and whirled around, exiting the office and stepping directly onto Callum's toes. "Excuse m—"

"Keep going," Callum whispered to her. He found a little dial and turned it up for a moment, like sunning himself. Warming himself on the hearth. Not that she seemed the type to give up, exactly, but still, it pleased him more to think that the fire was still lit, the lights still on. "Don't stop."

She looked up at him. She was small but sturdy somehow, a bit stocky. "Do I know you?"

He released her, leaning against the wall as he toppled for a moment. The bubbles of champagne that he'd drunk suddenly threatened to vacate his premises via belch. Or worse. He steadied himself with a deep inhale, seeing stars.

"Mr. Nova," came Atlas's voice. The woman was gone, then, presumably. "Perhaps you might try an appetizer. Or a reconciliation."

The latter, Callum felt sure, had been said in his head, which was a step too far. How unspeakably rude! How dastardly and invasive! What a great and terrible idea for which Atlas Blakely should pay, and swiftly.

"You killed them," Callum whispered to Atlas.

He would not remember Atlas's response, the rest of the night lost to fizzy haze, an indistinguishable blur. He thought he recalled seeing something from the corner of his eye. A halo of Nova-brand illusion spells, like a lawless nest of his family's fingerprints. And Tristan.

But by morning, Callum wouldn't know for sure.

· EZRA ·

H ello," said the most astonishingly beautiful woman Ezra had ever
seen. "You're about six feet tall, aren't you? Interesting. Bathroom?"
It took a moment for Ezra to respond. "That way," he managed,
clearing his throat.

"*And* you know your way around." She smiled dazzlingly at him. "Fascinating. Name?"

"Ezra." He had intended to lie, or rather, to not speak. Not that it mattered whether she knew his name or not. Nobody here would know him
aside from Nico de Varona, and to that end, Ezra's illusions—blandly for-
gettable hair, colorless eyes, the general look of someone that everyone had
gone to high school with—were secure.

He glanced around for Nothazai, who was elsewhere. Atlas had yet to
make an appearance. "Sorry, I'm just . . . looking for someone."

"Oh, don't worry, he's looking for you, too." The woman was smaller than
Libby, Ezra registered. He didn't know why he always compared women to
Libby, considering that she was quite an average height, or possibly even an inch
or so taller, but still. She was hardly an appropriate benchmark for *all* women.
This woman wore very high heels but was still not quite up to where Libby's
head typically reached. Why the fuck was he continuing to think about Libby.

"*Very* interesting," said the woman, lips curling up around the edge of her
glass.

Just then Ezra remembered what kind of den he'd wandered into.

"You're a telepath." His least favorite kind of specialty, and the only kind
for which his carefully illusioned face wouldn't do much good. "You're Parisa
Kamali."

Her eyes widened. Not, unfortunately, in surprise.

In . . . triumph. Or excitement.

"Oh, now this is just too delicious," said Parisa, toasting him with her
champagne flute. "I do so love a turn of events. Enjoy your evening, Ezra,"
she purred to him, sounding almost giddy with delight.

And then she vanished the glass and disappeared into the crowd, camouflaged among the other medeian elite before Ezra could ask her what was so

apparently delicious. In the same moment, Ezra caught sight of Nico, who was prowling around the house tugging at his neckline, the stiff collar of his shirt in plain collision with the protrusion of his Adam's apple. Ezra waited for Nico's distracted gaze to pass through him, then turned away.

He shook himself, glancing around again for Nothazai, or the professor. He didn't know what he had just been looking for—he felt like he did whenever he checked the fridge for the same contents he'd checked for five seconds earlier—or more importantly, what had possessed him to come to this event.

Well, not true. He did know. He knew exactly. Because he needed to show Atlas the kind of influence he commanded, the sorts of friends he had. Specifically, the kind in high places. Because Atlas, who was supposed to have changed things with Ezra, had chosen instead to become part of this thing they both hated, and now Ezra needed him to know that doing so was not impressive, it wasn't innovative, it was barely even powerful. It was uninspired and predictable and stale.

It was . . . *disappointing.*

But the suit was itchy and the house was far too warm and Ezra could feel it, the way he had been excised from the wards. They had been stitched up again. Which, in its own special way, hurt. He stood there, useless, like some kind of divested parasite.

"Was it 1988?" asked a voice in his ear. "Or was it '89?"

Ezra jumped, his pulse suddenly racing. "Was what '89?"

"The year your mother died." Atlas had sidled up to him, handing Ezra a glass of champagne. "Sorry, is that a painful memory?" Atlas commented, raising his glass to his lips. "I suppose I shouldn't ask." *As usual, Ezra, you're very easy to find.*

Ezra said nothing, accepting the glass without reply.

"You know, I actually can't stand Nothazai," Atlas remarked. "Not because he opposes me and everything I do or say," he added. "He's just such an ineffective communicator. Drones on and on." He glanced at Ezra. "I didn't realize you even owned a suit."

"Careful," Ezra warned, taking a sip from his glass. "You do appear to be speaking to someone young enough to be one of your initiates, in case you've forgotten the optics."

"I never forget the optics." True, Ezra thought grimly. "I'm just catching up with an old friend. I assume you came for the small talk, since I know you're not a fan of pâté."

Ezra slid a glance at Atlas, who was wearing an idle smile.

"Keeping an eye on her, I hope?" Atlas asked, taking a sip from his own glass. "I'd hate to think she might get into trouble. Think how guilty you'd feel if she got hurt."

Ezra said nothing.

"She's at LARCMA, by the way. But you already know that." Another sidelong glance as Ezra tried not to think of anything. Tried, purposely, to think of nothing. A blank canvas, an empty wall. "She's just spinning on a hamster wheel of your making, isn't she? Assuming she isn't far cleverer than you think, which is quite a dangerous assumption."

"I'm not letting you do it," Ezra said quietly. "I know what you're planning. And what you're doing—"

"What exactly am I doing? Having champagne at a party," said Atlas, toasting him with his glass. "To my knowledge I've never abducted anyone."

"You've found a way to trick the archives, I know you have." A bluff, but almost certainly accurate. The archives gave only the knowledge that was earned—and Atlas had in no way earned omnipotence. Ezra muttered it out of the side of his mouth, though no one was looking at him. "I know you must be getting someone to access the texts that you can't. And I know what you're planning to do with them." That, at least, was true. Even without the specifics of his plan—without witnessing the events leading up the outcome Ezra had seen—Atlas had shown Ezra who he really was over twenty years ago.

"You," Ezra said to Atlas, "are not a god."

"And I lament it every day," replied Atlas dryly.

The old spark of resentment in Ezra flared up in protest in twin flame with a memory of meeting Atlas for the first time, the kinship he had felt, the closeness he thought they had. He tamped both impulses down.

"Where is he? Your animator." Ezra didn't expect an answer, but he wanted Atlas to know that he was on to him. That someone, somewhere, was asking the right questions. Looking in the right places.

He wanted Atlas to know that someone knew what he really was.

"He stayed behind," Atlas said. "He's feeling under the weather."

Ha. Sure he was. "You sealed up the wards, I see. Was it difficult?"

"Very."

"Good." Ezra turned to shove the glass into Atlas's chest. "Thanks for the drink."

"Enjoy the party" was Atlas's absurd parting benediction.

Ridiculous. Clearly Ezra should not have come.

Only—

Only things were not entirely what he imagined. For one thing, Atlas was right about Nothazai. And although they had not discussed James Wessex, Atlas was probably right about him, too. Ezra still didn't know what to make of Professor J. Araña. At first she had been too quiet, but now she seemed . . . not loud, exactly, but not *right,* either. Her activism—which had drawn him to her to begin with—was beginning to strike him as . . . well, aggressive. Unspecific. Uncontained. He knew she'd been bullied into the cage of her alkalinity lab as some sort of institutional silencing technique, but to hear her speak her opinions now was less productive than he'd hoped. When she spoke, her vitriol did not seem to be about the task at hand, or about the initiates at all. There was something rumbling beneath her arguments, something coming loose. Like she was a frayed edge moments from disintegrating, and therefore liable to break from their plan.

He didn't know how to explain it because he wasn't a telepath, but the point was that the people he had selected for this task did not adequately grasp the urgency of the situation. He had warned them, had he not, what kind of omnipotence Atlas Blakely aspired to—what despotism his initiates would attempt, if given the chance? But increasingly, the others viewed Ezra as a tool, or possibly just a sentinel. He was Paul Revere crying that the British were coming, when in fact what he meant to do was point out that the British were already here.

The plan was growing more complicated by the day. In Ezra's mind it was simple: target each of the Society's newest members and neutralize the threat they posed before their influence—*Atlas's* influence—could be inflicted on the world. It was one thing to target the Society philosophically, for the purpose of unifying their mission, but in practice the Society was too large, too intangible an enemy to seek to destroy. Didn't his recruits understand that? That once Atlas Blakely was removed, the Society would simply return to being a collection of wealthy men and old books? Hardly a threat at all, except perhaps to one's ego should they not be admitted. Ezra cared nothing for egos. Ezra cared for the continuation of the world as they knew it. Thus, it was *Atlas* who was the problem, Atlas and his weapons who were the threat, and true, Ezra could kill him now and be done with it—but who was to say that Atlas had not already put his plan into motion? The newest Society members were well into their second year of independent study. What the archives had provided for them by now was incalculable, and that was the problem. Callum Nova was eliminated, Libby was trapped, but there were still four deadly weapons about to be unleashed on the world. And Ezra knew, even if they did not, that Atlas had a plan for them. Atlas had a plan for everyone.

As far as Ezra knew, none had tried to leave the house since Ezra's contingency plan had gone into effect. Still, eventually they would venture out, and what needed to be done then was clear: Parisa Kamali, Tristan Caine, Nico de Varona, and Reina Mori had to be stopped. They could not, by any means, be allowed to continue down the path that had been devised for them by Atlas—and, unwittingly, Ezra—so many years ago.

Ezra wandered moodily around the outskirts of the party's carousing bourgeoisie, narrowly skirting a blond man with glassy eyes who was practically sleepwalking through the house. Overindulgence, it seemed. God, Ezra loathed parties. All this excess, it was revolting, and worse, he did not know how to exist in it. He was reminded, too, of the last time he had been an initiate in this house. Only a few years ago for him, and yet almost two decades for Atlas. The other initiates of their class had not taken kindly to Ezra. He wondered where they were, what they were doing, whether they had toasted Atlas before the party and tinkled with laughter over Ezra's dearly departed loss. He had not seen any of them yet—Folade had loved a party, Neel had loved attention, and Ivy . . . hopefully no one was stupid enough to let Ivy loose in a crowd—but that didn't mean anything. Ezra assumed they would have blended into the crowd by now, already absorbed into the nucleus of privilege. (He shuddered to think of running into Alexis Lai again. She had given him the creeps badly enough when she was twenty-eight.)

Ezra was about to find Nothazai, to make his excuses—it wasn't as if there was much to learn from this gathering, and anyway, the Society had issued them all wristbands that were essentially dampeners, so he'd pass out if he even tried to open a door or break a ward from here—when someone paused him with a hand on his shoulder.

"Ezra, wasn't it?"

"Tristan," said Ezra, with reflexive alarm and no small amount of confusion, before softening it to something he hoped mimicked charmed surprise. Could it have been a mistake? Surely it must have been. After all, his illusions . . .

He turned to find a brooding Tristan Caine beside him, having only partially committed to the party's formal dress code. It seemed as if he'd wandered down the stairs in search of something and then given up.

"Didn't expect to see you here," said Tristan, who unfortunately showed no evidence of having been mistaken, despite his opportunity to take in the purposeful blandness of Ezra's illusioned face. "God, what a nightmare," Tristan added with a shudder, scouring the crowd with a grimace. "So many toffs in one room."

It was clear that Tristan had no reservations about who Ezra was, which at least addressed the mystery behind the source of his Society recruitment. Whatever it was Tristan could do, illusions must have been of no consequence, which wasn't related to any specialty that Ezra had ever encountered before. And which Atlas had never mentioned, of course.

(Truly, the list of reasons to kill Atlas was growing more plentiful by the day.)

"I didn't realize . . ." Tristan trailed off, frowning at Ezra with bewilderment. "You look younger than I recall, or I suppose younger than I expected. I rather thought you were from some other astral plane when I ran into you around the wards."

Ezra, who'd rather thought a lot of things before today, tried very hard to force a smile. Nico, thankfully, was too far away to notice. He was speaking with an Asian woman in a suit so black it appeared almost liquid, her hair pulled to one side while she stared listlessly out the window.

"It's my European lifestyle," Ezra said to Tristan, safely assured of Nico's ongoing distraction. "All that red wine and subsidized health care. I'm older than I look."

"Ha," said Tristan, who then glanced distractedly elsewhere in the crowd. "When were you initiated? I suppose I never asked."

"Oh, I'm—" Hm. Tricky. Luckily Tristan was not paying adequate attention. "And you?"

"Hm? Oh, sorry." Yes, Tristan was not listening at all. His gaze was following the intoxicated blond man, who had stumbled and then disappeared into a drawing room.

"They just let anyone into these things, don't they?" Ezra commented, which finally drew Tristan's gaze earthward.

"True. I hear there are members of the Forum here, too." Tristan shook his head. "I half expected to run into my old boss."

Ezra happened to know that James Wessex had not been invited. His assistant Eden had been incensed, ranting on about it to Ezra at length. "I suppose the Forum is more . . . enlightened, as far as enemies go," Ezra said, as Tristan shrugged his dismissive agreement. "Far more philanthropic, anyway."

This time the furrow of Tristan's brow was doubtful. "Are they?"

Wasn't that the question, indeed. "They're not a secret society," Ezra said. "They are committed to the distribution of information."

"Maybe so, but I doubt that information comes for free. Everything has a price." Tristan glanced around again, then back at Ezra. "You're not con-vinced, are you?"

"By the Forum?" He had been, once. He supposed, given everything, he was still willing to be.

"Well, you've been out in the world," Tristan qualified. "I assume you've seen them in action."

This was true. Ezra had seen Nothazai rub elbows with diplomats and politicians, same as he imagined of Atlas. It was a necessity, Nothazai had said, which was also true. Of course it was true. How could the Forum commit itself to the betterment of mankind if it could not afford to keep the lights on? What resources would they have possibly had without institu-tional backing? The point was the transparency, the way their members were informed of everything. The crucial thing was the distribution of informa-tion, the sharing of resources. Just last month they had challenged a medeian patent in the U.S. courts and won. Now everyone could use it.

Well. Everyone who could *afford* it could use it.

But functionally it was still better than the Society's archives, which were limited to only a smattering of people in this room. The champagne socialists—literally, Ezra thought, watching Tristan frowningly snatch a glass off a passing tray, waiting for Ezra's answer.

So, what did he think about the Forum?

"I think," Ezra decided, "that everyone is mostly full of shit."

Tristan choked on his swallow, spluttering a laugh. "True," he said, cut-ting another sidelong glance to Ezra in appreciation, or perhaps celebration. "I'll drink to that."

Ezra felt another sharp sting of impatience. No, of . . . not belonging. He did not belong here, never had. Nor did he want to be here.

He felt the flash of another life. A familiar bent head, an old furtive glance. The way Libby always chewed her fingernails while reading. She had asked Ezra to make her stop, but it had never bothered him, all her pesky little habits that she was so self-conscious about. He had liked it, being the person to soothe her agitation, to see all the cracks and flaws and pledge himself to protecting them, keeping them safe. It felt like making up for lost time. Saving someone, anyone, but all the better because it was her. Because she was kind, and more powerful than she knew.

Still, he reasoned, he would do it over, precisely the same way every time. Whatever she might have done after the Society, after knowing Atlas, it would ruin that fragile little glow of softness in her. Shouldn't he know that more than anyone? Atlas Blakely's version of the world was limitless and full of sharp edges, teeth waiting to puncture Libby's fragile optimism, her morality, her hope. If she hated Ezra forever, then so be it. He had saved more than her life.

He wondered how she was doing at LARCMA. He wondered what she was reading; what brilliant thing she'd thought of today that she was sharing with someone who wasn't him. It was not so bad, Ezra thought, because Libby was living a life. *Her* life, which he could only experience in miniature, witnessing it from a bird's-eye view.

A mall, most recently. The Galleria, where she had been inattentively listening to her companion, a rising professor whom Ezra already knew—time travel notwithstanding—would ultimately fail to attribute his groundbreaking research to a woman. *This* woman, Libby, though she should not have been so easily denied. She had worn electric-colored bike shorts, the pink a searing shock to Ezra's system. He had heard her laugh, insincere but reassuringly untroubled, and wanted, temporarily, to go blind.

He shook himself free of the memory, swallowing. This was not regret. Nor was it remorse. He wasn't wrong.

He could not, now, be wrong.

Ezra, trying his best not to look rabbity, glanced around for Nico to confirm that he was still in the corner with the Asian woman. To Ezra's momentary dismay, both of them were gone. It was supremely unlikely that Nico would take notice of him, but still. Suddenly the purpose of being here felt damningly insubstantial.

"Well," Ezra said to Tristan. "I've got to go. I fucking hate this."

Tristan's laugh in return was a low rumble. "To the Society and beyond," he said, already deeper in Atlas Blakely's pocket than he could possibly know. Like the animator, Tristan was at best one of Atlas's tools, at worst his disciple. If he wasn't already, he would be soon.

From the corner of his eye, Ezra caught a sickening glance of Atlas's laugh and thought perhaps he should take care of Tristan personally. Just to be sure.

But for the time being, Ezra tipped his head in farewell and turned away, recommitting himself to the promise of salvation ahead.

VII

SOUL

· TRISTAN ·

C an you use it yet?" Atlas asked Tristan as they sat cloistered in his office. The atmosphere had crackled with static, something electric. Not tension, not anxiety.

Excitement. Which was not something Tristan had been accustomed to feeling, perhaps ever.

"Almost," Tristan had said. "Nearly."

Atlas drummed his fingers on his desk, thinking. "You probably need something more efficient than your current tactics. However committed Mr. de Varona seems to be in that regard," he added wryly.

True. Not to mention that Tristan was beginning to wonder if being routinely scared to death might take a toll. "I can either do it quickly and emergently or slowly. *Very* slowly," Tristan qualified with a grimace. "Kind of an all-day task, if at all."

Atlas's expression didn't change. "And what happens? When you do it."

"I can shift reality. See things."

"Move them?"

Break them. "Sort of."

"Manipulate them?"

"In a sense."

Atlas looked thoughtful again.

"I had hoped you'd be able to spend the year perfecting your abilities," Atlas said after a moment. "But it appears we may have less time than I imagined."

"We?" Instantly, Tristan's guard flared up. "So you do intend to use me, then."

To that, Atlas gave him a look of something that might have been impatience on someone less aloof. "It is not what *I* intend for you, Tristan. We are, after all, beholden to the archives. We must contribute to them, as I told you from the moment you entered those doors."

We again. "Are you asking the same of Parisa? Or Callum?"

"I ask the same of everyone," Atlas said, "which is nothing. I do not have stakes except to further the aims of the library."

"The Society, you mean," Tristan observed gruffly.

"No." Atlas rose to his feet, pausing beside the window that overlooked the east side of the house's grounds. "I have a theory," he said eventually, turning over his shoulder to glance at Tristan. "I didn't want to share it with you before you understood your capabilities. But it is yours to pursue or not. It is, after all, within your capacity, not mine."

Tristan braced himself. "What is it?"

Atlas glanced outside again, then returned slowly to his chair, steepling his fingers at his mouth.

"I'm becoming aware that it will sound mad," he said.

"Try me," suggested Tristan, who had considered Atlas fairly mad for months, if not longer.

"Well." Atlas sighed, leaning back in his chair. "You are a physicist for which no name yet exists, Tristan. That has been my suspicion all along. You can see and manipulate quanta, which makes you even more powerful than an atomist, which most closely describes Mr. de Varona's skills. And it is your ability to see the world in a new dimension that opens the door for further testing."

"Testing of what?" Weapons, Tristan guessed, his insides souring. He had worked for James Wessex long enough to know that things eventually turned to violence. Money was in war—or perhaps more accurately, war was money.

"Worlds," said Atlas.

Which caused Tristan to blink, and then to frown. "I'm sorry?"

"Are you familiar at all with Mr. Ellery's research?" asked Atlas. "Or his specialty, for that matter."

Of course not. Tristan had never spared a thought for Dalton aside from wondering how Parisa could stand to be around him. "No."

"Dalton," Atlas began with another glance out the window, "is an animator. To some extent his abilities can produce sentience from nothing."

"But that's . . . impossible—"

"Yes," Atlas confirmed, glancing back at him. "Hence Dalton's area of research. For the past decade," Atlas explained, "Dalton has devoted his academic study to the nature of what appears to be, but cannot be, spontaneous creation. The library shows us that despite theological or scientific conviction, there is no primordial moment to this universe, no primeval atom from which our spark of life began. Millennia of our research suggest an alternative: that we are born from the void, a void that is not nothingness. Something preceded us, and it will outlast us. There is nothing special about this universe except that it's ours. And if we are not special, we are not singular. We are not unique." Atlas was staring at nothing. "The point," he continued, more to the line of dogwoods outside than to Tristan, "is that there must be some delicate but knowable balance, some quantity of matter and anti-matter, from which this world was formed—and if it could be identified, it could be re-created."

Here he turned to Tristan. "Dalton's research is these fluctuations. The possibility that the original chaos was not chaos at all, but some ordered force within a living, breathing void. Magic, perhaps—or perhaps you will prove it to be some arrangement of quanta." He shook his head. "That I don't know and can't guess. But here is what I do know," he concluded, leaning forward with a glint of something in his eye that could be described as sin-ister, or manic, or simply childlike—Tristan could not tell. "Miss Mori is capable of hosting such a spark. She can originate a primordial fluctuation. Mr. Ellery can summon the void, the element of cosmic inflation. You can see it. Mr. de Varona, Miss Rhodes, they can shape it, and—"

"You want us to create another universe?" Tristan cut in, unsure whether he had heard correctly.

Atlas shook his head. "Not create. Not from nothing. There is no creation from nothing, do you understand?"

"Then what—"

"There is nothing special about this universe," Atlas repeated. "There is nothing to suggest that this is the best that creation has to offer. Therefore there must be others."

Tristan felt he could not possibly be adequately following. "Others as in . . . ?"

"Other worlds." Here Atlas was adamant. "Other universes. Versions, per-haps, of this one."

Tristan frowned. "You mean a multiverse?"

"Maybe." The word left Atlas in a rush, like a sense of relief. "Maybe not. But the point is that with you, with your view of the world, then perhaps we could finally have an answer to that question. If the universe is not a void—if it is not *nothing*—and you can see its construction, then you can identify its shape. And if you can see where we are in this universe—"

"Then I will know where we are in the multiverse," Tristan abruptly con-cluded.

"*Yes.*" Here, now, this was Atlas's denouement. His entire purpose. "Yes. Precisely."

"But—" Tristan stopped to consider it, because by all accounts, everything he had just listened to should have been absolutely bollocks.

"The only principle I know to be true is that of balance," Atlas supplied for him. "Matter and antimatter. Order and chaos. Luck and unluck. Life and death." Atlas was outstretched in his chair, his long limbs expelling forward as he raised his arms over his head. "This cannot be the only world."

Tristan thought of Nico's mutterings, his many-worlds theory. "But what if it is?"

"If it is, then it is. Who cares? We'll all die and then nothing will matter." Atlas shrugged and carried on. "The point isn't the answer, Tristan, it's the question. It's the fact that it remains unknown."

"So you want to find out if Schrödinger's cat is alive or dead." Tristan could not believe the sound of his voice, which was neither toneless nor mechanical, but *intrigued*. By god, he actually found this interesting. Such incredibly poor judgment on his part.

"Yes," said Atlas, "I do."

"You want to open the box." Not just the box containing the cat. *Pandora's* box. The box containing an answer so massive that there would be, inherently, an ethical quandary.

What would happen if another universe could be found? Who would decide which universe was right, true, correct?

And more importantly, what would become of this one?

"No," said Atlas. "I don't want to open the box." A pause. "I want *you* to open the box."

"But—" And again a pause. "But if I refuse?"

Another shrug. "Then you refuse."

"What if I don't agree with your theory?" Tristan argued.

"Then you disagree. The purpose of the Society is to foster the knowledge within our walls. To be beholden to the archives as we are means to seek and keep seeking."

"But this is far more than a simple experiment." Tristan's head was beginning to hurt.

"It is no less an experiment than the medical cures within these archives," Atlas said. "No less ethical an inquiry than the research that already exists here that has never been shared."

"You want to open the door to the multiverse and . . ." Tristan blinked. "Keep it secret?"

"I want to open the door," Atlas said. "What happens afterward is nothing."

"Nothing," Tristan echoed blankly. *This* was the master plan of Atlas Blakely? To open a door without any regard for the consequences that followed?

To that, Atlas hastily shook his head, a sudden tic of self-consciousness. "Apologies. Not nothing. Of course it's not nothing."

But that slip had been telling, hadn't it?

Or maybe not.

"The point is," Atlas continued, "I believe that given the full scope of your power, Tristan, you would be capable of all of this and more. The answers to the universe's very foundation would be available to you. You are not beholden to my hypotheses," he added pointedly. "You are free to theorize at will. But the power you could wield, the answers you could provide—"

Tristan's hands were beginning to go numb. "I *would* be capable of it?" The conditional tense seemed foreboding. It implied, among other things, an *or else*.

Atlas gave him something of a sympathetic look. "I understand that it is a lot to ask of you. But surely it's not *my* asking, Tristan, so much as your own pursuit of—"

"You keep calling me Tristan," Tristan realized, looking up sharply from where he'd been staring at his lap. "You call the others by their surnames." Something else was tapping at his brain, prodding him from somewhere. Callum's voice.

Blakely hates me. Loves you.

Atlas, who had become very animated over the course of their conversation, suddenly paused. "Does it bother you?"

"You like me," Tristan said.

Atlas hesitated, then said, "As I once told you, I was once in your position."

"Which was what?" Tristan asked bluntly. "Venture capitalist? Future son-in-law of a billionaire? Engaged to a woman who was sleeping with your friend? Which part?"

Which was when Atlas fixed him with a long, deliberate glance.

"You know which part," said Atlas.

Inside Tristan's head, he saw the image of his father. No, not just the image, but the memory, the way his father loomed over him, towering above him, casting him in shadow. No—not the memory of his father but the fallout, the waves of loneliness, the sense of inadequacy, the pervasive, enduring gloom. The tiptoeing, the perilous sense that at any moment he might step wrong, might cause something to break, might awaken the beast inside his father's chest. Might summon to life the titan who ruled over his happiness, who dwarfed his own diminished sense of self. He felt the acrid sense of fear, the thought that was not really a thought, but just the heightened sense of *run*. That fight-or-flight, bitter and rancid. The rage in his heart, thud-thudding with his pulse. The fear that his anger was inherited. That his own soul, like his father's, was flawed.

When Tristan blinked again it was through tears, hot and stinging.

Shameful. He shook himself and swiped angrily at his eyes. "That's what you think we both are? Depressed?" he demanded.

Atlas said nothing and Tristan shot to his feet.

"Fuck you," Tristan said.

Then he turned and exited the office, blazing a path up the stairs.

In the weeks that had followed since that conversation, Tristan had been unsure what to do with himself. Unsure what to do with what he knew, or what Atlas thought he knew, or with whatever the fuck he was still doing there in that house, with all its secrets, its betrayal and its ugliness. Tristan hated Callum, hated Parisa, had never really liked Reina, and didn't know what to do with Nico, because the possibility that Nico might have gathered from Tristan's moment of unbridled honesty what Atlas had gathered from the inside of Tristan's head made Tristan feel something more than hatred.

He was feeling it again. Craving. A riotous thing, a need to be soothed. He had thought Libby was his existential crisis, but she meant more to him than just that, didn't she? She wasn't just the cause; she was part of it somehow. A piece of something his stupid brain couldn't figure out. She, he decided, was the reason he couldn't access his full powers. She was gone, and so long as she remained gone, there would always be something missing from him. His . . . goodness? His morality? Something critical. Something he didn't understand.

He hadn't intended to go to the ridiculous Society gala at all until he decided he was ravenously hungry and everything smelled good, like money. It was there he decided there was no point to hating Atlas. What was Atlas, anyway? As the other traveler, Ezra, departed, Tristan watched as Atlas lifted a champagne flute to his lips and made a demurred acquiescence to the prime minister of wherever the fuck.

It all struck Tristan as very stupid: the Society, the archives, the world, and—by extension—Atlas. He was, after all, just another human man with faults, with flaws and curiosities, and his own agenda. Worse men with bigger demands, more selfish expectations existed outside this house.

Ezra was right, whoever Ezra even was. Everything was fucked. It wasn't that Atlas Blakely was bad, or that the Society was bad, but that the world just was what it was.

Or maybe Atlas was correct, and this world was only one of many.

At precisely the moment this occurred to him, Tristan spotted Nico coming toward him. He gave an absent nod. "Weren't you just with Reina?"

"Well, she hates me and wants me dead for unknowable reasons. Or maybe she's just hungry. Who was that?" Nico asked, gesturing to Ezra's retreating form with his chin. "Someone important?"

"Oh, that was—" Tristan realized inopportunely that he had only the very faintest idea, having not been listening. "Ezra."

"Ezra?" Nico made a face. "Sorry. Force of habit. I only know one Ezra and he's got the personality of a slice of bread. I'd say he's my eternal enemy only I can't think how he could do anything worth hating." His gaze passed distractedly over the crowd, from Reina, who was sulking in the corner, to Parisa, who was laughing in the center of a small group of hyperattentive men. "But you've probably heard enough about him, I'm guessing."

Tristan slid Nico a glance of bristling annoyance, perhaps at the insinuation that he rabidly collected anecdotes about Nico's personal life, or some other inapt suggestion that they were friends. "Why would I know anything about a random person you have a vendetta against?"

Nico looked equally miffed. "Again, it hardly rises to the occasion of vendetta," he muttered, "and I assumed Rhodes would have told you."

"Rhodes?" Tristan's pulse ricocheted, then dropped. "What does she have to do with this?"

"Her boyfriend. Ex-boyfriend now, I suppose." For the first time in the conversation, they faced each other, equally bewildered. "Why are you getting all worked up?"

"Rhodes's boyfriend's name," Tristan said with a frown, "is *Ezra*?"

"Yeah. Well, was. I don't know. Not that he's dead now. Or maybe he is, it literally makes no difference to me." But at Tristan's expression, Nico's brow furrowed. "That wasn't him, anyway," Nico said, now doubly bemused. "That guy was even blander than Fowler, believe it or not, so I don't know why you look so thinky."

"He was illusioned." Tristan wasn't sure why this suddenly seemed to be of critical importance, given that the exchange was only a few seconds long. "But it's a party, a formal event." Nearly everyone in the room wore illusions or augmentations to some degree. "I assumed it was for normal purposes."

"That guy?" Nico stared after the place Ezra had been—unhelpfully, as he was no longer there. "Well, Fowler has black hair. A little shorter than you, maybe Callum's height. Generally looks like he would rather be somewhere else. Hasn't lifted more than a textbook in his life."

Fuck, thought Tristan. That could describe any number of people in the world. Surely this was nothing, and yet—"And that guy? What did he look like?"

"Uh, blond hair? Light brown? His face was, you know. A face—"

"No. No, that's—no." Tristan shook his head. "No. Black hair. Curls. And the first time I saw him he definitely wasn't wearing any illusion charms."

Nico blinked accusingly at him, as if this was something that should have come up while they were braiding each other's hair, bonding. "When did you see him before?"

"On the grounds. Near the wards."

"Which ward?"

"Does it matter?" Tristan felt twitchy with something.

"*Which ward?*" Nico repeated.

"I—" Fuck. "A time ward."

"Are you serious? A *time ward*." Nico looked furious. "I told you that time was the only dimension we hadn't considered, and yet it never occurred to you to mention that you'd run into Rhodes's ex-boyfriend on one of *our* wards?"

"How was I supposed to know he was her ex-boyfriend?" growled Tristan. "And what's his specialty, anyway?"

"It's—" Nico stopped. Frowned. "Fuck. Rhodes told me a hundred times, I swear, but it's something, I don't know. Something stupid, something like . . . *mind-numbingly* boring—"

"Is it?" hissed Tristan. "Or is he a goddamn *time traveler*?"

It dawned on them both in the same instant.

"Son of a bitch," said Nico, before abandoning his glass of champagne on a tray and careening recklessly into the hall.

Tristan went after him, barely restraining himself from breaking into a jog. "This could be nothing, you know." Someone in this situation had to be the adult, after all. Someone had to keep their wits about them. "We can't actually prove that she's lost in time, much less that she was stolen by a time traveler. We have no proof that your theory's anything but the ramblings of a madman." Unhelpfully, Tristan was panting as they wove between the party's roaming occupants. "This could be purely coincidence."

"*Could* it?" replied Nico scathingly, as if Tristan could not have said something more idiotic if he tried.

"You said yourself that he's nothing, he's dull, and anyway Rhodes, she would have—"

They skidded into the empty corridor as Tristan suddenly heard Callum's words in his head:

She knew the person who did this to her.

He blinked it away like a shudder.

It could have been a lie, he reminded himself. It could have been nothing. It was *Callum,* for fuck's sake, and—

"He's gone," pronounced Nico flatly, pausing in the empty hall before the transport wards. "Fuck. He's not here."

"Yes, Varona, I see that," Tristan snapped. They exchanged an irritated glance, both embroiled in silent arguments with people not present.

"You might have told me his name before," Tristan muttered after a moment, suffering a fit of unresolved frustration.

"And *you* might have mentioned someone on the wards!" snapped Nico.

"I thought it was—" Tristan's mouth tightened. It wasn't as if he could explain any of this to Nico. "Nothing. This is absurd." He cast an irritated glance at Nico. "You don't even know what his specialty is. Or if that was even *him.*"

"Oh, so I'll just go knock on his door, then? Ask him what he's up to and by the way, has he got Rhodes stashed in his closet?" The chandelier above them was vibrating at the low but unmistakable frequency of Nico de Varona's anger.

Nico's initial excitement, the adrenaline of the chase, was waning in favor of something older, more brittle. Fury. Bereavement. Disappointment. Perhaps because Nico, like Tristan, had realized that the leap they'd just had in judgment was not a guarantee of much—except that both of them were too emotionally tied to the whole situation to see things clearly, which was terrifyingly like admitting they would never find Libby at all.

"She's not here," said Nico, coming to the same conclusion Tristan had. That they had searched for Libby Rhodes on every inch of this earth and found nothing. The weight of it wilted Nico's shoulders as their joint moment of clarity fizzled out. "You know that as well as I do. She's not *here,*" Nico ranted, "and even if for some fucking reason I was actually right about Fowler being a useless piece of shit, my theory is still just a theory, and I still can't find her, which nobody can do anything about. Not," Nico added at something that faltered just shy of a bellow, "that anyone is even *trying!*"

He shot Tristan a look of uncontained loathing and stormed away, clipping Parisa's shoulder as he went. She frowned after him, then caught Tristan's eye.

"You've certainly riled him up," she commented. There was a man lingering slavishly at her side, and Parisa followed Tristan's eyeline of suspicion to her latest would-be paramour before turning back to him with a shrug. "Can't I have a hobby? Callum's got one."

"For *fuck's* sake," said Tristan to nothing, wanting desperately to punch something and opting, instead, to have a drink.

And then another.

Thankfully, time did tend to clear the head even if champagne was somewhat less helpful. After finishing his third glass, Tristan hurried bullishly up the stairs to bang on Nico's door, suddenly impulsive.

"Varona," he barked when there was no answer, slamming on the door again.

Across the hall, Reina emerged from her room in her pajamas to give Tristan the finger.

"Yeah, yeah," muttered Tristan, waving her away until Nico sleepily pulled open the door.

"Ugh, you again," he said without any particular bite, parsing the sentiment through a yawn. "So listen, I think I may have gotten a bit—"

"Get dressed," said Tristan.

Nico looked blearily at him. "Huh?"

"Get dressed," Tristan repeated crisply, before deciding that actually, there was no reason this errand required trousers. "Never mind. Let's go."

Nico frowned at him, rubbing one eye. "Go where?"

"Out. It'll be a drive."

"A *drive?*" echoed Nico, free hand falling to his side. "Where are you going to find a *car?*"

"Are you or aren't you magic, Varona?" Tristan snapped, which was nonsensical, but evidently made sense to Nico.

"Point taken. Give me five minutes." Nico reached for the door and disappeared behind it.

"You've gone insane, I see," commented Reina from behind Tristan.

He turned to look at her, realizing that before that evening, it had been weeks since he'd spoken to her at all. The suit jacket she had been wearing was draped atop a pile of books in the corner by the door. She looked different, somehow. More . . . focused. As always, she remained totally unknowable. "What have you been doing for the last six months?"

"Point taken," she said, and shut the door, though Tristan had been genuinely asking. He hadn't the faintest idea what she'd been doing or researching. Without their daily lectures from Dalton, there had been little to no reason for them to interact.

He wondered if she knew that Atlas considered her a piece of his plan. Had she been in on it from the beginning? He stepped forward to knock on her door and ask, but before he could, Nico flung his bedroom door open.

"So." Nico was absolutely buzzing. The floor hummed with energy and the sconces in the corridor were trembling. "Where are we going?"

"North," said Tristan, backing away from Reina's room. That conversation could wait. He wasn't even sure he wanted to hear the answer. What if everyone in the house had a purpose and Tristan was the last to know? Embarrassing. "*Very* north."

"Is this about Fowler? Are we going after him?" Nico asked as they descended the stairs. Below, the chandeliers were chattering like teeth.

"Anything you can do about that?" Tristan countered, gesturing at the lights. The party had moved into the great hall by then. Tristan wondered if Callum had gone to bed and then decided he probably hadn't. He had been wandering the house at all sorts of hours lately, not that Tristan cared.

"Right. Sorry. I hadn't realized how badly I wanted to leave until, like, this moment." Nico craned his neck around to peer into the corridor. "So are we hunting Fowler down, then?" he asked eagerly.

"No." Not yet. Not until they wouldn't sound like certifiable lunatics for suggesting it. "We don't know for sure that he took Rhodes, or that he can do anything remotely like what we think happened." Surely, Tristan thought desperately, Libby would have known if she'd put her life in the hands of an omnipotent psychopath. "And anyway, we're doing something much more important. Unless you have more pressing matters to attend to," he said, noticing out of the corner of his eye that Nico had been checking the screen of his mobile phone.

"Nothing." Nico shoved the phone back in his pocket. "I texted people I know in New York if they'd heard anything about Fowler, but no answer yet, not even from Max—"

"Other people have lives, Varona."

"I know, but—" Nico made a face as they reached the transports along the west side of the house. "Never mind. When you say *north*—"

"I'll know it when I see it," said Tristan shortly.

"Will you see it without me murdering you?" asked Nico, arching a doubtful brow.

"I'll know it when I see it," Tristan repeated, more emphatically this time. He jabbed the button to call the transport a second time, and then a third, which he knew contributed nothing. The lift-resembling doors remained placidly unmoved. "I'm looking for something big. A power source."

Nico's head bobbed in acknowledgment. "Because . . . ?"

"Because if your bonkers little theory is right and Rhodes is somewhere in time, then she's going to need something massive to power her way back," said Tristan matter-of-factly before deciding that was really quite a mad thing to say, so maybe neither of them was managing to keep a level head.

"Oh." Nico was thoughtful as Tristan pushed a button for King's Cross.

"We'll get a car and drive," Tristan said, not wanting to get into his whole theory. The more of it he confessed aloud, the dumber it sounded.

"Okay." Nico was uncharacteristically silent when the doors opened again, delivering them to the station. Inside, the moon came through the blend of industrial glass and old brick along the western concourse, oddly peaceful. Tristan had forgotten how quiet London could be in the wee hours. It had been a year since he'd last been out of the confines of the Society's manor house, and even longer since he'd called the city home.

They walked in silence for several minutes. They had already traversed the station's vestibule, Tristan striding ahead with more violence as his uncertainty increased, when Nico spoke again. "Auroras," he said.

"What?" Tristan's response was an unintentional snap. (It seemed having no fucking clue what he was doing had set him a touch on edge.)

"Auroras," Nico repeated. "They're electrical energy from solar flares."

Tristan came to a guarded halt. Last he checked he was not *Encyclopaedia Britannica*, but presumably there was a conclusion of some use. "Yes, and . . . ?"

"*And,*" Nico said, lifting his chin, "you're trying to find a power source that no one else can see. But it would probably give off energy the same way, right? So if you're looking for a bunch of, I don't know, waves—"

It would look like an aurora—to Tristan, and Tristan alone. Which was what he had irrationally, unscientifically suspected and thus not wanted to confess aloud, lest the idiocy pop out. Grateful, he mustered up a "Congratulations, Varona, you're a genius" and left it at that.

"It's true," Nico agreed. "They say God doesn't give with both hands, and yet—"

"Shut up. No, keep talking." Tristan took off again, this time in the opposite direction. "Come on, never mind about the car." That had been the plan of an optimistic maniac whereas this, while still technically the same in theory, was borderline informed. "We'll get a transport to Inverness, and then—"

"Ah, the Highlands? Magical," Nico chirped. Beneath the glimmer of station lights, Nico de Varona was suddenly the picture of health. He looked better than he had in months. Perhaps it was the promise of misbehavior, only Tristan, who had not committed a hijink in many an age, felt quite invigorated himself. Possibly it was the thrill of fresh air or general lack of empaths—though Nico, perhaps sensing Tristan's moment of peace, plowed on. "Although, riddle me this, Caine: When you find this mysterious power source, then what?"

That was the question Tristan had been trying very hard not to ask himself. He was very acutely aware that it was the middle of the night, and that he had gambled only on Nico's willingness to act rashly rather than his own lucidity with regard to this ongoing pursuit. He did not know what he would do when—or if—he found it. Darting off into the night to chase some unknown crop of fairy stones was hardly the scientific advancement of the century. Voicing it aloud would surely not help. Could he even put words to this urgency, this need to stretch out and see what his magic could do? Tristan was aware that he had all but admitted to Atlas how much his abilities still sorely lacked. He did not know what he was accomplishing, really, by trying to prove Atlas right or wrong, or whether that was even what he intended to do. Increasingly, Tristan's concerns had funneled tightly narrower and narrower until it all seemed to hinge on a single pressing need.

"Then we find a way to bring Rhodes home," he said quietly.

Which was, at least, the one thing Nico de Varona was never going to fight.

As expected, Nico's expression shifted to one of dawning clarity. He opened his mouth to answer, then stopped. "I," he began, and then frowned. "Tristan," he said, looking around. There was a beat of delay, or apparent confusion. "Does it seem . . . quite empty in here?"

"What?" asked Tristan, aggrieved at having yet another unrequited moment of spontaneous vulnerability. "It's the middle of the night, Varona, I hardly think—"

"Get down," Nico said suddenly, yanking Tristan to the floor.

In the same moment that Tristan's knees hit the hard floor, he registered the presence of someone—*two* someones, both covered by waves of magic—

just before something shot from the palm of Nico's hand. Then, ears ringing, kneecaps throbbing, Tristan registered something all too familiar.

The sound of a gun going off.

Tristan struggled to his feet and spun, everything around him shifting. It was happening faster now, the kaleidoscoping of his surroundings at his command, and then he was inside of the waves of Nico's magic—the shield that Nico must have erected like a sugar-spun globe around the place the two of them were standing in the vestibule. Within the span of a breath, Tristan dismantled the bullet—no wait, stop destroying things, *Caine for fuck's sake are you ever going to learn any offense!*—and put it back together again, recalibrating the force it had taken to send it backward the way it had come.

It occurred to Tristan just then that either Nico's attempts at spontaneous murder had spilled over into actual inconvenience or perhaps, more alarmingly, this was not Nico de Varona at all.

Tristan's redirected bullet found a home in the chest of the original gunman just before Nico, who had dissolved the shield he'd erected around them, landed a hard blow to the side of the second assailant's head.

"Did you see that?" Nico gasped, grabbing hold of Tristan's shoulder and taking off at a run. "His face, did you see it?"

"See what?" Tristan was panting, following with uneven strides as Nico leapt up the frozen escalator, evidently trying to find a vantage point on high.

"He was *surprised.*" Nico tugged Tristan behind a corner, pausing with a hand on his lips, listening. "They came for you," Nico mouthed in explanation.

"What?"

They waited for evidence that they were being followed. Highly unlikely, Tristan thought, considering that one man was bleeding out while the other was severely unconscious. Should they call the police? What did one do in the event of such an attack? This was no average mugging.

"They came for you." Nico nudged Tristan again, gesturing to a service exit. "Come on."

Nico vanished the alarms, which apparently did not have any medeian fail-safes. Figured. Tristan had valued medeian security systems for James Wessex and they were all privatized, trademarked and patented at costs that bordered on lunacy.

"What do you mean they came for me?" Tristan demanded.

Outside the air was biting. Tristan's lungs strained, and Nico's cheeks were red with effort.

"It's like they were waiting for you. Expecting you. But I was a surprise."

Despite the cold, and the sheen of sweat, Nico looked vibrant. "Someone," he deduced, "must have known you were going to be here."

"But I only decided to leave just hours ago. Tonight." Tristan frowned. "And who would want me dead?"

Nico's eyes were bright with calculation.

"I don't know," he said, "but I think we should probably find out."

· NICO ·

M id-morning on the day after he'd left the Society's manor house with Tristan, Nico arrived back within the wards of the west wing with a new, breathless sense of urgency that he had not had since . . . well, since Libby was still here. Ironically, he was pleased at the moment that Libby was gone, as she would not take news of his recent travels well at all. The lecture would have been interminable.

He entered the house's main corridor and took off at a jog, scanning the painted room first for any sign of activity, then traversing the ground floor to the reading room. "Parisa?" he yelled, making his way back to the entry hall.

No answer. He skidded to a halt beside the stairs, taking them two at a time to reach the bedrooms.

"Parisa, are you here?"

Silence. He knocked on her door, but when there was no response, he figured there was little chance she was inside it. There was no surly patrician growl of "Nicolás, your thoughts are too loud," which meant she was likely not here.

Fine. Time to check the gardens. Nico wandered back down the stairs, and was preparing to venture outside when his phone buzzed.

did I not make it adequately clear to you that this was an emergency

The contact name was "Asshole (Derogatory)" to distinguish it from Max's contact, which was "Asshole (Affectionate)."

get her, came the following message, *and then get back out here.*

"Very helpful advice, Caine, thank you," muttered Nico, shoving his phone back into his pocket and narrowly skirting the presence of an obstacle in his path.

"Watch it," muttered Callum, who was heading toward the dining room from the kitchen. "You smell like irresponsibility," he added disapprovingly, which was ironic considering that the half-eaten sandwich he was carrying almost certainly belonged to Dalton.

"Thank you," replied Nico, and then, because he was apparently bereft of better judgment, he asked, "Have you seen Parisa?"

"No." Callum's gaze was already distracted, his attention having passed through Nico and on to whatever matters lay ahead. "Goodbye forever, then."

Nico blinked, alarmed. "What?"

"Nothing. Just a little joke. Ha ha," said Callum in a disorienting tone, though he paused for another moment to stare at Nico through narrowed eyes.

"What?" asked Nico defensively.

Both of them looked down as Nico's pocket buzzed loudly with something. Probably some new complaint from His Eminence. *Tick tock, Varona,* et cetera, as if Nico were not also aware there was a pressing matter at hand. It wasn't his fault if Parisa couldn't be found, and what was he supposed to do about it?

Though, in lieu of Parisa—

Callum must have caught the change in Nico's expression. "No," he said with his usual air of condescension, and Nico sighed.

"Look, I need . . . a particular skill," Nico said.

Tristan, of course, was going to kill him for this. But then again, Tristan was likely going to be a bitch about it either way, and since Parisa wasn't currently in the house, it was either this or take a meandering stroll about the grounds.

"No," Callum repeated, turning away, but Nico waved a hand. Callum, uncharacteristically unsuspecting, walked directly into Nico's conjured wall of force as if he'd collided with an actual wall. "Son of a *bitch,*" Callum said, immediately drawing a hand to his face. "Mother of pearl."

"Busy?" asked Nico.

"You're a fucking child," mumbled Callum, who was daintily pinching the bridge of his nose between two aristocratic fingers.

"So I've heard," Nico replied, and then took Callum by the shoulder, hauling him toward the west entrance and beyond the safety of the house's wards.

Outside the manor house was a country lane, fields, all the expected pastoral tedium. That, plus a cheap rental car and an extremely aggravated Asshole (Derogatory).

"No," said Tristan instantly, his brow furrowing as Callum and Nico came into view from the other side of the house's protection wards. Tristan had been leaning against the car but launched himself upright, stepping halfway into the road the moment Callum's participation became obvious. "Absolutely not. We want him *alive*—"

"My goodness," said Callum spiritedly. He, Nico could see, had decided on elaborate theatrics as the vibes for the encounter. As usual, he was wearing only a plush robe that looked as if it belonged to a mad king. There was a spot of blood on his upper lip, which made him look especially unhinged, though as far as Nico could tell he was only tipsy and not actually drunk. "Varona, have you brought me a captive?"

Callum waltzed to the car and peered through the window, marveling at the contents of the backseat like someone observing a bear at the zoo. "Fascinating," he murmured, with a loaded glance over his shoulder at Tristan that even Nico could tell was far soberer than Callum himself seemed to be.

Meanwhile—"I told you to get *Parisa*," Tristan hissed at Nico.

"Yeah, well, you wanted someone manipulated, didn't you?" Nico muttered back. Unhelpfully, Callum, who had been taking a selfie with their slumbering captive through the window of the car's backseat, threw a grin over his shoulder, followed by a thumbs-up. "Don't need a telepath for that."

Tristan glared at him but said nothing, which Nico supposed was well within his rights. After all, it was day two of nearly being murdered, and Nico was pretty sure that such things did not generally do much for the disposition.

It had been happening almost like clockwork, every few hours, or so it seemed. Someone had suddenly thrown themselves over the rental car counter. Someone else had set a trap for their tires on the road. It was starting to feel like at increasing intervals, someone new would appear out of thin air to aim for Tristan Caine as if there had been a hit put out on him specifically, presumably on the off chance he left the Society's wards. At first Tristan and Nico had simply dispatched their bouquet of assassins, which varied from mortal to magical with seemingly no rationale, with an acceptable lack of effort. Finally, though, Tristan had pulled the car over and dragged the latest medeian (this one had pulled alongside them on the road when they were arguing about the contents of Nico's sausage roll) into the backseat, all while wearing a look of something far too methodical to be rage.

"This is getting ridiculous," Tristan had said, and turned the car around with such an unnecessary amount of force that Nico decided he was witnessing yet another layer of the Tristan Caine trifle. He hadn't known Tristan to possess such spectacular backbone before, so for a moment it was exciting enough to go along with it and forget that taking hostages was maybe not the best idea they'd had all day.

They weren't able to take the captive medeian into the house's wards—

among other things, it violated the Society's one (1) rule—so the plan had been for Tristan to wait by the car (and, by extension, its unwilling passenger) while Nico ran inside and grabbed Parisa. Presto change-o, a bit of mind reading, and boom, they'd know exactly why someone (aside from Nico) was so intent on Tristan's death.

But the reminder of Callum's existence was unfortunately also a reminder that sometimes a backup plan was key.

"What we do *not* want," Tristan seethed in Nico's general direction, "is a hobbyist's game of cat and mouse." Meaning he did not consider Callum capable of not playing with his food before he ate it, which was fair, albeit unhelpful. "We just need to get the answers and then deposit . . . this," Tristan decided as terminology for their rental car's occupant, "*elsewhere,* and then continue trying to figure out if—"

"Funny story, lads," announced Callum, opening the door to the backseat and slipping inside. "Your little witch friend here's awake."

"Witch?" asked Nico, which Tristan ignored. A witch would mean someone capable of magic, but without the university qualification that defined a medeian. All Nico really knew about witches was that they had their own rules and Tristan's father was one. "But he seemed so good at fucking around with the satellite signal—"

"And he's not awake," Tristan growled, launching forward with his knuckles clutched tight as if he intended to punch the entire situation in the nose. "I saw to it myself, he's asleep and he's—"

"A witch," Callum confirmed to Nico, who was now ignoring Tristan. "Proficiency with machines doesn't necessarily rise to the occasion of technomancy. Introduce yourself, if you please," Callum added to the witch, who was older than Nico but not old. If anything he looked like a duller version of Callum—a more weathered, less piercing manifestation of blond hair and blue eyes.

"Hello," obliged the witch, who rose from the car's backseat as if in a trance. "I am Jordy Kingsworth."

"Hello, Jordy Kingsworth!" replied Callum sunnily, tossing one arm around the witch's shoulders. "And tell us, Jordy Kingsworth, what business do you have with my friends here?"

"I'm their hostage," replied Jordy Kingsworth in a relaxed, affable tone that suggested he wasn't speaking of his own volition.

"Right, of course," agreed Callum, subjecting both an agitated Tristan and a slightly remorseful Nico to a bizarre show of pseudo-ventriloquism. "But before that?"

"Got a notification that Tristan Caine had left the Society's wards." The witch looked placidly glassy-eyed, as if he'd recently eaten quite a lot of Thanksgiving turkey. "Same warnings pinged Osaka, Paris, and New York for Reina Mori, Parisa Kamali, and Nicolás Ferrer de Varona."

"Should I be insulted?" asked Callum, alluding to his absence from the list with an exaggerated pout.

"Callum Nova: deceased," replied Jordy Kingsworth. "Whereabouts of the remaining initiates subject to change—"

"He sounds like he's reading from a dossier," Nico said with a frown, choosing for the moment to overlook Tristan's seething glances at Callum. "Someone's hunting us? Who?"

Jordy Kingsworth mumbled something in response, his words slurred.

"What's that?" asked Callum facetiously, cupping one ear. "Say it again?"

"The Forum is interested in the whereabouts of the Society initiates," repeated Kingsworth, louder this time. "In partnership with Metropolitan Police. The aforementioned medeians are to be immediately apprehended."

"Ah, that explains that," said Callum, removing a police badge from Kingsworth's breast pocket and offering it briefly to Tristan, before changing his mind and vanishing it into his own pocket at the precise moment that Tristan unwillingly put out a hand. "I'll take that. Any plans for your hostage?" he asked Nico.

A fair question. Nico glanced at Tristan, whose mouth tightened.

"Let him go," Tristan said.

"Are you sure?" chirped Callum, looking smugly delighted, as if he'd known the answer would be suitably uninspired. "Just let him go?" he pondered. "No further questions? No . . . special words of encouragement?"

The promise of something sinister seemed very, very palpable, which Nico doubted Tristan had missed.

"Let. Him. Go," repeated Tristan, to which Callum's smile stretched thinly across his face.

"There's just one other thing," Callum said, hand genially cupping the back of Jordy Kingsworth's neck. "You did say the Society members were to be *apprehended*, not attacked. So then who was it that put out the hit on our good friend Tristan?" Callum asked the witch, a deranged look of pleasure on his face.

This answer seemed to be extracted like teeth. Beside Nico, Tristan's breath faltered so sharply he seemed frozen in place.

"Adrian Caine," said Jordy Kingsworth.

"*Wonderful*," said Callum, clapping Kingsworth on the back before opening the driver's-side door and escorting him into it. "Enjoy," he offered, and cheerfully, Kingsworth waved back at them before taking off down the lane at an incredibly respectful speed.

"Where's he going?" asked Nico, stepping into the road to frown after the car.

"Off the nearest cliff," replied Callum, and then, to Tristan's scowl, he sighed. "Joking. He's just gone to the nearest pub for a pint. It seems he's suddenly feeling very thirsty." Still, Tristan said nothing. "Relax," Callum sighed. "He can't get to you within our wards, can he? So he's not a threat worth dealing with."

To that, Tristan turned on his heel and stormed into the house. Callum glanced at Nico, then shrugged.

"Seems like someone can't take a joke," Callum remarked.

Nico, who figured their quest for Libby was probably on pause due to unforeseen circumstances, arched a brow. "You might have left out the bit about his father wanting him dead."

Something glinted in Callum's eye. It was the first mark of true lucidity Nico had observed from him in weeks.

"Could have," Callum agreed. "Oddly, though," he mused, heading toward the house's grounds, "I found that rather the best part."

Nico let Callum walk inside the wards first, then followed, thinking as he went about the implications of being tracked by the Forum. What exactly did the Forum plan to do with the Society initiates? And was that yet another untold consequence of initiation? They had all been told, after all, that Society membership would mean wealth and prestige, not instantaneous arrest. Was this yet another lie from Atlas, or was it something related to Libby's abduction? Had it been the Forum after all?

Nico was so focused on his thoughts that he nearly stumbled into Callum's back upon reaching the house's west entrance, noticing that Tristan and Parisa were already mid-argument inside the house.

"—not exactly *news*, is it?" Parisa was saying. "I can't think why you're so surprised. Someone came for Rhodes. They'll come for us. And what were you doing out of the house, anyway?"

"That," Tristan huffed, "is *obviously* none of your—"

"Electromagnetic waves, really?" Parisa said, having chosen to read Tristan's mind in lieu of having it out like grown-ups. Beside Nico, Callum stood in the doorway looking amused.

From a distance behind where Tristan and Parisa were arguing in the corridor, Reina came to a halt from wherever she'd been walking. Probably the archives, although who knew. All that Nico had gathered from Reina in recent months was that she wanted him to disappear off the face of the earth as quickly as humanly possible, thanks.

"Don't tell me you were off searching for fairy stones and crop circles," Parisa was saying, in what Nico registered as quite a Rhodesian tone. "Varona," Parisa warned without looking at him, "just because a woman expresses that a man is being stupid does *not* mean—"

"Those myths have a reason for existing," Reina cut in from behind them.

"Nobody asked you," snapped Parisa and Tristan in unison.

"I do so love when we're all together," remarked Callum whimsically, leaning onto Nico's shoulder. Nico hurried to lean away.

"*Shut up,*" Tristan and Parisa replied.

"Creatures choose their ancestral sites for a reason," Reina continued academically as if no one else had spoken, then fixed a hard glance at Nico. "I read it in the book Varona gave me last year."

Nico sensed a wafting air of accusation from her somehow, which didn't make sense, as he was pretty sure he was innocent of nearly everything. "Oh?" he replied in an inoffensive tone that hopefully conveyed his confusion.

No luck. Apparently he'd find out what he'd done to Reina only when she was good and dead. "There are plenty of places in the U.K. that have increased electromagnetic activity," she went on, after looking at Nico as if he had personally ruined her day. "Clava Cairns, Loch Ness, Kilmartin—"

"Anything notable?" asked Tristan. He had abruptly forgotten his argument with Parisa, who was likewise frowning at Reina in thought.

Reina shrugged. "Maybe Callanish Circle? It's in Scotland. You could check the book."

"Great." Tristan was off like a shot, shaking off Parisa with a glare and leaving the rest of them behind as if they had never spoken.

"Were you looking for me?" Parisa asked, suddenly turning to Nico.

Fixed with the direct spotlight of her attention, he felt unexpectedly very awkward. "I was, yes, but—"

Before he could finish his sentence, Tristan had stormed back into the corridor.

"I would like to remind the lot of you that you all said you'd help Varona find Rhodes," Tristan announced in an irritable voice. "And ultimately none of you have lifted a finger. *You're* obviously no help," he added pointedly in Callum's general direction, "but still, the year's almost up, and not a single one of you have even mentioned her name."

"I—" began Nico, only to be cut off.

"Varona's the one searching for her," Parisa retorted, speaking to Tristan very slowly, as if she suspected him of suffering from a chronic state of idiocy. "What more do you want us to do? When he finds her, then we'll help."

"Well—" Nico attempted again.

"More pressing, I would think, is the fact that we're all about to be hunted down by some sort of hapless Forum task force," Parisa continued, to which Reina frowned.

"What?"

"Apparently they still prefer to have us within their possession and are no longer interested in asking nicely," Parisa muttered to Reina without looking at her, "which is so typical of so-called philanthropists, honestly—"

"What does it matter whether we're being hunted?" demanded Tristan. "We can't change that from inside this house," he growled, "but as for the matter of bringing back Rhodes—"

From Nico's pocket, his phone buzzed. Everyone seemed to have lost interest in him, so he pulled it from his pocket, glancing down to see if Max had finally deigned to answer his day-old text. (Mira, Libby's friend, had said only that she had not seen Ezra anytime recently, assuming he was smarting from the breakup. A follow-up text a day later said the unit had a new tenant, but who could be surprised about rental turnover in the city? The apartment was way too nice for one person and, anyway, Mira thought we hated him? *Oh and Nico, I know you're like super busy doing genius physicist-y stuff but if you could get Libby to please text back—*)

But it wasn't Max. Or Mira.

bonjour

Nico swallowed.

I came I saw I conquered
or whatever
the point is I have news
u up?

Nico's pulse careened with surprise/alarm/some egregious uptick of activity.

"Guys," he said, finding his throat dry.

"—could at least *strategize*," Parisa was still saying very loudly, "so as to not be sitting ducks when the time comes, yes?"

Reina's expression was tight with irritation. "That's what I just s—"

"Oh, but they think Callum's dead," Tristan said with a listless wave of a hand in Callum's direction.

"Well, obviously," replied Parisa, in a tone that seemed meant to annoy Tristan.

It worked, and Tristan rounded on her, plainly aggrieved. "What do you mean *obviously*? He was just wandering around in full view, how is that *obvious*?"

"Guys," Nico attempted again. "I'm just going to . . ."

He pointed to his phone, but then trailed off when he realized that nobody aside from Callum was looking at him.

"Hot date?" asked Callum with a mirthful smirk.

Nico gave a loud sigh and took the stairs two at a time, then three. From there, it was only a matter of moments to arrive in his usual cell of dream visitation.

"Oh, hi," said Gideon, the bastard. Nico wanted to punch him square in the mouth.

"Hi," Nico replied wildly. "*Cómo estás?*"

"*Bien, más o menos. Y t—*"

"Shut up. Just shut up." Nico walked toward the bars and felt elation of the most frustrating kind. "Hi."

"We did that already, Nicky." Gideon's smile in return was wan and unforgivable. "So, anyway," he continued, "good news. Libby's delightfully bad at this, but at least she's informative. And—what?"

Nico blinked, realizing Gideon was looking quizzically at him while waiting for an answer. "What do you mean what?" Nico demanded, suddenly self-conscious. "Keep going. You know where she is?"

"Yes, I was just . . ." Gideon's mouth twisted with amusement, then he shrugged. "I can keep it brief, if you want. I was just going to tell you she's—"

"Talk all day," Nico countered instantly. "Seriously. Recite poetry, I don't care."

"She's in Los Angeles," Gideon said. "In 1989."

Nico's heart swelled to bursting. "Is she?"

"Well, 1990 now, I suppose. What?" Gideon asked again, brow twitching with bemusement. "You're staring at me, Nicky."

"Am I?" Nico felt curiously breathless. "Never mind," he said. "Probably nothing. Anything else?"

"Yeah, I've got a theory," said Gideon.

They were the most beautiful words Nico de Varona had ever heard in his life. Never mind that he had just learned someone was out to kill him. Never mind that for the last two days, multiple someones had tried. All of a sudden, it was a very simple matter. Gideon was here, and he had answers.

He had a *theory*. Nothing had ever seemed like synchronicity of the most purely fucking divine.

"Tell me," Nico said, settling in for what would ultimately become a very long nap. "I'm listening. Go ahead."

· REINA ·

With Callum's help—"help" being quite a generous term—Reina had been able to extract (like teeth, or venom) from the library's archives a collection of books on mythology that for whatever reason it did not want her to have. Such things would have been amply available to her at any university. Every culture had an explanation for the universe, for life that was created in seven days or vomited up from a stomachache or transformed from a drop of milk, and to seek as much should not have been a problem. But the more she asked, the more the archives were resistant. Specifically, what the archives did not want her to have were the stories of gods who acted where man had failed: taming the wilderness around them, allowing a dying earth to be reborn.

The concept of samsara and its cycle of reincarnation was commonly misunderstood, which was something Reina had already known. Karma was routinely misrepresented as the scales of justice when really, it was a matter of eternal continuity. The wheel of fortune, turning and turning, was not a matter of any single point of high or low, but the absence of measurement, the irrelevance of time. There was no beginning, no end. There was only nature itself, and magic itself, which was not born and therefore did not die. It had existed and would always exist. There was no end to this world, no beginning, no salvation from on high, nor any need for it. Olympus was empty. The gods were already here.

Reina could tell the archives were beginning to find this train of thought worrisome.

Fortunately, she did not trust the archives or their brain, whatever it was. She assumed it was like programming, like code, where someone was still responsible for its biases. Whether that was Atlas Blakely or some other member of the Society on high was of no concern to Reina.

Well, not *no* concern. She was pretty sure there was something afoot, some mechanism of control.

Mother seeeeees, said the fern in the painted room. *MotherMother knows, but Mother wewewe are not alone!*

That was annoying. The whole thing with the plants was never not annoying, but they had grown increasingly vocal. They seemed to take issue with something, with the amount of reading she was doing, maybe, or with the comfortable softness growing around her middle as she remained in her bed, poring endlessly over piles of books. Vines were beginning to puncture the glass of her bedroom window, creeping into the cracks of her sill. It seemed that despite the fruitfulness of her studies, nature wanted increasingly for her to go outside and touch some grass.

It was a week or so after the ridiculous Society party ("You're welcome to attend," Atlas had said, which had caused the potted fig to outright guffaw at Reina's expense) that Reina finally gave in and wandered outside to the hard-packed ground, the uneven patches of snow beside the dogwoods. Below her footsteps sprang tiny green saplings, baby weeds.

Her timing was fortuitous. She heard tones of argument and paused among the giggling branches.

"—told you to leave it alone, but you didn't. You *couldn't*. You really can't love anyone, can you?"

It was Dalton's voice. Reina recalled, then, that Atlas had informed them the previous week of Dalton's illness. She had not thought much of it. Flu season. She forgot (out of a lack of interest, surely) that aside from Callum's ongoing flirtation with intoxication, they were medeians who did not get sick.

"That's what you think this is?" was Parisa's hard scoff in return. "Love? And how did you possibly see that ending?"

Dalton did not appear to be listening. "Because of you," he ranted, "I nearly couldn't finish what I started. Who knows if I even still can." His voice was hard-edged and unusually, uncharacteristically cutting. "Atlas is right. This isn't going to hold—it already isn't. And when it inevitably *fails*—"

"You want to hold me responsible for your choices? Fine. You seem to have forgotten that you knew exactly what you said yes to." Parisa sounded colder in response to Dalton's agitation, increasingly more aloof as his frustration grew. "You forget that *you* were the one who let *me* in."

Reina peered around the trunk of the nearest elm, watching as Dalton set his jaw in something she did not think was entirely frustration. Not entirely anger, either.

Saaaaaaaaad, sighed the elm.

"Fine." Dalton turned away from Parisa and was gone without another word, catching sight of Reina as he went but pushing brusquely past her.

Parisa, meanwhile, didn't turn from where she remained alone.

"I know you're there." Parisa flicked a glance down at the grass, then stared straight ahead again as Reina trudged reluctantly toward her. "I can hear everything you can hear, you know," Parisa added with pointed detachment. "And you're right, this lawn's a bitch."

Reina sidled up next to her in silence.

"You're not feeling sorry for me this time, I see," Parisa observed without looking at her. "I guess I've finally managed to convince you that I'm not worth the sympathy, then?"

"I think that whatever you did to him, you deserved that." Reina's voice felt unpracticed. She realized abruptly that she hadn't spoken to anyone in days. The last time she had needed Callum's help, she'd just roused him from where he'd fallen asleep in the dining room and dragged him to the archives. He'd stayed awake just long enough for her to pull the oral history of the Fulani herdsmen and then immediately put his head down again.

"Oh, I do deserve it," Parisa agreed. "Which is interesting, because I so rarely get what I deserve." She looked amused with herself, which was borderline revolting.

"You really think you're that desirable?" Reina cut a glance sideways. "You really just expect to be loved, no conditions met?"

Parisa shrugged. "Dalton doesn't love me."

"Maybe you only want to think he doesn't. Because you can't love anyone."

Parisa's laugh in response was dark and filled with a prissy sort of gloom. "Don't tell me you're a romantic, Reina," she sighed. "It'll ruin my high opinion of you."

"You don't have a high opinion of me," Reina muttered.

"Silly me, I'd forgotten." Parisa finally turned to look at her. It was a hard blow, a cold one, a shock of winter white.

Callum was right, her beauty was a curse. It masked the absence of something deeper.

Grimly, Parisa smiled. "I see you've given no thought to what you'll do when the year is over," she commented.

"Nor have you." Obviously not, given the conversation she'd just had with Dalton.

"Oh, I know what I'll do," Parisa said with a lofty air of condescension. "The same thing anyone does. Get old, spend money, die."

The grass beneath them cackled, or wilted. "Is that really all you came here to do?" Reina asked, irritated.

"No." A shrug. "Coming here was part of that."

"But don't you have research?" As always, Reina wondered why she was bothering to continue the conversation, but something about Parisa's foundational philosophy was maddeningly out of reach for her.

Was it her apathy? Her apparent insistence that being alive, being anything, did not matter?

"Of course I have research," Parisa replied. "But what good will that do, locked away in the archives for the next round of medeians to use in secret?"

"So then you'd rather give it away?" Like the Forum.

"Oh, fuck no." Parisa looked at Reina like she was the stupidest girl who'd ever lived. "No, are you joking? Humanity isn't meant to have everything that's hidden in there." She gestured carelessly over her shoulder to the archives. "The Society is right about at least that much."

Reina frowned. "But then—"

"Don't you get it? The world is meaningless and fucked," said Parisa. "I thought you understood that."

Reina cut her a glare. "You don't understand me."

"Actually, Reina, I do." Parisa sounded bored. "You're not that different from me. Or from Rhodes. Or from anyone. You don't want to be used," she said, "but you will be, you *are,* because even if you remain here—even if you die face-first in your *precious books*—" And there, the rare hint of actual anger. "—you will still be a tool of something. Of *someone.*"

Parisa folded her arms tightly over her chest. "The magic in the archives is sentient," she said, gesturing over her shoulder again. "It's tracking us, I know it is, and I know the Society is using it. That must be how they found us to begin with."

"So?"

"God, are you intentionally obtuse? So nothing. So everything." Parisa looked repulsed. "Either you care that something in there has a brain—or at the very least a set of eyes that's watching us," she amended, "—or you don't. And if you don't, then what the fuck am I even doing here explaining things to you?" Parisa threw her hands up in exasperation. "The point is that I know minds. *That,*" she said with another jerk of her chin to the house behind them, "is one. And you must know that," she added. "Because for all your insistence that you lack any sort of ability, what you do every single day is commune with something that lives and breathes and thinks for itself."

There it was again. Another person in this house treating magic like it was a god. As if naturalism was a force unto itself, with deliberate decision-making. "Nature doesn't think for itself," Reina said. "It wants me to think for it."

"No, it wants you to *speak* for it," Parisa corrected bluntly. "But it tells *you* what to think."

Reina scoffed. "Then nature is obviously very stupid."

"Not stupid." Parisa shook her head. "Well, for choosing you as a mouthpiece, maybe it is. Clearly it doesn't understand human nature well enough to know that forcing someone to do its bidding means she'll spend the whole time pointlessly struggling."

"So what would you do?" Reina demanded. "If you had my abilities instead of your own."

"Not confine myself to books." Parisa glanced sideways at her.

"Right. Well. If I had your . . . *talents*," Reina said with an equally dismissive glare, "I think I'd put myself to greater use as well, thanks."

"Oh, yes." Parisa's voice was riddled with sarcasm. "Because there's no difference between your power and my face." She laughed, bitterly. "You think this world is anything but a series of accidents? That's all anything is. There's no design, just . . . probability. Genetics are just a roll of the dice. Every outcome, every supposed gift or curse, it's all just one possible statistic." She sounded unusually defeated.

"God does not play dice," Reina murmured, feeling obstinate.

"Don't tell God what to do," Parisa replied.

She turned away stiffly then, having apparently grown tired of the conversation. In the moment she was about to leave, though, Reina realized that she was very angry about something she still didn't fully understand. "Dalton's right, isn't he?" she called to the rigid line of Parisa's shoulders. "You can't love anyone, can you?"

Below their feet, the roots of the elm trees stretched and cracked. Parisa flung a glacial look at Reina, and for a moment when their eyes locked, Reina felt a fissure in her chest. Remorse, maybe, or some inexplicable longing. She felt pried open and exposed, but it wasn't a thought. It wasn't an idea. It was just a different kind of pain.

Then Parisa looked away.

"I've met very few people worth loving," Parisa said, and then she blew on her fingertips to warm them, making her way back to the house.

The house seemed quieter in the weeks following that one. Reina realized eventually that there was a strange, growing tension between the occupants of the house as the days of their so-called fellowship became more perilously numbered. Odd that they had entered initiation with every intention of collaboration only for the initiation ritual itself to pull them apart, untangling everything that should have entwined them forever. The sacrifice they should have all made. Atlas had said the enchantments would hold, but something else, something just as fundamental, had fractured. Callum was alive, Libby was gone, and as a result everyone else was coming loose. Undone, as if the house itself were preying on their fault lines.

Parisa was right about one thing. Life in the Society's archives was pointless. Not because the research was not plentiful and rare—Reina would live a contented lifetime among the books if she wanted, but then she would hear it, for the next eight years and possibly her life: Parisa's scornful laughter, the derision of Reina's choice to remain behind. Increasingly, Reina became aware of the inadequacy of her singular, lifelong goal. Like Callum and wine, her vice was an unimaginative hindrance. It suddenly seemed intensely shameful that despite all the power in the world, the only thing Reina truly wanted was to hide.

That, too, was an area Parisa had intuited correctly. And if there was any further motivation Reina needed, it would be to prove Parisa wrong.

"Listen," Reina said to Callum, who'd put his head down beside the evening's rack of lamb and hadn't risen since. "Hey." She poked him and he jumped, squinted at her, then rested his head again, wiping his mouth on his sleeve. "Listen to me."

"What?" His voice was muffled into a napkin. "I'm reading."

She realized that he did, indeed, have a book somewhere below his drooling mouth, though whether he was actually reading it was a matter of opinion. "I thought you weren't doing any research?"

"I changed my mind. And go away." He shoved Reina's hand aside as she tried to pull the book out from below the crook of his elbow, scanning for the title. "I said *go away*—"

"You're reading about . . . physics?" Reina frowned at the book's title, which was in Greek. "You can read Greek?"

"What," Callum growled, "do you *want*?"

Fine. He could keep his secrets. "I want your help."

"With what, a book? I'm busy."

"No. With—" Reina hesitated. "A . . . plan. A thought, really."

"For what?"

"For after."

"After *what*?" Callum was clearly cranky when he was ill-rested.

"After this," Reina said, gesturing around the house. "After we all go back."

"Back." At that, Callum sat up slowly.

"Yes. The purpose of this Society should not be simply to contribute to the archives," Reina said plainly. "It should be to bring the archives into the world."

Callum seemed disappointed. Or annoyed, for having expected a better answer. "Are you suggesting that the Forum—"

"No, not distribution," Reina corrected. "Action."

"Action meaning . . . what, exactly? And I thought you were going to stay here." Now Callum was looking at her like she had food on her face, or possibly like light was leaking out of it.

Regardless, she ignored him. "The inevitable outcome of coming here is to see things differently. We come here to exist outside the world and then we reenter it. By necessity, we must change it."

The philodendron in the corridor was shrieking something unintelligible. Reina couldn't entirely grasp what, because in her mind she was on to something very exciting. Things, she realized, were about to change. Something innate and atavistic was calling. Wasn't that why she was here in this house, in these archives? Wasn't that why she was *born*? The world itself craved something. Some revitalization, some rebirth.

Why, in the age of the Anthropocene, with all the violence and destruction that had come with the rise of machines and monsters, would there be born a child who could hear the sound of nature itself? It was time for the wheel to turn. For the soul of the very universe to find balance. Dalton's area of study might have been genesis, the origins of life, but moving forward was not about how things began.

This was not about gossipy plants. It wasn't about creating or destroying life. Well, it was, but not in the sense that had always been impressed upon her by others: increasing harvests, bearing fruit. This was about resurgence, resurrection.

It was, like all things, about power. Power that, very soon, Reina would have the choice to either bury or to use. It left her with quite a philosophical conundrum—stay here, with the books and the research and the insulation from a greedy, gluttonous world, or rejoin it with a new purpose, a new outlook, a new understanding of who and what she was?

This was what it was to be a god, Reina decided. Not to live forever, but to restore the order of things. To bring about the age of something new.

Callum, meanwhile, was staring at her. "You want me to influence . . . the world? I assume you don't mean plants." It left his mouth in a rush, like his thoughts were colliding with each other.

"No, not plants." The philodendron was deeply insulted and told her so using very small words. "I think for better or worse the world consists of humans and things that humans have altered. You should understand that," she added as an afterthought.

Callum looked squinty-eyed and unamused, like a disappointed parent. "People don't normally agree with things as I happen to understand them."

"You're alive," Reina pointed out.

He toasted her with an invisible glass. "Not for lack of trying," he joked.

"No, I'm saying—" She exhaled sharply, annoyed. "You're alive. You shouldn't be. We agreed on you to die."

"Oh good," drawled Callum. "Please, don't spare my feelings. Tell me what you really think."

"The fact that you're alive and not apparently out for revenge," Reina continued, "means that you either have some idea how to spend the remainder of this time you've been randomly assigned—"

"Again," said Callum. "No need to be gentle."

"—or it means you're waiting for something. A purpose." She stared at him. "I'm here to give it to you."

He leaned back in his chair. "You're taking this god complex a little too far, Mori."

"It's not a complex," she muttered for the thousandth time. "And either you see this as having happened to you for a reason, or—"

"You don't think I'm out for revenge?" Callum interrupted.

Reina pursed her lips. "If you are, you're doing very badly. Tristan's alive. He's fine. His shirts aren't even wrinkled."

"Says you," replied Callum. "But I happen to know that all of his tags itch."

"The point is, you have time," Reina concluded, ignoring his very annoying pretense of ambivalence despite the more obvious indicators of existential malcontent—e.g., actively trying to drown in a proverbial barrel of wine. "You have time that you weren't supposed to have. So what are you going to do with it?"

"I thought I might buy another yacht," replied Callum.

Reina gave him a wordless look of complete and unadulterated loathing.

"Fine," Callum said. "I have no fucking clue. I'm just here to mess with Blakely and then, I don't know. Go back home, make money, and die."

Reina couldn't begin to fathom how the two people in the house who were the most intimately familiar with human nature—the most skillful at *manipulating* human nature—could think of nothing more pressing than wasting away under capitalism.

"Oh, and probably fuck," added Callum, who was apparently still considering his life goals. "And at some point develop what I can only assume will be terribly high cholesterol—"

"Stop," said Reina. "You're depressing me. And you can't go home," she added. "None of us can go *home*. The Forum knows who we are," she pointed out. "I doubt they're finished interfering."

"So what are *you* doing, then?" pressed Callum with what seemed to be genuine curiosity. "And don't think I can't feel you coming unglued," he added, waving a hand in Reina's general direction. "Zealotry is an odd flavor on you. Very unsettling."

"I'm not a zealot. I'm—" A pause to consider. "Inspired."

"A lovely word for madness," Callum remarked smoothly, "but still, madness nonetheless—"

"Better mad than drunk," Reina spat in return, before things suddenly went silent.

At precisely the moment the clock ticked from the mantel, Reina decided that spending the better part of a year trying to convince Callum to listen to her was going poorly. He clearly wanted to die, so fine. Perhaps she was wasting both her time and his by not letting him do as he wished. It was as if the house had taken ownership of the impurities of his soul, like it had with Nico's physical state. It was wringing all of them out, draining them of everything they hadn't willingly given. Libby Rhodes was gone, a cheap trick, and now they were being punished for it. Perhaps Reina most of all, by being led to believe that anything outside these walls could ever be different.

She whirled around, infuriated and oddly, humiliatingly small, when Callum rose to his feet and caught her by the wrist.

"I'm only going to say this once," he said. "I am not untalented. The powers I have, they are not—" He broke off, releasing her to let his hand tighten to a fist. "If I use them," he amended, choosing his words carefully, "the outcome will not be simple. This is not like physical magic, where you push up against something and something pushes equally back. There are no constraints of conservation with what I can do, no predictable laws of physics. People are more complex than that. And radically more fragile."

Reina waited for the point. "And?"

"And nothing." He shook his head. "Whatever you hope to achieve, you won't. But if it means I can achieve a moment of reprisal—"

Her mood darkened. "Reprisal against whom?"

"Is that any of your business? I haven't asked you *your* plan." He leveled a glance at her. "We're practical beings, aren't we? Task oriented. Results driven. If I thought you anything else, I wouldn't bother wasting my time."

Reina tried to summon the energy to care. It didn't outweigh anything else. The sense of overarching purpose was heavy now, magnetic. "Fine. Just don't influence me," she warned. "And I promise I won't interfere if you won't."

Ooooo MotherMotherMother, whispered a growing ficus, its leaves angling toward the frosted windowpanes. *Mother is balance, Mother is king—!*

"Fine," Callum said curtly. "Anything else?"

Yeah, she thought. Get your shit together.

But then again, that would be too much like offering him help.

"Try not to let anyone else kill you," she suggested instead, turning to leave the room.

Behind her, Callum had dug out his book from beneath his napkin. "Sage advice. Possibly more useful than you think."

Reina paused, frowning over her shoulder. "What does that mean?"

"That we'd all better hope Rhodes is dead, first of all. The rest I'll sort out and let you know." He winked at her, and she rolled her eyes. "Enjoy your delusions, Reina. Someone should."

When she turned away, heading up the stairs to her bedroom, Reina had the distinct feeling that she'd struck a deal with . . . not a devil, not that. Callum wasn't *that* far gone. But if balance was king, then perhaps it was a question of their natures. She had chosen him because her existence, her power that she could not wield, necessitated his—he was the Anthropocene incarnate, she was nature itself, and this was how the cycle would continue. The wheel would invariably turn. She heard her grandmother's voice in her head: *Reina-chan, you were born for a reason.*

Fine. So then she would be ready when the wheel was.

· PARISA ·

Parisa was no stranger to nightmares. She had had them all her life. Confusing ones, some belonging to others. Things she had read or intuited from other, external minds. But now, much to her private dismay, the dreams she had were entirely her own. A recurrence of the same panic, incepted from the same moment of unexpected error—

"Gideon?"

She kept reliving it: the moment of her hesitation that had led to the dreamer's sudden burst of energy. The strength he had summoned to rise to his feet and take hold of Dalton, yanking him out of the tower window, and—

In real life, Parisa had been dragged from Dalton's head, jerking awake from where she had been slumped over the reading room table.

It had been difficult to tell, in that first instant, what was dream and what was reality. The line between awake and unawake was blurry, like reaching across the divide between the living and the dead. The reading room was brighter than it ought to have been, illuminated by the shapes of things, ideas, memories, bursts of form and structure but less permanent, shifting and changing. Like watching a rose unfurl before her very eyes. Like ghosts, but alive, truly alive, at double, triple the speed of normal time, leaving Parisa dazed, disoriented, as she turned her head to see the source of the magic.

The animator himself.

The room and its phantasms weren't the only things that seemed to be operating in a separate continuum of time. Dalton the academic, Dalton the man, was contorted with pain, hunched over, his hands pressed to his temples, to his eyes. He seemed to shift with every degree of perspective, every trick of the light, like a cheap hologram. Parisa, unsteady, turned her head an inch to the right and there he was, emerging from Dalton's spine like a knife to the back: Dalton the memory. Dalton the medeian, who had been placed in a cage of someone else's making.

Dalton the Prince, who had built himself a kingdom inside his own mind.

She could see that only one of him was, for lack of a better word, *real*. Only one was physically present, visibly in pain. The other was like a shadow, a specter in silhouetted form, but that was the one she couldn't look away from. *That* was the Dalton she'd chased through time and consciousness, and he saw her now, apparitional eyes meeting hers like a shot finding its mark, and seemed, for a moment, to laugh.

But then—

"Get Atlas," Dalton had rasped, gasping for air—waking, submerged, from a trance. In the transition between astral plane and reality, Parisa, too, had momentarily lost her footing. She stumbled again at the sound of his voice, inhaling too sharply, and then choked, coughing on a misbegotten swallow. There was something noxious about the flickering light, some psychosomatic fume or miasma. She felt sick to her stomach, unable to breathe.

When she managed to catch her breath, it was lost again to the Prince—or rather, the sudden absence of him. He was no longer there, not in the same haunting silhouette that she'd first seen, but she could still feel the threat of him, the way an intruder does not simply disappear. She could still sense the presence of his thoughts, the arrhythmic and odd way they accordioned into each other, colliding in fits and starts, in warps and bursts. What was he doing to the walls, what were the translucent figures that danced and melted? It looked like he was speaking to the house, draining its memories like sap. The room was breathing, keening, howling, and its usual primacy of thought had inflamed to something viral, something pestilent and baroque in the corrupted sense, opulence to the point of grotesquerie. Was it seduction or torment? Even for Parisa, who should have known the difference, it was unclear. The house had always been sentient, but never like this. Never in pain or in ecstasy, whichever this was. Never *alive*.

Which begged the question: Was this real? Parisa felt dazed, staring at the pearls of sweat that clouded Dalton's meticulous brow. She'd been torn from his consciousness too quickly. Real life and telepathy had blurred, and her vision was cloudy. In and out of her periphery swam glimpses of another life, another version. A dream within a dream.

"Get Atlas *now*," Dalton shouted through strangled breaths, "bring him *now*—!"

There was a burst from the doors behind her as the animations along the walls rose up like tongues of flame, the archives themselves seeming to shudder. Dalton suddenly shoved her aside, rough in his haste, leaving her to collide with the table. A bruise that would last for weeks.

"You have seconds," Dalton was gritting out to someone behind her, "maybe less—"

"Sit down." Atlas's voice was superficially calm, transparently soothing.

"Sit. I'm going in." He glanced askance at Parisa, as if she were nothing but a distraction. "Leave."

She had dragged herself unsteadily to her feet, staring between them. "But—"

"*Leave*," Dalton snarled at her before Atlas sat him down firmly, wrestling him to the chair.

Go, Atlas said in her head. And again, the small tug of reflex propelling her to follow his instructions.

She had run from the room, racing to the first place she could think to go. Heart pounding, lungs throbbing, she needed somewhere she could remember where she was, *who* she was—somewhere she could find something else, anything else, to blame—

In the recurring dream, she always gasped awake before the aftermath. Before her arrival in Nico's room, wild with what she knew to be disarray. Desperate to find rest somewhere, to soothe herself. It was like the house was haunting her now with the recurrence of tension but without the relief, reminding her constantly of what it had seen. *You idiot, you broke your own rules, you stayed too long you cared too much—*

She inhaled, a hand on her chest, and exhaled.

One breath. Two. She counted up to twenty and then lay back down, closing her eyes and gradually drifting off again.

"—can't love anyone, can you?"

From the oncoming fog of sleep, Dalton's voice returned to her.

"I asked you to leave it alone," he ranted. "I told you to stay away from me—"

When he'd said it, Parisa had laughed bitterly, without humor. That wasn't how she remembered it. But apparently, in saving her life by revealing the Society's game all those months ago, Dalton now believed that he was owed her *heart.*

How stereotypically male of him. How fucking disappointing. "Since when was this about love?"

"What was it about, then?"

Power. Always power. Which she had ceded the moment she stayed here too long. Here, in this goddamn house, too fucking long.

Her eyes snapped open again, her memories replaying. Such a wonderful thing, the mind. So very, very helpful.

"What was that? The version of you in your head," Parisa had said to Dalton in real life. "I thought it was just an animation." It had been their first conversation after her mistake with Nico's dreamer friend—that little stumble of poor judgment. The percussive stammer of her idiot heart, which had accidentally stayed her hand.

"It was," Dalton said curtly. "And it wasn't."

That had been days later, nearly a week. Time had passed sluggishly while Parisa had waited for him to seek her out, to explain. She remembered the silence for its oppression—another unexpected weakness, a chink in her armor or, more fatally, an unexpected Achilles' heel.

She had never liked being punished with silence. It was her sister Mehr's favorite tactic, because for all Mehr's alleged uncleverness or unprettiness, she had always been gifted at being cruel.

"I asked Atlas to do it," Dalton had explained. He was himself again by then, mostly, or at very least the rasping urgency was gone. "My research, I needed to finish it. But the archives were keeping things from me." He gave Parisa a long look, a meaningful one. He wanted something from her, but was intentionally withholding whatever it was.

"I don't understand. That piece in there, it was . . . you?" Parisa asked, frowning. "An aspect of your consciousness, or . . . ?"

"Yes. A part of me. My—" Dalton stopped, looking elsewhere. "My ambition, I guess you could call it. My hunger."

For Atlas to dissect a piece of Dalton—a sliver of what was ostensibly his entire self, his actual *soul*—was beyond the power of a telepath. Unless Atlas had understated his abilities to her, which seemed unlikely. "How did he do that?"

"I had to animate it," Dalton said, looking revolted at confessing it. "That piece of me. That . . . flaw." He shuddered. "I brought it to life, then separated it from the rest of my consciousness. And then I did my best to forget it was there."

So he had done the dissection. Self-surgery. No wonder he looked repulsed. "And then?"

"Atlas built those wards inside my consciousness. He kept that part of me contained, by my request." Dalton dragged a hand around his mouth, looking older. Tired. "We agreed it would be the best way. The only way. I thought—" Another pause. "I thought it was only a fraction of myself. A small piece." A chink in the armor, Parisa thought. Funny how those things could undo you little by little over time. All it took was a tiny fracture to destroy an entire foundation.

"So then it *was* you who made the animation of Rhodes?" she asked.

"Yes. Somehow it must have been." Dalton's jaw tensed. "I suppose I hadn't considered the possibility of accessing my subconscious from the place he occupied in my conscious mind. I knew there was no chance of him escaping on his own, but I never thought—"

"Him," Parisa echoed. As if it were another person entirely. Evidently at Dalton's level of magical proficiency, a medeian split in two was functionally two medeians. Two animators. "So then Nico's friend, the dreamer. He let you out?"

"You helped." Dalton's look at her was stony and accusing, bitter and sure. "I was never meant to be aware of his existence. Atlas sealed him away. But the more you accessed that part of me, the stronger he got."

"You're talking about yourself, Dalton." How that part managed to repeatedly escape him was absurd. She'd known men who declined to take the blame before, but this, the actual personification of his own weakness, was bordering on too far. "*You* let me in. *You* confided in me, *you*—"

"Made a mistake," Dalton coolly agreed. "But you have to listen to me, Parisa, it has to stop. If I'm going to finish what I started, then you have to stay away."

"Stay away," she echoed. "From the you that you locked inside your own head?"

His response was a patronizing grimace. "From me. All of me." A pause. "Any of me."

Parisa sucked in a laugh. "I see." So he was breaking up with her? How absolutely hysterical. No wonder he was tiptoeing around, festooning her with tender glances. "You're letting me down gently, I take it?"

"It was going to end sometime. You were always going to leave."

"Dalton." Even he had to hear how stupid this sounded. "You locked yourself away again? And you expect that to last?" She thought of his other self's proclamation, that he wouldn't be able to manage it again. That his true self, his actual *truth,* would eventually come out.

"My days are numbered. But I'm close," Dalton said. "Too close to give up now. Atlas put him back, and now—"

"And now you're racing against the clock." This was all so ridiculous, so impractical. "Dalton," Parisa said in exasperation, "do you not understand the way your consciousness works?" Atlas should, if Dalton didn't. Atlas should have a grasp on the nature of the mind. A soul was inherent, practically ineffable, not something that could be drawn and quartered. That wasn't the nature of personhood, of humanity, no matter how skilled the medeian who did the casting.

"It doesn't matter," Dalton said. "I trust Atlas." Oh, so he was an idiot then. Great.

"Trust him or don't," Parisa continued, "the point is—"

"Parisa, if you loved me, you would leave it alone," said Dalton.

Which was approximately when, in real life, Parisa routinely shuddered with distaste, the acridness of memory. Intrusive thoughts. Terrible. She couldn't stop reliving the artificiality of the moment, the way she had realized *my god, we really have been playing entirely different games.* She said something like *I'm sorry,* and Dalton said something like *I'll always think fondly of you,* and together they playacted at romance. Until, of course, the inevitable accusation.

"Can you even love anyone?"

Absurd. What did he think love was—pain? Was that all anyone believed love to be? That if it didn't hurt, if no one pined, then it was as if it did not exist and had never existed—a tree brought down in the forest with no one to hear it fall?

Though she supposed it was not the first time she had been accused of lacking something. Like she was some kind of empty vase, waiting to be filled. Of course she loved. How else would she be riddled with holes like this if she were really so impermeable, so incapable of wounding? Just because to her, sex and love and desire and affection were different things— some of which she needed or wanted, and some she firmly did not? Because love, in the end, was not always pain, but it was routinely disappointment. Her sister Mehr's silence. Her brother Amin's betrayal. The tiny, terrible mistake of showing mercy to a dreamer she'd never met just because he had thought, perilously, in his final moments, of Nico de Varona, and thereby fucked everything up.

And for what it was worth, Parisa wasn't the one seeking Dalton. He didn't want her? Fine, she wasn't a masochist, and despite popular opinion she wasn't a sadist, either. She didn't chase him.

He was the one who found her, repeatedly. Because the other version of him, the one in his head, was the one who was right. Whatever magic had held for ten years until Parisa's arrival had been monumental the first time, just a breath shy of impossibility. It could not be done successfully twice.

Tiring of her efforts at sleep, Parisa rolled out of bed and walked quickly to the door, pulling it open. She brushed her knuckles along the walls, feeling for a particular pulse.

Unsurprisingly, she found Atlas in his office, head in his hands. "Please," he said without looking up. "Don't harangue me today."

She waved the door shut behind her and took the seat opposite his desk. "Headache?"

"Always." Oddly earnest of him. Too bad she didn't really care.

"You could have told me," she said, resting her bare feet on his desk. He flicked her heels away. "I would have left him alone, you know, if—"

"If what? If you had known that a sequestered part of his consciousness was operating independently inside his brain?" Atlas looked at her doubtfully. "Please. If anything I should have gone out of my way to make him more boring to you sooner."

She supposed he had a point. "How did you do it?" she asked, because she had to know.

"Every mind has its own structure." Another pointed glance. "You know that."

"You built him that castle?"

"God, no. I put him in a box. He put himself in the castle." Atlas leaned back, exhaling, as Parisa recalled the metallic sheen, the warping she had occasionally seen in the glitches of Dalton's mind prison. "He had nearly a decade to do it. I assumed it was a good sign—that maybe he'd done it because he was adequately bored and alone."

"What was he like before?" She had been wondering for ages about the version of Dalton she'd never met.

"Not that different from you." Atlas fixed her with a scrutinizing glance. "He was a person. Every person is complex."

"Interesting take from someone who collects talent," Parisa observed.

"I didn't collect you," Atlas said. "I chose you."

She didn't see the difference and didn't care. "So what made you hatch this little plan, then?" she asked. "Some kind of insane need to rule the world?"

"Rule it? No. Understand it, yes."

"But Dalton's research. It's . . . creation," Parisa summarized. "No?"

"Not exactly." To that, Parisa arched a brow. "Fine, essentially," Atlas conceded. "But I am still not the despot you suspect."

"I can't imagine what else you think would be done with research about the creation of the world," Parisa said with an unladylike snort of derision. "You think giving that kind of information to the archives is so innocent? Whatever you *personally* do or don't do is not the point."

"Give a man the world and he is hungry in an hour," murmured Atlas. "Teach a man to create the world and you do him a good turn?"

"I really can't decide whether I like you better or worse when you make jokes," Parisa said.

"True, that one was reaching." He scrubbed at the stubble on his chin, and Parisa again set her feet upon his desk. He watched her do it, then appeared to give up. "What are you doing awake?"

"Don't pretend you don't know." (Said one telepath to the other.)

"I thought I was being polite by letting you give me an answer." He glanced at her, resting both hands atop his head. "I have to admit, I'm surprised. I didn't think you cared much for Mr. Ellery."

"You know, being routinely accused of psychopathy is starting to get on my nerves," Parisa said dryly.

"Not psychopathy," Atlas corrected with a shrug. "You feel, that much is obvious. But I didn't pin you as a romantic."

Parisa looked out his window into the yawning black of night.

"He's seeking me out," she said.

It was starting over again. Anew. The lingering glances. The light touches. Every now and again he would brush past her in the corridor. She could hear him calling her name in his sleep.

She knew better than to chase him, only it was different this time. There was a subtle shift in flavor. He was like a mood ring now, changing color all the time. The old Dalton had been one pervasive taste, one lingering hint of smoke, a threat of intimacy, but this was like a treat for the telepathic senses. At any given hour he was a different version, more complex. She hadn't even realized before how much she had been starving until she tasted it. The difference. The newness of her palate was a new spectrum of temptation.

"Don't," Atlas warned.

Parisa turned to meet his glance. "So tell me the truth, then."

"What truth? I told you. His research is valuable."

"To whom? To you?"

Atlas said nothing.

"What did you want me for?" Parisa asked. "You didn't need me."

"Actually, I did," Atlas said, before amending, "I do."

"But you thought I'd be grateful, didn't you?" She shook her head. "You thought you could convince me to help you. To *soothe* you." She glanced at the twitch of his thumbs, feeling the thud against his temples like the bass of her own pulse. "You hate this, don't you? What you are?"

"Don't you?" he asked her.

She held his gaze for a long moment.

Then she rose to her feet with a sigh.

"All that self-pity," she commented, turning away from him and toward the door. "You wear it poorly." It was cold, suddenly. She wished she'd thought to put on a robe. "And more importantly, I have no interest in staying in this house."

He sounded amused. "Who says you'd have to stay here?"

"You." She rounded on him. "You want a sidekick. Someone loyal to your cause. You found it in Dalton, but you won't find it in me."

He inclined his head. Tacit agreement. "I didn't imagine I would. But I thought you might find more inside these walls than you could otherwise seek outside of them."

To think he actually believed that. "I was promised riches beyond my imaginings." Her smile in reply was mirthless. "I think the search will be very fulfilling indeed." *And why would I stay? Because you've asked?*

"Perhaps." *Call it what it is, Miss Kamali. That feeling you've been trying to fight is loneliness.*

They stood locked in silent battle before Parisa shrugged. "Ah, so yet another man who thinks he can save me. Tiresome."

Atlas's smile in return was equally long-suffering. "Indeed, it must be."

"Keep Dalton," she added. *Call it a parting gift.* "I won't interfere."

Atlas inclined his head in either acknowledgment or thanks. "Good night, Miss Kamali."

She recognized it for the farewell that it was. Several months early, but still. What reason did they have to continue the discussion? They had chosen their sides, their respective purposes in life. They had laid down their weapons and drawn them back up again. Which, in Parisa's mind, was really for the best.

This was not a normal house. The more she gleaned from the archives, the more she was sure of it. There were ghosts here, operations of a larger mind at work. Atlas was beholden to them, to some agenda he either did not know or had not shared with her. Whatever the archives might have hoped to gain from her, they would not. Whether they would seek reprisal for refusal was not, for the moment, her concern.

At the moment she left Atlas's office, she knew someone was waiting for her in the corridor. She had felt the unfamiliar presence and came to a halt when the backs of his fingers brushed her own, drawing her into the shadows.

"Of course you don't love him," said Dalton's voice in her ear, his lips beside her jaw. "But I," he murmured to the side of her neck, "don't care who or what you love."

The newness of him was familiarly intoxicating. Parisa closed her eyes and let his knuckles trace her cheek, her mouth.

"What have you learned?" he asked her. This new composite of him. The aggregate of him.

His true self.

"It's inevitable," she said, clearing her throat. "The drive to reach your full potential. It won't end here, never would." She recalled Dalton's lecture, the proof of fate that he'd derived from the body of Viviana Absalon, the medeian whose specialty was life. Life that had summoned her death, like two sides of a coin. A rise and fall, a turn of a wheel. Not that Parisa believed in such things.

But still, something about him had always called to her. Perhaps it meant something that she had been the one to draw him out.

Dalton took her chin between two fingers, lifting it to look at her. It wasn't the madness of his animation, the spark of manic energy, nor was it the solemnity he'd had before, the lofty angles. He was settling back into himself, into his own eventuality.

"I won't tell him if you won't," he said softly, tucking a loose tendril of hair behind her ear.

Ha. And to think Atlas considered her lonely. This was the problem with thinking her vulnerable, or constantly trying to uncover some inherent flaw. The presumption that she was in pieces just because she had once been broken was a dangerous one. Easy to misinterpret, and to underestimate in turn.

She hid a smile and touched Dalton's cheek. In a moment he would fade back into his former self, still wrestling with the demons no Atlas-built cage could hold, but the mask of his virtues wouldn't last. Not that this version of him was strictly evil and the other version good, or that any person could contain all of one inside themselves without the other. That was what Dalton, and potentially Atlas, had not understood. There was no unweaving Dalton's ambition from his work, not any more than Parisa could untangle her sadness from her purpose, her bitterness from her joy.

This was the danger in playing with a person's conscious mind, because nobody was made from only strong materials. They weren't gods—the flimsiness of imperfection still remained. Dalton had removed the shadow of himself that had made the archives wary, but there was more to hunger than badness. There was also boyhood wonder, the innate desire to grow. Contained in Dalton's hunger was the blueprint of his journey, the adaptation to his fate. The paths he would invariably take in order to become something more.

Sequestering his dangerous parts, his appetite for power, was enough to trick sentience, but not life. A person was only ever himself. So much of what they became, who they were, was inseverable, irreversible. If to others that meant irredeemable, then so be it.

That was the problem, wasn't it? The trouble with minds and souls.

"Until next time," Parisa murmured to Dalton in parting, stepping into the moonlit corridor alone.

· LIBBY ·

Libby gasped awake, panting, to find a fresh cup of coffee sitting before her on the table.

Right. Basement classroom. LARCMA.

Still trapped in time, but at least she knew where she was.

"You good?" asked Belen, catching the motion of Libby's startled jump. Belen was sipping from her own mug and staring at the map in front of them, having just finished charting a pentacle of energy lines from Siberia to Mesopotamia. The corner peeled slightly from where they'd taped it to the blackboard, gingerly preserving the majority of Mort's lecture from earlier that day. (It was nothing revolutionary, but still. Better not to anger anyone with her "ludicrous" research.)

Libby sat up slowly, wiping away a crease on her cheek from the folded cuff of her sweatshirt.

"Weird dream, I think." She shook herself. "Nothing important." It was another unsettling one, where Ezra was chasing her through some kind of corn maze—one of the ones with the clown mirrors, like from Libby's youth—and then all of a sudden Gideon was there.

She was starting to sense that the Gideon dream was recurring. That, or déjà vu. She could have sworn she and Gideon had been there before.

Libby stretched her arms overhead, looking at the map Belen had been working on while Libby slept on her own notes. "Sorry, did I miss much?"

Belen looked up from the map, and smiled.

As usual, Libby found Belen's presence soothing.

Libby had asked herself several times why Belen was even necessary, as she could surely do the research on her own, but in the end there were so few instances she still felt safe. And this—every iteration of *this*, which was sometimes a shared laugh over cold coffee or simply locking eyes over a map—this, for better or worse, was one of those moments of safety. An accidental intimacy of the strangest, most unexpected kind.

"You were only out for about twenty minutes." Belen slid a hand through her dark hair and yawned. "I don't blame you, honestly. But I've got to go soon, so—"

"Oh gosh, sorry. Work?" One of Belen's many side jobs was the early shift at a nearby Peruvian bakery.

"No, sadly not. I'm just going to get crucified by Professor Mortimer if I don't get his list of sources in on time," Belen replied cheerfully, though she followed it up with a reflexive sign of the cross, presumably for her blasphemy. She'd left her earrings in—she had begun abandoning her good-girl disguise gradually, one cardigan or strand of plastic pearls at a time, with every extracurricular hour spent with Libby—and the set of tiny silver padlocks in her ears jingled against the collar of the secondhand leather jacket she wore. It was at least four sizes too large. ("Fake, probably," Belen had assured Libby proudly the first time she'd worn the jacket, "but not bad, right? Even if it smells like my grandma's lechon.")

Libby fought a yawn, trying to recall if Belen had mentioned working on a list of sources before. "I thought you were done with that term paper?"

"Oh, it's not for class. It's something he needs for the Wessex grant." Belen rolled her eyes. "I volunteered, obviously, because I'm a glutton for punishment."

Libby's mouth felt cottony and dry. One of these days she'd have to manage a decent night's sleep and stop passing out over her notes. "Fission again?"

"Yeah, yeah, you know." Belen waved a hand dismissively. "For the weapons of mass destruction and whatnot. The usual."

"Wait, what?"

"I'm joking," Belen assured her, before amending, "Well, sort of. Unclear why else a British medeian corporation would need to have a testing site in the middle of the Nevada desert, but—" Belen shrugged. "I try not to accuse my faculty advisor of war crimes. Just as a measure of politeness."

"Understandable," said Libby dryly, to which Belen grinned.

"Yeah." Her shoulders disappeared inside the jacket as she shrugged. "So anyway, that's the rest of my night sorted. Unless you want me to stay . . . ?"

"No, you go ahead. Just, um. Did you look at Scotland at all?" Libby asked, wiping the corner of her mouth, which tasted a little like the blueberry muffin she'd eaten in lieu of an actual dinner. She discreetly licked the corner of her lips and then grimaced. "Did I already say to check the Callanish Circle or was it a dream?" The name was ready on her tongue, pre-formulated like something she'd said before, though she couldn't imagine why. It didn't sound familiar.

Belen laughed, black boots scuffing the linoleum as she set a blue pin atop one of the cross sections on the map. "Must have been a dream. Scotland? I thought we were focusing on Asia." Before Libby could answer, Belen added, "I mapped it, but you hadn't mentioned it before."

"Huh." Libby rose to her feet, staring at it. "Yeah, I don't know why it stuck out."

Belen glanced over her shoulder at Libby, half smiling. "Came to you in a dream?"

"Ha." Better that than her actual dreams, which now seemed to consist of Ezra chasing down everyone she'd ever loved. Or in Nico's case, wanted to set on fire. "Guess so."

"Well, it's not a bad idea. Probably easier to get to than most of the places we've talked about." Belen stepped back to stand beside Libby, who suddenly felt bland and ridiculous in her knockoff sneakers, her soulless jeans, her increasingly ragged ponytail that was so very . . . brown. Not that Belen seemed to disapprove, or mind. Instead Belen's shoulder grazed Libby's as both surveyed the map.

The tiny brush of otherwise unremarkable contact sent a shiver of recognition up Libby's spine, a resurrection of a dormant reflex. For a moment, she felt sure that Belen had noticed, or that the motion—no, the *closeness*—was intentional, calibrated, but she didn't know what such an observation might have meant.

"Anyway," Belen said quickly, turning to face Libby, "I don't know how you're going to begin testing them without actually going there. Did you get any word back on funding?"

"Oh. Um." Right, the small issue of nonexistent funding. That was a normal topic of conversation, or at least *more* normal than "hey thanks for the goose bumps, friend." "Not yet. Maybe it would be a good idea to try the U.K. first, though," Libby said. "There's a lot more established research about Gaelic ley lines."

"Ah yes, because if a British scholar says it, it must be important," yawned Belen, rubbing her eyes (rimmed, as of late, in kohl liner) before shrugging at Libby's glance of apology. "Hey, it's not your fault. Academia's naturally biased. There's money in U.K. research and not so much in—" She waved a hand over the Southeast Asia portion of the map. "You know. That."

"Would it cost much to get us to Scotland, you think?" asked Libby. "Assuming you had time," she added quickly, to which Belen yawned again, but hastily nodded.

"I would, of course I would. I'd love the opportunity to test it out. Plus, you know, getting my name on an academic paper . . ."

About that. "Right, of course."

"It would go a long way toward legitimacy around here." It wasn't the first time Belen had indicated that Libby's inability to pay her was worth the sacrifice if it meant uncovering more sustainable energy sources that required neither carbon emissions nor thousands of emigrated medeians to run. "And you should be able to use the medeian transports, right?" Belen asked, picking her backpack up from the floor and tossing it over one shoulder. "I mean, I know they're still being developed, but I heard academics got first dibs."

"Oh?" Libby hadn't realized that medeian transports were in use anywhere, though she supposed the system might have been in development for a long while before opening to broader use. "Yeah, I could ask Professor Farringer if he knows anything about that."

"Oof. Creepy." Belen made a face at the mention of Fare. "Sorry, I know you're friends—"

"Not friends, exactly." Not colleagues, either. Or anything at all. "And yeah, I guess he kind of is." Probably worse with his undergraduates, Libby realized. Particularly those of his undergraduates who were both very pretty and very unwilling to spare him the authority he thought he deserved.

(Ugh, men.)

"The point is you should be able to arrange a transport, I think," Belen continued. "I looked into it briefly earlier and I think the college will pay for it as long as you apply for some sort of educational grant." Belen stifled yet another yawn, followed by a bleary-eyed smile. "I'm *so* sorry—"

"Here, take this," Libby said, forcing her cup of coffee on Belen. "You need it more than I do."

"No offense, but I think that's probably false." Belen laughed and waved Libby off, exiting the basement classroom. "See you at noon?"

As usual, the thought of Belen's absence filled Libby with an upsurge of preemptive dread.

"Yes, yeah, thank you—"

In waving Belen away, Libby caught her reflection in the shiny aluminum paper-towel holder by the door. God, the bags under her eyes were getting absurd. She raised the cup of coffee to her mouth, then sighed. Cold now. Good thing Belen hadn't wanted it.

Warming the cup would probably cost her the same amount of energy as this amount of dismal LARCMA coffee might provide, so Libby poured it down the drain instead. It was freezing in the basement lab and she sighed, staring at the map.

As a potential source of power, the Callanish stone circle was a great idea, but it hadn't been on her short list. *Where* had the inspiration come from?

Nowhere that she could think of, so she gave up on wondering. She was exhausted. "Time to go home," she informed the map, rolling it up and tucking it away before Mort could ask her about it (and then ask her when she'd lost her mind, as an inevitable follow-up).

She locked the classroom door behind her, waving the ward into place. LARCMA had been more than generous in allowing her to work on campus, to stay in the nearby dorms. In return, Libby had been teaching a beginning section on force manipulation and physical magics. She had mostly kept her abilities to herself, knowing that anything *too* remarkable would lead to someone contacting NYUMA, which would in turn reveal her lack of existence. It was why she had not tried to get any actual grants or funding involved, either. But if Belen was right about the transports, it might be worth the pursuit now. Libby decided she'd have to try it sometime.

She stepped into the birdcage elevator and rose to the ground floor from the basement, then made her way outside. At night, downtown Los Angeles was more like a primitive version of her New York, albeit at a smaller, less towering scale. She walked a block to her room, in the nondescript warehouse building where LARCMA stowed their faculty and students. Libby's studio apartment, previously occupied by a medeian who now worked for the Department of Transportation, was a corner unit on the third floor.

She checked the deadbolt and wards behind her twice and then fell onto the pre-furnished sofa with a sigh, looking up at the string lights she'd found discarded in the trash chute some months ago. She had repaired them and strung them up like the strange magpie she was now, hoarding shiny objects to try and compile a life. She felt like she was living in suspended animation, waiting for something to happen. For someone to tell her this whole thing was just a joke. Or a dream.

She poured herself a glass of cheap wine and stood by the window, looking out. Downstairs, someone shouted at nothing, slurring their speech outside the building before hurling into the gutter. Beautiful. Libby shook her head, then glanced across the street.

Someone stood there, half ensconced in shadow.

The glass fell from her hand and shattered as she closed her eyes, then opened them.

She exhaled. The messy black hair was gone.

She pressed the heel of her hand to her pounding heart, feeling another wave of insuppressible nausea. This was getting out of control. The dreams, the paranoia, the sense that someone was watching her. It was relentless. Last week someone told her that a man had been asking after her and her first thought had not been oh god they're on to my lies but instead *Ezra, it's Ezra, he found me.* She was being haunted by him, like a ghost.

She needed to find a way out of here. Out of this time, out of this life. She remembered when her dreams had been eternally of Katherine—hard to believe that had been a simpler time. For so long, the grimness of death had shocked her. At one point Libby had realized that she would never be free of her sister, never stop turning corners and expecting to see Katherine standing there, and she had come to terms with that. But now?

There was a thin wisp of smoke from below the broken glass at her feet and Libby jumped, rushing to put out the small flame that had been smoldering in the aubergine fibers of the apartment's LARCMA-selected rug.

This, she thought again as she bent down to collect the pieces of her broken glass, her fractured mind. This would have to stop.

It took a few days to secure permission from the college.

Largely because it was rejected, first, on the basis of Libby not being full-time faculty, and so she had to forge the approval forms and submit them herself. She snuck in to receive them from the office fax and then flirted outrageously with Fare to convince him to let Belen take a week off from his totally banal (but brilliantly approached, as Libby assured him) course on chemical weathering, which was a requirement for Belen's scholarship and therefore her visa. Again, Libby asked herself whether Belen was actually necessary, and again Libby answered herself yes, undoubtedly so.

Within a week, they were ready to go.

"Is the Scottish Academy sending a team?" asked Belen, who was wearing plaid pants that should have been awful, while beaming with delight that should have been rage, given the fact that there would be no Scottish Academy involvement, would be no alternative energy source, would be no—well—anything. She didn't know this, of course. And Libby did not have the heart to tell her. Still, Belen couldn't stop going on and on about how impactful their subsequent paper would be. Libby, who had come from several decades into the future, already knew that the world as Belen hoped to make it would not exist by 2020. Perhaps much later, maybe. If at all. But saying so did not seem worthwhile.

"We're just going to do some testing," Libby reminded Belen. Libby hoped she could do the testing part alone, without revealing too much of what (and therefore who) she actually was. Assuming there was enough energy in the ley line. Assuming the ley line even *existed,* or that rotating magnetic fields could produce fractionally as much energy as she hoped. It would certainly not be nothing—Tesla's induction motor had already proved as much—but it would have to be unimaginably powerful in order to bring Libby from point A (1990—she'd said happy New Year to the new decade while ducking Mort's sloppy attempt at a kiss) to point B (as close as possible to the moment she'd been taken, depending on how accurately she could select her landing point).

"Right, okay." Belen was nervous about taking the medeian transports. Not that she preferred airplanes, according to her. She was superstitious and carried her grandmother's rosary—which she supposedly didn't believe in, but, at the same time, couldn't leave behind.

("I find it's better not to anger any spirits," she had said.

"Is that a Catholic thing?" asked Libby.

"Close enough? It's mainly the colonialism jumping out," Belen replied.)

Libby liked Belen a lot.

A troubling amount, really, because she needed Belen's help but also didn't want to tell Belen *why* she needed her help. How was she supposed to explain it? *Oh, Belen, by the way, I used to have access to a sentient magic library that I was willing to kill for? I liked it, I miss it, and now I want it back? Actually, Belen, I'm a time traveler from the future, you see, who maybe kind of slept with one or two of my coworkers, whom I would also (maybe) like to sleep with again.* (And there was also the small issue of her parents!! Don't forget them.)

But the transports, at least, were simple. They were the same. Libby's future version of them included more destinations, but Los Angeles to New York to London (there was a transfer, which wasn't ideal, but wasn't terrible) was simple enough. From there it was a train, and then there would be a bus. And a ferry. And eventually, once they reached the Isle of Lewis, on to a circle of stones.

"I don't know about you, but I'm exhausted," Belen said by the time the train pulled into Inverness. "Thoughts on getting a room for the night?"

Libby was practically dead on her feet. "Let's do it."

They found an eighteenth-century converted chapel with a single vacancy and accepted the charge without argument. The room itself was up an incredibly narrow staircase that Libby slammed her shin into twice before deciding to magically transport herself the rest of the way.

"Show-off," Belen panted when she opened the door several minutes later.

By then Libby was already on the right side of the single queen bed, halfway to passed out. "You don't mind," she mumbled, "do you?"

Belen fell into bed beside her. "Thank god," she said, and added something else, though Libby didn't hear her, having been lulled to sleep by the warmth of the room, the softness of the sheets.

"—there okay?"

Libby blinked, startled to find Gideon beside her once again. She was sitting in someone's backyard swimming pool with Katherine, only Katherine wasn't there. Instead, it was Gideon.

"You again," said Libby.

"Me again," Gideon agreed. He was wearing a bikini much like one Libby had coveted in the eighth grade and stood waist deep in the water, though he did not appear to be wet. "Someone's coming for you."

"What?"

"Someone's coming for you," Gideon repeated. Libby was trying not to look at his exposed chest, which was so pale it seemed more like a mirror than skin. "All of you."

Odd. It didn't feel like that kind of dream. It seemed more nostalgic than emergent. "All of who?"

"You, the rest of you. Nico, and the telepath. The whole Society."

"Oh," sighed Libby. "That. Yeah, I know."

Gideon tilted his head. "You know?"

"Well, there seems to be a whole plan. Something about taking all of us out in order to save the world." The sun was high and sweltering, or perhaps the heat was coming from somewhere else. "He knows all about us." At the mention of Ezra, the sky overhead grew darker. Libby was aware, vaguely, of the presence of debris, floating ash.

"He?" Gideon echoed, sounding slightly rueful. "Do you happen to know who? Because—" He inhaled sharply, battling with himself. "This is going to sound crazy, I know, but does it have anything to do with—?"

Something caught Libby's eye, distracting her. A little warp in her periphery, drawing her back from the edge of burning smoke. She smelled something different, something lighter. Rosemary, maybe. Some lavender.

"Oh, come on," said Gideon. "Libby, *wait*—"

Libby opened her eyes to the tickle of Belen's hair, her growing awareness of the unbearable heat of the covers. The smell of the hotel soap, herby and unfamiliar and dragging her back to the sudden reality of being here, in this tiny inn bed. She remembered something, a swimming pool, her sister. A harsh and blackened sky.

Ezra, who was trying to kill her.

Libby sat up with a gasp. Outside the sky was dark, and the clock read evening.

Early evening. Barely supper, and Libby was wide awake.

"Damn," she groaned, realizing she'd been foiled by time zones once again. She rose to her feet, padding softly to the window beside the bed. She ran a finger along the velvet cord of the drapes, contemplating the quietness of the narrow street.

"You're up too, then? Sorry." Belen sighed, flipping onto her back. "I didn't mean to wake you, but I'm kind of a flailer."

Libby turned over her shoulder. "A flailer?"

"Yes. I can't help it. I flail." Belen sat up, stretching, so her T-shirt rose up above her navel, which Libby tried not to notice. "We could keep going," Belen suggested, seeming not to have seen Libby's attention wandering. "If we're both awake."

Libby cleared her throat, grateful for a distraction. "At this hour?" She reached over to the nightstand for the bus schedule, glancing over it. "There wouldn't be a ferry running when we got there."

"Ugh, I forgot about that," Belen sighed. Then she patted the space on the bed next to her, picking up the remote. "Care for some telly?" she proposed in an outrageously incorrect accent.

Libby glanced out the window once more onto the darkness of the quiet street, a one-way lane of old brick town houses and quaint country guest rooms. A flicker of shadow sent a shiver careening down her spine, unwelcome, and she shut the drapes quickly. Awake or asleep, it was all the same.

Belen, she noted, was watching her.

"Finding anything good?" Libby asked, gesturing to the television and fiddling with her hair. Old habits. Gratifyingly, Belen chose not to comment.

"No idea." Belen turned back to the TV, sifting idly through channels and clearly trying to determine what to say. "I woke up a couple of times," she noted after a moment or two, adding, "You really don't sleep well, do you? You talk in your sleep."

Libby hugged her arms, suddenly freezing. "Do I?"

"You seem to talk to someone." Belen was silent for a moment. "Ezra?"

His name, which was not entirely unexpected, felt like another unlawful entry. A sudden assault on a hard-fought atmosphere of peace.

"Oh. That's—" An ambivalent denial rested near the tip of her tongue. *Really? Strange. It's nothing.* But after so many months of looking over her shoulder, the temptation—the *desperation*—to tell someone, anyone, was—

No, Libby thought with a swallow. Not just anyone.

This was *Belen,* who had been the only real friend Libby had had for nearly a year. Belen, who had confided in Libby, trusted her. Belen, who had let the illusion of herself fall away like cautiously shedding skin, revealing softness in the authenticity below: padlock earrings, fishnet tights, a small spider tattoo on the blade of her shoulder. Things she hid from everyone else in the world.

Time travel notwithstanding, it seemed fairly normal to have a romantic past. Or future. Whatever the chronology was at this point. The point was this was a safer secret of Libby's to share, and choosing not to would be to close a door that Belen had so gently left ajar for her.

"You don't have to," said Belen carefully, noting Libby's hesitation.

"No, I'm—" Libby took a deep breath. "I'm sorry. It's just . . . he's an ex. Ezra. He's my ex, from college. It was serious," she said in a rush. "Really serious. And in a way, I'm the one who ruined it—"

"I doubt that." Belen looked solemn.

"No, I did. But then he ruined it much worse," said Libby with a mirthless laugh.

She tried to summon the rest of the story, or at least a version of the story that she could tell without betraying the more complicated details of her situation. Unfortunately, nothing came to mind, and Libby glanced toward the window again, contemplating it in silence.

"You know," Belen remarked to Libby's back, "I did a little research on you."

"You did?" Libby turned sharply to look at her.

"Yes." As Libby's heart beat out a warning, Belen's dark eyes searched her face. "There was no record of you at NYUMA," Belen said quietly. "Libby, nobody seems to have heard of you there. That's not where you really came from, is it? No," she determined without hesitation. "Don't answer that. I already know it's not."

Libby waited, unsure what to say, but Belen didn't look accusatory. If anything, she looked . . . kind. Possibly soft.

"I also know you've been hiding something since the moment you got here. I know you've been afraid, maybe even terrified, and alone." Belen tilted her head then, smiling ruefully. "Libby, you don't have to tell me."

Libby swallowed. "I—"

"You don't have to tell me," Belen repeated, "because I already know. He threatened you, didn't he? Made you feel like he'd come for you? Punish you? Or maybe," she added in a low voice, "he already has."

With a shudder, Libby shut her eyes. She took a shaky inhale, then opened them.

"Wherever you came from," Belen said, "you can keep it to yourself. I won't tell anyone." Their eyes met briefly, and the corner of Belen's mouth twitched with sympathy, or with promise. "Your secrets are safe with me, Libby Rhodes."

Belen looked at Libby with an odd expression on her face, holding her gaze for a pulse or two of Libby's tired, aching heart.

Then Belen turned back to the TV, where some sort of comedy show was playing. Libby watched Belen smile to herself at a joke, the little rosebud of her lips alighting with a wistful calm before she looked down again, eyeing her hands. The laugh track was boisterous and Libby reached over, turning the sound down.

"We don't have to watch anything," Libby said, anticipation banging in her throat.

Belen followed the motion of Libby's fingers as Libby turned the television off. Then Belen lifted her gaze to Libby's face before returning with a beckoning motion to the covers, flipping onto her side. Libby did the same, climbing into the bed and mirroring Belen so their knees were touching beneath the duvet.

"It's warm in here," said Belen.

"Yeah," Libby agreed. It was. She no longer shivered or felt a chill and was enveloped, instead, in comfort. In the scratchy warmth of flannel. In the sense that here, if she kept all her arms and legs beneath the covers, no monsters of past or present could suddenly appear.

"Is this weird?" asked Belen suddenly. Her dark eyes were wide and liquid.

Only then did it become clear to Libby that she had reached one side of an intangible but critical bridge. To cross it was to confess all sorts of inadmissible things.

Libby swallowed. Then exhaled.

The answer was yes, of course, it *was* weird. The kind of weird that preceded a cliff's edge, a sharp drop. A sip of absinthe and a first kiss. Libby knew she was embedding herself too deeply in this time, which was not her own. Into this life, which was not for her.

But at the moment, those things felt trivial. Impossibilities, and inevitabilities, both too large to comprehend.

"You know I'm not really a professor, right?" she asked Belen, her mouth suddenly dry.

Belen's smile in response was a slow unfurling, her voice a husky murmur.

"Yes. But I don't mind calling you that if you ask," she replied, and drew Libby in with one hand.

Belen's lips were a whisper of cherry Pepsi and candy-coated chewing gum. But even this, a cautious kiss from Belen's careful mouth, was riotous with sensation. The hint of pressure was like a spark to Libby's imagination, igniting something dormant in her chest as a purr of satisfaction slipped from her parted lips into Belen's smiling mouth.

"I hoped you'd say that," Belen said hoarsely, the tip of her tongue brushing Libby's as Libby's fingers danced under her blouse.

The shock of Belen's smooth skin was enough to earn another small moan, an indulgent shiver of curiosity's satisfaction. Libby closed her eyes and let herself be rolled onto her back as Belen traced kisses along her jaw, behind her ear, down her throat. She exhaled as a growing heat unfurled in her belly, body complacently relaxing beneath the weight of Belen's hips. Belen slipped out of her sweater. Pulled her tank top over her head. Libby reached for her, watching Belen's stomach pebble lightly below her touch, and heard the vestiges of Parisa's voice in her head: *Have what you want, Rhodes.*

Take it.

"You," Libby began, and swallowed. Her pulse was racing. "You shouldn't."

Belen instantly froze, pulling away. "I'm so sorry, I should have asked. If you don't want t—"

"No, no, I meant—let me." With a nudge, Libby pushed Belen away and onto her back. "Can I?" she asked quietly, drawing a line from Belen's throat to her ribs with the tip of one finger.

"Yes." Belen looked enraptured. "Yes, please."

Libby positioned herself astride Belen's hips, easing Belen's arms above her head as Libby bent down again to kiss her, hair falling in waves around them both. Her hair was longer now, overgrown. Long enough for Belen to tangle her fingers in it while panting softly in Libby's ear.

Libby drifted away to tug her sweatshirt over her head, returning to let the flame of her skin meet Belen's and deliver them both to a communal shudder. Emboldened by the impact, Libby ducked to nip at Belen's clavicle, one hand fitting between their hips to stroke the curve of Belen's thigh.

"Maybe we shouldn't go so fast," whispered Belen, fingers tightening on the bare skin of Libby's waist. "I don't want to rush this."

"Is that the Catholicism talking?" asked Libby, and Belen gasped out a laugh.

"I wish I could say that even one of Lola's many lectures had proven effective," Belen mused as Libby buried a smile in her hair, "but alas, no. Tragically," she confessed, "it's my enormous crush on you."

"What?"

Libby pulled back, blinking, and Belen bit her lip.

"Sorry, was that too much?"

"I—" Yes. No. Not on its own, at least. Though it did beg the question of whether Libby wanted to do this again. Which was an easy yes, of course. Yes, definitely, more than once would be desirable, possibly even ideal. Belen, Libby suspected, was not the only one with a crush.

But time wasn't something Libby had to bargain with. The future—*her* future—was waiting for her somewhere else. She couldn't even promise tomorrow, much less the extent of tomorrows Belen might be entitled to, or want.

Libby had a feeling her hesitation was all too legible. Belen blinked, her expression carefully reserved when she said, "I didn't mean to make things too serious." She swallowed. "Ignore me, I was just—"

"No, you're right. We should slow down." Libby pulled away, disentangling. The air between them seemed cool with something, which she hoped Belen read as restraint and not rejection. "Plenty of time, right?"

Another lie upon a mountain of lies. But this one, at least, made Belen smile, if only for the moment.

"Yeah," Belen said, flipping onto her side to face Libby again. "Sure. Definitely."

Libby rolled onto her back, carefully preserving space for her limbs and falsehoods. The sheets were suddenly scratchy, too hot, and she had a feeling Belen would read far more into the cautionary distance she put between them than her chipper tone of reassurance. "Should we try to get some sleep?"

"Yeah." Belen's voice sounded far away. "Yeah, good idea."

When she glanced over again, it was to the view of Belen's back, her breathing so shallow and irregular that she could not have been asleep. Inwardly, Libby's gut roiled. It was one thing not to tell Belen of the future she already knew, the disappointment that was inevitable. It was quite another thing to lie as she was currently lying. To withhold a critical, defining truth.

The bus the next morning lurched along the narrow Scottish roads. The ferry was timely, voices carrying on the wind in a collection of incomprehensible brogues. They reached the inn that Libby had booked and then set off again for Callanish Circle, neither Belen nor Libby willing to subject themselves to the idle togetherness of slumber, their heads inches apart in the tiny room, the narrow crevice between twin beds. Their host joked about fairy circles, and dutifully Libby laughed; Belen's smile in return was somewhat more forced.

They departed the bus and followed a sparse traveling crowd, a handful of other tourists. Belen and Libby lingered behind, both of them abnormally quiet. Perhaps Belen was too perceptive. Or Libby was too poor an actress. Either way, they both shouldered a tacit sense of gloom.

"What if we get there and nothing happens?" Libby asked, if only to break the silence. Belen tensed at the sound of Libby's voice and looked down at her shoes. The sky overhead was swollen with the promise of rain.

"We go back home and keep looking, I guess."

"Right." It was surreal, the cleaving of possibility between nothing and everything. Between the likelihood of leaving here empty-handed and the distant prospect of return. Something would have to work, Libby thought in silence. If it wasn't this, it would be something.

It would have to be something.

From afar, the stone circle was like every picture Libby had ever seen of Stonehenge. She and Belen waited, respectfully or possibly just hesitantly, for the others ahead of them to take their pictures, to stake their claim to myth and legend and then wander back to their various hosts for a laugh and a pint.

Gradually the stragglers cleared, except for one. There was a man standing alone in the center of the circle, his back to the rest of them. He stood looking at the endless line of Highland fields, the rolling hills that ruffled the pristine state of his pressed collar. He raised a hand, tracking it over the back of his head, before he paused, as if he sensed something over his shoulder.

When he turned, it was like muscle memory. Like an old, unnatural pull; a wordless, invisible tug along a familiar current of time and space.

For a moment Libby was struck as if by lightning, by an ephemeral familiarity, the sudden presence of a prior version of herself. The drag and thump of her pulse, suspended and then resurrected. The man in the circle frowned, brow furrowed in thought or in expectation, and then their eyes met. Locked.

"Tristan," Libby exhaled without warning, her throat dry around the ghost of his name.

Tristan Caine's unsmiling mouth parted and in return, Libby's heart went frantic.

"Hello, Rhodes," he said.

VIII

FATE

· CALLUM ·

It took three days after the incident with the captive witch for Tristan to come find him. Ridiculous. As if they were schoolgirls waiting three days to text back.

"Finally," Callum said without looking up from his book. (Because yes, he did know how to read, thank you, Reina.) He'd been sitting on the painted room sofa before the hearth, one leg languidly crossed, effervescing patience. "Took you long enough, didn't it?"

It was the first time they had been alone together on purpose since that night nearly a year ago, which did not appear to escape either of their attention. Tristan seated himself at the opposite end of the sofa, primed inadvisably for a fight.

"Did you make him say it? My father's name," Tristan finally said in a voice throttled with tension. "You know it. And you know what it means to me. So I assume you know why I have to ask."

Callum set down his book with an irritated sigh, angling to face him.

"Yes," Callum replied curtly, and Tristan blanched, perhaps cleverly predicting what would inevitably follow. "I thought, 'You know what will be fun?'" Callum mused. "'I'll just make up a nice little story that will haunt Tristan for three days and then I'll simply tell him it was all a joke, ha ha.' Certainly it's not an *extremely fraught* situation," he added drolly. "After all, what possible knowledge would I have of such fragile emotional tangles? None whatsoever, methinks—"

"Fine. Point taken." Tristan's expression, a permafrost of sorts, still managed to sour. "So, my father wants to kill me. Wonderful. How new and exciting for me." He slumped lower in his seat, drumming his fingers along the sofa's armrest in agitation.

"I believe it's more complex than that," said Callum.

"In what way?" demanded Tristan with a sidelong glance.

"Oh, I have absolutely no idea," Callum assured him, shrugging. "I just typically assume these things to be complex, that's all. If not emotionally, then perhaps it's the matter of disposal that your father wishes to complicate. Either way, I doubt it's all that simple."

"You," Tristan said, rising sharply to his feet, "are an incurable dickhead."

"Yes, I know. By the way," Callum added, licking a finger casually and turning the page in his book. "About Rhodes."

Predictably, Tristan stopped.

"I actually had *not* forgotten our little agreement with Varona," Callum pointed out. "Not that anyone ever thought to ask me about it."

Tristan's desires to both flee and remain in place warred with each other in a most satisfactory way. "So you're telling me," he said in a strained voice, "that you've actually spent the last several months researching how to bring back the one person in this house you hate the most?"

"False," Callum said. "I do not hate Rhodes. I do not even dislike Rhodes. She simply does not matter."

"Okay, then why—"

"In fact, if Rhodes *does* come back," Callum continued, "I should think it would become very, very necessary to finish the job."

"I—" Tristan blinked. "I'm sorry, what?"

"That's an aside, of course. None of your business, really. The point is yes, I've done a bit of research," Callum remarked, producing a very neat and well-prepared document from the inside cover of his book—which was actually *How to Win Friends and Influence People,* chosen for its many wonderful techniques. For example, one way to make people like you was to smile, which Callum winningly employed now. "I know you and Varona have a very clever theory about dancing space waves, but consider that perhaps it's not enough."

Tristan was unhelpfully stuck on a previous topic. "What do you mean about finishing the j—"

"As it turns out, I have paid rather dutiful attention in class despite the wild accusations that I am here for all the wrong reasons. In fact, I've rather impressively done the maths on what's needed to bring Rhodes back," Callum said with a flourish, "and as you already know but are foolishly choosing to ignore, in order to create the wormhole that Varona and Rhodes manufactured, they also had to create a controlled explosion of enormous magnitude. It was still comparatively small, of course, because what they made was also small," Callum noted, "so how much energy do you suppose is enough in this particular case? Something far less innocuous. And with enough power to ensure precision? To land her *precisely* in the time that she left?"

Tristan said nothing.

"Even if you did manage to find the raw power necessary for that kind magical output, you still have to funnel it correctly. There is no *control* to be found in the wilds of Scotland," Callum concluded heartily. "Which is why the little jaunt you're still planning—unwisely and foolishly and with obvious stars in your eyes," Callum added, "is not going to work."

Tristan set his mouth stubbornly. "So you think it's not even worth trying, then?" He rolled his eyes. "Groundbreaking."

"No, no, wildly incorrect." Callum shut his book with an effortless snap and rose to his feet. "I don't just want you to try, Tristan. I want you to *succeed*. I want you to succeed so valiantly and with such flying colors that you believe yourself to be invincible and invulnerable and, ultimately, a more evolved version of your current self. But of course you won't do that," Callum finished, then added with a sigh, "Which is honestly very sad for me, because I really am an optimist."

The confusion wafting from Tristan's bewildered pores was an acrid tang. "You're manipulating me somehow. I know you're trying to talk me out of it."

"I'm doing no such thing, Tristan, my goodness." Callum thrust his detailed notes in Tristan's direction. "Here, I've even run the calculations for you. This is the output you need to generate a pure fusion reaction."

Tristan reached for the page of notes as if he thought it might bite. "Where did you get this?"

"Did you know there's a *whole library* back there?" Callum asked, widening his eyes appealingly to play-act Tristan's favorite fringed ingenue.

To Tristan's scowl, Callum breezily replied, "I told you, I did the maths. Ages ago. Three whiskies in, might I add. I'm really much smarter than anyone gives me credit for, which is absurd. And unfair. And unspeakably rude." Callum, who had not had a drop of alcohol in the last three days, felt intoxicated with delight. "And yet, I am the only one in this house who's been any help to you at all, Tristan, so you're welcome."

Tristan was scouring the page, looking for the trick as if it were written in invisible ink. "What's the catch?"

"The catch?" Hilarious. Absolutely hysterical. "You mean you don't already see it?"

The glare he received from Tristan was a ruthless thing of beauty.

"Rhodes," Callum explained, "can only transport herself through time through the creation of a massive explosion. How massive? Excellent question, Tristan. We're talking *nuclear*," Callum said giddily. "*Lethal* force. The bonding of hydrogen isotopes so heavy that it would be like regenerating a star. So enormous and frankly untested that the area may very well remain radioactive for years, to a magnitude that would cause certain death to anyone within miles of the area's vicinity." He checked to see that Tristan was following. By the ashen look on his face, he was. "Rhodes's only chance of creating a wormhole of this magnitude is, as I believe you already know, to leverage the energy created by a perfect fusion weapon—which has heretofore never existed," Callum sagely pointed out, "and which can only exist if *Rhodes herself* chooses to incite an explosion with exponentially greater potential for lasting damage than the atomic bomb."

Tristan said nothing. He knew this, the hopelessness of it, and equally, Callum knew there was nothing more dismally hollowing than determining yourself to have been right all along.

"You may be able to beat the laws of physics, Tristan," Callum said, "and with Varona's help, you *might* be able to win against the laws of nature—but."

Here Callum stepped closer, watching Tristan brace himself with a steady thud of preemptive rage.

"You will never beat *Rhodes's* nature," Callum triumphantly pointed out. "And that, my friend, is—as I've been warning you for nearly two years now—the absolute crux of the thing."

He could tell that Tristan knew he was right because he could taste it, the sinking feeling, the onslaught of dread. Tristan didn't look up from Callum's page of stunningly accurate calculations, because what would he find?

Ah. The delightful taste of withering hope.

There were no other conclusions to draw. There were no other alternatives. In order to bring herself back through time and space, Libby Rhodes would have to choose herself over everyone. Over *everything.* She would have to find the power to face down her own morality and say fuck it. I matter more.

Which was thoroughly impossible. A comedy of errors to the highest degree. And *this* was who Tristan had chosen over Callum! *This* was what he had done, and in the murky plumbing of Callum's allegedly nonexistent heart, he hoped that Tristan suffered for it. He hoped it would pain Tristan for the rest of his life, and if for some reason it didn't, then Callum had other plans in mind. He was, after all, cleverer than anyone gave him credit for. He'd spent a year getting fabulously sauced and coming to the inevitable conclusion that, actually, none of this would ever matter, because there was no big bad. There was no villain. Atlas Blakely might have wanted Callum dead, but that didn't make him the bad guy. Tristan might have betrayed Callum, but he wasn't the bad guy, either. This was just the world. You trusted people, you loved them, you offered them the dignity of your time and the intimacy of your thoughts and the frailty of your hope and they either accepted it and cared for it or they rejected it and destroyed it and in the end, none of it was up to you. This was just what you got. Heartbreak was inevitable. Disappointment assured.

This was the conclusion Callum had landed upon, and he didn't like it. He accepted it. Understood it. Didn't care for it.

Still wanted to fuck around for a bit before he was done, though, so.

Here. "I have no dog in this fight," Callum told Tristan, withholding a smile. Poor Tristan was still staring numbly at the calculations in his hand, and so of course could not see Callum's barely withheld delight at his delivery of this most delicious and most perfect blow. "I know you know I'm right. Both about this," he said, flicking the page in Tristan's hand, "and about Rhodes. But I also know that you'll come to whatever conclusions you choose, and none of that is up to me."

"So then why do it?" asked Tristan. His voice was gravelly with resentment, maybe bitterness. Maybe even sadness, but what was Callum supposed to do with that?

"Because I said I would," Callum said coolly. "Because on the day we took our initiation rites, someone asked me for a promise. I gave it and I kept it." It was really very simple. These were the decisions that Callum could live with. He didn't care what happened to the world or whether Atlas Blakely created a new one. Atlas Blakely could create an entire fucking universe and it wouldn't matter, because nothing mattered. And wasn't that such lovely irony! Atlas Blakely wanted to make a new world because he was a clinically depressed magical bureaucrat *who already knew that nothing mattered.*

Honestly, Callum was doing just fine with his grief.

"I'm still going to bring her back." Tristan looked up and now—god, exhausting—he was aflame with certainty.

"It's possible," Callum said mildly.

"We're different," Tristan insisted. "All of us. For having been here. For having walked these halls, read these books—"

"Yes, a magical experience, truly," Callum blandly agreed.

"You can laugh," Tristan snapped, "but we're not the victims of our weaknesses that you so obviously believe we are."

Interesting, Callum thought. He seemed not to have heard himself.

"This was nothing to you," Tristan continued. "Just another opportunity in a life of opportunity, so fine. You can walk away from this unchanged, good for you. But for the rest of us—for *me*—"

"Did I say this was about you?" Callum cut in, carefully neutral, but for once, Tristan managed to surprise him.

"Of course it's about me." Tristan was snarling, and from the hearth was a coincidental series of cracks and sparks. "I was there, Callum. I was fucking *there*."

Tristan's chest rose and fell with anguish and Callum sat still, bearing the unexpected weight of it.

"Whether you put it there or not," Tristan said, his voice heavy with irony, "this—between us—it was real for me. You can pretend that it didn't matter. That I was the one who wronged you. That you had no hand in how things happened. That I made a choice based on nothing, based on my own insecurities and flaws. But I am not such an idiot—I'm not so devoid of *feeling*," Tristan spat, "to not be perfectly aware that you and I had something rare and difficult and fucking significant, and in the end it only broke because I broke it."

Callum's chest suddenly felt as if it had been compressed with a cartoonishly large mallet.

"So, yes," Tristan concluded with a jerk of the muscle beside his jaw. "I know this is about me."

They didn't speak for several minutes. It was the first time that Callum could recall not being able to sense something intangible about the room or the feelings within it. He realized later that it was because *he* was the one feeling things. He felt his victory ballooning into rage, pure rage. He felt anger with an intensity that was incandescent with bereavement. He wanted, just as he had wanted at the beginning of this godforsaken year, to murder Tristan. To take him by the throat and slice him into ribbons and serve him like a roast—and also, to meticulously and with great inconvenience to himself weave a flower crown laden with unrequited meaning, with which to adorn Tristan's incredibly stupid and perfectly functioning head.

Mostly, though, Callum wanted Tristan to suffer profoundly for every honest word out of his mouth.

So he was back where he started, really.

Relieved with the eventual stasis of his conclusion, Callum exhaled. And smiled. People did not like to be contradicted, said Dale Carnegie, master of influencing, apparently. It was best not to criticize, even when people were wrong about silly things like where they had placed their loyalties.

"Good luck," said Callum. "With everything. Hope it works out between you and Rhodes."

Tristan's expression darkened. "Did I not *just say*—"

But Callum walked past him, ignoring the impulse to stop and listen. Also ignoring the impulse to get a drink. Ignoring most impulses, really, because now he had a plan, and that was more important. Like Atlas Blakely, Callum was going to stick to his plan, even if it was objectively flawed and would lead to either despotism or tears.

He bumped into Dalton on his way out of the painted room.

"Sorry," said Dalton under his breath, nodding to Callum while hastily averting his glance.

Callum paused.

Glanced over his shoulder.

It was unusual to see Dalton, whom Atlas had said was feeling ill, which Callum of course did not care about, although as far as he could tell, Dalton was perfectly healthy. No, what was odd wasn't Dalton's presence, which was never a matter of relevance to Callum. It *was* something, though. A distinctive and noticeable newness.

Had it been . . . ?

Salt. Smoke. A mix of both. Unusual for Dalton. Something was off, Callum deduced with a frown. There was something deeper, there, than what had been there before.

But that was Parisa's problem—or certainly anyone else's but his—so he ignored it, setting off up the stairs while whistling "La Vie en Rose." It was very freeing to have a plan, Callum thought, passing an open window with a deep breath of wintry air. He could see why Atlas clung so desperately to his own. Spring would come soon, followed by summer, followed by the inevitable smiting of all his enemies—or more accurately, the unavoidable despair and sense of loss that came with being human and alive. Marvelous.

For a man responsible for the brutal deaths of four people—his friends, at that—Atlas Blakely was really on to something.

· REINA ·

Reina suspected she'd had a dream about her grandmother, or maybe it was just her grandmother's house. She never kept track of her dreams much, but she woke up that morning with the sense that she had recently been very small.

No, she remembered now, through a flash of something, a hint of steam. It wasn't her grandmother making her feel small—it was the Businessman, her stepfather. It was a memory again, the same one she'd had while watching Nico's initiation ritual. He was looking through her in her café in Osaka. The Businessman, or rather the reaper, whose business was war, and therefore death. She dreamt of the same scene, the same foreign name, the same angry words.

He did it once, he can do it again!

She had not thought about this event since the day Nico had brought it to mind, but doing so must have triggered something slow-acting in her brain. Something just on the tip of her tongue, because here she was, thinking about the Businessman again, which she almost never did, and about the Englishman who'd so angered him, which was not something she'd considered relevant at the time. It had seemed ubiquitous then. Meaningless. But now she remembered the name again retroactively, with a sudden significance, as if a color lingering in the background had recently come to light.

"I had a strange dream," Reina commented as Nico strode past where she'd been waiting beside the foot of the stairs. He had been whistling something as he took off toward the reading room but froze at the sound of her voice, startled.

"Jesus." Nico pressed a hand to his chest like she'd shot him, then back-stepped to face her. "Sorry, didn't see you there—"

"I hadn't forgotten, you know. About Rhodes. Actually," she added, "I thought we were going to work together to find her." She paused. "Wasn't that the agreement?"

Nico blinked, looking like a small boy awaiting a scolding. Then he carefully recovered. "We still can, can't we? It's not like the year is over yet."

"What did Tristan do for the Wessex Corporation?" Reina asked, ignoring Nico's response. Too little, too late. "I know he was a VC. What kind of technology did he fund?"

"Hell if I know." Nico shrugged. "Tech, I assume? Software? Doorknobs?"

"You don't know?" asked Reina blandly.

"We're not exactly friends." Nico was looking at her with a strange expression on his face. "You don't think I somehow replaced you with Tristan, do you?"

"I was just thinking," Reina said, "that last year, you and Rhodes . . . the wormhole. The reaction you caused. It was to release enough energy to create it, yes?"

"You helped us do it," insisted Nico. "Without you, we wouldn't have—"

"What else could cause it?" asked Reina, who wasn't looking for flattery. "Fusion. At that size."

"Oh. Uh." Nico looked wobbly and destabilized. "I don't know."

That didn't sound like the whole truth. "You don't know?"

Nico rubbed his temple, thinking of how to explain. "Most things like that, big energy outputs, they require fission to start the reaction." Fission: splitting an atom into smaller nuclei. "That's what generates the energy necessary for fusion." Fusion: combining different particles for the release of energy. "Usually there's energy lost in fission, which prevents a more explosive fusion reaction, but Rhodes and I—*and* you," he clarified quickly, "we were able to bypass that energy loss, so the reaction was—" He frowned, concluding suboptimally, "Well, bigger, I guess."

"Right." Reina had already known that. "So then what could replace you and Rhodes?"

"Um. Nothing, to my knowledge." He looked no more smug than usual, so it must have been true and not hyperbole. "That's kind of the problem," he admitted, which explained his tone of hesitation before. "Creating a pure fusion reaction like that would have to be magical, and the energy released would have to be channeled by a medeian of really proficient skill. But for it to work at any significant size, it would also have to be a reaction bigger than anything a single medeian could produce, so even someone really, really skilled would still need to be able t—"

"Would you have killed me?" Reina asked.

At that point Nico looked lost. "What?"

"Would you have killed me?" Reina repeated. "If it had become a race."

"Oh. You mean last year? No. God, no. Of course not." He shook his head vigorously.

"Easy to say that now," Reina observed. "Now that nobody else has to die, right?"

"Well, still. I wouldn't have." He shrugged.

"Would you have killed Callum?" Reina asked.

"I—I mean, no," Nico said, sounding troubled. "No, probably not—"

"Or Tristan?"

By then, Nico's brow was creased with conflict. "I don't—"

"Definitely not Parisa or Rhodes," Reina commented, "so basically, you wouldn't have killed anyone." She was trying to decide why this realization was so disappointing when Nico abruptly took the defensive.

"Where is this going?" asked Nico irritably. He was annoyed, obviously, not because he hadn't considered this before, but because he had been trapped into admitting something that he had not intended to confess.

"Well," said Reina, "I guess I'm just wondering what the hell you're doing here."

Nico stared at her.

"That's . . . it?" he asked. Or rather, demanded. "You don't talk to me for months and this is what you have to say? To ask me why the hell I exist?"

"Not exist," she said impatiently. "Just . . . here. You were willing to kill someone *hypothetically*."

He frowned. "Yes, and—?"

"But it wasn't a theory. Or a hypothesis. It was a real requirement."

"So?" He folded his arms testily over his chest. "You've been extremely weird for almost an entire year and now you're mad because I wouldn't have murdered you?"

Yes. "Maybe."

"*What*—" Nico inhaled. Exhaled.

"You also wouldn't have killed someone else to keep me alive," Reina noted.

Nico visibly bristled. "Look, if Nova came for you with a knife I'm pretty sure I wouldn't just *stand* there—"

"Pretty sure," Reina echoed, and then Nico's face contorted into a mask of itself. Boyish frustration.

God, he suddenly seemed so young.

"Okay, what the fuck?" Nico demanded, before scoffing transactionally, "Like you would have saved me. It apparently makes no difference to you whether I'm alive or dead."

Reina felt a sharp plummeting in her chest that she worried was some kind of loathsome sentimentality. Luckily it was gone now. Dead. Drowned. A mercy kill, really. Because the price of admission was too much. The cost of confession was too high. No, Nico, I would have lit on fire anyone with even the slightest intention of harming you, and that is the kind of friend I am, when I choose to be a friend. Which I have never dared to dream of doing.

Until you.

"Okay," she said, and turned away to climb the stairs.

"Reina," Nico called after her, sounding frustrated. "Reina!"

She told herself that actually, this was tactical. Responsible, even. Callum had made that plenty clear.

"Look," Callum had said to her the night before, accosting her when she was busy looking over the notes they had submitted to the archives during their first unit on space. "I'm only telling you this because I think it's important that you not do anything stupid," he said, "and I have a suspicion that in order to keep your wits about you, you're going to need all the facts."

"Which are?" asked Reina without looking up. She didn't typically associate Callum with facts. He seemed exceptionally emotional, which was what the others seemed to be missing about him. If he actually *was* a psychopath, he'd probably get a lot more done.

Callum slid into the chair opposite hers, immediately taking up too much space.

"Atlas Blakely is depressed," he said.

"Okay," Reina replied dully. "Who isn't?"

"And *because* he's depressed," Callum continued as if she hadn't spoken, "he's looking for a way to open a portal to a different strand of the multiverse. I think, anyway," Callum qualified. "Since I doubt he's trying to actually start a new universe from scratch."

"Oh." Reina blinked. "He can . . . do that?"

"He thinks he can," Callum agreed, "but he needs you to do it. He has every piece he needs except one. Well, two," Callum clarified, "because of the whole Rhodes issue, but that's not important. It's you that I'm concerned with."

"Why?" Reina asked crossly.

"Because," Callum said, "his time for recruiting you is about to end. And I think he's actually quite good at ensuring that people make the decisions he wants them to."

Reina arched a brow in order to indicate that yes, manipulative people tended to do that. Present company included.

Callum smirked. "Compliment taken," he said. "But there's a catch. Something he won't tell you."

"Something in his file?" Reina guessed, wondering if it was something ridiculous like Parisa's marriage. Presumably something unrelated and personal that Callum would find interesting but that Reina would not, because Reina was not a—

"He killed four people," Callum said. "His friends."

"*What?*" The word left her with a deep blow, like a gust of surprise.

"Well, okay, not *really*," Callum said with a little laugh. As if to say, Ha! Semantics. "But he feels responsible for the deaths of the other four initiates in his Society cohort."

Again, a blur of surprise and confusion. "What?"

"I'm not clear on the details," Callum admitted with a shrug, "but I know that something that Atlas did caused the other four to die. Not all at once. Not in some freak accident or anything. But by the time the next class of initiates was recruited to the Society, they had each met an untimely end. One was shot through the chest. Another poisoned. A third got an aggressive form of cancer." Reina winced. "The last one died in her sleep. Allegedly."

That sounded Shakespearean and annoyingly dramatic. "Okay. So?"

"So, I have a guess that something must have gone wrong with Blakely's initiation ritual. It's not in his file, which I can't explain. Maybe he got to it first, I don't know. But he's the one who supposedly killed the fifth member, the sacrificial lamb—and I can tell," Callum said in a low voice. "I can tell that the blood on his hands is purely secondhand."

Troubling, if true. Which was a very big if.

"This is guesswork," Reina pointed out. "Not fact."

"Fine. I just thought you'd consider it relevant—you know, since nobody in *our* initiation class was killed," Callum pointed out, rising to his feet. "Which means the archives are still owed a body."

"But—"

"Think about it." Callum's expression was oddly candid. "It's been stealing something from each of us, hasn't it? Varona's a mess. Parisa's jumpy as fuck. You're—you," he said with an arched brow that Reina wanted to slap away. "And we're all decaying further the longer we stay here. So if Atlas convinces you to *continue* to stay, which obviously won't be difficult—"

"No," said Reina. "No, I told you. I already decided I'm getting out."

"You say that now," Callum said. "But deep down you can't resist being told that you're special. *Unique*," he said, his voice a little too close to her ear. "Necessary."

"I know what I am." She glared up at him, swatting him away like a mosquito, but he only laughed.

"No, you *think* you know what you are, but you don't. You think you're cold, unfeeling, but you're not." He leaned forward again, and she went rigid. "The moment you let yourself love, Reina Mori, it will be the death of you. I promise you that."

Remembering it now, Reina shivered. It wasn't cruelty, and it was all the worse for that. It was honesty, prophetic and intrusive, and whether it was true or not, inside her something was burning. The humiliation of having been seen.

Lost in thought, Reina nearly bumped into Parisa, who was lingering obnoxiously on the stairs. Perhaps she had heard Reina leaving the argument with Nico and had placed herself there, paying Reina back for what Reina herself had once overheard.

"Careful," Parisa warned.

If she looked more smugly omniscient than usual, Reina didn't have time for it. Not for this, or anything. She shoved Parisa back against the wall as if they were sparring, though of course Reina didn't do that anymore. Now, she only fought.

"Touchy," observed Parisa, and Reina realized she was breathing hard. Not because it was difficult work pinning Parisa, who was smaller than Reina had ever realized, but because Reina suddenly felt like something inside of her was shattering. Her sanity, or her heart.

She wasn't going to tell anyone what she'd found, she decided. Nothing about the Businessman, or about James Wessex or his weapons-testing site. Nothing about her suspicions. If Libby Rhodes came back or didn't, that was no longer Reina's promise to keep. She was done with it, this damn Society. She was done with the old feeling of being inconsequential and small.

"I hate you," she whispered to Parisa, eyes stinging.

Parisa searched her face and nodded.

"I know," Parisa replied.

The fight went out of Reina as abruptly as it had been lit. She released Parisa and walked calmly to her room, the tension expelled from her at long last. She stepped inside, shut the door, and then stood with her back to it, closing her shaking hands into a set of fists. She was done with this, with all of it. She was glad now for her chosen secrecy, and for the reminder that she walked alone. It was easier that way. Safer. Less complicated.

And if what Callum said was true—if anyone else came for her? That was even less complicated.

She would strike to kill.

· TRISTAN ·

Nico had been right about the electromagnetic radiation. Beyond the edges of the stones at Callanish Circle—which, according to Nico, was a "nice" but otherwise unremarkable view—was, to Tristan, a ribbon of fluorescence, greens and purples that braided into each other and then frayed out like flares of light. The colors sailed up to the sky and departed in waves, crystalline auroras, beneath which stood Libby Rhodes. A year older. No more fringe. No books in hand. She wore a yellow raincoat, a black turtleneck under the faded gray sweatshirt she'd tucked into jeans. She seemed thinner than he remembered, and taller, like she was standing up straighter but hadn't slept well in months. He took in the little particulates of her and found them altered. Changed.

"Fancy meeting you here," she said, and laughed nervously, almost hysterically, like at any moment (perhaps even this one?) she might burst into tears.

"Rhodes. Don't do that." Tristan took a step toward her and she laughed again, this time apologetically, retreating half a step.

"I . . . How are you doing this? Or is it even real? I've been having very vivid dreams lately." She was staring at him like she could look for hours, days, months, lifetimes.

"I'm not physically there with you, Rhodes, so don't get too excited. I'm still standing in my own time." Sharing her dimension on an astral plane had been simple enough, but it was still like peering through a lens. He had traveled, but not physically. Or rather, not in the sense that all of his body could come along. The rest of him stood in precisely the same geographic location, but at a distance of over three decades away. "But it's definitely not a dream."

He wondered whether time was passing the same way for Nico, whom Tristan had brought along to stand guard. Tristan was currently floating between states of permanence, with Nico on one side of him and Libby on the other. As if he'd climbed some kind of crow's nest and looked down, but could look in only one direction at a time.

He didn't imagine that Nico was taking the silence well. Partially because Nico was Nico and had no proficiency with waiting, but also because there was reason to believe an attack was imminent. The others had also indicated that they did not appreciate the absence of two medeians from the wards of the house, which they were still tasked with protecting. *Are you an idiot* was the general chorus from Parisa (echoed by Reina's look of pursed disapproval) until Nico had reminded them that they had all made him a promise, et cetera et cetera, and of course it had been Callum who'd jauntily said they had things well in hand lads, ta.

Tristan grimaced at the thought of Callum, who could well and rightly fuck off. Not that he had time for any ill-wishing at present. With as much magic as he was using, he'd be incredibly easy for the Society's enemies (and his father) to track, which meant he had minutes to talk to Libby, at best.

"It's quanta, isn't it? I knew it," Libby was babbling. "I *knew* there had to be something—"

"Rhodes," Tristan said in a quiet voice that he hoped would convey the dual meaning of *I mean business* and also *I've missed you, hi, hello.* "I've got bad news."

"Worse than me being trapped in the past?" Libby asked. She seemed in oddly good spirits, as if all of this was very funny indeed.

"Have you found a way out?" he asked her.

"I'd hoped this would be it," she said. "I'm going to test it."

Alas. Here came the drop.

"It won't work," said Tristan. "I'm sorry."

She frowned at him. "How can you know that? I haven't even begun t—"

"I know, Rhodes, but it's not enough. I'm sorry, but it's not."

He watched this information settle confusingly into her brow. "But . . . then how—? Are you saying I'm . . . ?"

Her face was pale with finality. Oh god, she thought he was telling her she really was trapped there.

"There's another way," Tristan rushed to say, though he dreaded the conversation to follow. It would only get worse, but it had to be done. "I don't have much time, so you'll just have to listen, okay?"

She seemed instantly concerned, even suspicious, as if she should have known that he was a silly boy who couldn't take care of himself. "Why, what's wrong?"

"Nothing. I'm being bounty-hunted. But mostly nothing." He laughed, and familiarly, she looked alarmed. Seeing her that way, anxious again, was an unexpected salve. "Don't worry about me, Rhodes, I've got Varona keeping watch." There was a brief flicker in her eyes at the mention of Nico, like a dance of recognition, which he chose at the moment to ignore. "The point is you need a reaction, Rhodes, a big one. A place like this is an amplifier, but you still need more than that."

"Damn." Her voice got quiet. "I was afraid of that."

Tristan felt a tug at his back, like the crack of a whip. "You need a power surge that's essentially—"

"Nuclear." Her expression plummeted. "But something that big, even if I could do it, the effects would be—" Her throat visibly tightened. "The fallout would last for years. It could affect people for decades, or generations. I . . . I could never."

And here came the worst part.

"The thing is, Rhodes, I think . . . you already did," Tristan said.

It hadn't been Tristan who found the answer—or perhaps the more appropriate word was "loophole." He had tried for weeks to find it himself, but in the end it was Parisa, because of course it was. Weeks after Callum had so delightedly sprung the news on Tristan that Libby Rhodes would rather eat her own foot than commit the brutality necessary to bring herself back, Parisa had kicked out the chair beside Tristan's in the reading room and settled herself into it daintily, like a fawn perched over spring meadow grass.

"What did you do for James Wessex?" she asked.

She did not seem to acknowledge Tristan's unwillingness to talk to her. He supposed he was holding a grudge overlong at this point, but it was hard to let go of things once he'd already decided. "What?" he said gruffly.

"For Wessex Corp." Parisa was looking at him with an odd, reflective intensity. "You were a venture capitalist, right?"

"Yes." It came out in a sulky mutter, perhaps because the question seemed to have been following him around for the last year. "I did valuations on magical technology."

"Any weapons?" she asked.

This again. "No. James did those himself. Why?" he demanded, all in one intake of breath.

"You said Rhodes is in 1990?" she asked.

That was the information Nico had given them. Tristan had pushed him on how, determining that information somewhere between unlikely and impossible, but Nico was adamant, and in the end Tristan simply decided that Nico was the least likely of all of them to lie. "What does that have to do with anything?"

Parisa waved his concern away. "I'll get there. But she's in 1990, right? In Los Angeles?"

"According to Varona," Tristan muttered like a child scorned.

"Look," said Parisa.

She slid the book across the table to Tristan, which was not actually a book, but a very lengthy report. A file. He opened it to see a newspaper article on top.

"Reina didn't think it worth mentioning to you," Parisa remarked, "but I thought you'd like to know. I assume you can piece together what this is all about."

Tristan scanned the page, then turned it. The next page was a map of the state of Nevada, with the desert just outside Las Vegas outlined in red. "James never let me near any weapons technology. He wanted it set aside for him, but that's it. He—"

Tristan turned to the next page. "Wait," he said, frowning as he scanned the report. "Where did you get this?"

Parisa shrugged.

Tristan read the page.

Blinked. Read it again. "No. Seriously?"

"Your interpretation is as good as mine." Then Parisa got to her feet and moved to saunter away as if nothing had happened. As if what she'd just found had been nothing at all.

"Parisa," Tristan said through his teeth, leaping to his feet and catching her by the crook of her elbow. "You don't think—?"

"Look. Here's what I know." She detached herself from Tristan's grip with a glance of lofty impatience. "We're all different people for having come here. Some of us," she added with a flick of disinterest over him, "more than others."

"Okay, insult taken," Tristan said, because although he didn't know exactly what she intended to imply, he could guess it accurately enough.

"You like her because she's innocent, Tristan. Because she's moral. Because she's *good*. Because she represents something to you that the rest of us no longer have, because we came here. And because we made choices." Parisa's expression was stiff and hard and slightly punitive. "But she made a choice too, Tristan. She knew what the consequences were."

Parisa was silent for a moment before she touched Tristan's temple gently. Almost tenderly.

"Libby Rhodes is not your goodness, Tristan," she cautioned. Steadying him, as if for disappointment. "She's her own open flame."

Tristan had been waiting to see Libby again, to be able to tell with certainty that Parisa was wrong, that of course Libby was not his goodness but also of course, of course she was *good*, and that was what he had been missing all along.

He had been living his life since that day in idle paralysis, unsure whether he wanted Parisa to be right, or himself. To prove that the Libby he had known, the Libby she had become, these were just refractions of a fundamental truth: That she was not corruptible. That unlike him, she could not be wrong.

But if that was true, then *Callum* was right, and that was the worst of the possible outcomes.

Because Tristan would rather have whatever version of Libby she had become than face the prospect of having no Libby at all.

Tristan blinked away the memory and looked at Libby's face. The one that was at once familiar and not. The one that, for better or worse, was real, and not the tortured ideation of his thoughts.

"In May of 1990," Tristan said, "there's an explosion in Nevada. In a stretch of desert between Reno and Las Vegas that is owned by the Wessex Corporation." His voice was measured and careful. "No one is harmed. No one is—no one's killed. But the size, it's . . . significant." He cleared his throat, bypassing the other things he knew. That there would be radiation. Sickness. Disability. Cancer. People would be affected. But no one would die *then*, in the inferno of the blast. He didn't need to mention the aftereffects aloud. "Atomic weapons, nuclear weapons, they depend on fission to create the energy necessary for an explosion," Tristan continued, which was the same information he had told her once before. "But this particular explosion . . ." He wanted to sigh, maybe. To express regret.

He didn't. "It's magical," he said. "It's a perfect fusion weapon that has never been replicated by anyone since. Started by a power source incendiary enough to generate energy without the use of fission. Enough, by your own calculations, to open a wormhole through time. And therefore, it's enough," he clarified with a guillotine of finality, "to send you back."

For a long time, she stared at him. Waiting, as if for a better punch line. But he had none.

"Wait. You're saying—" Libby's forehead was creased with conflict. "What are you saying?"

"A *perfect fusion* weapon, Rhodes?" he sighed, trying to be patient, though in fact he, too, was bracing for her reaction. "Only two medeians in the world could possibly do it," he pointed out. "But only one of you is alive in 1990."

"No." Immediately, she shook her head. "No, I won't . . . there's no way I could—"

This would begin an endless spiral if he let it. Unfortunately, neither of them had the time.

"Rhodes," Tristan said firmly, "look at the facts. You're gone. All traces of you. We found nothing." She stared at him, uncomprehending. "If you had stayed in the past, there would have been something, some thread for us to pull. You would have aged, caught up with yourself, and we would have found you. Even if you'd—died—" The words left him in a rush. "We would have found you," he said again, clearing his throat. "You have no idea what kind of resources we have, the way the Society can—"

"Fuck the Society." Libby was breathing hard, backing away. "I can't, Tristan, no. I couldn't."

There was a blur of motion beside her as Tristan realized, belatedly, that she wasn't alone. There was another woman beside her, dark-haired and silent, wearing a worn leather jacket like it was a shield or a cape. He wondered if he should have avoided any mention of the Society, but then there was a whipcrack from the other side of his astral projection again, another small fissure of urgency.

"Rhodes, it's already done," Tristan exhaled quickly. "You mitigate the risks. You must have." He didn't have proof of that aside from who she was, from having known her, but he trusted that. He trusted her. "You do it carefully, so carefully, I'm sure of it. And—" He shook his head. "And you need to come back. I need—" He interrupted himself. "Look, you can't stay there. You'd be absolutely mad to stay there."

She winced. "Tristan—"

"Please," he said. He was pleading, which ought to have been repulsive, but he didn't know what else to do. "Rhodes, *please.*"

"Tristan, you can't possibly—!"

There was a piercing, terrible pain in his shoulder, unmissable this time and unignorable. Tristan let out a soundless yell, plummeting backward as if he'd been ripped from the sky. The aurora overhead dissipated and was gone, the force of Nico's magic enough to nearly divorce his lungs from the inside of his chest.

"*Varona*—" Tristan coughed.

"We've got company," Nico offered in non-apology, sweat beading on his brow as he forced Tristan to his feet, both of them staggering from the shift in momentum. "I took out two," he added, inanely, as if Tristan couldn't count the two bodies lying prostrate on the ground, "but they're in communication with someone. By the sounds of it, there's more coming."

Tristan, who was struggling to his feet, stumbled over the boot of one of their assailants, taking off after Nico toward the nearest road. "Two what? Medeians?"

Nico shook his head. "Not sure. No specific magic, just some combat proficiency. Not mortals, though."

"So witches, then." Oh no. No, not today, not seriously. If they were his father's brand of thugs, they were definitely organized and on their way. Tristan stopped running, pausing to look around and reassess their points of access. "We're on a fucking *island*, Varona. Where the fuck are we going to go?"

"If you want to stay and fight, I'll stay and fight." Nico's expression looked grim as he came to a breathless halt beside Tristan. "I just didn't think you'd want to be trapped in your little astral trance while potentially getting shot at. Or whatever it is they've got," he said, showing Tristan the burn on his shoulder.

Of course. Of fucking course. Tristan remembered the first time he'd seen that particular injury. It was meant to teach him a lesson, to make sure he didn't touch daddy's weapons again. *Stay away, Tris, you're not equipped to handle this, you know what this cost me to come by?* Tristan felt a ghost of the sting in his hand, the graze he'd taken that day to the backs of his knuckles. The hard look on his father's face: *You're lucky I don't make it worse.*

Right then. This was happening. "No, we've got to go." He'd prefer to stay—*Who's useless now, Dad?*—only there were better ways to come by vindication that didn't include letting his father's whole gang descend on him now.

Tristan turned to Nico, contemplating him. "How far could you take us? If I moved things out of the way." Nico was essentially a human battering ram. Tristan was at least adept enough to assist.

Nico offered him a glance of calculation. "Like a medeian transport?"

"Close enough." He figured it had to work. "Can you do it?" It was an explosive output of energy, but at least they didn't have to travel through time.

"I had a good breakfast," Nico said. "We can make it a solid few miles."

A car skidded up the road, tires screeching to a halt as Tristan's hand met Nico's shoulder. He felt the scorching heat of a blast below his palm, the ground beneath them shaking. Tristan imagined rustic picture frames rattling, sheep loudly voicing their displeasure, the locals reaching in bewilderment for the trembling surfaces of their pastoral walls.

In response to Nico's explosion, Tristan's powers ignited, the world pixelating and rearranging itself into particulates and waves, auroras and grains. Nico's magic was itself a wave, so clearing a path of least resistance for it was a matter of expelling Tristan's own energy outward. It was, as Nico had said, the equivalent of using a medeian transport, only it was powered by only the two of them, with what energy they had left. It wasn't enough to get them to Edinburgh, which would be the simplest place to get a magical transport back to the house, but by the time they crash-landed in a car park, it was clear they'd gone at least a far enough distance away to avoid the coven at their heels.

"*Go,*" gasped Nico, who was on his feet first. He lunged for the nearest vehicle and shot through the alarm system with a bolt of whatever it was that ran through his veins. Tristan followed, dazed, and collided with Nico, who had made an accidental beeline for the driver's side.

"Other side, Varona," he hissed, throwing himself into the driver's seat of a car made for a much smaller person. "Stornoway," he read aloud from a nearby souvenir shop, still breathing hard. They'd transported themselves clear across the Isle of Lewis. Comparatively, the wormhole to the kitchen looked positively dull. "We can get the ferry to the mainland from here." Tristan's vision blurred from exhaustion. He could only imagine the state Nico was in.

"Nice. Not bad for a first try." Nico looked both pale and smug, checking the objects in the car while Tristan threw the gearshift into reverse. "It's a rental."

"What?" asked Tristan, who was busy looking for the nearest road to the ferry.

"It's a rental car. Hopefully insured. What did Rhodes say?"

It was clear that Nico was trying desperately not to look desperate.

"Don't know," Tristan said while he took the nearest turn. "I only had enough time to tell her and get out."

Nico nodded, looking drained. "Do you think she'll do it?"

"Told you, Varona, she already has." Tristan didn't voice his own doubt: that maybe, just maybe, it was purely a coincidence. Or that maybe by *not* doing it, then she could alter the future. How did time work, exactly?

But a louder voice, one he tried to quiet, told him precisely what Parisa had told him. That they were different now, all of them. The grip the archives had on them was strong, stronger than anything. Because how could a person see what they had seen and still decide that fate was anything aside from what they shaped it to be with their own two hands? This was the paradox. That Libby Rhodes could, at the same time, both travel through time and refuse to. That she could know how to save herself and still be forced to decide whether that knowledge was hers to turn away from or use.

This was the same thought ringing through Tristan's head when they abandoned the stolen car, boarded the ferry, made their way south to London. That sense of portent, the looming call of the as yet unknown, it only grew louder. He wondered if there was any way around it, but as with Rhodes, he already knew that there wasn't.

He was beholden to the archives as they were beholden to him.

"Okay," Tristan said, pausing in the doorframe of Atlas Blakely's office, and Atlas looked up.

"Okay?" Atlas echoed.

"Okay." Tristan's heart thudded in his chest, no longer the beat of rage. Well, not rage alone. Not the anger of someone whose father wanted him dead for a price. Nor the fury of a man who'd just fled from Scotland, where he had seen the woman he loved for the first time in a year, and realized he would do anything for her. No, instead it was the agony, the inevitability of a boy who'd been burned, and who had now become a man impervious to flame.

"Let's make a new world," said Tristan. His lungs were aching. "New rules."

"You'd stay here, then?" Atlas asked, arching a brow.

"Yes." Tristan already knew what awaited him outside this house. His father's petty gang of witches. Stolen rental cars that he didn't actually give a fuck about. Nico still cared, so there was hope for him. But not for Tristan. Tristan wanted only to let the bridges he'd burned light the path ahead.

"Very well, Mr. Caine." Atlas's expression was unreadable, but Tristan didn't care. Somewhere a clock was ticking; the edge of a knife was waiting, calling, flashing.

"I look forward to working with you," said Atlas, and Tristan nodded grimly. He knew it like he knew his own pulse: Libby Rhodes would be back, and he would be here. Waiting.

When the wheel inevitably turned, Tristan Caine intended to be on top.

· LIBBY ·

W ho was that?" asked Belen, startling Libby so acutely she jumped. "And what's 'the Society'?"

Libby had forgotten for a moment that Belen was still standing next to her. Not next to her, actually, but at a slight distance behind her, hovering just outside her periphery.

"What?" Libby asked, dazed. The sight of Tristan had felt like time travel in itself—the rush of being herself, only exactly one year ago. The mention of Nico, which should have been met with an eye roll, had only produced a severe tearing of something in her chest. Something necessary, like an artery. She was bleeding internally and yet was somehow perfectly fine.

Trapped, but perfectly fine.

"That guy, he said something about a society. And why are you talking about time travel?" Belen's dark brow was furrowed with something that wasn't quite confusion. In fact, it was significantly less confused than Libby hoped it would be. "I thought the purpose of this whole trip was to find an alternative energy source."

Libby played a now-familiar game with herself of weighing the value of telling the truth.

"Well, right, of course. But I am a physicist," Libby said in a rush. "I've done some work with quantum gravity in the past, so. It's obviously a matter of consideration."

It was a flimsy excuse and she knew Belen knew it. Belen had heard, after all, everything that Tristan said, and even if she didn't understand what it meant, she wasn't an idiot. "Why are you *really* looking for ley lines?" asked Belen in a tone that Libby had heard her use before. Usually in response to Mort or Fare. It had a dangerous edge to it, like the sense that at any moment, something might snap.

"You know why. Alternative energy. That's always been the point." Libby felt suddenly out of breath.

In response, Belen's expression was stiff with careful concealment. "Why did he mention the Wessex testing site?"

"I don't know. I have nothing to do with that." And she didn't.

Probably.

Belen's eyes narrowed. "Who is he?"

"A colleague." Libby inhaled sharply. "An old friend."

"How old?"

"Earlier. From my previous research."

"At wherever you were that wasn't NYUMA." Belen's voice was thick with something. Doubt, maybe.

Libby turned to look at her.

"I thought you had finally decided to be honest with me last night. But you're still lying, aren't you?" Belen said flatly.

"I'm not," Libby began, "*lying*, I just—"

"I wanted to trust you," Belen said, the divot between her brows deepening. "I *want* to trust you," she emphasized, looking stung, "and if you tell me it's something stupid, some clerical error or a records mistake, I'll believe you." A heavy swallow. "But it isn't, is it?"

Belen's eyes were swimming angrily with tears. Libby could relate. There was something awful about feeling rage and wanting to strangle something but instead falling prey to the softness of hormones, welling up with the inadequacy of sadness when what she meant to do was scream.

"What do you want me to say?" Libby asked helplessly.

"Tell me the truth." Another small group of tourists was approaching behind them, but Belen was immovable. "The whole truth. Now."

Fine, Libby thought with an inward sigh. Fine. This had probably always been inevitable.

"I was born in 1998," Libby said. Belen blinked. "I *did* graduate from NYUMA, but not in 1988 like I said I did. I graduated in 2020." She cleared her throat. "That same year, I was recruited by the Alexandrian Society, the caretakers of—"

"Stop. Shut up. Stop." Belen was blinking rapidly now. "No. That's not possible. There are laws . . . Thermodynamics, entropy, I—" She stopped. "That's not possible."

"I didn't *want* to be deposited here," Libby said quickly. It felt important, somehow, to point that out: that she had not asked for this. Any of it. "My ex, the one I told you about, he's a medeian. He did this. He's trying to kill everyone I care about from that place—that *time*—that I left. And I'm pretty sure he's been stalking me ever since he put me here, so—"

"So you *have* been lying to me." Belen swallowed. "About the grant. The research. And about—" The look on her face was ghostly with anguish. "About everything."

Libby had always known it was a mistake to get close to Belen. She had known it, perilously, with her lips pressed to Belen's neck, she had known it as she leisurely bisected Belen's chest with her finger, and she had known it earlier, too, when she looked across a table littered with lukewarm coffee thinking: *I cannot do this without you.* "Belen, listen to me, if I hadn't thought it was—" She hesitated. "That *you* were necessary—"

"We should go." Belen folded her arms tightly over her chest, like she suddenly worried that Libby might see through her. "Right? Since you got the answer you needed. We're done."

Libby's heart swelled and ached. "Belen, it's not like this was pointless. You heard him," she said pleadingly. "There actually *is* some kind of power surge around here—"

"But not enough. Right? Not enough. So it doesn't matter." Belen turned and started walking. Libby, unsure what to do, hastened after her.

"Look, I know this seems . . ." Libby hesitated. "I know it sounds bad, but—"

Belen whirled to face her. "You're saying that in the future, there's a society that actually knows how to do this? Time travel? Wormholes?"

"Yes." Libby was slightly taken aback. "Yes, and—"

"So then they *fix* it, right? Everything wrong with the world. Carbon emissions, viruses, poverty—they reverse them, right?" Belen was staring at her with something different now. Hope, maybe.

"Well . . . sort of." The answer fell clunkily from Libby's mouth. "I mean, yes."

Belen's eyes narrowed. "Is it 'yes' or is it 'sort of'?"

"Well—" Libby exhaled. "The stuff you can do, the alkalinity . . . it slows everything down. But for things to actually be *fixed*—"

Belen took a step back. "They don't fix it?"

"I mean." Libby fumbled for words. "I don't . . . I don't totally understand it. The politics of it. But there's research!" she suddenly decided, because of course! That was obvious! "There are labs all around the country in my time, and one of them might be yours—"

"You think that's *good news*?" Belen asked in a voice that suggested Libby was actually an incurable moron. "Thirty years from now, you think it's *good* that someone has ignored everything that we already know about the world *right now*? And there's an entire society that knows how to fix it but *doesn't*?"

"It's not like some secret society can just take over the world." Libby's defensiveness was turning rapidly to frustration. "Just because information exists doesn't mean that people will act on it. Isn't that the point? You can say things all you want," she pointed out, "but it doesn't mean people will believe it."

She knew it was a mistake when she watched Belen's jaw tighten. The concept of belief was a blow to Belen's loyalty, to her tender, well-meant faith. The words *your secrets are safe with me, Libby Rhodes* seemed to strike them both at the same time.

Belen's liquid eyes were red-rimmed now. "You manipulated me," she said, voice faltering.

"No." Libby shook her head, adamant. Callum was the manipulative one. Parisa was, and Ezra, and Atlas. She had only done what was necessary, and it had pained her the whole time. "No, I never meant to hurt you, Belen—"

She took a step toward Belen, who hastily jerked away, hugging herself tighter. "You didn't?" Belen scoffed. "Because for an entire year, you have watched me put aside my life and my family for something *you knew* was never going to happen."

Belen turned around, shaking her head while she stared, hard, at the ruins beside them.

But it wasn't like this was some kind of trick. This wasn't some villainous orchestration by Libby, who had never asked for any of this. She felt an upsurge of the anger she'd repressed for nearly a year, which had been so long eroded by fear and loneliness. The rage was suddenly difficult to bite back, and from the tip of her tongue, Libby tasted smoke.

"What was I supposed to say?" Libby demanded. "'Just give up, there's no point'? How would that have worked? What good would that have done?"

Belen said something Libby couldn't understand.

"What?"

It took a moment for Belen to face her. And when she did, Libby could see there was a wealth of things she'd overlooked in her haste to bring them both here.

"My grandmother *died*," Belen snapped. "Last week. And I came here. With *you*. Because you said you needed me. Because you made me think—" She stopped, wiping her nose hard on her sleeve. "Because *you* needed me."

"I—" Libby melted, then decided to stiffen. "I'm sorry, Belen, of course I'm sorry." Her voice sounded hard even to her, but there was nothing for it now. "You could have just *told* me that, but—"

"You're going to do it, aren't you?" Belen cut in. She swiped a hand across her eyes accusingly, as if she was daring Libby to notice the tear tracks, to witness firsthand the damage she'd caused.

"Do what?" Libby said, though she knew. She knew precisely what.

"That. The explosion, the fusion weapon that guy was talking about—that's *you*." Belen spat it out, letting the impact land near Libby's feet. "You did notice that he didn't say there were *no* effects, right? He said that nobody *was killed*. That's very specific phrasing."

"I haven't said I'll do it," said Libby warily, or perhaps testily, and then Belen's face contorted in something manic. A hysterical, mirthless laugh.

"Of *course* you'll do it!" she snarled. "I've always known you've been hiding the real extent of your magic. I thought it was because of Fare and Mort, that maybe you didn't want your research stolen, or that maybe you just didn't want your ex to find you, but—" Belen shook her head, suddenly scornful. "I saw your face, Libby. He told you that it was predestined, that it was already done, and in that moment, you decided to do it. You don't care about the costs. I see it there, on your stupid fucking face."

"You can't know that," Libby countered. Belen wasn't Parisa. She wasn't Callum. She wasn't any of the six of them and how could she be, how could she possibly know? How could anyone else understand what it meant to have seen what they'd seen and chosen what they'd chosen?

In Libby's mind, something horrifying turned, not unlike a key in a latch. Something, for Libby Rhodes, unlocked. Perhaps it was cruelty. Or necessity. Because the truth, as Libby could now see, was that Belen was actually not much of anything.

Belen had enough magic in her blood for some modern form of alchemy, but that was it. Her grandmother might have died, but at least her grandmother had lived a life, she'd had children, someone had loved her. Libby's sister had died and she'd had none of those things. Belen wanted Libby to make a moral choice based on Belen's limitations but Libby *had* no limitations, because what *she* had was a fucking ex-boyfriend with a god complex and the means to bring herself home in a way that no one else on earth had ever done. When no one else alive *could* ever do it.

This was the thing, the crux of it all, that Libby had the power, she had the formulas, the calculations—she had the *goddamn means*—and so what would it mean for her to live her life now, to decide to be small, to be powerless *on purpose*? What was she supposed to do, locked inside her mind, her mind that held all the answers, her life that had been stolen from her, that she—and *only she*—had the means to get back? If she already knew that Belen would spend a lifetime fighting a political battle that never bore fruit, then what kind of life remained for Libby?

And what was the *fucking point* of outliving Katherine if Libby never did anything with her own goddamn life?

"I can't believe you." Belen was stepping away from her now, shaking her head as if she could see where Libby's thoughts had gone. "Lie after lie after lie. For what? Just so I'd help you? Why did you even need me involved?"

"I didn't." It took hold of Libby hard, gripped her like a vise. "I don't," she realized with a sharp exhalation. All this time she'd been desperate for help, for someone else to reassure her, for some form of comfort, or for anything that could make her feel she wasn't alone—but she *was* alone. She was alone, and this decision was hers to make. Alone.

So that was that, then.

"I don't care what he says." Belen's voice shook. "I don't care if you say that it's already done. I don't believe you. I—" The tremor in her voice became a fracture. "I can change things. I have to be able to change things."

Libby heard the doubt and tried not to comment on it. "I don't know what you want me to tell you."

"I want you to tell me that you've got some goddamn *morals!*" Belen snapped. "I want you to tell me that you're not going to go to Nevada right now and blow up thirty miles of desert just to *bring yourself home*—"

"And why is going home such a small thing, hm?" Libby asked, the air thick with smoldering ash like one of her ongoing nightmares. "What if this were *your* life, Belen? What if *your* life was stolen from you? What wouldn't you do to win it back?"

"My life is being stolen from me every day!" They were facing off angrily now, quarreling like lovers in front of fairy stones. "You just told me that I gave up my family so that . . . what?" Belen spat. "So that one country, or maybe two or three at best, can carry on as normal?"

"I'm not the one who makes decisions about who gets to live or die," Libby snapped, and Belen gave her a look like she wanted to slap her.

"Keep telling yourself that," Belen said. Her tears were dry now, pale channels of foregone misery on her face. "I doubt you're the only one who does."

She turned and walked away. Libby stared after her angrily, then remorsefully. The moment in the quaint country bed, their knees touching like prayer hands, seemed impossibly far away.

"Belen," Libby called, the bubble of fury in her chest rupturing, the thrill of the fight gone out to leave her with nothing but emptiness. "Belen, come on, you need me to get back home."

Belen wasn't listening.

"Belen, do you want me to say I won't do it?" Libby was shouting now as she jogged after her. She probably looked deranged to the passing sheep. "Is that what you want? For me to just give up, stay here?"

With you? she did not add.

Belen didn't pause. Didn't turn. Eventually Libby let her go, assuming they would discuss it back at the inn. She waited by the stones of Callanish Circle and took the last bus.

By the time she got there, the room was empty. When she arrived for their transport, there was no sign of Belen.

·   ·   ·

A month later, Libby Rhodes woke up in a motel room outside of Las Vegas, her eyes snapping open as the VACANCY sign flickered outside her window. She ran a hand along the scratchy sheets, idling in the sensation that she'd had another of her recurring dreams.

Gideon was there. She was pretty sure he'd told her that Nico said good luck today. Then he'd said something else. He had asked her something about Ezra—and here, another hole in her memory; she couldn't recall his question and she wasn't sure if she'd answered. Or maybe Gideon hadn't said anything about Ezra at all and Ezra had simply shown up uninvited, like Ezra tended to do. But by then in the dream Libby couldn't feel her legs, so she had tried to run but couldn't. And then, thankfully, she woke up.

Libby climbed out of bed and faced the bathroom mirror, staring at her reflection. Although only a few weeks had passed since her journey to Scotland with Belen, she felt like she was a different person now, even if she didn't look much different. Just tired. She rubbed a knot out of her neck and bent her head, gathering her hair to one side. She picked up her toothbrush. She brushed her teeth. Then she walked to the wardrobe and gathered her clothes—purchased from the Las Vegas airport gift shop—and applied her name tag for the day's work.

She hadn't gone back to LARCMA. She couldn't. Instead she'd taken a job as one of the medeians doing security for the Wessex Corporation's U.S. testing site. It had been government owned before, but since geoengineering was being privatized, then why not military defense technology, too? Magic could save the world—and end it. Libby herself had helped to figure out how.

She fingered the edge of her name tag, watching as her reflection failed to change. She knew how to do it. She knew what to do. The question was how she would live with it, but that wasn't much of a question at all, given the alternative.

Libby thought suddenly of their lessons in the painted room. Luck and unluck. Lethal arrows. Fate. Before, she had been a believer in destiny—

would readily admit to thinking about her own from time to time. Now, however, she actively hated it. Because if her life story was falling for a man who would only betray her, abduct her, and stalk her like prey until she caved under the weight of his control, then fate was *nothing*. No piece of her was willing to submit to the way her path had altered.

She would have to find her way out.

She eyed her reflection again. This time, she forced herself to stand taller. To hold her shoulders straighter. To cast off the burden that this would inevitably cause. Who lived without guilt? No one. What Libby could not live with was regret. She knew too much. That was the trick of it all, the knowing.

Nico had been right, all those years ago.

If she didn't use this life, then she was wasting it.

Today was the day. Two versions of her existed at once: the Libby Rhodes who was enough and the one who never would be.

Put in those terms, it was a simple matter. She would first make a small, controlled fire to set off the alarms and evacuate the building. Followed by a tiny reconfiguration of the security cameras. The containment structure of the Wessex nuclear reactor that did not work—that could not, and would not without the magical assistance of someone yet to be born—consisted of a reactor, control rods, steam lines and turbines and pumps. It was all very soulless dystopia, glossy machinery and unfanciful sterility.

Well, except for her. The medeian who could power the stars.

She would stand there beneath the generator. She would close her eyes and call to mind the fever in her veins, the fury in her lungs. The rage and disquietude. The hurt and the helplessness. For as much as she had learned about medeian theory, about her calculations, about what it meant to bind atomic nuclei together and force two stubborn things to fuse, she understood that this was not a matter of exactness. To do this would mean holding a supernova in the palms of her desperate, human hands. To let herself collapse and then explode through time was not a matter of holding things together inside herself. She had been angry before, but she had directed it all inward, lonely and humiliated and heartsick. That would not work for her this time.

This time, she would close her eyes. She would inhale deeply. She would do what she had done before but this time she would not let herself fail, because she was no longer frightened. She was no longer aching. She was no longer desperate for the crutch of someone else's faith. For the first time since leaving the Society's walls—for the first time since walking into the dean's office at NYUMA—for the first time since meeting Nico de Varona—for the first time since the death of her sister, the day Libby lost half her heart—she would not presume herself to be deficient. She would not doubt the power in her body. She would not question what was earned.

She would do this, and she would do it alone.

Later she would not remember the details, only the surge. The course it took inside her chest, to use herself as both the conduit and source of power that no other machine or man or myth could ever reach. She would not remember the hysteria, the absolute lunacy of carrying stellar energy inside the same heart that had been broken in periodic increments since she was twelve. She would not recall the details of what it took from her, would not catalogue the force exertion or sweat excretion, would not be able to chart the temperature changing in her blood or the cramping in her muscles, the trembling in her fingers or the dehydration, the excruciation, the agonizing drive of her staggering pulse. She would experience in retrospect the moments, the flashes, but not the blindness—the absolute *carnage* of the pain.

For all the hazy aftermath, the only thing she would recall for certain was that morning. The way she had put on her badge, straightened it, polished it until it shone and then thought to herself: Destiny was a choice.

Time to torch this outcome and let the fucker burn.

IX

OLYMPUS

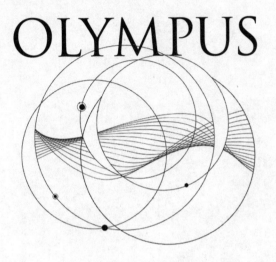

· BELEN ·

Later in life, Belen Jiménez would look back on the days following her argument with Libby Rhodes at Callanish Circle and determine her response to be both an egregious waste of money and the act of a child scorned. For one thing, Belen had spent the entirety of her checking account on a plane ticket with multiple stopovers, which meant that by the time her anger had faded a little bit (somewhere above the Atlantic) she realized that she could have just gone home for free and been able to afford groceries when she got there. So, the tantrum, while hopefully effective at proving a point, was not altogether her smartest decision.

But that was later in life. The version of Belen who arrived back at LARCMA was starving and angry and failing her physicist course—the one that she'd taken *because of* Libby Rhodes, who never came back to Los Angeles. Probably because she set off a bomb and then rode it into the future, sayonara, amen.

The craziest thing was that Belen didn't hear a word about it. Not a peep. It took her years, in fact, to discover that there even was a patent filed for a pure fusion weapon by Wessex Corp, which she only uncovered after accepting a government contract and sneaking around behind a bunch of red tape, risking her security clearance. But by then, it was the mid-2010s and she no longer gave much of a damn about things like security clearance. She had once—in her more optimistic days, circa the aughts—predicted supranationalism to be the future of international politics (the European Union! the North American Free Trade Agreement! the motherfucking United Nations!), but optimism had not served her nearly as well as, well, rage. The kind of rage that made her dig through confidential documents, find the never-replicated 1990 explosion, decide that she was actually extremely fucking sick of laboring under a colonist country's bullshit contracts, and proceed to strike out on her own.

It did not take long to find the Forum, whose pristinely sans serif logo and beautifully curated website had a very pleasant user interface and an obvious agenda. Every month their press releases were full of all sorts of "groundbreaking transparency" and "calls to action" and "bright futures" for the "global community" that meant absolutely nothing besides signaling that they had money that came from somewhere. Belen had by then come to understand that much about the world: that where there was a clean user interface and promises of groundbreaking transparency, there was probably also money. Massive and massive amounts of money. The Forum had "no hierarchy of leadership, Professor, we're all equals here" (bullshit) but eventually Belen sniffed out Nothazai, a man about her age who was paradoxically full of clear-eyed purpose despite his relatively few accomplishments, much in the way men her age so frequently were. As if the catastrophic political and economic failures they had lived through were someone else's fault. Not theirs, of course. After all, *they* were breaking ground on transparency. Had to have hope, they said, because when the hope died, that's when everything went downhill. But it wasn't hope, Belen wanted to say, it was some bizarre sense of entitlement. The failure to believe in failure—or even to accept the nature of things and adapt—felt like an extreme form of narcissism. She didn't tell Nothazai that. Not that he would believe her.

Not that anyone believed her.

It was cute when she was a college student. Her, that is. Her hope, specifically. Her sense that there was a way forward, a necessity to not give up. Adorable! There were a few major articles about her, actually. Praising her as a hero. She was named *Time* magazine Person of the Year one year, alongside a mortal software developer and also, everyone (that was the year global user-generated content became a thing, so, the average consumer was now Person of the Year . . . gimmicky, but not exactly false). Clips of Belen's speech on the floor of the United Nations went . . . well, not *viral* (that was not such a thing yet), but they were certainly acknowledged widely in progressive-leaning academic circles. Her home country of the Philippines cheered her and her adopted country of the United States offered her several ceremonial grants (they did not make any changes to their policies, but that was to be expected). She was even considered for a Nobel Peace Prize. (She lost it to the American president that year, who had apparently avoided war with some other first world country possessing equal opportunity to cause lasting global damage, so she supposed she couldn't be mad.)

When her hope started to lose some of its shine, Belen decided to be angry. Developed countries were stealing, she pointed out. They used more resources and blamed the third world for everything it lacked just because *they*, with their invisible-hand free markets, had afforded themselves the technology to offset their mistakes. (Nobody could remember why the countries that had once been generously colonized by other countries somehow hadn't evolved. Perhaps they were simply . . . stupid? Who could remember that far back.)

Then the cheering got a little bit muddier.

Some people still thought Belen had a point, but others began to suspect that she might have been shouting about nothing. People started asking questions like, was this perhaps reverse racism? Didn't *all* lives matter? Perhaps these smaller island nations should simply embrace recycling as a way of life. Or eat less meat! The carbon footprint of meat was really something. And really, at this point, weren't we *all* equally well-informed, given the philanthropic measures taken toward global transparency?

Wasn't it up to the individual consumer to *choose* to be socially conscious? What was the United States supposed to do about it if people in Africa kept burning down trees?

And, anyway, they asked, how exactly did she foresee this going? The actionable items were intangible (no, Belen said repeatedly, actually it was very simple, all you had to do was hold corporations responsible for their emissions, but for whatever reason her voice seemed to get drowned out by something, usually heartwarming ads where oil was being cleaned off of ducks with Very Effective dish soap). And also, they noted with importance, where were they supposed to get *the money*? Belen said wealth tax, and the wealthy said hm sorry what? And anyway, it probably came down to communication issues. She wasn't pretty anymore, not like she used to be, and since most people could go about their day without feeling the effects of whatever it was Belen was mad about, lots of other issues were much sexier to them. More desirable. The whole thing was like a marriage gone stale.

So, by the time she sat in a room watching a young man babble at her about the Alexandrian Society that she'd first heard about when she was twenty-two and still believed in things, Belen—who was by then fifty-two going on two hundred, or so she could only assume given the premature ache in her bones that would turn out to be just sciatica—had already begun her transition to childless chaos grandma, letting her hair turn gray like the proverbial village witch. She was quietly publishing her old fission research and the research she'd squirreled away from other positions, stubbornly funding the inevitable IP lawsuits with the profits from her government lab. The Western world, the rich Asian countries, they could afford the medeian technology offsetting carbon emissions, but others were still struggling, still on track to lose billions of dollars and millions of (apparently insignificant) lives if things got any worse. Belen was funneling time and money and care—*her whole fucking life*—into people who wanted the world to burn, so when Ezra Fowler, that poor idiot baby, began to talk about saving the world from the six most dangerous people on the planet as if they were someone other than the people sitting next to her (James Wessex, for example, or Nothazai, who had made a fortune off of something Belen doubted was philanthropy) Belen suddenly became overcome with the desire to torch the whole place to the ground. The damage to the ozone would be offset by the work she had done in her twenties, which had ensured the planet's survival for just long enough, for just enough parts of the world, so that she could sit here, in this room, listening to a child talk about the end of the world.

Belen knew instantly who he was.

Ezra.

She remembered the name, as she remembered everything that had ever passed Libby Rhodes's lips back when Belen was still starving for something. Recognition or affection or love. Failing a course for Libby Rhodes had nearly lost Belen her scholarship to LARCMA, but luckily she provided such a valuable service to the American military-industrial complex that, instead, she was required to do the course over, twenty-six units in one semester. A study load that eclipsed her ability to work. She lived for four months off microwavable noodles and did not call home too often. During that time, her mother was one of the casualties of a massive earthquake in Luzon—not from the impact, but from the inability to receive sufficient global aid. American military personnel had been there, which was how Belen eventually found out, but there was only so much the American military could spend on something so . . . inconsequential.

Belen's mother died a few months after the eruption of Mount Pinatubo, which was caused by the earthquake. So, when you thought about it, Belen's mother dying from "complications" only meant that what she really died from was bullshit.

Everything was related. This was what nobody seemed to understand. That although some corn-fed family in Iowa might not feel the loss of the Philippines now, they would someday, they would have to, because ecosystems were connected, because life *mattered,* because nothing in this world could disappear without a trace—and thus, gone was Belen's reason to ever return home.

She was feeling very murderous indeed when she got the invitation from Atlas Blakely to go to London for the Alexandrian Society's farce of a ball. How ironic, really, to be so casually invited in after half a lifetime's effort to drag the Society's secrets to light. It was idiotically transparent, the attempt to welcome her as if she actually had anything left to offer, or as if anyone wanted to listen to anything she had to say. Nothazai was already meeting with governments by then, trading the knowledge Ezra had given him of the Society's tracking systems for other countries' military cooperation, the assistance of their police. All to hunt down the six most dangerous medeians in the world, led by Atlas Blakely, a known associate of a secret society who could change all of this *but wouldn't*. A man who sat on access to archives that were so precious, so priceless, they could change the course of human existence. And all he did was sit.

The congratulatory self ceremony in the Society's great hall was too disheartening. Bad enough to drive her to irrationally seek out the Caretaker himself, thinking that might liven up her evening. A little power play, for the palate. But no, she couldn't even have that, because standing in Atlas Blakely's office was easily the most depressing moment of Belen Jiménez's life.

Which was ridiculous, actually. Because by most measurable standards, her life was very depressing.

She had no close friendships. Her family was gone. She had never married. Never had children. She had had many affairs but nothing of substance; no small things to later look back at as the big things. Nothing to romanticize at all.

She had once fallen in love with a professor who was not a professor, who represented power and femininity and the promise of taking the things she deserved, who turned out to be just another white girl who thought that whatever obscure thing she was born to accomplish was worth more than Belen's entire future. Congratulations, Belen had wanted to shout, on being you! on being pretty! on being full of magic that you have no actual use for! on being born in a country that said you had the right to strike out and *be great*!

But, no. Even that moment, standing in Scotland with Libby Rhodes, had not been as depressing as looking at Atlas Blakely and realizing, with a deafening ring in her ear, that he, too, was just . . . a man.

"Professor J. Araña," he said, wielding her name like a threat. "Your reputation precedes you. Tell me, the *J* is for . . . ? Ah yes, Jiménez." Belen flinched at the reminder. She had done away with her old name, her old life, back when it was too closely associated with the person that the eminent Dr. Maxwell T. Mortimer—the boy-man formerly known as Mort who was now a founding quantum theoretician—had once failed, and who, subsequently, had gone so far as to laugh at the mention of Belen Jiménez during his Fields Medal interview.

"Are you married now," Atlas asked, "or just pseudonymous?"

Surely he knew the answer. Dick. "It's my grandmother's maiden name."

"I see." Atlas was younger than she had thought, and older, too. He seemed just as tired as she was despite being nearly ten years her junior. "And what can I do for you, Professor?"

"Die," she said. "Slowly. Painfully." She was disappointed to discover that she did not hate him. She felt nothing for him, which was almost worse. It was . . . anticlimactic. Pathetic.

Sad.

"Understandable," said Atlas.

"In fact, I only came here to kill you," Belen said. Which was true. She was beginning to think this Ezra child's little runaround could be much more efficiently solved with a healthy dose of preemptive strike, like killing baby Hitler. "But the truth is it's not about you," she sighed, putting an end to all sorts of homicidal fantasies, which were all that she even had left these days. "If you die, someone else will just replace you. Like the hydra's heads."

"True," said Atlas.

"The poison is institutional. It's bigger than you." Fuck.

"It always is," Atlas replied, and okay, she did hate him a little bit for that, because what did he know, actually? Nothing. He was so British she could spread him on a crumpet. "I regret not being able to offer you more, Belen," he said.

"Right." So this was it. She had peeked behind the veil and it was just some English guy. So *this* was the villain? He was nothing. And she was even less than nothing after all.

"Well." Belen cleared her throat. "So much for the party, then."

"I'll take a sock to the jaw if it helps," said Atlas. He seemed to think this was funny. He was looking at her oddly, as if he knew exactly how depressing this whole thing was and he felt sorry for her.

Great.

"Very patronizing, thanks," Belen replied, wondering if she shouldn't kill him anyway just for fun. But what would be the point now?

What was the point of anything?

During her *Time* magazine interview, Belen had been asked by a Pulitzer-awarded journalist named Frank about why she had fought so hard that year to lobby Congress for institutional environmental policy. It was a stupid question and she had treated it as such. It was like asking her, "Hey, why do you think it's important that every human being should be treated with dignity, almost as if they matter or something," and she had been tempted to say, "Well, Frank, why should I even deign to answer your question, hm? You have a family, a ring on your finger, a roof over your head—why should I treat you as if *you* matter, when you could have been born a woman, or a mosquito, or a resident of my mother's hometown?" The reality, that the thought would never have occurred to him, had angered her at the time, but now it only deflated her. She had hated him for years but nothing happened as a result of that hate.

Her hair had turned gray. He had been the basis of an Oscar-winning film.

What was the point, what was the point, *what was the point*?

Eventually she whirled around, exiting Atlas Blakely's office and stepping directly into someone's path. "Excuse m—"

She didn't know exactly what happened. It was like a bomb went off somewhere in her head. Something explosive, from which she could not return. She couldn't give up, she realized. Because if she gave up, *then they won*. She didn't know exactly who *they* were, but that was not important. *She* would win. She would not let the future that Libby Rhodes had predicted be the only future there was. Belen would *make* someone listen to her. She would make someone hear her and it suddenly no longer mattered how, or how long it would take, or which of her principles she cast aside to do it.

. . .

After the party, Belen increased the productivity of her lab.

She no longer refused projects on the basis of moral concern.

She left Nothazai's calls unanswered, dismissing his goals as too lofty, his beloved transparency too high a price.

For years she had had access to precisely the kind of medeian research that would fetch a pretty penny on shadow markets. If money made the world go round, then fine. If money was what she needed to make people shut up and listen, then money she could get.

Not to have, of course. Not to collect. To *spend*.

She was now actively arming guerrilla environmentalists who opposed governmental policies in countries ruled by idiot men.

In places like Indonesia and Vietnam, she began quietly funding union revolts. *Fuck the supply chain!* she roared while she wired money to the many enemies of the state.

She would violate every fucking patent and reveal every goddamn trade secret and thus, the meek would inherit the earth. They would have to! They would be the only ones left to do the inheriting, because Belen would personally make every bespoke-suited capitalist *bleed*.

"I worry you're losing sight of our purpose," said Nothazai, who felt it appropriate to pay a visit to her lab. Ezra was with him, the little twerp. He couldn't have been more than twenty-five and yet here he was—*corralling* her. Like she was some kind of teenager gone wild. As if he were not waging some kind of ideological war with his own guilt.

(Not that it mattered now, but when Belen was his age, she had been hotter than him.)

"I have no idea what your purpose is, Nothazai," replied Belen calmly, though her appearance might well have suggested otherwise. She had not washed her hair in several days and she had thrown out all her lipsticks, her foundations, the illusion charms that she had once used to make herself appear dignified and/or sane. "Do *you* know what your purpose is?"

"Our goal is the same as it's always been," Nothazai replied stoically. "To reveal the truth of the Society. To make public the precious knowledge they hide behind closed doors. To—"

"First of all," said Belen, "everything worth knowing is already known. People *know* about slave labor," she pointed out. "They know about the politics of geoengineering. They know about unethical business practices. They know about corporate bailouts and tax loopholes and the fucking Cayman Islands. What do you do about *that*?"

She realized she was speaking quickly, perhaps too quickly. Nothazai did not seem to understand her. Ezra, if he understood anything at all, had fixed his attention far too firmly on his shoes.

"What people do with information is not our business." Now Nothazai was the one speaking calmly, as if to soothe a growling tiger, which Belen was not. She was an extremely sane woman who had simply had it *up to here* with everyone who had ignored her for thirty literal years. "We cannot control what the world chooses to do with knowledge. It is not ours to possess."

"Bullshit," said Belen. "So whose job is it, then?"

"J.," offered Nothazai soothingly. "Be reasonable."

"My name is not J., you pompous twit," she said. "My name is Belen. I was named after my mother's cousin. My mother who died, by the way," she informed Ezra, who was looking everywhere but her face. "And her cousin who died too, and sure, maybe that was just in the cards for her, but did anyone care? Does *anyone* care?"

"Professor," said Nothazai.

"You're doing this all wrong," Belen said to Ezra, because for now, he was a child who could still maybe learn something, not an old dog with old tricks. She couldn't imagine how this had been the man that had filled Libby

Rhodes with such mind-altering terror, but then again, she had clearly not understood Libby Rhodes.

"You think this is about *six people?*" she asked Ezra, watching his expression blanch. "You're wrong. It's not about six people. It's not even about the world." Okay, maybe that time her laughter sounded a little deranged, even to her. "It's never about *the world,* Ezra. It's only about one person," she said, and gratifyingly, he seemed to be listening, at least. "Everything you do. Everything you believe. Every mistake you ever make and every dream you ever have. It's not about the ten billion fucking people you'll never meet—it's only ever about one. It only comes back to one person after all."

Libby Rhodes, you bitch. I miss you and I hate you.

That was the last conscious thought that Belen remembered. Everything else was a blur. A motion of Nothazai's hands (biomancer scum), a sickened glance from a shamefaced Ezra, the sudden tilting up of the old linoleum floors. Belen, at the time, was laughing, her throat starting to hurt with it, the laughter. She had one thing left in her tired, angry mind. Just the one thought, on repeat—

Fuck you, Libby Rhodes!

Fuck you, *Libby Rhodes!*

Fuck you, Libby Rhodes!

—until, quietly, the little flame of rage that had burned for three decades in Belen Jiménez's heart finally spluttered and went out.

· NICO ·

W here is everyone?" demanded Nico, after five minutes of awkward silence in the painted room. The date had been marked on the syllabus for nearly a year; their independent study was to have concluded today, to something Nico assumed would be pomp and circumstance, or some casual pageantry, at least. Tristan, who was sitting at the table, shrugged. Callum, who was staring out the window, didn't turn. "I thought we were supposed to be sharing our research."

Nothing. Crickets.

"Seriously?" Nico said.

"You really need to spend more time out in the world, Varona." Parisa, at least, had finally strolled into the room, sunglasses on, as if she'd taken herself out for a stroll and only come in because the weather had taken a turn. Which it hadn't; it was beautiful outside. This was exactly what was so frustrating. "You're not here to present a final exam," she said, sitting on the edge of the sofa as if she expected someone to fetch her a drink.

"Like hell I'm not," said Nico, whose notes had all been painstakingly prepared with no time to spare over the course of the long night before, just as he had done with all his previous courses. "And where's Reina?"

"Here" came from the painted room's entryway. Reina slunk in and sat down at the opposite end from Parisa, an enormous tome clutched sullenly to her chest.

"See? Reina brought . . . something." Nico waved a hand in her direction. "I mean, we *were* assigned independent study for a reason, weren't we? Go forth and research? Do unto the archives as they do unto you?"

"You're confusing Atlas with the Bible," said Parisa, as Callum and Tristan both snorted under their breaths and then immediately strove to undercut the synchronicity by facing in opposite directions. "Nobody said we had to present our findings," Parisa added. "We were always told this wasn't a school. Our only instruction was to contribute our personal research to the archives."

"*Make them grow,* as it were," Callum recited, affecting a deep, Atlas-adjacent tone.

"Okay, *and*?" Nico prompted, waving a hand. "Where is this alleged research?"

"Contributed," Parisa replied. She glanced at Reina, who was still hugging her notes to herself, and then away. "But I think the question is where is Atlas, isn't it?"

"He's not coming," said Tristan.

"Are you his disciple now?" asked Callum without turning.

"Fuck you, and no," Tristan snapped. "He's just not here."

"What about Dalton?" asked Nico.

"Sick," said Callum with an elusive glance at Parisa, which she ignored.

"Oh." Nico blinked, then frowned. "So then what are *we* doing here?"

In answer, Reina rose to her feet and turned to the doorway to leave until Parisa sighed and caught her by the wrist, stopping her.

"Look, this is our last week here," said Parisa, who then glanced at Tristan. "Well, for most of us."

Tristan said nothing. Nico, who had heard no such thing, rounded on him. "What?" he demanded. "Since when? I thought Reina was going to—"

"No," said Reina irritably. "Are we done now?"

She glanced at Parisa with a sullen look of resentment.

"Sit," Parisa told her.

Irritably, Reina sat.

"Good girl," Parisa said, and Reina rolled her eyes. "Anyway, in case you've all forgotten, someone is coming for us." She glanced at Nico, who grimaced, and Reina, who looked away. "So we ought to discuss our exit strategy amongst ourselves, whether Atlas is going to be here or not. After all," Parisa added, "*he's* not the one who'll be hunted down the moment he sets foot outside these wards."

Reina cast her a look of stubborn irritation. "They'll only know how to find us if we go where they expect us to go," Reina muttered. "So we can just go somewhere else. Done. Problem solved."

"They'll find us eventually," Parisa pointed out. "Which I find a bit too inconvenient for my taste."

Nico recognized the tone in Parisa's voice as the one that he enjoyed the most—the timbre of plan formulation. "You have my attention," he said, to which Parisa gave him an ironic salute.

"Look," she said. "We know the Society has enemies. We know they've decided to come for us. After two years in this godforsaken place, they almost certainly expect us to go back where we came from. And we know they expect at least one of us to have already been killed." She looked pointedly at Callum, who was considering her in silence from a distance. "My guess is they'll be sending someone to pick us off one by one until the job's done. So rather than sit around and wait for the inevitable, I say we dismantle the threat by making our own—with someone they won't be expecting."

Nico felt his brow furrow. "You mean—"

"Someone sent to catch a telepath in Paris might be ill-prepared for a physicist," Parisa supplied with a shrug. "Likewise, someone expecting a physicist in New York may be easily defused by an empath. Particularly one with . . . Callum's particular specialty." She gave him a smirk of mock deference and he arched a brow in acknowledgment, but said nothing. "The point is," Parisa continued, "we have the opportunity to take things into our own hands one last time before we resume occupancy in the world at large. Which," she added dryly to Nico, "is not a world where you're required to submit your homework anymore, just so you know."

There was a little drumbeat of excitement in Nico's chest despite the jab. "You're saying you want us to fight back?"

"Why not?" Parisa shrugged, then looked at Reina, challenging her to argue. "Unless you have another idea."

"No." Reina's answer was surprisingly quick. "No, I think it's a good plan."

"So do I," said Callum smoothly.

Parisa rose to her feet, straightening her dress. "Well, that was easy. You can go to London," she told Reina, divvying up the remainder of the unassigned destinations, "and I'll go to Osaka."

"Okay," said Reina, who seemed oddly unaffected by the suggestion. Nico supposed she really was done with all of them.

"Great. Excellent. We're all set, then." Parisa turned to the door, preparing to leave.

Reina stood up to follow, and Tristan, and then, before Nico quite knew what he was saying, he had already blurted out, "But aren't we going to say goodbye?"

The others turned slowly to stare at him.

"Sorry," he said, and then blinked. "No, I'm not sorry. I don't think it's *unreasonable* for me to think that we might consider speaking to each other in some capacity before we leave! And how the fuck is Dalton still sick?" he added hotly, partially because nobody had seen Dalton in weeks and also because the presence of Dalton typically indicated an Official Academic Event, which was something Nico was disappointed to learn this wasn't. "You can't honestly think we're all going to walk away and then . . . *nothing*," Nico stammered. "Right?"

Reina looked blankly at him. Parisa was holding her mouth with charitable affection, like he'd said something especially charming and adorable. Tristan sighed loudly.

"Fine," Tristan said in a long-suffering voice, as if no one had ever been as tired as he was and thus they could not even dream of imagining his trauma at the thought. "Dinner together? Our last night?"

"A last supper?" Parisa said. "Typically those are hit-or-miss."

"Nobody bring knives," Callum remarked from his spot by the window.

"Fuck you," said Tristan. "Is that a yes?"

"It's not a no," said Parisa.

"Fine," Tristan said before glancing at Reina, who shrugged her ambivalence. "There," Tristan concluded, turning back to Nico. "We'll see each other at the end of the weekend. Satisfied?"

"I mean, I guess," muttered Nico, who hadn't expected to feel like the neediest kid at sleepaway camp. But apparently that was enough for the rest of them, because a couple of minutes later, they had all vacated the room.

"I suppose you can't blame them," Gideon said from outside the usual cage of Nico's dreams. "This was always just a job to them, wasn't it? You're the only one who hasn't had one of those yet."

"I guess," Nico muttered, though he brightened at the reminder that in a matter of days, he would no longer have to occupy a jail cell in order to talk to Gideon. "Want to meet me in Paris?" he asked, feeling unexpectedly upbeat.

"Aren't you supposed to be fighting someone?" Gideon asked.

"Yes," said Nico.

"Then yes, obviously," Gideon replied. "Though I feel like my corporeal self probably needs to take some vitamins first."

"Stretch," Nico advised.

"*Gracias.*"

"*De nada.* And bring bagels."

"No," said Gideon. "You can get those yourself."

"Unless I get murdered," said Nico.

Gideon arched a brow.

"Just kidding," Nico said. "I'd never get murdered unless it's by an ex, in my sleep. In which case it's justly deserved."

"Richly so," Gideon agreed.

"Speaking of exes." Nico made a face of repulsion, which Gideon helpfully interpreted.

"No sign of him," Gideon said with a shake of his head. "I sent Max to ask around, but so far no one's heard from Fowler in over a year."

Unsurprising. "What about—"

"Libby's parents? Weirdly, they've been in touch with her, or think they have." To Nico's look of surprise, Gideon shrugged. "Apparently someone's been messaging them from Libby's phone at semi-regular intervals. Normal check-in texts to say *hi, love you,* that kind of thing."

For fuck's sake. "Who would do that?" Nico muttered, disgusted. "Some kind of sadist."

"Or someone who cares," Gideon suggested neutrally, using his best Saint Gideon voice.

Unbelievable. What a menace. "Could your overbearing sense of compassion please find rational limits?" Nico growled. "For once, Gideon, just stop trying to force me to love people and accept that I've been extremely reasonable and correct this *whole time—*"

"Shouldn't you be pleased?" Gideon countered. "I'm only bolstering *your* theory, after all, that someone who cares about her did this."

Nico fumbled, sensing a trap. "Yeah, well—still, I—" He cut himself off, flustered. "As if he could possibly do this and still *care about her.* Honestly, how would that even—?"

Infuriatingly, Gideon smiled.

"Any word from Rhodes?" Nico demanded instead, his chest suctioning bizarrely at the thought. He supposed it was no wonder that he'd done something so completely embarrassing as to ask his fellowship cohort to hang out with him one last time. He'd had no Libby for a year, which apparently meant he'd become her in her absence.

"I passed along the message," Gideon said with a shrug. "And for what it's worth, I can't find her anywhere else in the realms, so either she's done it, or . . ."

He trailed off, looking particularly ethereal in his reluctance.

"She won't die," said Nico quickly. "Rhodes would never get killed."

"Unless it's by an ex, in her sleep?" asked Gideon quietly.

As much as Nico loved the idea of being right about Ezra Fowler, he hated it in equal measure. Better to assume that the worst was not actually *the worst.*

"She wishes," scoffed Nico, shoving aside any semblance of real concern. "She's probably nothing but considerate to her lovers."

"So sad for her to have so few enemies," Gideon whimsically agreed. "Unlike you."

"Exactly," said Nico.

Gideon's smile in response was demonic with fondness.

"See you soon, Nicky," he said.

"Bagels," said Nico.

"I'll tell Max," Gideon replied, snapping his fingers for Nico to wake.

The day that followed went by with an absurd quickness. Nico couldn't believe it, that something so allegedly impactful could fall away like this, with no ceremony, no notice. Then again, he supposed that someone who'd started the fellowship was usually dead by now, so maybe he was the one being strange.

"You can call me any time," Nico offered to Reina at their final dinner. Callum was late. Parisa was across from him, looking over a map of Osaka's magical epicenter. Tristan was stabbing his salad furiously with his fork.

"Thanks," said Reina. Nico had been hoping to mend whatever it was that had come loose between them, but it didn't look likely. She seemed eager to leave, which he couldn't understand.

"I thought for sure you'd want to stay," he murmured in an aside, and she glanced at him as if he'd said something horrifically vulgar.

"Why? You wouldn't," she muttered.

He hesitated, unsure of his footing. "Well, no, but—"

"There's no winning this one," Parisa advised him from across the table. "Just tell Reina she's very clever and dangerous and she'll feel much better."

"What?" said Nico, turning to stare at Reina. "Is that true? Because—"

"Good night." Reina shoved her chair out and let her utensils fall with a clatter before leaving the room. She clipped shoulders with a whistling Callum, who had finally deigned to show up.

"What was that? Oh, don't tell me," he said, waving his concern away. "Never can tell with her. Did you know she thinks she's a god?"

"What?" demanded Nico.

"It's not important," Parisa said. "Eat your salad."

"I regret this *so much*," Nico sighed.

"So do I," contributed Tristan, who looked as if he was trying to explode a cherry tomato with his mind. Which was a thing he could kind of do now, thanks to Nico, but bringing it up felt a little sad. Like watching a video of their best moments and saying "aww" as a crowd.

"Has anyone spoken to Atlas?" asked Nico, in lieu of something sentimental. (In fairness, "I'll miss you" or "Have a great summer" did feel misplaced.)

"Yes, actually, I just did," said Callum with a jerk of his head to the corridor. "Apparently he was going to join us this evening but was called away. He said someone from the Society will be in touch with us after we leave here."

"That's it?" The whole thing was exasperating Nico. "Who will it be?"

"Whoever's in charge of careers, I imagine." Callum was obviously joking.

Well, presumably joking. To be fair, Nico could not imagine the logistics of the Society, which would only get . . . well, less magical the farther he got from it. Though he was fairly certain the distance from the archives would do him good.

"Oh." The clock on the mantel ticked as they ate in silence, Nico eyeing his fork. "Well," he began, and then Parisa kicked him under the table.

"We know, Varona," she said. "Don't make it weird."

"But—"

"It's just a thing we all did," Tristan said.

Callum added, "Try to make the next thing interesting."

"But—"

"Bread?" asked Parisa, offering Nico the basket.

He had never felt more like a child.

"Fine," Nico said, exhaling.

The next day Dalton finally had the decency to show up, though it was only to explain the process of transport, as if Nico had never been magically transported anywhere before.

"And should you ever need to consult the archives, you'll need to contact the Caretaker," Dalton added, handing Nico a card that said ATLAS BLAKELY, CARETAKER, as if that, too, were something he had never seen before.

"Wow," said Nico. "Wooooooooow."

"Indeed," said Dalton. He stood very still, as if he assumed the interaction was already over.

"Well, bye, then," Nico muttered, glancing over his shoulder for Reina. No sign of her. Parisa's bedroom was already empty. He hadn't bothered to say anything to Tristan because he felt pretty sure he knew how that would go, and Callum . . . was Callum.

"Ah, Mr. de Varona," came Atlas's voice, and Nico let out a heaving sigh of relief. This, at least, would be important. Perhaps a plaque would be involved.

But instead, Atlas was merely holding out a hand. "Safe travels," he said. "Hopefully we'll see you again soon."

"Did you see my research?" Nico asked, sounding more Rhodes-like than ever.

"I did." Atlas nodded. "Very thorough."

That appeared to be it. Nico reached a hand forward to place in Atlas's.

Then, because he was an idiot, he asked, "Why didn't you ask me to stay?"

"Hm?" said Atlas.

The answer left Nico in a rush. "You asked Tristan to stay. And Parisa.

And, well, Callum is a whole other thing, but—" Nico chewed his lip. "I thought you'd find my research, you know, interesting."

God, he felt like a catastrophic fool. It was even worse when Atlas smiled at him.

"You'll be back," he said to Nico in a paternal way, patting his shoulder. "I have a feeling I'll see you again quite soon, Mr. de Varona."

"Why?" Nico asked desperately. "How?"

"Because," Atlas said, "Miss Rhodes will be back."

This information dawned on Nico forcefully. Like the sun hitting his eyes, dazing him.

"Oh," he said dizzily, and Atlas stepped aside, gesturing him toward the transports on the west side of the wards.

"Safe travels," Atlas said, nodding obligingly as the transport doors closed.

Nico swallowed, pausing a moment in silence. Then he jerked an elbow into the button for Paris and waited for the transport to deliver him as the doors once again opened, releasing him blinking into the light.

The sun was high over Pont Neuf, the Seine glistening below him. He realized for the first time how unaccustomed he had become to noise over the last two years. The sound of cars and passing strangers was almost alarmingly loud, the sights and smells an overwhelming rush of newness, aliveness. A bike went by on the cobbles and Nico wanted to fall to his knees and kiss the ground.

"Fancy meeting you here," came a voice to his left.

Nico turned to find Gideon leaned up against one of the iconic lamplights, looking pale and sleepy and generally unkempt. Nico's pulse thud-thudded in greeting, like the wag of a loyal dog's tail.

"*Bonjour,*" he wanted to say, or something otherwise cultured and clever, but Gideon's brow stormed with intensity before he could.

"Nicky, behind you—!"

But even before Gideon had called out to him, he had felt it. The earth below him rumbled with oncoming thrill and Nico turned, giddy with anticipation, to lock eyes with the latest person who wanted him dead.

· CALLUM ·

By the time he stumbled upon Reina in the narrow street behind St. Paul's, she had narrowed her four attackers down to two. Still, Callum had a feeling she was regretting the time she'd spent reading books and ruminating on divinity (or whatever it was she did in her bedroom) rather than sparring, as she'd done the previous year, because the toll it was taking on her was considerable. She was obviously slowing down, with the bursts of physical magic she was able to produce becoming wispier each time she centered on her target, so Callum did the gentlemanly thing and tapped one of her assailants on the shoulder—the more hulking of the two. That man was obviously used to accepting commands from people who were smaller but smarter, which was a convenient starting place.

"Leave," Callum suggested, and the guard dog of a witch seemed to think that this was an excellent idea. He straightened and walked off at once, quicker even than the dolt Callum had once persuaded to leave his older sister alone, whom Callum had previously believed to be the most brainless arse on the planet. So, it seemed some people did not choose their soldiers well.

In the meantime, Reina had gotten herself fairly well cornered. Not that Callum fought much, or ever—funnily enough, he had not had many enemies before this—but he was pretty sure she had violated some essential law of combat by letting herself get backed into a wall. She at least had a weapon on her, some sort of thin stiletto knife, which was sartorially adorable and not completely useless, seeing as the witch she was facing off against had to keep care of his eyes. But other than her knife, Reina seemed ill-prepared for the trap that had awaited her, and Callum could see her struggling to take in breath, her hair stringy with sweat and falling into her eyes right at the moment she caught sight of him. Presumably her stores of unpolished battle magic had already run out.

Reina's brow furrowed at his approach, a moment's delay nearly trapping her into a face-first introduction to her attacker's incoming fist. Callum helpfully dog-whistled and took advantage of the moment's distraction, pausing the smaller witch with a hand on his shoulder.

"Stop," Callum said.

The witch stopped, looking dazed.

"Sit," Callum suggested.

The witch sat.

"Stay," Callum concluded, and when he was confident the situation was handled, he turned to a gasping Reina, who looked as if she might collapse. "Poor choice," he said with a small tut of disapproval. "Didn't anyone warn you there was a whole gang of witches out for Tristan Caine's blood?"

"I'm assuming Parisa must have accidentally left that part out." Reina's chest rose and fell with such sluggish jerks that for a moment Callum was almost concerned for her physical well-being. But then she scowled at him, so he guessed she was mostly fine. "What are you doing here?"

"You and I had a deal, didn't we?" He shrugged. "And anyway, the situation in New York was easily handled."

Actually, it was stranger than he had expected, because in addition to the magical thugs he had anticipated, there was also a blue-veined mermaid who seemed *very* disappointed to see him. Callum had never tried manipulating a creature before—she, in fact, had nearly used some sort of manipulation on *him,* which of course he was able to evade on the basis of having no interest in fucking a mermaid—and he couldn't be sure whether the full effect had kicked in. In any case, he was here now, and Nico de Varona clearly had a very valuable friend if the mermaid was to be believed, which was good to know. (He would look into those details later, if necessary.) The point was that everything was fine there, and now Callum was here, and there were no more sentient houses breathing down his neck, and everyone was behaving themselves very nicely. Even, or perhaps especially, the witch who sat placidly at their feet.

"I didn't need your help," said Reina, which was patently false. Callum could feel every modicum of remorse that had wrung out of her since she'd left the manor house that day, pearls of doubt that clung to her like dewdrops, clouding the surface of her skin. She was exhausted, and furious that there wasn't more that anyone had tried to do to help her. No useful trees, no helpful vines, no Nico, not even a word from Atlas, whom she had expected to beg her to stay but who obviously hadn't. She was sick with sadness and she thought it was anger, which was probably why she thought Callum was to blame. Because Callum could not, would not, make her sad.

He had no effect on her whatsoever. Which was better for both of them in the end.

"I'm not here to help you," Callum said. "But I do think there is a benefit to making sure that you don't wind up unhelpfully dead."

Her breath was slowly coming back to her. She grimaced, then flicked a glance to the witch at her feet. "So are you going to take care of this, then?" she asked with a jut of her chin. "Send him off to his own private nightmare like you usually do?"

"No, I rather think not. Lead on," Callum said to the witch, who clambered eagerly to his feet. "My goodness, so well-behaved. Come on, Mori," he called to Reina, who was frowning after him even though Callum had already started to walk.

She caught up to him, then staggered a bit. "Cramp?" asked Callum jovially.

She glared at him while pressing a hand to the stitch in her side. "It's nothing."

"You'll live," Callum agreed. Nothing to worry about, unlike what he suspected would happen to them if they didn't find a way to complete the Society's ritual before the effects of the distance started rotting them like a thick mist of decay. Or, he thought with an upward squint, like London fog.

"So," he added. "Anything I should be aware of as far as goals?"

She was still concentrating on the pain. "What?"

"You're planning to fulfill your divine purpose, right? So where do you start? I don't think anyone will be impressed if you walk on water," Callum pointed out, gesturing to the witch who was leading them down a winding street away from the Thames. "Magically speaking, even this guy can probably do that."

Reina grimaced. "I don't want attention. I don't need anyone to see me."

Actually, Callum thought, that was precisely what she needed. But if she didn't already know that then he wasn't going to be the one to tell her. "Going to start your own Forum?" he asked. "Distribute information to the masses? Community of one world?"

"No." She was making a face, either of repulsion or pain. Unclear. "I just want things to be different."

"What things?"

She shrugged. "Everything."

"Set achievable goals, I always say," Callum offered with a dry nod of approval. She glared at him, and he shrugged. "It sounds like you're still going to use me, then, yes? So perhaps you did need my help," he added with a flutter of his fingers to the witch leading them ahead.

"I—" Yes, she knew it. Oh, she didn't care for it. There was another wave of nauseating doubt coming from her general direction. "I told you. We can help each other."

Ah yes, so egalitarian of her. So very quid pro quo. "For what it's worth," Callum remarked, "I doubt this is the last you'll hear from Atlas Blakely." She cut an angry glance at him. "Don't deny it," he warned. "You were hoping for a chance to tell him to fuck off, but he didn't even give you the opportunity, did he? He will," Callum assured her. "He just knows better than to ask you right now, when you're already sure to say no." He waited for her to say something, to disagree, but she had fixed her scowling glance on the cobbled path before them. "He will wait until you're desperate," Callum said. "Until every other plan of yours has failed. When you have nothing else, then he'll come for you."

"You sound almost admiring," Reina muttered, which wasn't entirely the reaction Callum had expected, though he supposed she might have been right. He *had* come to admire certain aspects of Atlas Blakely's style. Ironically, the more he understood Atlas, the more he respected him. (This did not get in the way of Callum's hatred for him, of course. That went on unimpeded, staying its invariable course.)

"He's very effective at what he does," Callum said curtly. "Which is why it matters that you achieve your very achievable goals."

"Right," said Reina bitterly.

"Because if you don't—"

"Yes, I understand," Reina snapped. "I'm not stupid."

"Of course you're not. If you were, you'd probably be better off." He smiled in advance of her oncoming scowl. "Have a little more blind faith, Reina. Or blind rage. Whatever you do, do it blindly," he suggested. "Much easier that way."

She flipped him off as the witch turned a corner. The last one, Callum suspected, and he was correct. A pub that looked nearly Dickensian came into view as they approached.

"We can find our way from here," Callum said, pausing the witch. "You can go off and have a swim if you like."

The witch fought him for a moment—they were close, clearly, to the source of the witch's usual instructions, but Callum was not untalented— and then turned blankly in the direction from which they'd come.

Reina turned her head, dark eyes following as the witch disappeared. "You didn't actually suggest he drown himself, did you?" she asked Callum, still watching even after the witch had gone.

"Of course not," said Callum, who then knocked on the pub's back door. He was met with yet another man who was probably a witch, this one doused in putrid fumes of expensive cologne with a film of cheap tricks and unseen armor. "Take us inside," he said.

The witch cocked his head. "Go fuck yourself," he suggested.

Reina, sensing an opportune moment, stepped closer. Callum set a hand on her shoulder.

"Take us inside," he suggested again, his magic grabbing hold of Reina's and taking off with a cannon-fire kick start.

The result was a bit much, Callum suspected. The witch looked comatose as he turned and staggered in the direction of the back office, hardly able to walk. Next time, Callum thought, a bit of moderation was in order. Reina turned to look at him, then shrugged.

They both followed the witch into the guts of a respectable galley kitchen. There was at least a somewhat functional business here. Clearly the establishment was used as an actual pub, though it was probably also a front for something. Money laundering? Weapons dealing? Probably all of the above. This witch, the one who smelled aggressively of greed, knocked twice on the back-room door and muttered, "Boss. Visitors."

"Thank you," said Callum, who had not been raised by wolves.

The witch grunted and fell back as Callum entered the room, Reina half a step behind him.

"Afternoon," Callum offered as the witch at the desk looked up, sparing him a thin slice of derision between familiarly narrowed eyes. "I'm here about an acquaintance we have in common."

"Is that so?" asked the witch, eyes flicking to Reina and back to Callum. "Nice muscle," he congratulated Callum, gesturing to Reina with an obvious look of mockery. Beneath the desk, Callum was comfortably certain a pistol was currently aimed at his cock.

"We're just here to talk," Callum assured him, taking a seat. Reina shot him a look of *this isn't what I agreed to,* but she'd piece things together in a moment. Perhaps even less. She was not, after all, stupid.

"As I said," Callum continued, "we're here about a mutual acquaintance."

"And who is it we both know?" the witch rumbled with feigned disinterest.

Ah, wonderful. Even the skepticism tasted familiar.

"Your son," Callum replied.

Beside him, Reina stiffened. Adrian Caine's narrowed eyes took on a dawning look of clarity, and briefly, Callum wondered whether it would break Tristan's heart to know he had grown up to possess all of his father's mannerisms. Callum dearly hoped so.

"Well then," said Adrian Caine, lifting the pistol for both of them to see before unloading it, setting it on his desk as a measure of peace. "Let's talk."

· PARISA ·

You don't want me.
Look away.
I'm not what you came for.

One by one, the four would-be attackers—each of them in a separate part of the plaza at the center of the square—turned their attention back to whatever covert position they had assumed at her moment of arrival. One was reading a newspaper. The other was having a fake phone call. The third was pretending to alter the charms of the central fountain, dressed as some kind of maintenance worker. The fourth was a woman, pushing a stroller that did not contain a baby, and whose hair was held in place by two knives.

Contrary to her suggested course of action prior to leaving the manor house, Parisa did not plan to kill any of her attackers. They would take care of each other later, once she'd enjoyed some milky tea and left them to whatever their minds decided (courtesy of the power of telepathic suggestion) was a good use of the afternoon. For now they would go on about their business, and so would she. She had learned something from Callum after all.

Parisa stepped into a café, signaling the waitress. Then she sat down at a table in the corner, pulling out a book. It had been so long since she'd read purely for pleasure. She had always loved a cozy mystery. There was something so relaxing about not putting her mind to work.

Her tea arrived and she sipped it comfortably, listening to the scattered thoughts around her. Someone worried about their ailing mother. Another worried about their troublesome children. Someone else was looking at Parisa's legs. Normal, mundane things. Someone had recently had a dream about their dead aunt staring over at them from the foot of their bed.

Parisa had had a strange dream, too.

"You're the telepath who set up the subconscious wards," said the man in her dream, who was not quite blond, and not even entirely anything. Up close and under less urgent circumstances she could see he had a mixed look to him, ethnically speaking, and also in relation to whether he was a person or not. At first glance he was one thing, but it was obvious now that there was something else not quite right. He had a look of impermanence to him in general.

"I am," Parisa confirmed, sitting up to take in her surroundings. She had never been inside her own subconscious wards and regretted that she had not spent more time making them less prisonlike. The bars were not a pleasant atmosphere. "You're Gideon," she said.

"I am," he confirmed. "And I came here to thank you for not killing me, though I'm feeling a little less grateful after what you put me through just to say it." He gestured over his shoulder, presumably to whatever trap he'd just escaped.

Parisa had some idea of what he would have had to sift through in order to arrive within the Society's telepathic wards. Pain, mostly. She was very good at pain. "I had a job to do."

"And you did it well."

She nearly allowed a grimace at that. "Minus letting you escape."

"Minus that." Gideon gave her a long look of something that she had every intention to read until he said, "Did it work?"

It caught her off guard. (His thoughts were another thing that wasn't entirely normal.) "What?"

"The Prince," Gideon said. "I never found out if it worked. And Nico doesn't know."

"Oh." Well, Nico knew very little. Poor thing. He would be back within the Society's walls within a month, maybe less. Parisa was sure of it. "No, it didn't take."

"Oh." Gideon's voice sounded flat with disappointment. "That's too bad."

"Why?"

"My mother is—" He grimaced. "She'll be looking for me."

Ah. "Men with dysfunctional mothers are the worst," said Parisa.

"Totally," Gideon agreed, and sighed, "Oh well."

"Indeed." Parisa rose to her feet to stand opposite him, scrutinizing him from her position behind the bars. "Do me a favor," she said. "Don't tell Nico exactly what happened when I encountered you last." Even with the relatively benign outcome, she didn't like recalling the carelessness of what she'd done. Or *not* done, as the case may have been.

"Why?" Now Gideon looked amused. "Afraid he'll think you like him or something if he knows you saved my life?"

"Of course not. I don't like anyone. And more importantly, I didn't save your life. I made a mistake and you got away. Which," she pointed out, "will not happen twice."

"Fair," said Gideon graciously, with a hint of a twinkle in his eye.

"Though, look out for Nico," Parisa added. "He's an idiot."

"*Oui, très vrai,*" said Gideon.

They smiled politely at each other the way people occasionally did right before facing off in the ring.

"*Bonne chance,*" said Parisa. "*Ne meurs pas.*"

Good luck. Don't die.

"I'll tell Nico you said that" was Gideon's reply. And then she woke up, and a few hours later, the strangest two years of her life were over.

She wondered if she would miss them. She never liked nostalgia. Better to just move on.

Just then someone else entered the café, their steps quiet and familiar. Parisa looked up just as the seat across from her was filled.

"Hello," she said.

Dalton crossed one leg over the other, slinking down in the chair.

"That," he said, "was exhausting."

His thoughts had completely changed in recent weeks. They had gone from orderly to overgrown, reaching, like vines or weeds, spreading out further and further. His handwriting had changed. His voice had changed. His mannerisms had changed. Keeping it from everyone else had been a herculean effort. If it hadn't been for the others being absorbed in their own lives, someone would surely have noticed. Luckily, if people could be counted on for anything, it was a narcissism of sorts. Everyone was somewhere on the spectrum of self-obsession, and under the circumstances, the other four were further to one axis than most.

"Well, it's over now," said Parisa pragmatically, reaching for her tea. "Did Atlas say anything?"

She wondered if Atlas knew. She was wondering, lately, how much Atlas actually knew in general. It was possible that Atlas had made several critical mistakes, including underestimating her.

But that seemed . . . somehow out of character. She couldn't help feeling like she was still part of a plan. Still a piece, or a gear, or a mechanism, part of the invisible workings of something she couldn't quite see. Or maybe she'd just unwisely started to like him.

"No," Dalton answered, sounding bored. "What would he say? I finished the research. He can play his little games if he likes." Dalton glanced over his shoulder at the woman in the courtyard, the one with the fake baby. "I always wanted one."

"Hm?" said Parisa, who had still been thinking about Atlas before realizing Dalton was now fixated on the pram outside. "What, you're serious? A baby?" she asked, wanting to laugh.

"Yes. But no." He turned and smiled at her. It was a new smile, mischievous, and slightly knowing. Parisa found she quite liked it. "I just enjoy life, that's all."

She thought of Dalton's boyhood memory, reviving a sapling that had later died anyway, because such things happened. Because all of life had an end. She was starting to notice his odd fixation with death, which was almost a paranoia. Like he wanted desperately to outlast it.

This was a new observation, because whatever that fixation was, the previous version of him had not had it. She realized that without the entirety of himself—with *no* ambition, and indeed, no formulation of the future, which was a thing she had thought they had in common until she realized that, actually, his version of a blank page was wildly different from hers—she had never seen the other intricacies of him.

His dreams. His longings. His fears.

"I never thought I'd be much of a mother." Parisa thought of the plants in Reina's head, the way they clung to her like children. Speaking of unnatural mothers. "I don't think I have the capacity to not be selfish."

"I think having progeny is inherently selfish," said Dalton, who instantly grew bored. He turned to Parisa, itching with something. The fractures had not entirely healed, and now the Frankensteining of Dalton's consciousness had left him with slight gaps, overlapping pieces. He was a poorly set break. "Forcing something to exist that has no choice over the matter," he said, "is an act of pure selfishness."

Parisa chuckled into her tea. "True. And yet you'd do it anyway?"

"I never said I wasn't selfish." He smiled at her so sweetly it reminded her a bit of Gideon. She almost regretted lying to him, given his obvious concern about his mother, though there had been no benefit to her telling him the truth. (And anyway, if he had mommy problems, those weren't going away anytime soon. Or ever. Look at Callum.)

"So," Dalton said. "What are we doing?"

"I thought we'd dig up the Forum," Parisa suggested. "See what kind of resources they have, who they really are. I have a guess they're primed for a hostile takeover." Or a very well-dressed one, at least. She crossed her new Louboutins below the table.

"That sounds good." Dalton jiggled his knee, restless. "What about the physicists?"

Parisa paused. "What about them?"

"I want them," Dalton said. "Where is the other one again?"

Parisa set the teacup on the table. "You know their names."

"Right. Varona and Rhodes." He gave her another reassuring smile. "And the other one, too. The battery. We'll need her."

Parisa opened her mouth, then paused again. "Are you saying you want to beat Atlas to his own research?"

"My research," Dalton clarified.

"Right." That was true. That was fair. "I just didn't think you were interested in creating another world."

"Oh no, it's not about creating a completely new one," Dalton said quickly, with a slight brush of impatience—as if he had spent the last ten years proving that was nonsense, which admittedly, he had. "It's to find a way into an existing one. To open a door to another world. To many worlds. All the worlds. Though that is, in a sense, making a new one." His words were running into each other the way they often did now, his speech patterns rushed and manic.

"And you want that?" Parisa asked. "A door?"

Dalton smiled into nothing, then reached across the table for her hand.

"I want everything," he said. "Don't you?"

Hm, thought Parisa. Troubling.

Potentially there was a dangerous undercurrent, a little thrum of madness. Something ever so slightly discordant, like a violin plucked out of tune. Nobody had ever asked her what she wanted before, not really. Not in any way that mattered. People wanted *her,* and that was quite another thing. Still, the reality was that wanting everything was dangerous, and that seeking power for the sake of power was futile. That there was probably such a thing as too much knowledge, because having even a little bit could make a person sick for want of more.

But at the same time, he had a fucking point.

"What do you need me for?" asked Parisa, because she still had a brain and a healthy sense of caution.

Dalton shrugged. "The same reason he wants you."

"Wanted," Parisa said, and Dalton shook his head.

"Wants," he repeated.

Again, Parisa wondered where she was in the current of Atlas Blakely's plans. Had she already been in the middle before she even knew she had begun? She remembered her first meeting with Atlas, the mirror he had shown her. The way she had stumbled upon her own face in the midst of his thoughts.

Jung said the self was the sum total of a person's psyche. The part that looked forward, the process of individuation, the quest to become something more. Perhaps this was the part that Parisa had been missing after a year of researching the collective unconscious, the atavistic sense of humanness, the oneness of existence. An existence that was full of betrayal and staggering around blindly for meaning. An existence, as Dalton himself had said, that was an invariable guarantor of pain.

She had been wondering if she owed something to the world—some sense of when to stop, to find her limits—but fuck it. What had the world ever done for her?

"Let's make a new one," she said to Dalton. His princely angles caught the light; refracted it with a smile.

"I thought you might say that," he replied, leaning across the table to reach her as her cup of tea went cold.

Ezra distinctly remembered that it had been early morning when he had first arrived in the Society's manor house; the light had been shining overhead from the high, narrow windows of the house's great hall. He remembered the windows seeming snakelike, light flashing through blinding slits. Even now, when he thought about his time there, he still saw it in flashes, troublingly gilded and bright.

Now, though, the house was somber, the shadows falling like curtains as he walked, light illuminating the crafted moldings along the floor. There was something funereal about it. Quiet.

He paused in the doorway of the Caretaker's office to find Atlas looking out the window, his fingers steepled at his mouth. Once again, Ezra was struck by how old Atlas looked. How changed he was. Ezra assumed Atlas already knew as much—could feel Ezra's presence, and presumably also his thoughts.

"You let me in," Ezra remarked aloud.

Atlas's eyes flicked in his direction, studious, and then back to the window.

"You came back," Atlas replied.

Ezra wandered into the office, taking a seat in the chair opposite Atlas's desk.

"So. Was it everything you dreamed it would be?" Atlas asked in a tone that was almost juvenile. A not-quite-accusation that was certainly derisive, because he must have already known the answer was no.

"I couldn't let you go through with it." Ezra glanced at his hands. "I saw the path you were on, Atlas, and I had to stop you. I'm sorry."

"*Are* you?" Finally Atlas turned to him, his dark eyes flat with disinterest. "If that's true, I should think you're worse off than you imagine."

"I said I was sorry, not remorseful. They're still dangerous. They still have to be stopped." A pause. "You," Ezra clarified. "You have to be stopped." Whatever it cost him. Which seemed with every passing moment to be more than he could stand.

Things, Ezra thought, were going awry. Tristan, whom Ezra had planned specifically to meet, had not gone where he was expected. Maybe he was in Osaka instead, where no alarms had gone off, or in Cape Town. They must have known someone was coming; Atlas's remaining tools had obviously been prepared for ambush, and now, despite a year to plan, Ezra had lost the element of surprise.

A blow, though his window wasn't yet closed. How long could the four most easily trackable medeians stay hidden when half the world knew they existed and wanted them gone? Surprise was only one weapon among many, which surely Atlas already knew.

The room, like the house itself, was eerily quiet. Ezra wondered if Atlas had any plans to defend himself, or if perhaps this was a trap. Possibly the animator still remained somewhere nearby. Dalton Ellery seemed, after all, to have bought into everything Atlas offered that Ezra had rejected in the end.

"No," Atlas said in answer to Ezra's thoughts. "Dalton is gone."

Ezra bristled. Unwelcome telepathy was the least of Atlas's sins, but still. "Where?"

A shrug. "I don't think it's any of my business."

That was surprising. Or possibly just embarrassing. "So you don't actually know?"

"I have my guesses." Atlas traced a line contemplatively along his bottom lip. "But he is not mine to control. Nor are you."

"You tried, though," Ezra muttered.

Atlas shook his head. "No."

"Yes, of course you tried." At that, the rewriting of his experience, Ezra was filled with a sudden tremor of frustration. "Are you serious? You made it very clear that if I didn't agree with you—"

"Are you here to kill me?" Atlas interrupted. "Because if so, you might as well get on with it." He sounded bored, perhaps even exhausted. "I'm not sure I have the energy for another of our lovely heart-to-hearts."

"Bullshit." Atlas loved his rhetoric. Surely he'd want to give a speech, to make the whole thing needlessly ceremonial.

"No, actually, I'm far more of a realist than you imagine. And anyway, Ezra, I've already run the scenarios." Atlas looked at him squarely. "If you don't kill me, then all of this has been for nothing. Everything you sacrificed has been entirely in vain."

Ezra lifted his chin, defiant. As if Atlas, who'd done nothing but rise, could understand sacrifice. "What is it you think I've given up? Libby? Because I assure you," Ezra scoffed, "she'd have broken up with me anyway."

"Yes, Miss Rhodes is one thing you've unwisely cast aside," Atlas agreed as if Ezra had said nothing. "But it's more than that. It's not just her."

Oh good, another poignant insight into Ezra's lived experience. Lucky him! "I do so love when you take the time to regale me with my own thoughts," Ezra sighed, though of course Atlas continued.

"You threw away your chance at a life," Atlas said. "Your peace of mind. You threw away your convictions, Ezra." A pause. "You realized once again that you are not in control, and how are you meant to live with that now? After everything you've already had to live with." Atlas seemed borderline sympathetic, which to Ezra was proof that he had always been a complete and utter sociopath. "You are forever haunted," Atlas said again, "by the moment you saw death all around you, and you chose to stay alive."

No. No, that wasn't fair. "You don't get to tell me what I feel, Atlas." Ezra's mouth tightened. "My life is not yours to mold."

"We were friends once," Atlas pointed out. He drummed his fingers on the desk. "I didn't steal that insight from you. You gave it to me."

"Ha," said Ezra with a scowl. "I would *never*—"

"Ezra," Atlas cut in wearily. "Please. Give me some credit."

Again, Ezra felt the onslaught of agitation. A lightning rod of sudden fury, at the thought that *somehow,* Atlas still considered himself the victim in all of this. As if the betrayal had been Ezra's alone. "I've given you plenty of credit."

"Yes. More than I deserve, clearly," Atlas graciously allowed, "or you wouldn't still concern yourself with me."

"Excuse me?" Ezra shot to his feet at that, staring at Atlas. "What do you mean *concern* myself with you? Do you not understand that everything I've done has been *because of you*?" Clearly he didn't, which was delusion of the highest degree. "You're at the heart of all of this!"

"And what is it that you imagine I have caused?" Atlas asked in a tone of gentle amusement, which made Ezra even angrier. Presumably that had been Atlas's intent, to taunt him with his helplessness. "Clearly you think you are keeping me from terrible, dastardly things," Atlas said dryly, "or you would not have killed five people to achieve it."

Hearing the accusation aloud was unexpectedly gutting. Temporarily, Ezra was stunned. "I haven't killed anyone."

"Really. You think your hands are clean?" This time, the amusement was far from gentle. It was pitying, really. As if Atlas felt that Ezra was the one who had sins to confess. "You've effectively arranged for the deaths of five Society members," Atlas reminded him. "You abducted the sixth."

So this was Atlas's game plan, then. Save himself by turning the tables on Ezra, making Ezra the one to blame. "One was already dead," Ezra said irritably, "thanks to your precious Society—"

"No." Atlas's interruption was jarring, and temporarily Ezra reeled. "Callum Nova left here alive this morning."

Ezra blinked. "I—" He stopped. "I still never said they'd be killed. And as for the empath, he was—"

"Do you really still believe things will go according to your plan?" Atlas cut in. "What do you think will come of revealing their names, their magical specialties, their families and friends? Their locations? Do you really suppose that information will only be used to *apprehend*?" To Ezra's silence, Atlas concluded, "You know human nature as well as I do, Ezra, and so you know what is coming for them. You made them targets, and their deaths are on your hands."

"*You* made them weapons," Ezra snapped. "Without *you*—"

"Without me they might have never discovered the things they discovered. Or perhaps they would have, who knows?" Atlas remained seated, his eyes slowly following Ezra as he shifted from foot to foot, agitated. "But without you, they certainly would not have walked into a series of traps. So it seems we're at an impasse."

Was that supposed to be a joke? "You don't know that they'll be killed." But Ezra heard his own hesitation, the hitch of doubt, and knew Atlas heard it, too.

"You'll have to kill me," Atlas repeated with a shrug. "You will have to, or everything you have done to lead you to this moment becomes a waste. A betrayal of your own beliefs."

He rose to his feet, hands open, as if to make the target wider, more accessible. Ezra had never wanted him dead more. Was Atlas completely suicidal? Ezra wanted, ideally, for Atlas's death to happen via some kind of divine smiting, like a lightning bolt from above. He waited, but evidently no one was home. Olympus was empty and so was hell. The devils were all here, in this house.

"You're right," Ezra said. "I will have to kill you."

Regrettably, he sounded like he was still trying to convince himself. Poor form, given the stakes, but then again Atlas had always brought out the meek in him, the small, the insignificant. Atlas had a vastness, a brightness that was impossible to snuff out—only now, Ezra would have to do it. He would have to.

"But that's not why you're here," Atlas noted, and Ezra's attention snapped back to him.

"What?"

"You have to kill me," Atlas said. "Believe me, I know. I understand. I can see how the path of logic takes you back here, to this room. To this moment. It has to end here." A pause. "But it's not why you came."

"Oh, great." Ezra's laugh was sickly, thick with bitterness at the prospect of another cerebral gift from Atlas Blakely. "So tell me, then," he beckoned, listless. "Why am I here, if not to finally be rid of you?"

Atlas looked sorry for him. "Because," he said. "You finally realized that there is something out there worse than me."

For half a second, Ezra stiffened. As if, once again, Atlas had read his mind.

Then, because Ezra was using every telepathic block known to man, he scoffed, "Oh, *please*—"

"No, you're right, that's not it," Atlas agreed. "But you did realize that there are only others like me. That *I* am not the problem," Atlas guessed, "because the problem is you, because *you* don't fit. Because what you believe, what matters to you, does not measurably improve the world for anyone else, and thus they will never believe you, never listen to you. You came here to save this world, and all you did was destroy things—all you did was give destructive men the justification for their violence." Atlas was silent again for a moment. "I wasn't what you wanted me to be, Ezra, but neither were they. None of this was what you wanted. It wasn't what you thought."

Ezra turned away, staring out the window. "You have no idea what I—"

"What you gave up?" Atlas supplied for him.

Ezra could feel Atlas watching him, but didn't turn.

"You think I don't understand everything at war within you right now, Ezra?" Atlas laughed. "Twenty years ago, I chose a loophole. I decided to make my own plan, my own world. And do you know what happened because I made that choice?"

Fuck you, Ezra thought. Fuck you, Atlas Blakely, don't even try—

"The other four died," Atlas said, and Ezra turned to him by accident; without even noticing he'd done it until it was already done. "Do you remember them? Maybe not. I remember never thinking much of them either, and at first it didn't seem to matter. Maybe it was an accident, I thought. Maybe just bad luck." Atlas idled in nostalgia, toying with the knuckles of his right hand. "But then I realized it was my fault, because I was told to make a sacrifice, and instead I chose myself. I chose to stick to the plan I made with you. And then I chose this," he said with a reference to his office, "because after a certain point, I came to the same conclusion you did: that if I did not make myself Caretaker, if my plan did not succeed, then I would forever have the blood of four people on my hands for nothing."

Ezra found it impossible to swallow, to breathe. To think. "They're dead? The others?"

"Yes."

Ezra frowned. "But then why—?"

"Why am I alive?" Atlas guessed, and shrugged. "Presumably because I stayed here, close to the archives. Still here in this house, where it can still use me, where the magic can still rot me from the inside and take from me whatever I have left. I care for the archives and they allow me a certain degree of freedom," he said with a sense of deference, "but my life is what's owed. My sacrifice is still owed."

"You *want* me to kill you." Ezra's breath came short. "You actually *want* me to do it, don't you?"

"Why not? If not you, it will be someone." Another shrug. "Perhaps one of your new friends. Possibly the archives themselves. Either way, I will die, Ezra, someday. What could I possibly accomplish before then that can make up for the weight of my sins?"

The Atlas that Ezra had known had not been so defeated. It almost felt pointless now, Ezra's entire purpose. His vision. His drive, his sense of meaning, his reason for existing. If Atlas was gone, if the Society continued without him, then what had Ezra's entire life been for?

"Is this—" Ezra paused to moisten his lips. "Is this some kind of reverse psychology? You're trying to convince me to do it so that I won't?"

Atlas gave a grim laugh, then shook his head. "No. What I think is that there is a blueprint to our lives, Ezra. And I think we chose the wrong paths, you and I." Atlas was staring at him strangely, with an expression Ezra couldn't read. "I think that if you let me finish my research, then I have a chance to right it. To fix where things went wrong."

"My god." Ezra almost laughed. "So you're trying to *recruit* me? All over again?"

"No." Atlas shook his head blandly. "I'm trying to explain to you that everything I've done—everything I've tried to do," he amended, "has been in service to my conscience. Because yes, I have allowed you to believe certain things of me in my failure to tell you the truth, but I did so because I didn't feel that the truth was your burden to carry."

"Oh, well thank god for that," said Ezra, half snarling at Atlas as he began to pace furiously before his desk. "Thank *goodness* you kept it from me so that I wouldn't have to suffer at all, not even *remotely*. How *magnanimous* of you," Ezra said with a congratulatory sneer, "to decide for me what I was meant to know—"

"What will you do with her?" Atlas asked. "Libby."

"I wasn't—" Ezra faltered at the sound of her name. "What?"

"You know that I cannot succeed without her, which I readily admit is true. So you've removed her from the equation for now," Atlas said, "but if you don't kill me, then she remains a threat to you and your plans. She is the piece you already know I need. So, what will you do with Libby?"

"I—" Again, a pause. "That's irrelevant, because I'm going to kill you. That's—" Ezra faltered, inarticulate in his frustration. "That's why I'm here, Atlas. Because you can't be allowed to continue, you can't—" A splutter. His throat was incurably dry. "You can't just *play god*, Atlas—"

"You want to hate me, Ezra," Atlas observed. "But you don't."

"Shut up," Ezra snarled. "You don't get to tell me what's in my own head, Atlas. This was *our* plan, not yours—"

"She won't stay lost to the past," Atlas said. "*She's* your true error, Ezra. Your biggest mistake was not in leading her here, to me, but in allowing her to become dangerous." Where, Ezra thought desperately, was the smiting? How was this not ending for Atlas in fire and floods, in pestilence and violence? It certainly felt like war inside his chest, like devastation, a litany of plagues. "If you had really wanted to stop me, you already knew how. And you should have known long ago," Atlas cautioned, "that if you couldn't kill her, she would forever be your Achilles' heel."

"Don't tell me what Libby is to me." Even to himself, Ezra sounded strained, imbalanced. "You have no idea what she is to me—"

"Is that what you think? That I don't understand?" Atlas's voice was gravelly with something. Not honesty, Ezra thought. It could not be honesty. "Ezra, just end it here," Atlas sighed. "Let me finish my research, then let the whole thing end here with me."

Ezra's eyes were blurring with something. Conflict. Misery. Hate. "I can kill her," he flung at Atlas like a threat.

"You can't." Again, the pity. "Ezra, you won't, because you can't."

"Yes, I can. I have to. I would not have done this if not for—" He took a deep breath. Exhaled shakily. "If not for something I believed *unquestionably*—"

"Change your path," Atlas said. "Ezra. Change it."

"No. No." His vision was swimming. "I can't. I've gone too far. I can't come back from this."

"It will only get harder to live with, Ezra."

"Don't tell me what I can live with. You have *no idea* what I can live with!" His voice was breaking, and something in Ezra thought: Now, it will have to be now. It will have to be now, this moment, because if you don't, the world will end. The world as you know it, the world that has for so long turned its back on you, the world that you did everything in your power to save—it will end.

It's not about the world, the professor had said to him, which sounded like a warning now. *It's never about the world.*

It is, Ezra thought desperately. It has to be. It *has* to be, because if it is not about the world, then I have spent the last year in agony for nothing. I have betrayed the woman I love, I have watched her suffer without lifting a finger to help her, I have turned my back on the only friend I ever had. I betrayed myself, my beliefs, the books that were nothing, that weren't ever *anything,* because knowledge is a fucking curse. Knowledge is nothing, I could have lived a whole life and never known the meaning of it or the reason for existence and I still might have had joy, or sweetness, or softness—

"She has to die," Ezra said, the words numb between his lips. "She has to. You don't understand." It was hollow, tunneled out with sorrow, or perhaps with falseness, because surely Atlas knew he didn't mean it. Atlas, that motherfucker, knew weakness when he saw it, and he knew, finally, the truth: that Ezra was weak. That he had come not for vengeance, not for reprisal, but for redemption. For forgiveness. To confess that yes, he had made a mistake, he had thought he was choosing the lesser of two evils but it was still evil, it was still the wrong choice—but now, that was impossible. Now he could never say it. "You don't understand."

He didn't hear the sound of footsteps behind him.

He didn't even notice the presence in the doorframe, not until Atlas's eyes lifted.

It was only when he realized that he had lost control of the moment, lost his recognition of himself in time and space, that Ezra turned over his shoulder to come face-to-face with his moment of reckoning.

So this was what he'd been waiting for.

The conclusion of a lifetime's worth of waiting; the knowledge that eventually, his time would come. Ezra's knees buckled in fear, which was simultaneously relief.

She was smoldering. She was singed. Her clothing had burned away and she stood before him in the doorway like an angry, avenging goddess.

"Fuck you, Ezra," said Libby, her chest ragged with anguish.

The explosion from her palm was white-hot behind his eyes, and for once, there were no doors to fall through. No sliver to crawl through. No way to escape, and in the moment that he burned, he pined, he perished, Ezra Mikhail Fowler looked into the eyes of his death and thought ah, so then this is destiny.

So this, then, was fate.

· END? ·

Gideon Drake had never been much for combat. He wasn't very combative as a person, really. Not much of a fighter. There were a lot of things he hadn't found worth the time or the energy; he didn't really have a violent streak, or much of an ego, either. He had always considered himself relatively bland, actually, and the only proof to the contrary was his friendship with Nico de Varona, who was so un-bland and alive it was almost a shame that he wasted his time on Gideon.

That being said—to suggest that Gideon was not a fighter by nature did not mean that he wasn't formidable when given a chance.

"Nice one," panted Nico, who, true to form, had paused to backhand Gideon's chest after a particularly well-thrown blow to the side of his attacker's head, which was designed to discombobulate and temporarily destabilize the inner ear. Gideon was particularly good at those types of specialty impacts. Unlike Nico, he didn't like to draw things out.

This, though, was less a matter of Nico's enjoyment than it was a genuinely well-constructed snare. Ironically, the trap that had been set for Parisa Kamali was not unlike the traps that Parisa herself had set for Gideon in the past. These were not regular people, not police, not witches like the kinds of assailants that Nico had described encountering in England. These were medeians, each one specifically selected to face off against the most talented telepath Gideon had ever met. One was a biomancer who seemed to have control over muscle matter—Gideon kept feeling abrupt muscle spasms, fighting through the sense that he might spontaneously collapse. Another was a specialist in multipotence, who could replicate her consciousness to be several places at once—a clever form of combat against telepathy, presumably to create an echo chamber of thought, although it wasn't terribly efficient against Nico's use of force. The third was a physicist who specialized in energy conversion, which was an inconvenience for Nico (and slightly more than that for Gideon). It was ultimately a test of who could outlast, outman, and magically outgun.

This was also not a dream. This was reality, where mortality was an issue, perhaps more so than pain. Pain was temporary. Pain would end. Consciousness could blink out, which was the far more troubling outcome. Gideon felt Nico's scapulae align with his, the two of them back-to-back as the three medeians circled their periphery, formulating their next attack.

"I'm going to need you to do something dumb," Nico said to Gideon between breaths. He conjured a thin shield of something, which held against a blow from one of the medeians—the multiplier, who had split herself in thirds.

The other two, who were waiting in the wings for their next attack, were essentially physical specialists, which Gideon was not. He turned over his shoulder to listen for Nico's instructions. "How dumb, exactly?"

"Need you to go that way," Nico said with a jut of his chin toward the Seine. "But then, like, duck."

"Okay," Gideon said uncertainly, wondering if there was room for a veto. "So when exactly would you want me t—"

But Nico was already rolling away, and the shield he'd conjured dissipated at the moment his strike hit the cobbled path. Gideon sighed, but he did as he was told, waving a streak of sparks as he dove for the opposite side of the bridge.

Someone had shouted to follow him, Gideon knew that much, and if he knew Nico—which he did—then something explosive was coming next, so Gideon closed his eyes and careened over the edge of the bridge, aiming himself in a high arc, more up than out.

Time slowed, wind whistling in his ears, while something loud as a gunshot went off overhead. Then everything sped up again, too fast, adrenaline coursing through his veins, the primal rush of mortality. The impact against the river would be hard and there was no way to break the surface tension. *Just live,* Gideon told himself. *Just live.*

In the half second before he made contact with the water, eyes closing against the glassy oncoming surface of the Seine, the force of Gideon's momentum suddenly collapsed beneath him. He gasped, breathing hard, with his face no more than an inch above the water as something reversed his course, propelling him backward and onto the now partially deconstructed cobbled stone bridge. There was a chunk missing from the wall, the scorched pile of rubble in its wake concealing a glimpse of unmoving limbs.

Gideon, who landed on his back, took another moment to recover from his temporary brush with doom. "Nice catch," he offered breathlessly to Nico, who grinned in his maddeningly arrogant way.

"Always," Nico replied, offering a hand.

Gideon took it, accepting the lurch to his feet and glancing around at the small crowd that had gathered around them. "Are you worried about this?" he asked, gesturing to the oncoming siren of metro police.

Naturally not. Nico shrugged. "I'll just put it on Blakely's tab."

Gideon figured that was reasonable. Though he had evidently suffered what was either a blow to his head or a disorienting flash of sun, because he thought he caught a little blur of something as he rose. "Where are the other two?"

"One, uh, fell," said Nico vaguely, with a hand in his hair. "And the other—"

Gideon caught a swarm of light from his periphery, more motion than object.

"Nico, get down!"

He shoved Nico out of the way and felt something singe the side of his head, as if he'd smacked it on the corner of a table. It rattled his brain, the skin of his temple searing from the impact, eyes watering so thoroughly he heard but didn't see the blast from Nico's palm, aimed upward from Nico's position where Gideon had flung him near the ground. Gideon spun with a grunt of pain, blindly tossing out an arm and catching the medeian around the throat, holding him still while Nico, still dropped in levels, took the medeian out at the knees. Gideon caught the medeian as he went down, this time with another of his specialty combat moves. This one he'd learned as a foster kid from their neighbor, a hunter who was known for putting down rabid bears. It was quick and brutal, with a sound that Gideon would never unhear.

The moment it was over, Gideon wanted to be sick, but instead he reached out for Nico's hand, grasping it sightlessly. "You good?"

"I'm good, Sandman." Nico sounded dazed, euphoric, awed. "Where the fuck did you learn that? I told you to stop playing video games."

"Shut up, asshole." Gideon was panting, almost retching with fatigue, when his vision finally cleared enough to see that Nico was laughing at his expense. The two of them stood like mirror images, both folded at the waist and grasping at their knees.

There was a streak of blood on Nico's cheek when Gideon looked at him. A slow trickle from Nico's hairline, a cut along his jaw. There was a roar of something furious and fierce in Gideon, who reached up to brush the blood away and then stopped.

"What?" said Nico, who swallowed a laugh. The muscle in his jaw jumped, then stilled.

"Nothing," said Gideon.

"What?"

"Nothing."

"Gideon, come on, *no te hagas rogar—*"

Don't make me beg. Ha, as if he would. As if he *could.*

Nico laughed again and it hurt Gideon somewhere deep, jellying his legs with delayed paralysis. That, or a timed-release breakdown. Fear, firstly, that they had skirted something narrowly, so narrowly that it was almost a disaster, a disaster from which Gideon would never recover. Relief, that no one had put a stop to that arrogant laugh. That Nico de Varona had never learned how fragile Gideon really was. That because Nico believed himself to be invincible, Gideon sometimes believed it, too, right up until the terrifying moments when he didn't. Like now.

"I always forget how good you are at stuff," Nico was babbling appreciatively, still talking, still laughing, still blissfully, ridiculously alive, and some madness inside Gideon's chest made up his mind for him. He leaned forward and caught Nico's mouth with his in something of a punitive force, a captive blow. More of a gasp than anything else, really.

Although technically it was a kiss.

Nico's lips were dry and his mouth was hot, taken aback, unprepared and metallic with concentration. Gideon felt Nico's breath catch on his tongue, an audible hitch of surprise, and then Nico pulled away and Gideon thought *no, no, no—*

"Oh. So it's like that?" Nico said. His eyes were searching and bewilderingly, confusingly bright. In response Gideon felt unopened and raw, like he'd cracked his chest in two and presented the evidence for Nico's evaluation.

"Yeah." It left Gideon in a rasp, but fuck it. It had lived in his throat long enough. "Yeah," he attempted again, "yeah, it's like that."

Nico's smile broadened.

"Good." Nico caught him by a fistful of his T-shirt, tugging him in again. "Good."

Gideon's heart banged in his chest, his lips parting in absolute rapture, when he heard another noise behind him. It was unmissably magical, unavoidably so. The opening of a transport ward.

Gideon spun, one arm thrown instinctively into Nico's chest to put himself between Nico and his latest assassin, when instead he blinked in surprise. Behind him, Gideon felt Nico's pulse stutter and quicken; heard the confusion in his voice.

"Rhodes?"

Libby Rhodes stood before them on the sidewalk. There was blood on her clothes—clearly someone else's—and ash in her hair, but there was no question it was her. She had found her way back, through time and space and impossibility. It was Libby Rhodes, and she was here.

To say she was unharmed would be false. Her eyes were unfocused except for the way they met Nico's. He, Gideon noted, seemed for once too stunned to speak, one hand still pressed to his mouth and the ghost of Gideon's kiss.

"Varona," Libby said, taking a step toward him. "We need to talk."

Then she collapsed into Gideon's arms.

ACKNOWLEDGMENTS

That you hold this book in your hand is (1) confirmation that we are in the weirdest timeline and (2) a real testament to what can be accomplished on so little sleep that I wouldn't have trusted myself to operate a vehicle. I must first thank my mother, because if she had not dropped everything to live with me and my family for four weeks while my son was a newborn, there would never have been a first draft. I must also emphatically thank everyone who read the early drafts of this book, because it was edited on my iPhone and therefore contained every manner of chaos that autocorrect could dream up. To Molly McGhee and Lindsey Hall, my brilliant editors at Tor, I am beyond grateful for your genius, your insight, and your fantastic ability to decide how much hotter I can make a scene if I really try. To Amelia Appel, my beloved agent and most discerning editorial eye, I owe you something critical. If ever you require a kidney, I am there on bended knee. (And also, profound thanks to my tied-for-first fans, Debbi and Sam.)

To Little Chmura, my illustrator and friend, it never fails to boggle the mind how lucky I am to be working with you. Every new adventure we embark on together is a reminder of how much I love creating art with you, and you always bring out the best version of the creator in me. Working with you is a pleasure and a gift.

To my team at Tor: another round of thanks to Lindsey for signing on, guns blazing, to whatever it is I'm doing here. To my unfailingly excellent cover designer Jamie Stafford-Hill, and interior designer Heather Saunders. My publicists, Desirae Friesen (constantly in my inbox saving my life) and Sarah Reidy. My marketing team, GIF queen Eileen Lawrence and flawless genius Natassja Haught. Dakota Griffin, my production editor, my managing editor Rafal Gibek, my production manager Jim Kapp, and my incredible publishing operator Michelle Foytek. My publishers, Devi Pillai and Lucille Rettino. Chris Scheina, my foreign rights agent. Christine Jaeger and her incredible sales team. To Steve Wagner and fantastic voice actors James Cronin, Siho Ellsmore, Munirih Grace, Andy Ingalls, Caitlin Kelly, Damian Lynch, Steve West, and David Monteith. To Troix Jackson, for sticking around to read on.

To my team at Tor UK/Pan Macmillan: much gratitude to my editor Bella Pagan, with much appreciation too to Lucy Hale and Georgia Summers in editorial. To Ellie Bailey and the rest of the marketing team—Claire Evans, Jamie Forrest, and Becky Lushey, as well as Lucy Grainger in export marketing and Andy Joannou in digital marketing. To Hannah Corbett for brilliant PR wizardry as well as Jamie-Lee Nadone and Black Crow for an incredible publicity campaign. To Holly Sheldrake and Sian Chivers in production and Rebecca Needes in editorial services. To UK cover designer Neil Lang. To Stuart Dwyer, Richard Green, and Rory O'Brien in sales; Leanne Williams, Joanna Dawkins, and Beth Wentworth in export sales; and to Kadie McGinley in special sales. To the audiobook team, Rebecca Lloyd and Molly Robinson. And last but not least, thanks to Chris Josephs for handling a beautiful mess of couriering.

To the translators and editors who've brought this book to the rest of the world in the many, many languages I can't speak: thank you endlessly for living in my words and for telling my story for me.

To Dr. Uwe Stender and the rest of the team at Triada. Thank you to Katie Graves and Jen Schuster at Amazon Studios and Tanya Seghatchian and John Woodward of Brightstar for being my creative partners.

Enormous thanks to the good citizens of BookTok, BookTwt, BookTube, and Bookstagram. You guys are absolutely insane (affectionate). To all the incredible booksellers I've had the fortune of meeting since this bizarre fever dream began. To anyone who has ever taken to the interwebs (or even—gasp—gone IRL) to reverse-gatekeep other people into reading this book. There are so many footprints in the sand. All of the footprints but mine. (You get it? It's because you carried me.)

To the boys: Theo, Eli, Clayton, Miles, Harry, and their respective parents: Lauren and Aaron, Kayla and Claude, Lauren and Matt, Carrie and Zac, Krishna and James. To my family, especially Megan, my fellow air sign, and Mackenzie, who read my books before they were BookTok approved. To David. To Nacho and Ana. To Stacie. To Angela. To Melina. To everyone who helped me stay sane, or something close to it.

To Henry, my boy king, my chaos goblin, my squishiest boy, may this embarrass you well into your teen years and beyond. My little mischief prince, how lucky I am to be your mom. You came into my life and made a whole new world for me. I love you and your dad so very much.

To Garrett. Oh, fuck. I can't thank you without tearing up. I'll run out of dumb poetry for you someday, but not today. You're my safe harbor, my favorite place. You are my privilege in life. Thank you for believing in me. Thanks for choosing me. I pick you every time.

To you, reader: without you I am nothing but a sleepless goon, shouting hopelessly into the void. Thank you for listening and for giving my story somewhere to land. I hope something in here makes you think, or wonder, or smile, or laugh, or dream. I hope it makes you feel. And even if it doesn't—it is, as it always is, an honor to put down these words for you. I sincerely hope you enjoyed the story.

xx, Olivie